My Heart Pounding, I Opened the Door and Let My Twin Sister into the House. . . .

"Our stepmother would bust a gut if she saw how well you've done for yourself, dear sister," Gisselle said, as she gazed at the grand entryway, my paintings and small statues, the long marble floors and grand stairway. . . .

"Where's Beau's baby?" she demanded.

"Pearl's asleep, and no one knows her as Beau's baby here," I said.

"Of course." She smiled with satisfaction.

"If you've come here to make trouble for us . . ."

"Why should I do that? I don't care what you've done, although I know you did it just to spite Beau."

"That's not true, Gisselle."

"Don't you want to hear about him?" she teased. I didn't reply. "He broke up with his fiancée in Europe, so you see, if you hadn't rushed into this sinful arrangement, you might still have won him," she said with great self-satisfaction. I felt the blood rush into my face so quickly, it felt as if it had drained completely out of my legs and I might tumble down the stairs. Then she laughed and put her arm through mine. "But let's not talk of old romances. I do have a lot to tell you, a lot you will enjoy . . . and a lot you won't. . . ."

V.C. Andrews® Books

Published by POCKET BOOKS

All That Glitters

V.C. ANDREWS®

POCKET BOOKS

New York   London   Toronto   Sydney   Tokyo   Singapore

Following the death of Virginia Andrews, the Andrews family worked with a carefully selected writer to organize and complete Virginia Andrews' stories and to create additional novels, of which this is one, inspired by her storytelling genius.

An *Original* Publication of POCKET BOOKS

POCKET BOOKS, a division of Simon & Schuster Inc.
1230 Avenue of the Americas, New York, NY 10020

ISBN: 0-671-87319-9

First Pocket Books paperback printing June 1995

10 9 8 7 6

V.C. Andrews is a registered trademark of the Virginia C. Andrews Trust.

POCKET and colophon are registered trademarks of Simon & Schuster Inc.

Cover and stepback art by Lisa Falkenstern

Printed in the U.S.A.

All That Glitters

Prologue

In the early evening just after the sun has slipped below the tops of the cypress trees in the western bayou, I sit in Grandmere Catherine's old oak rocker with Pearl in my arms and hum an old Cajun melody, one that Grandmere Catherine used to hum to me when she put me to sleep, even when I was already a little girl with pigtails bouncing over my shoulders as I ran across the fields from the banks of the swamp to our toothpick-legged shack. I can close my eyes and still hear her calling.

"Ruby, it's time for supper, child. Ruby . . ."

But her voice fades from my memory, like smoke from someone's potbelly stove drifting into the wind.

I am nearly nineteen now and it has been almost three months since Pearl was born during one of the most vicious hurricanes to hit the bayou. Trees that were blown over the roads have been pulled aside, but still lay along the macadam like wounded soldiers waiting to be healed and restored.

I suppose I am waiting to be healed and restored as well. In a real sense, this was the true reason for my return to the bayou from New Orleans. After my father, who had suffered great guilt for what he had done to his brother, my uncle Jean, died of a tragic heart attack, my stepmother, Daphne, took over our lives with a vengeance. Daphne resented me from the day I had arrived on their doorstep, the hitherto unknown twin daughter, the one Grandmere Catherine had kept secret so I wouldn't be sold away from her by Grandpere Jack like he had sold Gisselle.

Until I arrived, Daphne and my father, Pierre Dumas, had managed to keep the truth buried under a pile of lies, but after I had appeared, they had to create a new deception: claiming I had been stolen from my crib the day Gisselle and I had been born.

The truth was, my father had fallen in love with my mother, Gabrielle, during one of the hunting trips he and his father frequently made to the swamps. Grandpere Jack was their guide, and once my father set eyes on my beautiful mother, a woman Grandmere Catherine described as a free and innocent spirit, he fell head over heels in love. She fell in love with him, too. Daphne was unable to have children, so when my mother became pregnant with Gisselle and me, Grandpere Jack agreed to a deal proposed by my Grandfather Dumas. He sold Gisselle, and Daphne pretended Gisselle was her daughter.

Grandmere Catherine never forgave him and chased him from our house. He lived in the swamp like a swamp rat and made his living trapping muskrats and harvesting oysters, as well as guiding tourists when he was sober enough to do so. Before Grandmere Catherine, who was a *traiteur,* a spiritual healer, died, she made me promise I would go to New Orleans and seek out my father and sister.

But life proved even more unbearable for me there. Gisselle resented me from the beginning and made my life miserable in New Orleans as well as at Greenwood, the private school we were made to attend in Baton Rouge. She was particularly peeved at how quickly her former boyfriend, Beau Andreas, fell in love with me, and I with him. Later, when I became pregnant with Beau's child, Daphne sent me to have an abortion in the back room of some horrible clinic, but instead, I ran off and returned to the only other home I had ever known: the bayou.

Grandpere Jack drowned in the swamp during one of his drunken rampages, and I would have been left alone from the start if it weren't for my secret half brother, Paul. Before we knew our real relationship, Paul and I had been young lovers. It broke his heart to learn that his father had seduced my mother when she was very young, and to this day, he has refused to accept the reality.

Since I have returned to the bayou, he has been at my side daily, and daily has proposed that we marry. His father owns one of the biggest shrimp canneries in the bayou, but from an inheritance of land, Paul has become one of the richest men in our parish, for oil has been discovered on that land.

Now Paul is building a grand home in which he hopes Pearl, he, and I will someday live. He knows our relationship would have to be limited, that we couldn't be lovers, but he is willing to sacrifice so he can spend his life with me. I am tempted by his offer, for I have lost Beau, my one great passionate love, and I am left alone with our child, scrounging out the same sort of living Grandmere Catherine and I scrounged out when she was alive: weaving blankets and baskets, cooking gumbos, and selling it all to the tourists at our roadside stand. It's not much of a life and holds no promise for my beautiful baby.

Every night I sit in the rocker as I am now doing and rock Pearl to sleep while I ponder what I should do. I stare hopefully at the picture of Grandmere Catherine I had painted before she died. In it she is sitting in this very rocker on our front gallery. Behind her in the window, I painted my mother's angelic face. The two of them stare back at me as if they expect me to come up with the right decision.

Oh, how I wish they were alive and here and could tell me what to do. In less than a year and a half, I will have money because my inheritance as a Dumas will come due; but I have such a distaste for that world back in New Orleans now, despite the beautiful house in the Garden District and all the riches it promises. Just the thought of facing Daphne again, a woman who once tried to have me incarcerated in a mental institution, a woman whose beauty belied her true cold nature, makes me shudder. Besides, if there was anything I learned while I lived in the Dumas house surrounded by servants and valuable possessions, it was that money and riches won't buy you happiness if you don't have love.

There was no love in that house once my father died, and while he was alive he suffered so under the dark shadows of his own past sins. I tried to bring sunshine and happiness into his world, but Daphne and Gisselle were too determined and too selfish to let me succeed. Now they are both satisfied that I have gone, that I got caught up in my passion and became pregnant and proved to be what they always claimed I was . . . a worthless Cajun. Beau's family sent him to Europe, and Gisselle can't wait to write me about his girlfriends and rich, happy life there.

Perhaps I should marry Paul. Only his parents know the truth about us, and they have kept it a deep, dark secret. All of my grandmere Catherine's old friends believe Pearl is Paul's child anyway. She has his *chatlin* hair, a mixture of blond and brown, and she has both our eyes: cerulean blue. She has such delicate fair skin, pale yet rich and glowing that brought pearls to mind the moment I set eyes on her.

Paul pleads with me to marry him every chance he can get, and I haven't the heart to make him stop, for he has always stood by me. He was there when Pearl was born, protecting us during the hurricane. He brings us food and gifts every day and spends his every free hour fixing things around my shack.

Would it be a sinful alliance if we don't consummate

our relationship? Marriage is more than simply something that moralizes and legalizes sex. People marry to love and to cherish in greater ways. They marry to have someone who will stand by them through sickness and hard times, to have companionship and to protect each other until death. And Paul would be a wonderful father for Pearl. He loves her as if she were really his own. Sometimes I think he believes she is, really believes it.

On the other hand, would it be fair to Paul to deny him what every man expects and needs from a woman? He claims he is willing to make that sacrifice because he loves me so, and he points out that our Catholic clergymen make such a sacrifice for a higher love. Why can't he? He has even threatened to become a monk if I reject him.

Oh, Grandmere, can't you give me a sign? You had such wonderful spiritual powers when you were alive. You drove away evil spirits, you healed people who were so sick, you gave people hope and lifted their souls. Where should I look for the answers?

As if she understands my turmoil, Pearl stirs and begins to cry. I kiss her soft cheeks, and as I often do when I gaze into her precious little face, I think about Beau and his handsome smile, his warm eyes, his tempting lips. He has yet to set his eyes on his own daughter. I wonder if he ever will.

Pearl is all my responsibility now. I have chosen to have her and to keep her and to love and cherish her. The decisions I have made from her birth on are decisions that will affect us both. I can no longer think about only what is good for me, only what is right for me. I have to think about her welfare, too. The choices I am about to make might be painful ones for me, but they might be better ones for Pearl.

She quiets down again. Her eyes close and she falls back into her restful sleep, trusting, comfortable, oblivious to the storm of troubles that rage around us. What does fate have in store for us?

If only all this had happened years later, I think. Beau

5

and I would have married and had a wonderful home in the Garden District. Pearl would have grown up in a house of love in a world as precious as the make-believe worlds of our dreams. If only we had been more careful and . . .

If's, I realize, have no meaning in a world of reality, a world in which dreams often turn into shadows anyway. No more if's, Ruby, I tell myself.

I rock on and hum. Outside, the sun disappears completely and darkness falls thick and deep with only the eyes of the owl reflecting the starlight. I get up and put Pearl in her crib, a crib Paul bought her, and then I return to the window and gaze out at the night. Alligators slither along the banks of the canal. I can hear their tails slap the water. Bats weave through the Spanish moss and dive to scoop up insects for supper, and the raccoons begin to cry.

How lonely my world has become, and yet I have never been afraid to be alone until now, for now there is someone else to worry about and protect: my precious Pearl, asleep, dreaming baby dreams, waiting for her life to start.

It is up to me to make sure it starts with sunlight and not with shadows, with hope and not with fear. How will I do it? The answers linger in the darkness, waiting to be discovered. Were they left there by the spirits of good or the spirits of evil?

Book
One

1

Choices

The growl of Paul's approaching motorboat annoyed a pair of grosbeak herons that had been strutting arrogantly on the thick branch of a cypress tree, and they both spread their wings and dove into the Gulf breeze to glide deeper into the swamps. Rice birds flicked their wings as well and soared over the water to disappear into the marsh.

It was a very warm and humid Thursday afternoon in late March, but Pearl was very alert and active, twisting and struggling to break free of my embrace and crawl toward the dry domes of grass that were homes to the muskrats and nutrias. Her hair had grown faster this past month and was already below her ears and at the base of her neck. It was leaning more toward blond than brown now. I had dressed her in an ivory dress with pink fringes on the collar and sleeves. She wore the little cotton booties I had woven out of cotton jaune last week.

As Paul's boat drew closer, Pearl raised her eyes. Although she was a little more than eight months old, she seemed to have the alertness and awareness of a one-year-old. She loved Paul and took such delight in his every visit, her eyes brightening, her little arms and hands waving, her legs kicking to break free of me so she could rush to him.

Paul's boat came around the bend and he waved as soon as he spotted us on the dock. I had finally agreed to let him take us to see his grand new home, which was close to completion. Until now, I had avoided doing so, for I feared that once I set foot in the mansion, I would be tempted to accept Paul's proposal.

Perhaps it was only in my eyes, but to me Paul had grown leaner, more mature, since I had returned to the bayou. There was still that boyish glint in his blue eyes from time to time, but most always now, he was pensive and serious. His new business duties as well as the supervising of the building of his home, combined with his worrying about Pearl and me, kept a dark shadow over his face, a shadow that troubled me, for I was afraid I was dragging him down along with me. Of course, he spared no effort to convince me I was wrong. Every time I suggested such a thing, he laughed and said, "Don't you know that when you returned to the bayou, you brought the sunshine back into my life?"

Right now his face was full of smiles as he brought the boat up to the dock.

"Hi. Guess what," he said excitedly. "The chandeliers were just hung and turned on. Wait until you see them. It's a spectacle. I had them imported from France, you know. And the pool is filled and running. Do you know the stained glass in the Palladian fan window comes from Spain? I paid a fortune for it," he added without taking a breath.

"Hello Paul," I said, laughing.

"What? Oh, I'm sorry." He leaned forward to kiss my cheek. "I guess I sound a little excited about our house, huh?"

I looked down. I couldn't keep my heart from fluttering every time he said *our* house.

"Paul . . ."

"Don't say anything," he said quickly. "Don't come to

any conclusions or decisions. Let the house and the grounds speak for themselves."

I shook my head at him. Would he ever take no for an answer? I imagined that even if I married someone else and lived to be a hundred, he would be coming to my door, waiting for me to change my mind.

We all got into his boat and Paul started the engine again. Pearl laughed as we spun around and into the breeze, some spray raining on our arms and faces. The early spring had brought the hibernating alligators out. They dozed on the mounds and in shallow water, their sleepy eyes barely showing any curiosity as we rushed past them. Here and there clumps of green snakes came apart and then entwined again like threads being woven together under the water. Bullfrogs hopped over lily pads, and nutrias scurried into the safety of shadows and small openings. The swamp, like some giant animal itself, seemed to stretch and yawn and take shape as spring arrived and marched its determined way toward the heat of summer.

"Number three well exploded this morning," Paul shouted over the roar of the engine. "It looks like it will produce four, maybe five times what was estimated."

"That's wonderful, Paul."

"The future couldn't look brighter, Ruby. We could have anything, do anything, go anywhere.... Pearl would be a real princess."

"I don't want her to be a princess, Paul. I want her to be a fine young lady who appreciates the value of important things," I said curtly. "I've seen too many people fooled by their own wealth into believing they were happy."

"It won't be that way for us," Paul assured me.

Paul's rich acres of oil land and the homesite was southwest of my shack. We wove our way along, passing through canals that were so narrow at times, we could thrust out our arms and touch the shore on either side of the boat. We cut through some brackish ponds and into an entire new web of canals before turning dead south into his property. I hadn't been here since I had left for New Orleans, so when I saw the roof of the great house rising above the sycamores and cypress before us, I was overwhelmed. I felt like Alice being swept off to her own private Wonderland.

Paul had already had a dock built and there was a gravel path from the swamp that led up to the beginning of the house property. I saw the pickup trucks and vehicles that belonged to the workmen who were still hard at their labor, for Paul had put a rush on things and was willing to pay everyone time and a half to get the house completed ahead of schedule. To the east we could see the oil rigs at work.

"I bet you never dreamed the Cajun boy who motored about on his little scooter would own all this," Paul said proudly, his hands on his hips, his smile stretching from ear to ear. "Imagine what your grandmere Catherine would say."

"Grandmere probably would have expected it," I replied.

"Probably," he said, and laughed. "Whenever she looked at me, I felt she could not only see my thoughts, but my dreams."

He helped Pearl and me out of the boat.

"I'll carry her," he offered. Pearl was dazzled by the vastness of the house before us. "I'd like to call it Cypress Woods," he said. "What do you think?"

"Yes, it's a wonderful name. It is overwhelming, Paul. The way it just pops up out of nowhere . . . it's magical."

He beamed a broad smile of pride.

"I told the architect I wanted a house that resembled a Greek temple. It makes the Dumas residence in the Garden District look like a bungalow."

"Is that what you wanted to do, Paul . . . overshadow my father's home? I told you . . ."

"Don't take me to task just yet, Ruby. What good is anything I have if I can't use it to please and impress you?" he asked. His eyes hardened to rivet on me.

"Oh, Paul." I wagged my head and took a deep breath.

What could I say to counter his enthusiasm and his dreams?

As we approached the house, it seemed to grow even bigger and bigger before us. Across the upstairs gallery ran a diamond-design iron railing. On both sides of the house, Paul had wings constructed to echo the predominant elements of the main house.

"That's where the servants will live," he indicated. "I think it gives everyone more privacy. Most of the walls in this place are twenty-four inches thick. Wait until you see how cool it is in there, even without fans and air-conditioning."

A short slate stairway took us up to the portico and lower gallery. We walked between the great columns and into the Spanish-tile-floored entryway, a foyer designed to take away the breath of a visitor the moment he or she set foot in this mansion, for it wasn't only vast and long, but the ceiling was so high, our footsteps echoed.

"Think of all the wonderful art you could hang on these huge walls, Ruby," Paul said.

We passed one spacious and airy room after another, all opening onto the central hallway. Above us hung the chandeliers about which Paul had expressed so much pride. They were dazzling, the teardrop bulbs looking like diamonds raining down over us. The circular stairway was twice as wide and as elaborate as the one in the House of Dumas.

"The kitchen is at the rear of the house," Paul said. "I have equipped it with all the most modern appliances. Any cook would be in heaven working back there. Maybe you can find where your Nina Jackson went and convince her to come live here," he added as a bonus. He knew how fond of Nina, my father's cook, I had been. She practiced voodoo and had taken an affection to me from the first day I had arrived in New Orleans. After she was convinced I wasn't some sort of zombie made to look like Gisselle, that is.

"I don't think anything would tempt Nina from New Orleans," I said.

"Her loss," Paul replied quickly. He was so sensitive about the rich Creoles, interpreting any comparisons as a criticism of our Cajun world.

"I mean she is too attached to her voodoo world, Paul," I explained. He nodded.

"Let me show you the upstairs."

We went up the stairway to find four spacious bedrooms, each with a dressing room and walk-in closets. There were two master bedrooms, something Paul had definitely designed with his proposal of marriage in mind. Each looked out over the swamps. However, there was an adjoining door.

"Well?" He waited anxiously, his eyes searching my face.

"It is a magnificent house, Paul."

"I have saved the best for last," he replied with that impish twinkle in his eyes. "Follow me," he said, taking us to a door that opened to an outside stairway. It was at the rear of the mansion, so I hadn't seen it when we first approached.

The stairway led us up to an enormous attic with hand-cut cypress structural beams. There were large windows looking out over the fields and canals, but none on the side that faced the oil rigs. The great skylights provided illumination and made it bright and airy.

"Do you know what this is?" he asked, and flashed me a brief, amused smile. "This," he said, holding out his arms, "will be your studio."

I widened my eyes, overwhelmed with the possibilities.

"As you can see, I've provided the best views. Look, Ruby," he said, going to the window, "look at what you could paint. Look at the world we love, our world, a world that could surely inspire you to return to your wonderful artistic talents and create masterpieces that your rich Creole friends would beat each other down to possess."

He stood by the window and held Pearl. She was intrigued and fascinated by the view. Below us, the construction workers had started their cleanup. Their voices and laughter were carried up to us in the wind. In the distance the canals that wove their way through the swamps toward Houma and my shack home looked unreal, toylike. I could see the birds flitting from tree to tree, and off to the right, an oyster fisherman poling his way home from a day's harvesting. There was a store of pictures and ideas for any artist to choose and embellish with his or her imagination.

"Can't you be happy here, Ruby?" Paul asked, pleading with his eyes.

"Who couldn't be happy here, Paul? It's beyond words. But you know what has made me hesitate," I said softly.

"And you know that I have thought it all out carefully and proposed a way for us to be together and not be sinners. Oh, Ruby, it's not our fault that our parents created us with this stain on our heads. All I want is to provide for you and Pearl and make you happy and safe forever."

"But what about . . . Paul, there is a side of life that you would be eliminating for yourself," I reminded him. "You're a man, a handsome, virile young man."

"I'm willing to do that," he said quickly.

I looked down. I had to confess my true feelings.

"I don't know if I am willing to do that, Paul. You know that I have been in love, passionately in love, and you know I have tasted the ecstasy that comes in touching someone you love and someone who loves you."

"I know," he said sadly. "But I don't ask you to give up that ecstasy."

I looked up sharply. "What do you mean?"

"Let us make a pact that if either one of us finds someone with whom we can find that ecstasy, the other won't stand in his or her way, even if it means . . . parting.

"Meanwhile, Ruby, put your passion back into your art. I will put mine in my work and my ambition for all of us. Let me give you what would otherwise be the most perfect world, a world in which you know you will have love and in which Pearl will have security and comfort

15

and not suffer the miseries we have seen so many suffer in so-called normal families," he begged.

Pearl looked at me as if she were joining his plea, her sapphire eyes soft and quiet.

"Paul, I just don't know."

"We can hold each other. We can be warm to each other. We can look after each other . . . forever. You've been through more tragedy and misery than someone your age should have experienced. You're far older than your years because of it. Let wisdom replace passion. Let faithfulness, devotion, and pure goodness be the foundation of our lives. Together, we'll create our own special monastery."

I gazed into his eyes and felt the sincerity. It was all so overpowering: his devotion, this wonderful house, the promise of a secure, happy life after having lived through the misery he mentioned.

"What about your parents, Paul?" I asked, feeling myself slipping toward a yes.

"What about them?" he said sharply. "They brought me up in deception. My father will accept what I decide, and if he doesn't . . . what of it? I have my own fortune now," he added, his eyes narrowing and darkening.

I shook my head with confusion. I remembered Grandmere Catherine's dour warning about separating a Cajun man from his family. Paul seemed to hear my thoughts and soften.

"Look, I'll speak to my father and get him to see why this is a good decision for both of us. Once he sees that goodness in our choice, he will understand."

I bit down on my lower lip and started to shake my head.

"Don't say yes, don't say no," he said quickly. "Say you will think more, think seriously about it. I'll haunt you forever, Ruby Dumas, until you become Ruby Tate," he said. Then he turned to show Pearl the view.

I stepped back and gazed at them. He would be a wonderful father, I told myself again. Maybe it was time to make a decision solely for Pearl's sake and not for my own.

I gazed at what would be a magnificent studio, imagining where I would put my tables and shelves. When I turned back, both he and Pearl were looking at me.

"Could it be yes, finally?" he asked, seeing the expression on my face.

I nodded and he flooded Pearl's face with kisses so that she giggled.

Twilight had begun in the bayou by the time we started back to my house. The Spanish moss draped over and under the cypress trees and vines took on a soft, wavy look. We passed through the shadows cast by overhanging willow trees, and the soft, undulating motion of the boat rocked Pearl to sleep. It was beautiful here, I thought. We belonged here, and if it meant living with Paul under our special arrangement, then perhaps that was what destiny had in store for me and Pearl.

"I've got to get back to dinner at the house," Paul said after we pulled up to the dock and he helped us out of the boat. "Uncle John, my mother's brother, is here from Clearwater, Florida, and I promised," he said apologetically.

"It's all right. I'm tired and I want to go to sleep early tonight myself."

"I'll stop by as soon as I can tomorrow. Tonight, if I can get an hour alone with my father, I'll tell him about our decision," he added firmly. My heart began to pitter-patter. It was one thing to talk about all this, but another to actually start the series of events that would make us man and wife.

"I hope it's the right decision, Paul," I said.

"Of course it is. Stop worrying. We'll be very happy," he promised, and leaned over to kiss my cheek. "Besides, God owes us some happiness and success," he added with a smile.

I waved good-bye as he started away in his boat. After I

17

fed Pearl and put her to sleep, I ate a little gumbo, read by the butane lantern, and went to sleep myself, praying for the wisdom to make the right decisions.

Mornings began for me now just the way they had when I had lived here with Grandmere Catherine. After I carried out the blankets, baskets, and palmetto hats I had woven in the loom room, I set Pearl out in her carriage in the shade beside the roadside stand and did some needlework to pass the time and wait for any tourist customers. It was a quiet morning, but I had nearly a half dozen cars stop and sold most of my blankets and baskets by lunch. I had only a few customers for my gumbo, and then the long, quiet, and hot afternoon settled over the bayou. When the insects began to bother Pearl, I decided it was time to take a break and brought her into the shack for her afternoon nap. I had expected Paul to drop by during lunch, but he didn't, and he had still not arrived by midafternoon.

I made myself some cold lemonade and sat on the front gallery just thinking about the past. In my pocket I had crumpled the most recent letter from my twin sister, Gisselle. She was attending a ritzy private college in New Orleans that sounded more like a place to dump spoiled rich young people than a real institute of higher learning. Her teachers, from what she wrote, let her get away with not doing her reading or homework or paying attention in class. She even bragged about how often she cut classes without being reprimanded for doing so.

But in all of her letters she loved to include some news of Beau, and even if it was news that brought me pain, I still had to read it repeatedly. I unfolded the letter and skipped down to those passages. "You might be interested to know," she wrote, knowing how much I wanted to know . . .

that Beau is getting more serious with this girl in Europe. His parents told Daphne that Beau and his French debutante are only inches away from announcing a formal engagement. All they do is rave about her, how beautiful she is, how wealthy she is, and how cultured she is. They said the best thing they could have done for him was to send him to Europe and keep him there.

Now let me tell you about the boys here at Gallier. . . .

I balled the letter in my fist and shoved it back into my pocket. Memories of Beau seemed stronger now that I was thinking about marrying Paul and choosing a safe, secure life. But it promised to be a life without passion, and whenever I thought about that, I thought about Beau. His soft smile appeared before me and I recalled the morning when Gisselle and I were leaving for Greenwood, the private school in Baton Rouge. He had arrived just in time and we had only a few minutes to say our good-byes, but he surprised me by giving me the locket I still wore hidden under my blouse.

I pulled it out and opened it to look at his face and mine. Oh, Beau, I thought, surely I will never love another man as passionately as I loved you, and if I can't have you, then perhaps a happy, secure life with Paul is the right choice. The feel of warm tears on my cheeks surprised me. I wiped them away quickly and sat back just as a familiar big automobile pulled into the yard. It was Paul's father, Octavious. I closed the locket and quickly dropped it back under my blouse where it rested between my breasts.

A tall, distinguished-looking man who was always well dressed and well groomed, Mr. Tate stepped out of his car. His shoulders dipped like a weary old man's and his eyes looked tired. Paul got most of his good looks from his father, who had a strong mouth and jaw with a straight nose, not too long or too narrow. I hadn't seen Mr. Tate for some time and I was a bit surprised at how much he had aged in the interim.

"Afternoon, Ruby," he said when he reached the steps. "I was wondering if I could talk to you sort of privately."

My heart was pounding. I couldn't remember passing

more than a half dozen words between us, mostly hellos and good-byes at church over the years.

"Of course," I said, standing. "Come inside. Would you like a glass of lemonade? I just made a fresh pitcher."

"I would. Thanks," he said, and followed me into the house.

"Please, sit down," I said, nodding toward my one good piece of furniture: the rocker.

I poured his glass of lemonade and returned to the living room.

"Thank you," he said, taking the glass, and I sat across from him on the worn, faded brown settee, the threads so thin on the ends of the arms, the stuffing of Spanish moss showed through. He took a sip of the lemonade. "Very good," he said. Then he looked about nervously for a moment and smiled. "You haven't got much here, Ruby, but you keep it real nice."

"Not as nice as Grandmere Catherine used to keep it," I said.

"Your grandmere was quite a woman. I must confess I never took much stock in faith healing and the herbal medicines she concocted, but I know many people who swore by her. And if anyone could stand up to your grandpere, it was her," he added.

"I miss her a great deal," I admitted. He nodded and sipped some more lemonade. Then he took a deep breath. "I guess . . . I guess I'm a little nervous. The past has a way of coming back at you and punching you in the stomach when you least expect it sometimes," he added, and leaned forward, his sharp, penetrating gaze fixing on me.

"You're Catherine Landry's granddaughter and you've been through a helluva lot yourself. I can see in your face that you're much older and wiser than the pretty little girl I used to see march up to the church beside her grandmere."

"The past has punched us both in the stomach," I said. His eyes brightened with more interest.

"Yes. Well then, you'll understand why I don't want to

beat around the bush. You know some of what happened in the past and you probably got some ideas about me. I don't blame anyone but myself for that. Twenty-one years ago, I was what you'd call a very young man, full of himself. I'm not here to justify anything or make excuses for myself," he added quickly. "What I did was wrong and I've been paying for it in one way or another all my life.

"But your mother . . . Gabrielle . . . she was one special young woman." He shook his head and smiled with the memory. "Being your grandmere's daughter and all, I used to think she was one of them swamp goddesses about whom the old folks whispered and most Christian folks half believed in in spite of themselves. Seemed like you could never come upon her, never surprise her without her looking beautiful, so beautiful, it was . . . spiritual. I know it's hard for you to understand about a woman you never set eyes on, but that's the way she was."

Deep in my heart, I felt waves of dread. Why was he telling all this now?

"Every time I set eyes on her," he continued, "my heart would pound and I'd feel like tiptoeing around her. When she looked at me . . . it was like that Greek thing . . . you know with that cherub and his bow and arrow?"

"Cupid?"

"Yeah, Cupid. I was married, but we had no children yet. I tried to love my wife. I did," he said, raising his hand, "but it was as if Gabrielle cast spells or something. One day I was poling through the swamp alone, returning from a little fishing, and I came around a turn and found her swimming without a stitch of clothing. I thought all time had stopped. I froze and held my breath. All I could do was watch her. She had the most youthful, happy eyes, and when she set them on me, she laughed. I couldn't help myself. I peeled off my own clothes as fast as I could and dove into the water. We swam side by side, splashed each other and tormented each other by embracing and breaking away. I followed her out of the water to her canoe and there . . .

"Well, the rest you know. I owned up to what I had done as soon as it was revealed. Your grandpere Jack came after me.

"Gladys, well, she was devastated, of course. I broke down and cried and begged her to forgive me. In the end she didn't, but she was bigger about it than I thought possible. She decided we would pretend the baby was hers and she began this elaborate ruse, faking her pregnancy.

"Your grandpere wasn't satisfied with the initial payment. He came after me time after time, demanding more until I finally put an end to it. By then Paul was a little boy and I realized no one would believe any story Jack Landry spun. He stopped bothering me and the whole affair ended.

"Of course, I've spent most of my life ever since trying to make it up to my wife. She never let Paul think she was anything but his mother either, and until the time Paul found out the truth, he never felt anything toward her but a son's love. I'm sure of that. In fact, I go so far as to say he still feels that way toward Gladys. He's just an awfully confused young man sometimes. We've had our arguments about it, and I thought he understood and accepted and finally forgave."

He paused and anxiously, with narrow eyes, waited for me to digest his tale.

"That's a great deal to ask anyone to forgive, especially Paul," I said. His lips grew tight for a moment and then he nodded as if confirming a thought about me.

"I got to tell you," he continued, "when you ran off to New Orleans, I was happy. I thought he would start looking for a nice young lady to be his wife and the turmoil would be over, but . . . you came back, and last night . . . last night he came to me and told me what you two had decided. All the time he was having that mansion built, I feared something like this, but I hoped I was wrong."

He sat back, exhausted for a moment.

"Our plan is to just live together, side by side," I said softly. "So many people around here think Pearl is Paul's child anyway."

"I know. Gladys even feared it herself for a while until Paul explained, but now she's in a deep depression. You see," he said, sitting forward, "we both want only the best for Paul. We want him to have a normal life, to have the things any man should have, especially children of his own. I don't think he realizes what he's proposing to do.

"In short, Ruby, I come here to plead for my son. I come here to ask you to refuse to marry him. There's no need for him to pay for his father's sins. Maybe this one time, the son don't have to have his father's mistakes and pain on his head. We can change it, stop it from happening, if you'll only turn him away. Once you do, he'll settle down and marry some nice young girl and—"

"The last thing in the world I want to do, Mr. Tate, is hurt Paul," I said, the tears streaming down my face. I made no effort to wipe them away and they dripped from my chin.

"I'm really asking for my wife, too. I don't want her hurt anymore. It seems this sin I committed won't die. It's reared its ugly head again to haunt me even twenty-one years later."

He straightened up in his seat. "I'm prepared to offer you some security, Ruby. I can give you what you need until you find yourself another young man and—"

"Don't!" I cried. "Don't offer me a bribe, Mr. Tate. Seems like everyone wants to buy away their troubles in this world, that everyone, whether it's rich Creoles or rich Cajuns, everyone thinks money has the power to right every wrong. I'm doing just fine right now, and soon I will be inheriting money from my father's estate."

"I'm sorry," he said softly. "I just thought . . ."

"I don't want it."

I turned away and a heavy silence fell between us.

"I'm begging you for my son," he said softly. I closed my eyes and tried to swallow, but my throat wouldn't work. It felt as if I had already swallowed a small rock and it was stuck in my chest. I nodded.

"I'll tell Paul I can't do it," I said, "but I don't know if you understand how much he wants it."

"I understand. I'm prepared to do all I can to help him get over it."

"Don't offer to buy him anything," I warned, my eyes full of fire. He seemed to shrink in the rocking chair. "He's not like Grandpere Jack."

"I know." After a moment he added, "I got another favor to ask of you."

"What's that?" I flared, my rage simmering just like milk boiling in a pot.

"Please don't tell him I came here today. I had him do an errand for me that took him out of the area just so I could pay you this visit without his knowing. If he found out . . ."

"I won't tell him," I said.

"Thank you." He stood up. "You're a fine young woman as well as a very beautiful one. I'm sure you're going to find happiness someday, and if there's anything you need, anything I can do for you . . ."

"There's nothing," I said sharply. He saw the fury in my eyes and the smile left his face.

"I'll be going," he said. I didn't get up. I sat there staring at the floor until I heard him walk out and heard him start his car and drive away. Then I flung myself down on the settee and cried until I ran dry of tears.

2

Unfinished Business

After Pearl woke from her nap, I gave her a bottle and took her out again while I sat by the roadside stand watching out for any late afternoon business. There was a flurry of activity for about an hour and then the road became quiet and empty, the dwindling sunlight casting its long shadows across the macadam, bringing the curtain down on daytime.

My heart felt so heavy. Mr. Tate's visit had cast a deep pall over everything. I felt as if Pearl and I had no home. We didn't belong here and we didn't belong in New Orleans, but I thought it was going to be even worse living here after I had turned Paul away. Every time he visited, if he ever wanted to visit again, there would be this storm of sadness hanging over our heads.

Maybe Mr. Tate was right, I thought. Maybe after I had rejected Paul, he would find someone new, but even if that loomed as a possibility, I knew it would have a much greater chance of happening if Pearl and I were truly gone and out of his life. Once he saw our marrying and living together was impossible, he might seek happiness elsewhere.

But then, where should we go? What should we do? I wondered. I had no other relatives to whom I could run. I took Pearl into the house and brought in what was left from the stand, desperately trying to think out some sort of future for us. Finally an idea came to me. I decided to swallow my pride, sit at the table, and write a letter to Daphne.

Dear Daphne,

I haven't written to you all this time because I didn't imagine you cared to hear from me. I am not going to argue that you shouldn't have been upset to learn I was pregnant with Beau's child. I am old enough to realize I must be responsible for my own actions, but I couldn't go through with the abortion you had arranged, and now that I have my daughter, whom I have named Pearl, I am happy I didn't, although I know our lives will be hard.

I thought if I could return to the bayou, to the world in which I had grown up and been happy, all would be well and I wouldn't have to be a problem for anyone, least of all you. We never got along when my father was alive, and I don't anticipate us ever getting along.

But circumstances here are not what I thought they would be, and I have come to the conclusion, I can't stay here. But don't be afraid. I'm not asking you to take me back. I'm only asking that you give me some of my inheritance now so I can make a life for myself and my daughter someplace else . . . someplace not in New Orleans, and not in the bayou. You won't be giving me anything that's not coming to me; you'll only be giving it to me sooner. I'm sure you would agree that it would be something my father would want you to do.

Please give this consideration and let me know as

soon as you can. I assure you, once you do this, we will have little or no contact.

                                        Sincerely yours,
                                        Ruby

While I was addressing the letter, I heard a car pull into the yard. I stopped writing and hid the letter in the pocket of my dress quickly.

"Hi," Paul said, entering. "Sorry I wasn't here earlier. I had an errand that took me to Breaux Bridge. How was your day? Busy?"

"A little," I said. I shifted my gaze downward, but it was too late.

"Something's wrong," he said. "What is it?"

"Paul," I said after taking a deep breath, "we can't do it. We can't marry and live at Cypress Woods. I've thought about it and thought about it, and I know we shouldn't do it."

"What's changed your mind?" he asked, grimacing with surprise and disappointment. "You were so happy yesterday in the house. It was as if a dark cloud had been lifted from your face," he reminded me.

"You were right about Cypress Woods. The house and the grounds cast a spell. It was as if we had entered a make-believe world, and for a while I let it convince me. It was easy to pretend and to ignore reality there."

"So? It is our world. I can make it as wonderful as any make-believe world. And as long as we don't hurt anyone . . ."

"But we are hurting someone, Paul. We're hurting each other," I pointed out painfully.

"No," he began, but I knew I had to talk fast and hard or I would break into tears.

"Yes, we are. We can pretend. We can make promises. We can make special arrangements, but the result is the same . . . we're condemning each other to an unnatural life."

"Unnatural . . . to be with someone you love and want to protect and . . ."

27

"And never to hold passionately, and never to have children with, and never to reveal the truth about . . . We won't even be able to tell Pearl, for fear of what it will do to her. I can't do it."

"Of course we will be able to tell her when she's old enough to understand," he corrected. "And she will understand. Ruby, look . . ."

"No, Paul. I . . . don't think I can make the sacrifices you think you can make," I concluded.

He stared at me a moment, his eyes small, suspicious. "I don't believe you. Something else happened. Someone spoke to you. Who was it, one of your grandmere Catherine's friends, the priest? Who?"

"No," I said. "No one has spoken to me unless you want to count my own sensible conscience." I had to turn away. I couldn't stand looking at the pain in his eyes.

"But . . . I had a talk with my father last night, and after I explained everything to him, he agreed and gave me his approval. My sisters don't know anything about the past, so they were overjoyed to learn you would be my wife and their new sister. And even my mother . . ."

"What about your mother, Paul?" I asked sharply. He closed and then opened his eyes.

"She will accept it," he promised.

"Accepting is not approving." I shook my head and fired my words like bullets. "If she accepts it, it will be because she doesn't want to lose you," I said. "Anyway, it's not her decision. It's mine," I added a little more sternly than I had intended.

Paul's face whitened.

"Ruby . . . the house . . . everything I have . . . it's only for you. I don't even care about myself . . . you and Pearl."

"You must care about yourself, Paul. You should. It's wrong of me to be so selfish as to let you deny yourself a normal marriage and a normal family."

"But that's for me to decide," he retorted.

"You're too . . . confused to make the right decision," I said, and looked away.

"You'll think more about it," he pleaded, and nodded to convince himself there was still hope. "I'll come by tomorrow and we'll talk again."

"No, Paul. I've decided. There's no point in our continually talking about it. I can't go through with it. I can't," I cried, and turned away from him. Pearl, sensing unhappiness between us, began to cry, too. "You'd better go," I said. "The baby's getting upset."

"Ruby . . ."

"Please, Paul. Don't make this any more difficult than it has to be."

He went to the door, but just stood there gazing out.

"All day," he said softly, "I was like someone traveling on a cloud. Nothing could make me unhappy."

Although I was really feeling sick now, I still managed to find a voice. "You'll feel that way again, Paul. I'm sure you will."

"No, I won't," he said, turning back to me, his eyes full of pain and anger. His cheeks were so red, he looked like a sunburnt tourist from the North. "I swear I'll never look at another woman. I'll never kiss another woman. I'll never hold another woman." He raised his right fist and shook it toward the ceiling. "I'll take the same vows of chastity our priest has taken and I'll turn that great house into a shrine. I'll live there all alone forever and ever and I'll die there with no one beside me, nothing but the memory of you," he added, and then he shoved open the door and ran across the gallery and down the steps.

"Paul!" I cried. I couldn't stand to see him this angry and hurt. But he didn't come back. I heard him start his engine and spin his tires on the gravel as he shot away, his heart shattered.

It seemed that everyone I touched, I managed to hurt. Was I born to bring pain to those who loved me? I swallowed back my tears so Pearl wouldn't be upset, but I felt like an island with the sea eddying around me. Now I truly had no one.

After my heart stopped pattering like a woodpecker, I began to prepare us some dinner. My baby sensed my unhappiness despite my attempts to bury it under busy-work. When I spoke, she heard it in my voice, and when I gazed at her, she saw the darkness in my eyes.

While the roux simmered, I sat with her in Grandmere Catherine's rocker and stared at the painting. Both Grandmere Catherine's and my mother's faces looked sad and sympathetic. The vivid memory of Paul's distraught face hung like the threat of a storm in the air around me. Every time I looked toward the door, I saw him standing there, glaring back, reciting his vows and threats. Why was I hurting the one person who wanted to love and cherish my child and me? Where would I ever find such affection again?

"Am I doing the right thing, Grandmere?" I whispered. I heard only silence and then Pearl smacking her lips.

I fed her, but her appetite was as curtailed as mine. She really only sucked a little of her bottle, and as she did so, she kept closing her eyes. It was as if she were just as emotionally exhausted as I was, as if every feeling, every emotion, went from me to her over the invisible wires that bound mother and child. I decided I would take her upstairs and put her to bed, and had just gotten up to do so when I heard a car approaching. Its headlights washed over the house and then it came to a stop and I heard a car door open and slam. Had Paul come back with new arguments? Even if he did, I thought, I couldn't weaken my resolve.

But the heaviness of the footsteps on the floor of the gallery told me it was someone else. There was a loud rapping at the door, making the entire shack shake on its toothpick legs. I walked slowly from the kitchen, my heart beginning to pound almost as hard as that rapping.

"Who is it?" I asked. Pearl gazed curiously toward the door as well. Instead of replying, the visitor pulled the door open so roughly, he almost lifted it off its hinges. I saw this hulk of a man enter, his messy brown hair long and straggly to his dirty thick neck. He had hands as big as mallets, the thick fingers caked with grease and grime. When he stepped into the light of the butane lantern, I gasped.

Although I had met him only once and seen him only a few times before, Buster Trahaw's face loomed in my memory beside my worst nightmares. He was even uglier than he was the day he had come to the house with Grandpere Jack to solidify their agreement that I would marry him if he would give Grandpere as much as a thousand dollars. What was even worse was, Grandpere was going to let him sleep with me beforehand, to test me as if I were some kind of merchandise.

I remembered him then as a man in his mid-thirties, tall and stout with a circle of fat around his stomach and sides that made it look as if he wore an inner tube under his shirt. He had added to that girth since, and his facial features, distorted by his weight, were now so bloated, he looked like a cross between a pig and a man. Only now he had a stringy beard, untrimmed around the chin, with hairs curling off his neck and joining to make it seem as if he were part ape, too.

When he smiled, his thick lips practically disappeared under the mustache and chin hairs, revealing the loss of most of his front teeth. The ones that remained were stained with tobacco juice, making his mouth resemble some cavernous charred oven. The skin on the exposed parts of his cheeks was flaked and peeling, reminding me of a snake shedding. There were thin, wiry hairs emerging from his huge nostrils, and his eyebrows joined to form a thick, dark line over his bulging dull brown eyes.

"It is true," he said. "You're back. The Slaters told me when I brought my wagon in to be repaired."

He leaned back, opened the door a bit, and spit out a wad of chewing tobacco. Then he returned his gaze, his smile wide.

"What do you want?" I demanded. Pearl held tightly to me. She began to whimper like a puppy at the sight of him.

31

His smile evaporated quickly. "What do I want? Don't you know who I am? I'm Buster Trahaw and I want what's comin' to me, is what I want," he said, and stepped forward. I retreated as many steps. "That your new baby there? She's a honey child, all right. Been makin' babies without me, have you?" he said, and laughed. "Well, that's over."

I felt the blood drain down to my feet as his intentions became clear.

"What are you talking about? Get out of here. I didn't invite you into my house. Leave or—"

"Hey now, whoa horse. You forgettin' what's coming to me?"

"I don't know what you're talking about."

"I'm talkin' 'bout the deal I made with your grandpere Jack, the money I gave him the night before you run off. I let him keep it 'cause he said you was comin' back. Course, I knew he was an old liar, but I figured the money was well spent. I said to myself, Buster, your time will come, and here it has, ain't it?"

"No," I said. "I made no agreements with you. Now, get out."

"I ain't gettin' out till I get what's comin' to me. What's the difference to you anyway? You make babies without a husband at your side, don'tcha?" He flashed that toothless smile at me again.

"Get out!" I screamed. Pearl started to cry. I started to turn away, but Buster moved quickly to seize my wrist.

"Here now, be careful you don't drop the baby," he said with a threat in his voice. I tried to keep my face turned away from him. His breath and the odor from his clothes and body was enough to turn my stomach. He started to pry my arms from Pearl.

"No!" I cried, but I didn't want the baby hurt. She was screaming hysterically when he put his big, dirty hands around her waist.

"Let me just hold her a moment, will ya? I got babies of my own. I know what to do."

Rather than pull and tug with Pearl between us, I had to release her.

"Don't hurt her," I begged. She cried and waved her arms toward me.

"Hey, now, hey . . . it's your . . . uncle Buster," he said. "She's a pretty one. Goin' to break someone's heart, too, I betcha."

"Please, give her back to me," I pleaded.

"Sure. Buster Trahaw don't hurt babies. Buster Trahaw makes babies," he said, and laughed at his own joke.

I took Pearl back and stepped away.

"Put her to bed," he ordered. "We got business to conduct."

"Please, leave us alone . . . please. . . ."

"I ain't leavin' till I get what I come for," he said. "Now, is it goin' to be hard or easy? I can take it either way. Thing is," he said, smiling again, "I kinda like it the hard way more. It's like wrestlin' an alligator." He stepped toward me and I gasped. "Put her to bed less'n she's going to get an early education, hear?"

I swallowed hard. It was difficult to breathe and not be drowned in what was happening so fast.

"Put her down on that sofa there," he ordered. "She'll cry herself to sleep jist like most babies. Go on."

I eyed the settee and the door, but despite his stupidity, he had enough sense to anticipate that and stepped back to block my escape. Reluctantly I brought Pearl to the settee and set her down. She screamed and screamed.

Buster took my wrist and pulled me to him. I tried to resist, but it was like holding back the tide. He wrapped his enormous arms around me, crushing me to his stomach and chest, and then he pinched my chin in his powerful fingers and forced me to look up so he could bring those spongy lips to my mouth. I gagged under their wet pressure, holding my breath and trying to keep myself from falling unconscious. I was terrified that if I did, he would just rip off my clothes and have his way with me.

33

His right hand moved down my waist until he cupped my rear in it and lifted me, bouncing me in his hands as if I weighed only a little more than Pearl.

"Whoa, now. This is a fine piece of merchandise here. Your grandpere Jack was right. Yep."

"Please," I pleaded, "not near the baby. Please."

"Sure, honey. I want a real bed for us anyway. You go on and lead the way upstairs."

He turned me roughly and pushed me toward the kitchen and the stairway. I gazed back at Pearl. She was crying hard and her whole little body was shaking.

"Go on," Buster ordered.

I started forward, searching for a means of escape. My gaze went to the roux I had left cooking on the stove. It was still simmering.

"Wait," I said. "I've got to turn this off."

"That's a good Cajun woman," Buster said. "Always thinkin' about her cookin'. Afterward, I might sample some of your gumbo anyway. Makin' love usually makes me hungry as a bear."

He stepped up behind me. I knew I had only a few seconds and if I didn't make the most of it now, I would be doomed to go up those stairs. Once up there, I was trapped and at his mercy. Even if I could jump out a window, I wouldn't, for I would be leaving him alone with Pearl. I closed my eyes, prayed, and took the handle of the pot firmly in my fingers. Then I spun around as quickly as I could and heaved the hot contents into Buster's face.

He screamed and I ducked under his arms and shot out of the kitchen. I scooped Pearl up and rushed out the door of the shack, pounding over the gallery and down the stairs. I ran into the night without looking back. I heard his shouts and curses and I heard him flailing about within, knocking over chairs, breaking dishes, smashing a window in his rage. But I didn't stop. I hurried into the darkness.

Pearl was so shocked by my actions, she stopped crying. She was shivering with fear, though, for she felt the trembling in my own body. I was afraid Buster would come running after us, but when he didn't do that, I was afraid he would get into his car and come driving after us, so I stayed in the ditches off the side of the road, ready to lunge into the brush and hide the moment I saw car headlights.

I don't know how I managed not to trip and fall with Pearl in my arms, but I was lucky there was some moonlight peeking in and out of the clouds. It threw enough illumination ahead of me to show me the way. Fortunately, I never saw his car coming. I arrived at Mrs. Thibodeau's house and pounded on her front door.

"Ruby!" she cried as soon as she set eyes on Pearl and me. "What's happened?"

"Oh, Mrs. Thibodeau, please help us. Buster Trahaw just tried to rape me in my house," I cried. She opened her door and hurried us in, locking the door after her.

"You just sit right there in the living room," she said, her face white with shock. "I'll get you some water and then I'll ring up the police. Thank goodness I got one of them phones put in last year."

She brought a glass of water back from the kitchen and took Pearl into her arms. I gulped down the cool liquid and sat back, my eyes closed, my heart still thumping so hard, I thought Mrs. Thibodeau could see it rising and falling against my blouse.

"Poor baby, poor child. Oh, my, my . . . Buster Trahaw, you say. My, my . . ."

Pearl stopped crying. She whimpered a bit and then closed her eyes and fell asleep. I took her back into my arms while Mrs. Thibodeau went back to the kitchen to call the police. A short while later, a patrol car arrived, and when the two policemen came in, I described what had happened to me.

"We've had more than one run-in with that good-for-nothing," one of the officers said. "You just stay right here until we come back."

I wasn't about to move an inch. About an hour later, they returned to tell us they found him still at my shack.

He had done some damage and then dug a bottle of rotgut whiskey out of his car to sit and wait for my return. From what they described, they had to have another pair of policemen come by to help subdue Buster.

"We got him in the cage, where he belongs," the policeman told me. "But you'll have to come down to the police station and swear out a complaint. You can do it now or you can do it in the morning."

"She's exhausted," Mrs. Thibodeau said.

"Morning will be fine," the policeman told us. "You don't want to go back to your house just yet anyway," he added, gazing at Mrs. Thibodeau. "It will take a bit of work."

"Oh, Mrs. Thibodeau," I wailed. "He's ruined the only home I have."

"Now, now, child. You know we'll all be there to help you fix it up again. Don't you fret about it. Just get some sleep so you can be bright and cheerful for Pearl in the morning."

I nodded. She brought me a blanket and I slept on her sofa with Pearl in my arms. I didn't think I could sleep, but the moment I closed my eyes, exhaustion set in firmly, and the next thing I knew, the morning light was warming my face. Pearl moaned when I stirred. Her little eyelids fluttered open and she gazed into my face. The realization that she was safe in my arms brought a smile to her lips. I kissed her and thanked God we had escaped.

After Mrs. Thibodeau made us some breakfast, I left Pearl with her and walked to town to go to the police station. They couldn't have been any nicer to me, getting a seat for me immediately and making sure I was comfortable. A secretary brought me some coffee.

"You don't have to worry about proving anything," the policeman sitting at the desk told me. "Buster doesn't deny what he did. He's still complaining about not getting his money's worth. What's that all about?"

I had to tell what Grandpere Jack had done. I was ashamed of it, but there was no other way. All of the policemen who heard the story nodded in sympathy and disgust. Unfortunately, some of them remembered Grandpere Jack vividly.

"He and Buster are cut from the same cloth," the desk policeman told me. Then he took down my statement and told me not to worry. Buster Trahaw wouldn't bother me again. They'd see to it that he was put away someplace where they lost the key. I thanked them and returned to Mrs. Thibodeau's.

I think the reason some people in the bayou still didn't have phones and television sets in their shacks was that news traveled almost as fast without them here. By the time I picked up Pearl and headed back to our home, there were a dozen or so of our neighbors working on the house. In his rage, Buster had ripped off the front door and broken almost every window.

Miraculously, Grandmere Catherine's old rocker survived, although it looked like he had kicked it over a few times. Two of the kitchen chairs didn't do as well. Both suffered broken legs. Fortunately, he started drinking before he decided to go upstairs, so nothing up there was touched. But he did wreck a good deal of my kitchen. Once the details were known, my neighbors provided.

As I came up to the house, I saw Mr. Rodrigues repairing the front door. I remembered when Grandmere Catherine had been called to his home one night to drive away a *couchemal,* an evil spirit that lurks about when an unbaptized baby dies. He was very grateful and after that night, couldn't do enough for us.

Inside the house, Ms. Rodrigues and the other women were cleaning up. A collection had already been made to replace the broken dishes and glasses. Before afternoon, it resembled a shingling party, a gathering of neighbors to help finish a roof, after which there would be a feast with everyone providing something. The goodness of my neighbors brought tears to my cheeks.

"Now, you don't cry, Ruby," Mrs. Livaudis said.

"These people here remember the good things your grandmere Catherine did for them, and they're just happy they can do something for you."

"Thank you, Mrs. Livaudis," I said. She hugged me, as did all the women before they left.

"I don't like leaving you alone," Mrs. Thibodeau said. "You're welcome to come back to my house."

"No, we'll be fine now, Mrs. Thibodeau. Thank you for your help," I said.

"Cajun people don't hurt each other," Mrs. Thibodeau emphasized. "That Buster, he was just a rotten egg from the day he was conceived."

"I know, Mrs. Thibodeau."

"Still, dear, it's not right that a young woman like yourself be left alone here in the swamp with an infant to raise." She shook her head and pursed her lips. "Him who shared the pleasure of making her should share the responsibilities, too," she added.

"I'm all right, Mrs. Thibodeau. Really."

"I hope you don't mind me saying what I think, Ruby, but I know your grandmere would want me to care, and I do care."

I nodded.

"Well, that's all. I spoke my piece. Now it's up to you young people. Times have changed," she said, wagging her head. "Times and people. Good night, dear." We hugged and she left.

By early evening everyone was gone and things settled down again. I put Pearl to sleep, humming to her awhile, and then went downstairs to have some coffee and sit out on my gallery. Mrs. Thibodeau's words returned. I knew they were the words not only thought by other neighbors, but spoken by them behind my back as well. This incident with Buster Trahaw would only make the topic that much more vocal.

When I had changed dresses, I found the letter I had written to Daphne still in my pocket. More than ever now, I felt I should mail it. I went back into the house and finished putting the address on it and then went out to put it in the mailbox for the postman to pick up in the morning. I sat on the gallery again, finally feeling myself relax.

But moments later, a rippling sensation on the back of my neck gave me the awareness that someone was near and watching. My heart contracted. I held my breath and turned to see someone silhouetted in the shadows. I gasped, but he stepped forward quickly. It was Paul. He had come by boat and walked up from the dock.

"I didn't mean to frighten you," he said. "I wanted to wait until everyone left. Are you all right?"

"Yes. Now."

"How long after I left yesterday," he asked, coming farther forward into the glow of the gallery light, "was it before Buster came here to attack you?"

"Oh, it was quite a while," I told him. "Nearly dinnertime."

"If I had been here . . ."

"You might have gotten hurt, Paul. I was just lucky to escape."

"I might have gotten hurt or I might have hurt him," he said proudly. "Or . . . he might not have come in," he added. He sat on the gallery step and leaned against the post. After a moment he said, "A young woman and a baby shouldn't be alone." It was as if he had heard Mrs. Thibodeau's words.

"Paul . . ."

"No, Ruby," he said, turning to me. Even in the subdued light, I could see the fires of determination burning in his eyes. "I want to protect you and Pearl. In the world you think is pure make-believe, you would not have to confront Buster Trahaws. I can promise you that, and Pearl wouldn't either," he pointed out.

"But, Paul, it isn't fair for you," I said in a small, tired voice. All of the resistance was slipping away.

He fixed his eyes on me a moment and then nodded slowly. "My father came here to see you, didn't he? You don't have to answer. I know he did. I saw it in his eyes last night at dinner. He's only worried about the weight of his own conscience. Why do I have to suffer for his sins?" he cried, not waiting for my answer.

"But that's just what he doesn't want you to do, Paul. If you marry me . . ."

"I will be happy. Don't I have a say in my own future?" he demanded. "And don't tell me it's fate or destiny, Ruby. You come to a fork in the canals and you choose one or the other. It's only after you've made your choice that fate or destiny takes control, and maybe not even then. I want to make that first choice and I'm not afraid of the canal I'll be poling our pirogue through as long as you and Pearl are at my side."

I sighed and lay my head back on the chair.

"Can't you be happy with me, Ruby? Even under the conditions we outlined? Can't you? You thought you could. I know you did. Why don't we give it a chance, at least? Why don't you let me try? Forget you, forget me. Let's just do it for Pearl," he said.

I smiled at him and wagged my head. "Dirty pool, Paul Marcus Tate."

"All's fair in love and war," he said, smiling back.

I took a deep breath. Out of the darkness could come all the demons of our childhood fears. Every night we put our heads to our pillows, we wondered what loitered in the shadows about our shacks. We were made stronger by our trepidations, but we were haunted by them nevertheless. I was not so naïve to think there would be no other Buster Trahaws waiting, hovering in the days to come, and that was why I put the letter to Daphne in my mailbox.

But what was the world I wanted Pearl to grow up in . . . the rich Creole world, the Cajun swamp world . . . or the magical world Paul was designing for us? To live in that castle of a house where I could spend my time painting in the great attic studio, feeling and actually being above all that was hard and dirty and difficult below, did seem like a long, golden promise come true. Should I run away into my own Wonderland? Maybe Paul was right, maybe his father was worried only about soothing his own troubled conscience. Maybe it was time to think of ourselves and to think of Pearl.

"Okay," I said softly.

"What? What did you say?"

"I said . . . okay. I'll marry you and we'll live in our own private paradise above and beyond the troubles and turmoil mired in our pasts. We'll obey our own covenants and take our own oaths. We'll pole down that canal together."

"Oh, Ruby, I'm so happy," he said. He stood up and came to me, taking my hands into his. "You're right," he said suddenly, a new excitement in his eyes. "We must have our own private ceremony first and foremost. Stand up," he said.

"What?"

"Come on. There's no better church than the front gallery of Catherine Landry's home," he declared.

"What should we do?" I asked, laughing.

"Take my hand." He seized mine into his and pulled me to my feet. "That's it. Now face . . . that sliver of a moon up there. Go on. Ready? Repeat after me. I, Ruby Dumas. Go on, do it," he said.

"I, Ruby Dumas . . ."

"Do hereby pledge to be the best friend and companion Paul Marcus Tate could have or want."

I repeated it and shook my head.

"And I promise to devote myself to my art and become as famous as possible."

That was easy to say.

"That's all I will ask of you, Ruby," he whispered. "But I have more to ask of myself," he added, and then he looked up at the moon. "I, Paul Marcus Tate, do hereby pledge to love and protect Ruby and Pearl Dumas, to take them into my special world and make them as happy as it is possible to be on this planet. I pledge to work harder and keep all that is ugly and unpleasant from our doorstep and I pledge to be honest and truthful and understanding of any and all Ruby's needs, no matter what I might feel."

He kissed me quickly on the cheek.

"Welcome to the land of magic," he said. We both laughed, but my heart was pounding as if I had really been part of some sacred and important ceremony. "We should have something . . . a toast to our happiness."

"I found a little of Grandmere Catherine's blackberry brandy in a jar at the bottom of a closet," I said. We went inside and I poured the few precious drops into two glasses. Laughing, we tapped our glasses and swallowed the brandy in a gulp. It did seem fitting that we top our pledge with something my grandmere had made.

"No ceremony, nothing any priest or judge could say, will top this," Paul declared, "for this comes from the bottom of our hearts."

I smiled. I didn't think I could feel so good so soon after my ordeal with Buster Trahaw.

"How should we get married?" I wondered, and thought about his parents again.

"A simple ceremony . . . Let's just elope," he decided. "I'll come by tomorrow and we'll drive up to Breaux Bridge. There's a retired priest there who will marry us, legal and all. He's an old friend of the family."

"But he'll want to know why your parents aren't at our sides, Paul, won't he?"

"Leave it up to me," he said. "I'm to start taking care of you from the moment I wake up tomorrow until the day I die," he said. "Or as long as you'll have me around to do so," he qualified. "Be ready at seven. Just think," he said, "all the old biddies who have been quacking about us will finally stop."

Paul remained with me talking about the house, the things we had to buy and do even after we moved in. He was so excited, I barely got in a word. He talked until I grew so tired, I couldn't keep my eyes from shutting.

"I'd better get going and let you get some sleep. We have a big day tomorrow." He kissed me on the cheek and then I watched him go off toward the canal to take his boat home.

Before I went back into the house, however, I walked

out to the mailbox and took back the letter to Daphne. I wouldn't mail it, but I couldn't get myself to tear it up. If I had learned anything in my short life, it was that nothing was forever, nothing was certain. I couldn't close all the doors. Not yet.

But at least tonight, I thought, I would go to sleep easily, dreaming of that great attic and my wonderful studio and all the exciting paintings I would do in the days to come. What a great place for Pearl to grow up in, I thought when I looked in on her. I fixed her blanket, kissed her cheek, and went to bed looking forward to my dreams.

3

My True Wonderland

Pearl's baby babble woke me. It was a heavily overcast day, so there was no warm sunlight to slip through the curtains and caress my closed eyelids until they fluttered open. As soon as I awoke, the significance of what I was about to do returned. I'm going to elope, I thought. Questions rained down from everywhere. When would I actually move Pearl and myself into Cypress Woods? How would we announce our marriage to the community? Had he informed his family by now? What, if anything, did I want to take from the shack? What kind of a wedding were we about to have?

I rose, but I had the strange sensation that I was caught in a dream. Even Pearl had a distant, quiet look in her eyes and was more patient than normally, not crying for her breakfast, not demanding to be plucked out of her crib and held.

"It's a big day for you, my precious," I told her. "Today I'm giving you a new life, a new name, and an entirely different future, one I hope is full of promise and happiness.

"We've got to pick out a nice dress for you to wear. First, let me feed you, and then you will help Mommy choose her own wedding dress, too.

"My wedding dress," I muttered, my eyes suddenly filling with tears. It was in this shack, in this very room that Grandmere Catherine and I talked about my future wedding.

"I always dreamed," she had said, coming over to me to sit beside me and stroke my hair, "that you would have the magical wedding, the one in the Cajun spider legend. Remember? The rich Frenchman imported those spiders from France for his daughter's wedding and released them into the oaks and pines where they wove their canopy of webs. Over them, he sprinkled gold and silver dust and then they had the candlelight wedding procession. The night glittered all around them, promising them a life of love and hope.

"Someday you will marry a handsome man who could be a prince, and you, too, will have a wedding in the stars," Grandmere had promised.

How sad she would be for me now. How much I was feeling sorry for myself. A young woman's heart should be filled with so much excitement on the morning of her wedding day that she would be afraid she would simply burst, I told myself. Every color should be brighter, every sweet sound, sweeter. It should seem like every single creature that lived around her was delighted, too. There should be happy, deliriously excited voices around her, and everywhere she looked, she should fix her eyes on some preparation, some activity related and solely devoted to the wonderful ceremony she was about to undertake with the man she loved.

And love . . . it should have blossomed and overwhelmed her. She would stop for a moment and wonder if it was possible to ever again be as happy and content as she was. Could any event bring her as much joy? She should be surrounded by dozens of friends, each and every one electrified, thrilled, the whole bunch of them chattering away, no one particularly listening to anyone else, but everyone listening to everyone, a cacophony of laughter, giggles, shrieks, and exclamations.

The kitchen should be filled with the sounds of clanking pots, nervous cooks, aromas of wonderful fish and chicken dishes, cakes and pies. Orders should be shouted across rooms, cars pulling up and driving off, their drivers assigned various errands. Little children would be charged with some of the electricity, making mischief and being shooed from one place to another. The older women would be pretending to be annoyed and concerned but stopping every once in a while to recall their own special day, their own excitement, and now feeling overjoyed that they were sharing in hers, drawing from it like a bee drawing pollen from a flower and turning that excitement into honey-filled memories and moments of their own pasts. She should see it on every woman's face when they finally set eyes on her in her wedding dress.

I continued to envision my dream wedding. The limousine would be waiting outside, its engine idling like a horse anxious to get galloping. The door would be flung open. Everyone would start cheering and clapping as I made my way down the gallery steps and into the car. And then the whole entourage of friends and relatives would follow behind as I was brought to the steps of the church where inside, my wonderful, loving husband-to-be stood shifting his weight from one leg to the other nervously, flashing handsome smiles at his own parents and relatives but watching that doorway for signs of my arrival.

And then the music would begin and everyone would sit solemnly, but be eager to set eyes on me starting down the aisle toward the altar where the holy sacrament waited. My feet would never touch the ground. I would walk on a shelf of air and glide slowly toward the vows.

When I closed my eyes and thought of all this, my pictures were as vivid as my paintings, but I surprised myself when I saw myself in the wedding sequence I had conjured, and when I lifted my eyes, I saw not Paul waiting, but Beau . . . my precious love . . . Beau, at last.

I sighed deeply. It was not Beau who would be coming to fetch me shortly, I reminded myself. Another shivering thought came: I was probably not even in his thoughts this day, the day I would take the vows that would tear me away from him forever. Pearl's wail reminded me, however, that I was not doing this for myself. I was doing it for her and for the promising future and the security it would bring to her.

I chose a simple light pink cotton dress with a square collar and a skirt that fell an inch or so above my ankles. I still wore the locket Beau had given me more than a year ago just before I had left for the Greenwood School in Baton Rouge, but it was wrong to wear it now. I took it off and buried it under some of my other precious things in Grandmere Catherine's old oak chest.

I had a bright pink outfit for Pearl. It had a white bow at the collar. After I fed and dressed her, I placed her in the crib, dressed myself, and then sat down and brushed my hair, deciding I would simply tie it with a ribbon and let it lie as softly as possible over my shoulders and down my back. I had let it grow long, and when I brushed it out, it reached my shoulder blades. I put on a little lipstick, found a bonnet that had once belonged to Grandmere Catherine, so I felt I had her with me, and then went out on the gallery with Pearl to wait for Paul.

I heard him honk the car horn before he pulled into my driveway. His car was all washed and shiny and he wore a new blue suit, his tie loose around his collar. His *chatlin* hair glittered when he stepped out of the car, the strands still wet from brushing.

"Good morning," he said. We were both so nervous, it was as if we were about to embark on our first date. "Let's get going. Father Antoine in Breaux Bridge is expecting us." He opened the car door for us. "You look very pretty."

"Thank you, but I don't feel pretty. I feel . . . anxious."

"You're supposed to," he said. He took a deep breath, started the engine, and drove out.

A light drizzle began and the windshield wipers went from side to side, resembling two long forefingers wagging warnings and predicting shame. I heard it in the rhythm . . . shame, shame, shame.

"Well, the house is ready for us to move into it. Of course, I just have the most basic furnishing right now. I thought after a day or so, you and I would take a trip to New Orleans."

"New Orleans! Why?"

"So you could shop in the best places and have more choices. I don't want you to worry about cost either. Your job is to make Cypress Woods into something very special, a house and grounds that even the rich Creoles in New Orleans will envy.

"You should set up your studio as soon as possible," he continued with a smile. "As soon as we return from New Orleans, we'll interview prospective nannies to help you with Pearl so you can have the time you need for your work."

"A nanny? I don't think I'll need one, Paul."

"Of course you will. The mistress of Cypress Woods will have all sorts of servants. I have already hired our butler. He's a quadroon named James Humble. He's a man about fifty and he's worked in the finest homes."

"A butler?" It didn't seem that long ago when he and I poled in his pirogue through the swamp and fantasized about the very things we were about to do.

"And our maid. Her name is Holly Mixon. She's half Haitian, half Choctaw Indian, and in her mid-twenties. I got her from an agency, too. I know you are going to enjoy our cook the most," he said with his impish eyes twinkling.

"And why is that?"

"Her name's Letitia Brown, but she wants to be called Letty. She'll remind you of your Nina Jackson. She won't say her exact age, but I think she's somewhere around sixty. She practices voodoo," he said, lowering his voice to make it sound ominous.

"You've done all this already?" I asked, amazed. He blushed as if he had been caught naked.

"I've been planning for this day from the moment you returned to the bayou, Ruby. I just knew it would happen."

"What about your family, Paul? Did you tell your parents this morning?" I asked.

He was quiet for a moment. "No, not yet," he said. "I thought it would be better to tell them afterward. Once it's a fact of life, they'll be quicker to accept it all. It will be all right. It will be fine," he assured me, but that didn't quiet my thumping heart.

Although the rain stopped completely by the time we arrived in Breaux Bridge, the sky remained dark and ominous. Father Antoine lived in the rectory beside the church with his housekeeper, Miss Mulrooney. He was a man about sixty-five with thin gray hair cut so short, the strands popped up like a paintbrush on the sides, but he had gentle, blue eyes and the sort of soft smile that would make someone relax and be at ease in his presence. Miss Mulrooney, a tall thin woman with dark gray hair, looked stern and unapproving. I knew why.

Paul had told Father Antoine that Pearl was his child and he wanted to marry me to do the right thing, only he wanted the marriage to be a quiet one, away from the disapproving eyes of his neighbors and his family's friends. Father Antoine was understanding and happy Paul had decided to go through with the marriage and uphold his moral responsibilities.

Our wedding ceremony was as quick as a religious one could be. When it came time for me to recite my vows, I did what might have been a sinful thing: I conjured up Beau, and I told myself I was pledging my heart and my soul to him.

Getting married had all been so much easier and quicker than I had imagined it would be. I didn't feel any different, but I knew from the beaming smile on Paul's face every time he looked at me that everything had changed. For better or for worse, we had gone ahead and bound ourselves and our destinies.

"Well, that's that," he said. "How do you feel, Mrs. Tate?"

"Terrified," I said, and he laughed.

"You have no reason to be terrified anymore. Not as long as I'm around," he vowed. "So what, if anything, do you want from the shack?"

"I have Pearl's and my clothes, the painting of Grandmere Catherine, and her rocker," I said. "Maybe her old chest and the armoire her father had made for her. She was so proud of that."

"Fine. I'll send some of my men over with a truck this afternoon and they'll get the furniture. It looks like the rain has stopped for a while. You can follow in your car," he added nonchalantly.

"My car? What car?"

"Oh, didn't I tell you? I bought a little convertible for you to get around in . . . for your errands and such," he added. I could tell from the way he was behaving that it was more than just a little convertible, and sure enough, when we pulled up to Cypress Woods, I saw a candy-apple red Mercedes with a white ribbon around the hood parked in the driveway.

"That's mine?" I exclaimed.

"Your first wedding present. Enjoy," he said.

"Oh, Paul, this is too much," I cried, bursting into happy tears. Here was the grand house with our servants awaiting us, our beautiful grounds, our oil fields in the background, and my new studio waiting. Had we defied Fate, blown smoke in the face of Destiny? Would Paul's newfound wealth be enough to keep the howling winds and cold rains of misery outside our doors? For the moment, at least, I couldn't help but be as optimistic and as happy as he was.

Maybe I was Alice in Wonderland, I thought. Maybe this was what was meant to be all along and I had had no business in the rich Creole world of New Orleans, and that was why all the terrible things had happened there, things to drive me back to the bayou where I belonged. Paul took Pearl into his arms.

"Instead of carrying you over the threshold, I'll carry Pearl," he said. "After all, she will be the princess."

I noticed the white powder sprinkled on the front steps. Paul noticed too.

"Letty's work, I imagine," he said.

The large, tall door was opened by our butler, James Humble. He was at least six feet two inches tall, a lean man with curly brown hair, caramel skin, and bright hazel eyes. He looked like the proper butler with his perfect posture, awaiting our beck and call.

"This is James," Paul said. "James, Madame Tate."

"Welcome, madame," he said with a small nod and bow. He had a deep voice with a cultured French pronunciation.

"Thank you, James."

When I entered the hallway, I found Holly Mixon standing to the side, waiting for us. She was a large-boned woman with stout arms and shoulders.

"And this is Holly," Paul said. "Holly, Madame Tate." She curtsied.

"Hello, Holly."

"How'd ja do, ma'am," she said.

"Where's Letty?" Paul asked.

"She's in the kitchen, monsieur, preparing for tonight's dinner. She don't want none of us in there when she works," she added.

"I see," Paul said, winking at me. "Why don't you take Pearl up to the nursery first then, Ruby. I want to go over to my parents and inform them myself. That's probably best. If you agree, that is."

"Yes, Paul," I said. The thought of their reactions put something hard and heavy in my chest.

"As soon as I return, we'll see about getting your things, okay?"

"Yes," I said, taking Pearl into my arms.

He leaned over, kissed me quickly on the cheek, and then hurried out.

"Now then," I said, turning to Holly. "Why don't you lead the way to the nursery and we'll see what has to be done."

"Yes, ma'am," she said.

If I hadn't lived in the House of Dumas with its servants around me, I would have felt uncomfortable having a maid and a butler and a cook. I was hardly one to put on airs and act like some grand lady, but Paul had really built a mansion and it required household help. There was nothing to do now but assume my place and become the mistress of Cypress Woods.

Letty did remind me of Nina Jackson. She wore the same sort of red kerchief with seven knots whose points all stood straight up, a tignon; but she was much taller and much thinner, surprisingly thin for a cook, with long hands ribbed with veins against her chocolate skin. She had a narrow face with a slender mouth and a thin nose. She told me her eyes were too close together because her mother had been surprised by a rattlesnake the day she became pregnant. I saw she wore a camphor lump around her neck, which I knew was to keep germs away.

Letty was a more formal cook who had learned from educated chefs. The first meal she was preparing for us proved it. We were to begin with oysters Bienville for an appetizer, followed by turtle soup. The main dish was *filet de boeuf aux champignons* with yellow squash with peas. For dessert she had prepared an orange crème brûlée.

"I noticed you put white powder on our front steps," I told her after we were introduced and had spoken awhile. Her small dark eyes grew smaller.

"I be not workin' in a house without it," she replied firmly.

"I don't mind, Letty. My grandmere Catherine was a *traiteur* woman," I said, and she brightened, impressed.

"You be holy child, then."

"No, just her granddaughter," I corrected. There was nothing holy about me, I thought.

I heard Paul return and went to greet him. He smiled, but I saw the pain in his eyes.

"They were very upset, weren't they?" I asked.

"Yes," he admitted. "My mother cried and Daddy sulked, but after a while, they'll warm up to the fact and accept it, just like I told you they will," he promised. "Of course, my sisters think it's wonderful," he added quickly. "They'll all be here tomorrow for dinner. I thought we should have the first night to ourselves. I have two of my men outside with the truck waiting to go to the shack for your things."

"Pearl's still sleeping," I said. Paul's report had quickly extinguished the excitement and happiness.

"Go on, lead them in your new car. I'll be here for her when she wakes. Go on. I've got Holly to help," he assured me.

"She'll be afraid, waking up in a strange place."

"But she's not with a stranger," he replied confidently. "She has me." I saw how much he wanted to establish himself as her father as soon as he could.

"Okay. I won't be long," I said.

At the shack I pointed out the pieces of furniture I wanted. I told Paul's men I would take the painting myself. After I put it safely in the car, I went back inside the house and stood in the living room gazing at everything. How empty and sad it looked without the few pieces of furniture. It was as if I were losing Grandmere Catherine once again, cutting off whatever spiritual attachments still bound us together. Her spirit couldn't go with me. It belonged here in these shadows and corners, in the little toothpick-legged shack that had been her mansion, her palace, her home, and mine, too, for so long. All the days here weren't happy ones, but they weren't all sad ones either.

Here she had comforted me during my moments of fear and anxiety. Here she had woven the stories and conjured up my hopes. Here we had worked side by side to make our living. We had laughed and cried and collapsed with fatigue beside each other on the old settee that Grandpere Jack had practically beaten to death in his drunken rages. These walls had soaked up the laughter and the pain and inhaled the wonderful aromas of Grandmere's cooking. From these windows at night, I had looked up at the moon and the stars and dreamt of princes and princesses and wove my own fairy tales.

Good-bye, I thought. Finally good-bye to childhood and all the precious innocence that kept me from seeing and believing there was any real cruelty in this world. I thought I had moved into Wonderland at Cypress Woods. So much of it seemed too wonderful to be real. But here was my true Wonderland. Here I had felt the special magic and here I had done some of my best art.

Tears trickled down my cheeks. I wiped them away quickly, took a deep breath, and hurried out of the house, down the steps of the gallery, and into my car. Without looking back, I left my past behind me a second and perhaps final time.

Now it was Paul's turn to see the sadness in my face when I returned. He had Holly and James take my things up to my room and to Pearl's nursery and then he took me out back to look at our pool and cabana. He talked about his plans for landscaping, the trees and the flowers and the walkways and fountains he envisioned. He talked about the parties we would have, the music and food. I knew he was talking a blue streak just so I wouldn't have time to brood on the past and be sad.

"There's so much to do here," he concluded. "We don't have time to feel sorry for ourselves anymore."

"Oh, Paul, I hope you're right."

"Of course I'm right," he insisted. We heard someone calling and turned to see that his sisters had arrived.

Jeanne had been in my class when I lived in the bayou. We had always been good friends. She was about an inch or so taller than I was, with dark brown hair and almond-shaped eyes. She looked more like their mother and had her deep, dark complexion, her sharp chin and nearly perfect nose. I always remembered her as a bright and happy girl.

Toby was two years younger, and although she didn't look like her mother as much, she had her mother's serious demeanor. She was a little shorter but with broader hips and a fuller bosom. She kept her dark brown hair trimly cut. Her eyes were more perceiving, studious and inquisitive. She had a way of twisting the corner of her mouth downward when she doubted or disapproved of something someone else had said or done.

"I told them to wait until tomorrow," Paul said angrily.

"It's all right. I'm glad they've come," I said, joining them. They both hugged and kissed me and then followed me up to the nursery, Jeanne chattering away as I changed Pearl's diaper.

"Of course, this is all a shock," she said. In a breathless gush, her words spilled forth. "It's so unlike Paul, Mr. Perfect Little Man."

"Why did you two do it now?" Toby asked. "Why didn't you do it as soon as you knew you were pregnant?"

I didn't look at her when I spoke, for fear she would see the lies in my face.

"Paul wanted to," I said, "but I didn't want to ruin his life."

"What about your life?" Toby countered.

"I was all right."

"Living by yourself with a baby in that shack?"

"Oh, Toby, why drag up the past? It's over now, and now look where they are," Jeanne cried, her arms extended. "Everyone's raving jealous over this house and Paul's good fortune."

Toby came up beside me and looked down at Pearl. "When did you two . . . make her?" she asked.

"Toby!" Jeanne exclaimed.

"I'm just asking. She doesn't have to say if she doesn't want to, but we're all sisters now. We shouldn't have secrets from each other, should we? Well, should we?" she asked me.

"No, not secrets, but each of us has something private in our hearts, something best kept locked up. Maybe you're still too young to understand that, Toby, but you will," I said. It was the sharpest thing I had ever said to her. She blinked and pulled her lips thin for a moment and then she nodded after considering what I had said.

"You're right. I'm sorry, Ruby."

"That's okay," I said, smiling. "We should be sisters now in every way possible."

"And we will!" Jeanne declared. "We'll help with the baby, won't we, Toby? We'll be real aunts."

"Sure," Toby said. She gazed at Pearl. "I've baby-sat enough to know how to take care of an infant."

"Pearl will get more love and attention than she can stand," Jeanne promised.

"That's all I want," I said. "That's all I really want. And all of us to become a family."

"Mother is still quite speechless, isn't she, Toby?" Jeanne said.

"Daddy isn't exactly bursting with pride and happiness either," she said.

"Maybe Daddy doesn't want to face the fact that he's a grandpere so soon," Jeanne quipped. "Don't you think that's it, Ruby?" she asked.

I stared at her for a moment and then smiled. "Yes, probably," I said. It was uncomfortable to stand waist-high in deceptions and half-truths, but for now there was no other way, I thought.

Jeanne tried to wrangle a dinner invitation out of Paul, but he insisted they leave and return with their parents tomorrow.

"When we'll have a real celebration," he said. "Ruby and I are just very tired and we need to be alone, rest up," he explained.

Toby smirked, but after Jeanne flashed her face of disappointment, she burst into a smile and exclaimed, "Of course you should. It's your honeymoon!"

Paul shifted his eyes toward me quickly and blushed.

"As usual, Jeanne puts her foot in her mouth," Toby said. "Come on, sister dear, let's go home."

"What did I say?"

"It's all right, Jeanne," I told her. We all hugged again and they left.

"Sorry about that," Paul said, glaring after them. "I should have warned you about my sisters. They've been spoiled and think they can have anything and everything. Don't put up with their antics. Just let them know their place and everything will be fine," he assured me. "Okay?"

"Yes," I said, but it was more of a prayer than an answer.

That evening we were served the wonderful dinner. Paul talked about his oil fields and some of his other ideas for business. He told me he had made reservations for us in New Orleans and we would be going the day after tomorrow.

"So soon?"

"No sense in postponing what has to be done here. And remember, I want you at your art," he said.

Yes, I thought, it was time to return to my second great love—painting. After dinner, Paul and I wandered through the great house and discussed what we would do to complete the furnishing and the decorations. I finally realized how big a task it was going to be and wondered aloud if I was capable of doing it.

"Of course you are," he assured me. "But maybe I can get Mother to help. She loves doing this sort of thing," he said. "You can learn a lot from my mother," he added. "She's a woman of refined taste. Not that you aren't," he added quickly. "It's just that she's been buying expensive things longer than you have," he said, smiling.

"How rich are we, Paul?" I asked. Was there no end to the possibilities?

He smiled. "With the price of oil rising and the wells producing four to five hundred percent more than predicted . . . we're millionaires many times over, Ruby.

Your rich stepmother and your twin sister are paupers next to us."

"Don't let them know it," I said, "or they'll be heartbroken."

Paul laughed. I confessed to being tired. Exhausted was more like it. It had been a roller-coaster day emotionally, one moment full of depression and sadness and the next moment taken to the height of happiness. I went upstairs and prepared for my first night in my beautiful new home. Once again, Paul surprised me. I found a pretty nightgown, robe, and slippers laid out on my bed. Holly had been in on the surprise. When I thanked Paul, he pretended he didn't know a thing about it.

"Must be your fairy godmother," he said.

I looked in on Pearl. She slept so contentedly in her pretty new crib. I leaned in and kissed her on the forehead and then I returned to my own bedroom and slipped into my own large bed with its fluffy pillows and soft mattress.

The overcast and rain had moved southeast and the cloud cover had broken up to permit some moonlight to fall over our great house and spill through my windows. I lay there, comfortable, but still full of trepidation about all our tomorrows. Then I heard a gentle knock on the adjoining door.

"Yes?"

Paul opened it and looked in. "Are you all right?"

"Yes, Paul. Fine."

"Comfortable?" he asked, remaining in the doorway, silhouetted.

"Very."

"May I kiss you good night?" he asked in a small voice.

I was quiet a moment. "Yes," I said.

He approached, leaned over, and pressed his lips to my cheek. I thought that would be it, but he moved toward my lips, so I turned away. I could feel his disappointment. He lingered inches from me and then straightened up.

"Good night, Ruby. I love you," he said. "As much as any other man could," he added.

"I know, Paul. Good night."

"Good night," he said, his voice soft and small, like the voice of a little boy again.

He closed the door between us and a cloud closed the gap that had permitted the moonlight a window on my new world. For a while the darkness was thick and deep again.

However, although they were on the other side of the house and some distance away, the oil pumps could be heard delving into the bowels of the earth to draw up the black liquid that would ensure our future and build walls of riches around us, keeping out the demons. Paul had created a moat of oil between us and the hardships that marred so much of the world beyond.

I could cuddle in my luxurious comforter and I could close my eyes and put aside my own fears and think only of the wonderful things to do. I could dream of Pearl as a little girl with her own pony. I could dream of lawn parties and birthday parties and grand dinners. I could dream of my studio bright and full of new works.

What else should I wish for? I thought.

Wish for love, a tiny little voice whispered. Wish for love.

4

Another New Family

Very early the next morning, I heard the adjoining door open and saw Paul poke his head around to check if I was awake. He was about to retreat when I called to him.

"Oh, I didn't mean to wake you," he said quickly.

"What time is it?"

"It's very early, but I wanted to check on the wells before going over to the cannery this morning. I'll be home for lunch. Did you sleep well?"

"Yes. It's a very comfortable bed," I said. "And these pillows . . . it's like sleeping in a vat of butter."

He smiled. "Great. See you later, then." He closed the door and I rose and got dressed before Pearl woke. By the way she was giggling and playing in her crib, I saw that she, too, had enjoyed her first night in her new home. I dressed her and took her downstairs. After breakfast, I took Pearl up to the attic to plan out my studio and make a list of what I would buy when we were in New Orleans. When Pearl took her late morning nap, I went out to the side patio to watch the men Paul had hired work on our landscaping.

The scent of new bamboo was in the air, and off in the distance, a pair of snow white egrets soared into the blue sky. I sighed with pleasure, dazzled. I was so entranced in my own visions of the rolling lawns, the flagstone walkways, the flower beds and bushes, that I didn't hear a car come up our drive, nor did I hear the door chimes.

James came out to the patio to inform me I had a visitor. Before I could go back into the house, Paul's father appeared. As soon as James retreated, Octavious hurriedly approach me. A chilling shiver ran down my spine.

"I told Paul I'd join you two for lunch and then go over to the wells with him, but I left early so I would have a chance to speak with you alone," he quickly explained.

"Mr. Tate . . ."

"You might as well start calling me Octavious or . . . Dad," he said, not quite bitterly, but not quite willingly either.

"Octavious, I know this is something you left my house believing I wouldn't go through with, but Paul was so heartbroken, and after I had been attacked by Buster Trahaw—"

"Don't explain," he said. He took a deep breath and gazed out at the swamp. "What's done is done. Long ago," he continued, "I stopped believing that Fate or Destiny owes me anything. Whatever good fortune I have, whatever blessings I receive, I don't deserve. I live only to see my children and my wife happy and secure."

"Paul is very happy," I said.

"I know. But my wife . . ." He looked down a moment and then raised his dark, sad eyes to me. "First off, she's terrified that somehow, because of this marriage, the truth will rear its ugly head in our small community and all of the make-believe she has constructed around Paul and herself will come crashing down. People think because we are a rich, successful family that we are as hard as rock, but behind closed doors . . . our tears are just as salty."

"I understand," I said.

"Do you?" He brightened. "Because I've come early to beg a favor."

"Of course," I said without hearing his request.

"I want you to keep the . . . for lack of a better word . . . illusion alive whenever you see her. Even though you know the truth and Gladys knows you know."

"You didn't have to ask me," I said. "I'd do it for Paul as well as for Mrs. Tate."

"Thank you," he said with relief, and then gazed around. "Well, this is quite a home Paul is building. He's a nice young man. He deserves his happiness. I'm very proud of him, always have been, and I know your mother would have been proud of him, too." He backed away. "Well . . . I . . . I'm just going out to speak to one of the workers in front," he stammered. "I'll wait for Paul. Thanks," he added, and quickly turned to disappear into the house.

My quickened heartbeat slowed, but the emptiness in my stomach that made it feel as if I had swallowed a dozen butterflies live continued. It would take time, I thought, and maybe even time wouldn't smooth the rough edges between me and Paul's parents, but for Paul's sake, I would try. Every day of this specially arranged marriage would be a day full of tests and questions. At least in the beginning. Despite all we had and all we would have, I had to question whether or not I could go through with it.

James returned to interrupt my heavy thoughts. "Mr. Tate is on the phone, madame," he said.

"Oh. Thank you, James." I started for the house, realizing I didn't know exactly where the closest phone was.

"You can take it right here on the patio," James said, and nodded toward the table and chairs. A telephone had been placed on a small bamboo stand beside one of the chairs.

"Thank you, James." I laughed to myself. The servants

were more familiar with my new home than I was. "Hello, Paul."

"Ruby, I'll be home very soon, but I had to call you to tell you about this stroke of luck. At least, I think it is," he said excitedly.

"What is it?"

"Our foreman here at the cannery knew this nice elderly woman who just lost her job as a nanny because the family's moving away. Her name is Mrs. Flemming. I just spoke to her on the phone and she can come to Cypress Woods this afternoon for a personal interview. I spoke with the family and they can't stop raving about her."

"How old is she?"

"Early sixties. She's been a widow for some time. She has a married daughter who lives in England. She misses her family and seeks employment to be around children. If she works out, maybe we can hire her immediately and leave her with Pearl while we go to New Orleans."

"Oh, I don't know if I can do that so soon, Paul."

"Well, you'll see after you speak with her. Should I tell her to come around two?"

"Okay," I said.

"What's the matter? Aren't you happy about it?" he asked. Even through a telephone, Paul could sense when I was nervous or anxious, sad or happy.

"Yes, it's just that you keep moving so fast, I barely have time to catch my breath over one astounding thing when you present me with another."

He laughed. "That's my plan. To overwhelm you with good things, to drown you in happiness, so that you will never regret what we have done and why we have done it," he said. "Oh, my father is going to join us for lunch. He might arrive before I do, so . . ."

"Don't worry," I said.

"I'll call Mrs. Flemming and then I'll start for home. What's Letty making?"

"I was afraid to ask her," I said, suddenly realizing. He laughed.

"Just tell her you'll put the hoodoo on her if she doesn't behave," he said.

I hung up and sat back. I felt like I was in a pirogue going over one waterfall after another, with no chance to catch my breath.

"The little one's up, Mrs. Tate," Holly called from an upstairs window.

"Coming," I said. There wasn't time to think about anything now, but maybe Paul was right. Maybe that was for the best.

At lunch neither I nor Paul's father did or said anything to reveal we'd spoken earlier, but we were all nervous. Paul did most of the talking. He was so full of excitement, it would have taken a hurricane to slow him down. His conversation with his father finally centered around their business problems.

Promptly at two, Mrs. Flemming arrived in a taxi. Paul's father had left, but Paul had remained to greet her with me. The first thing that struck me about her was how close in size she was to Grandmere Catherine. Standing no taller than five feet three or four, Mrs. Flemming had the same doll-like, diminutive facial features: a button nose and small, delicate mouth with two bright grayish blue eyes. Her light silvery hair still had some strands of corn yellow running through it. She kept it pinned up in a soft bun with her bangs trimmed.

She presented her letter of reference and we all went into the living room to talk. But none of her previous experience, nor an arm's length of references, would have made any difference if Pearl didn't take to her. A baby is completely reliant on its instincts, its feelings, I thought. The moment Mrs. Flemming saw my baby and the moment Pearl set eyes on her, my decision was made. Pearl smiled widely and didn't complain when Mrs. Flemming took her into her arms. It was as if they had known each other from the day Pearl had been born.

"Oh, what a precious little girl," Mrs. Flemming declared. "You are precious, you know, as precious as a pearl. Yes, you are."

Pearl laughed, shifted her eyes toward me as if she wanted to see whether or not I was jealous, and then gazed into Mrs. Flemming's loving face.

"I didn't get much chance to be with my own granddaughter when she was this small," she remarked. "My daughter lives in England, you know. We write to each other a lot and I go there once a year, but . . ."

"Why didn't you move there with her?" I asked. It was a very personal question, and perhaps I shouldn't have asked it so directly, but I felt I had to know as much as I could about the woman who would be with Pearl almost as much as, if not more than, I would be.

Mrs. Flemming's eyes darkened.

"Oh, she has her own life now," she said. "I didn't want to interfere." Then she added, "Her husband's mother lives with them."

She didn't have to explain any more. As Grandmere Catherine would say, "Keeping two grandmeres under the same roof peacefully is like trying to keep an alligator in the bathtub."

"Where are you living now?" Paul asked.

"I'm just in a rooming house."

He looked at me, while Mrs. Flemming played with Pearl's tiny fingers.

"Well, I don't see any reason why you shouldn't move right in, then," I said. "If the arrangements are satisfactory for you," I added.

She looked up and brightened immediately.

"Oh yes, dear. Yes. Thank you."

"I'll have one of my men take you back to the rooming house and wait for you to get your things together," Paul said.

"First let me show you where you will sleep, Mrs. Flemming," I said, pointedly eyeing Paul. He was doing it again, moving along so fast, I could barely catch my breath. "Your room adjoins the nursery."

Pearl didn't complain when Mrs. Flemming carried her out and up to her room. I kept feeling there was almost something spiritual about the way the two of them took so quickly to each other, and sure enough, I discovered Mrs. Flemming was left-handed. To Cajuns that meant she could have spiritual powers. Perhaps hers were more subtle, the powers of love, rather than the powers of healing.

"Well?" Paul asked after Mrs. Flemming had left with one of his men to get her things.

"She does seem perfect, Paul."

"Then you won't be upset leaving her here with Pearl?" he followed. "We'll be away only a day or two." I hesitated and he laughed. "It's all right. I've come up with the solution. I have to be reminded from time to time how rich I really am. *We* really are, I should say."

"What do you mean?"

"We'll just take Pearl along, reserve an adjoining room with a crib," he said. "Why should I care what it costs, as long as it makes you happy?"

"Oh, Paul," I cried. It did seem like his newfound wealth could solve every problem. I threw my arms around him and kissed him on the cheek. His eyes widened with happy surprise. As if I had crossed a forbidden boundary, I pulled back. For a moment my happiness and excitement had overwhelmed me. A strange look of reflection came into his blue eyes.

"It's all right, Ruby," he said quickly. "We can love each other purely, honestly. We're only half brother and sister, you know. There's the other half."

"That's the half that worries me," I confessed softly.

"I just want you to know," he said, taking my hands into his, "that your happiness is all I live for." His face became dark and serious as we just stared into each other's faces.

"I know, Paul," I finally said. "And that frightens me sometimes."

"Why?" he asked with surprise.

"It's . . . it just does," I said.

"All right. Let's not have any sad talk. We have to pack and plan. I have to go make some arrangements with the oil drill foreman and then go back to the cannery for a few hours. In the meantime, draw up your shopping list and don't spare a thing," he said. "My family will be here about six-thirty," he added, and left.

I had forgotten about that. Facing Paul's mother was something I dreaded. It started my heart tripping with anxiety. Despite the promise I had made to Paul's father, I wasn't good at looking someone in the face and ignoring the truth. My twin sister, Gisselle, was the expert when it came to that, not me. Somehow, though, I had to do it.

I changed my dress five times before deciding on the one I would wear to dinner with my new family. I couldn't decide whether I should pin up my hair or wear it long. Every little detail suddenly took on paramount importance. I wanted to make the best impression I could. In the end I decided to pin up my hair and went down to dinner just as the Tates arrived. Paul was already dressed and waiting in the entryway.

Toby and Jeanne entered first, Jeanne bubbling over with excitement and eager to describe how the community was reacting to our elopement. Octavious and Gladys Tate followed; she clung to his arm as if she were afraid she wouldn't be able to stand straight or keep from fainting if she were on her own. She kissed Paul on the cheek and then gazed up at me as I descended the stairway.

A tall woman, only an inch or so shorter than her husband, Gladys Tate usually projected a regal stature. I knew she had come from a wealthy Cajun family in Beaumont, Texas. She had attended a finishing school and college where she had met Octavious Tate. It often surprised me that more people didn't suspect Paul was not really her child. Her features were so much sharper, thinner. There was a hardness in her face, a look of superiority and arrogance, and aloofness, that set her apart from most of the women in our Cajun community, even the ones who were wealthy, too.

She usually kept her hair stylishly cut and wore the most up-to-date designs, but tonight she looked so dark

and depressed that not even the most fashionable clothing or best hairstylist could change her sad appearance.
She gave me the feeling she was attending a wake rather
than a family dinner. Her eyes searched my face anxiously as I approached.

"Hi," I said, smiling nervously. I gazed at Paul and
then said, "I guess I should start calling you two Mom
and Dad."

Octavious smiled nervously, his eyes shifting to Gladys,
who, only because Paul's sisters were present, let her lips
slip into a quick grin. Immediately she returned to her
more formal expression.

"Where's the baby?" she asked in a cold, hard voice,
directing the question at Paul rather than me.

"Oh, we've just hired a nanny today, Mom. Her name
is Mrs. Flemming. Both she and Pearl are upstairs in the
nursery. She fed Pearl earlier, but she'll bring her down
after we eat."

"A nanny?" Gladys said, nodding, impressed.

"She's very nice," I offered. Gladys Tate's lips softened
slightly when she gazed at me. I felt we could slice the air
between us, it was that thick.

"I'll go see about dinner," I said. "Why don't you show
everyone into the dining room."

"I haven't really seen your house, Paul," Gladys complained.

"Oh. Right. Let me take my mother around first,
Ruby."

"Fine," I said, happy for the chance to get away. This
was going to be harder than I had imagined, I thought.

Letty, as though she knew the deepest, darkest secrets,
prepared a meal that was even more special than the first
she had prepared for us. Octavious kept saying how
jealous he was that his son had a finer cook. For her part
Gladys complimented everything properly, but every
time she spoke, I sensed a control wound so tight that at
any moment it could spring loose and become hysteria. It
was as if she might burst out in shrill screams suddenly
over the slightest thing. It kept Paul, his father, and me

on pins and needles. I was relieved when we had gotten through the dessert, which was a chocolate rum soufflé Paul's father said rivaled any he had ever had.

Just as Molly refilled everyone's coffee cup, Mrs. Flemming appeared with Pearl in her arms.

"Isn't she gorgeous, Mom?" Jeanne cried. "I think she has Paul's eyes, don't you?"

Gladys Taté stared at me a moment and then looked at Pearl. "She is a pretty child," she said in a very noncommittal tone of voice.

"Do you want to hold her, madame?" Mrs. Flemming offered. I held my breath. Mrs. Flemming was a grandmere who knew how much any grandmere would want to hold and kiss her own grandchild.

"Of course," Gladys said with a forced smile. Mrs. Flemming brought Pearl to her. She squirmed uncomfortably in her arms, but didn't cry. Gladys Tate stared into her face for a moment and then kissed her quickly on the forehead. She smiled up at Mrs. Flemming and nodded to indicate she wanted her to take her back. Mrs. Flemming's eyes narrowed for a moment and then she hurried forward.

"How does it feel to be a grandmere, Mom?" Jeanne asked.

Gladys Tate smiled coldly. "If you mean do I feel any older as a result, Jeanne, the answer is no." She turned and fixed her gaze on me across the table, and then Paul suggested we all go into the library.

"It's not much yet. Nothing is, but after Ruby and I return from New Orleans, this place is going to be a showcase."

"Why don't you two tell your mother some of your plans for the house decor," Octavious suggested. He turned to me. "Gladys did most of our decorating."

"Oh, I'd love to get some suggestions," I said, turning to her.

"I'm not a decorator," she snapped.

"Now, don't be modest, Gladys," Octavious said, undaunted. He nodded at me. "Your mother-in-law knows her way around when it comes to furnishing and decorating expensive houses. Why, I bet she could just walk through this house with you and make suggestions off the top of her head."

"Octavious!"

"You could, Gladys," he insisted.

"You two go on," Paul suggested. "I'll entertain everyone else in the library."

Gladys looked enraged for a moment. Then she gazed at her two daughters, who looked puzzled by her reluctance.

"Of course, if Ruby would really like that," she said reluctantly.

"Please," I said, my lips trembling.

"Fine," Paul said, and rose.

"What should we look at first?" I asked Gladys Tate.

"You should do your bedroom first," Jeanne suggested. "They have separate bedrooms with an adjoining door. Isn't that like a royal couple, Mother?"

There was a deep moment of silence. Then Gladys smiled and said, "Yes, it is, dear. Very much so."

As we walked upstairs and down the hallway, Gladys remained a few inches behind me. She said nothing. My heart was thumping as I searched frantically through my mind for small talk that wouldn't make me sound silly or nervous. I started to talk about the colors I was considering, babbling quickly about color coordination, furniture design, and accent pieces. When we paused in the doorway of my bedroom, she finally looked at me.

"Why did you do it?" she asked in a hoarse whisper. "Why, when you knew the truth?"

"Paul and I have always been very close, Mother Tate. Once before, I was forced to break Paul's heart so that I could hide the truth from him. You know what it was like for him once he found out," I said.

"And how do you think it was for me?" she demanded. "We weren't even married that long before Octavious . . . before he was unfaithful. Of course, your mother wove a

70

spell over him. Catherine Landry's daughter wasn't without mystical powers, I'm sure," she said.

I swallowed hard. I wanted to defend the mother I had never known, but I saw how Paul's mother had developed this theory to accept her husband's infidelity, and I wasn't about to poke holes in her balloon.

"But what did I do?" she continued. "I accepted and I covered things up and I made it possible for us to remain respectable and for Paul to grow up protected. Now the two of you . . . go off and . . . It's sinful," she said, shaking her head, "just sinful."

"We're not living together that way, madame. That's why we have separate bedrooms."

She shook her head, her flinty eyes unrelenting in their condemnation. Then she sighed deeply and took on an expression of self-pity.

"Now I must pretend again, swallow my pride once more and do what I must do so that my children are not disgraced. It isn't fair," she said, shaking her head. "It isn't fair."

"No one will know anything from my lips," I promised. She laughed a short shrill laugh.

"Why should you say anything? Look at all you have now," she added harshly, and lifted her arms. "This house, these grounds, this great wealth . . . and a father for your child." She fixed her eyes on me.

"Madame, Mother Tate, I assure you—"

"You assure me. Ha! I'm sure you cast the same sort of spell over Paul that your mother cast over Octavious. From mother to daughter, only I'm the one who pays for it all . . . not my dear husband, not my dear adopted son. Funny," she said, pausing. "I have never used that term once, never; but now, here with you, I can't say anything else but the truth: my adopted son."

"It's not the truth," I spit back. "You love Paul in your heart the same way you would had you been the one to give birth to him, and he loves you that way, too. I will make you one promise, Mother Tate, and that is that I

71

will never do anything to interfere with that love. Never," I insisted, my eyes narrow and fixed with determination on hers.

She smiled coldly as if to say I couldn't even if I wanted to with all my heart.

"But you should know that Paul loves Pearl as much as he would had she been his from the start," I warned. "I hope you will accept that and love her as much as a grandmere should."

"Love," she said. "Everyone needs so much of it, no wonder we're all so exhausted." She sighed again and then looked into my room, her face hardening with criticism. "You should do something nice with drapes on those windows. The sun will be setting on this side. And those colors you were thinking about . . . I thought you were supposed to be an artist. You'll use beige with a little pink in it in here," she commanded. "Now, when you get to New Orleans," she continued as she walked on, "there's this place I know on Canal Street . . ."

I followed along, grateful for the truce that had fallen between us, even though it was a truce on her terms.

We rose early the next morning for our trip to New Orleans. Fortunately, the morning overcast broke and the patches of blue with the bright sunlight seeping through made the trip more enjoyable. I hated going long distances in the rain. But as we traveled the familiar highway, I couldn't help but feel like someone reliving an old nightmare. I recalled my first trip, when I had run away from Grandpere Jack. I had arrived in New Orleans during the Mardi Gras and was nearly raped by a man in a Mardi Gras mask who pretended to help me find my way through the city.

But that was the day I had met Beau for the first time, too, I remembered. Just as I was about to give up and turn away from my father's house, Beau arrived like some dreamboat stepping off a movie screen. I knew from the first moment I set eyes on him that he was special, and from the way he gazed at me once he knew I wasn't my twin sister, I knew he thought the same about me. When Lake Pontchartrain came into view with its water a dark green and its small waves capping, I vividly recalled my first date with Beau and how passionate we had been even then.

I was so lost in these memories, I didn't even realize Paul had driven us into the city until we pulled up to the Fairmont Hotel. Pearl had slept for most of the trip, but when we stepped out, she was fascinated with the sounds of traffic and people and all the activity around us as we checked into our suite of rooms. Paul had arranged for us to have a room with two double beds that adjoined a room for Mrs. Flemming and Pearl.

After we had a little lunch in the hotel, Mrs. Flemming took Pearl up for a nap, and Paul and I began our shopping spree. I had forgotten how much I loved the city. It had its own special rhythms that changed as the day grew into night. In the morning it could be so quiet. Most of the shops weren't open and the shutters and balcony doors were closed, especially in the famed French Quarter, the Vieux Carré. The shadows were still deep and the streets relatively cool.

By late morning the shops were open and the streets were filling with people. The scrolled balconies above us were bursting with flowers. Hawkers called out their wares; music started to draw the tourists to the doors of restaurants and bars. Then, as the afternoon continued, the rhythm quickened. Street performers took their positions on the corners, tap-dancing, juggling, playing guitars.

Paul had a list of places to go, a list he revealed his mother had prepared.

"She knows a lot more about all this than we do," he stated, and then he showed me a list of items she had dictated we buy. "What do you think?" he asked.

"Fine," I said, although many of the things were not particularly things I would have chosen.

Paul and I went from store to store, buying the furnishings, lighting fixtures, lamps, and tables, as well as accoutrements, his mother had suggested. I began to feel as if I were just tagging along.

"My mother is a woman of great taste, isn't she?" he declared before I had much of a chance to comment.

"Yes," I said. It was as if she were right there beside us.

Late in the afternoon, Paul and I took a break and went to the Café du Monde for coffee and their famous beignets. We could watch the artists at their easels and the tourists marching by, their eyes big, their cameras swinging on their necks. There was a cool breeze off the river, and the magnolia blossoms that lifted and fell in the air seemed particularly brilliant.

"I've made a dinner reservation for us at Arnaud's," Paul declared.

"Arnaud's?"

"Yes. Mother suggested it. Don't you think it's a good choice?"

"Oh yes, it's nice," I said, quickly smiling. How was Paul to know that it was to Arnaud's that Beau had taken me on our first formal date? However, to me it seemed as if the city were conspiring to stir up each and every memory I had of living here, whether they be good ones or bad.

We had a wonderful dinner and Pearl was well behaved. Afterward, Paul wanted to sit in the hotel lobby and listen to the jazz. We did so for a while, but the day's traveling and shopping with all its emotional implications had been more exhausting than I believed. I couldn't keep my eyes from closing. Paul laughed and we went up to our room.

This was the first night we spent together sleeping in the same bedroom, and although we weren't sharing a bed, there was an intimacy that at first made me a little uncomfortable. As I stood before the sink and mirror dressed only in my slip and washed the makeup off my face, I saw Paul in the mirror, standing behind me, staring, the blue in his eyes so deep, I felt naked. Once he saw my gaze go to him, he moved away quickly.

I went into the bathroom and dressed for bed. Paul was

already in his when I put out the light and crawled under the cover.

"Good night, Ruby," he said softly.

"Good night." The silence and the darkness seemed to grow thicker between us. We would share everything a man and a woman who married and became one could share, except one thing: each other. That thought lingered in the darkness above me, taunting, tormenting. I turned on my side and when I closed my eyes, my thoughts fled back to my memories of Beau and our passionate lovemaking. For now, those recollections were all I had.

We continued our shopping safari the next day, following the list Mrs. Tate had written. I went to an art supply house and gave them my list. Everything would be delivered. After lunch, Paul and I walked through the French Quarter, now looking for gifts for his sisters and parents.

"You haven't mentioned it yet," he said, "but do you intend to see your stepmother? She has yet to learn about us."

"I was thinking about it, yes," I said. "Although I'm not eager to do it."

"I'll go with you."

"No. I think I'd better do this alone for now," I said.

"Okay." He smiled. "Should I get you a cab or . . ."

"No, I think I want to take the streetcar," I said. I had done it so often when I had lived in my father's great house in the Garden District. It was still a quaint and delightful ride for me, but the moment I stepped off the car and began to walk toward the mansion, I felt my heart begin to pound.

Could I do this, walk back into that house and face my stepmother after I had run away? I knew Gisselle was at school, so I wouldn't have to contend with her, but to go into that great house knowing my father was gone, Nina was gone, and Beau was off in Europe involved with some other young woman seemed like self-imposed torture.

I paused across the street and gazed at the ivory white mansion. It looked unchanged, frozen in time. Maybe if I crossed this street, all that had happened since the day I had arrived would disappear and I would be starting over again, I thought. Daddy would still be alive, vibrant and handsome. Nina Jackson would be in the kitchen mumbling over some ingredients and complaining about some evil spirits that had camped in the closets, and Otis would still be at the door, waiting to greet me. I would hear Gisselle shrieking some complaint from upstairs.

I started to walk across when the familiar Rolls-Royce pulled into the driveway. I watched it come to a stop in front of the house and then Daphne step out. If anything or anyone looked unchanged, it was she. Still the ice queen, she rose to her statuesque posture instantly and uttered some command to the driver. The car pulled away and she started up the steps. A new butler, a shorter man with dark gray hair, instantly opened the door. It was as though he did nothing but wait just behind it for her return. Without acknowledging him, she marched into the house. He bowed slightly and then looked out as if he were looking at freedom. A moment later the door was closed and I stepped back onto the walk.

Suddenly nothing seemed more frightening and unpleasant than the thought of facing her. I pivoted quickly and hurried away, walking so fast, I'm sure I looked like someone in flight. But I was fleeing, after all. I was fleeing from the horrible memories of Daphne's spiteful ways, her attempt to have me committed and locked away, her jealousy of my father's love for me, her eagerness to make me look terrible in the eyes of Beau's parents. I was fleeing from the emptiness of that great house once Daddy had died, from the shadows and the darkness that lingered in its corners.

I didn't get back onto the streetcar for blocks, and by the time I arrived at the hotel and Paul opened the door for me, I looked frenzied, my hair disheveled, my face full of agony.

"What's wrong?" he asked. "What did she do?"

"Nothing," I said, throwing myself down on the bed. "I never spoke to her. I couldn't do it. I'll write to her," I said. "And leave it at that. Let's go home . . . now!"

He shook his head. "But we still have a few things to get. Mother thought we should have—"

"Oh, Paul," I cried, seizing his hand. "Take me home. Please . . . just take me home. You can get the rest yourself, can't you?"

He nodded. "Of course," he said. "We'll leave immediately."

It wasn't until we had arrived in the bayou and began up the drive to Cypress Woods that I felt a sense of relief again. Our new great house loomed before me and I realized this was my home, even if my mother-in-law was the one decorating it and not me. Now, more than ever, I was happy I had made the decision to marry Paul and come here. It was far enough and isolated enough to keep out the ghosts of my horrid past.

I couldn't wait to begin setting up my studio and painting again. The swamps and our great acres of land and our oil wells would comprise the walls keeping the demons away. I was safe here, I thought . . . safe.

5

Sad News

Each day of my first six months as mistress of Cypress Woods was so filled with responsibilities and activities, I barely had time to ponder over the life I had chosen for myself and my daughter. I don't think I noticed the winter until I saw the snow geese leaving and realized it had ended. The first buds of spring were opening in an explosion of flowery splendor the likes of which I had never seen. Furnishings and decorations for the great house had begun arriving shortly after our trip to New Orleans. Painters and decorators, tile and carpet people, drapery and mirror people, a parade of artisans, marched through the house daily.

Paul's mother arrived nearly every morning to supervise. When I commented about it, Paul either misunderstood or ignored my meaning.

"Isn't it wonderful how much interest she's taking in us," he replied. "And her being here, running from room to room, upstairs and downstairs, answering questions, frees you to work on your studio."

I did direct my attention to it because it was the one place Gladys refused to enter. Paul was caught up in a flurry of activity, too. His days were divided between his work at the cannery and his supervision of the oil wells. Two weeks after our return from New Orleans, a new well was drilled. He called it Pearl's Well and decided that all the proceeds from it would go into a trust for her. Before she was a year old, she was wealthier than most people were by the end of their productive lives.

On weekends we had grand dinners for the husbands and wives of the people whom Paul dealt with in his oil business. Everyone was impressed with our home and grounds, especially the ones who came from Baton Rouge or Houston and Dallas. I knew they had all expected quite a bit less in the Cajun bayou. Paul never stopped bragging about me, bragging shamelessly about my artistic talents and successes.

I finally did write my letter to Daphne, but not until nearly a month had passed since my attempt to confront her in New Orleans. Paul would occasionally inquire if I had done so and I would say, "Soon. I'm just composing my thoughts." He knew I was procrastinating, but he didn't nag. At last, one afternoon while I had a chance to catch my breath, I sat on the patio with pen and paper and began to write.

Dear Daphne,

We haven't written or spoken to each other for nearly a year now. I know you have little interest in what's happened to me and where I am now, but for my father's sake and memory, I have decided to write this letter.

After my horrible experience at that disgusting clinic where you sent me to have an abortion, I ran off and returned to my roots, to the bayou. For months I lived in my grandmere's old shack, doing the things she and I had done to keep ourselves alive. I gave birth to a beautiful daughter whom I have named Pearl, and for months I struggled to provide for both of us.

I realized that my first responsibility now was to

my daughter and her welfare, and with that in mind, I have married Paul Tate. I do not expect you to understand, but we have a very special life together. We are more like partners, devoted to making each other happy and secure and providing a secure future for Pearl, than we are husband and wife. Paul's inherited land turned out to be rich with oil. We have a beautiful home called Cypress Woods.

I ask nothing of you, certainly not your forgiveness, nor should you interpret this letter as my forgiveness of you for what you have tried to do to me in the past. Actually, I feel pity for you more than anger. I do expect, however, that what my father had decided to give me will be given to me. My love for him has not diminished one iota. I miss him dearly.

Please see that the attorney in charge of my trust has my new address.

Ruby

I received no reply, but that didn't surprise me. At least I had put myself on record and she couldn't claim I had disappeared and disavowed all contact and connection with my father's estate. I really had never accepted her as a mother or as family. She was a stranger to me when I had lived in the House of Dumas, and she was even more of a stranger to me now.

Jeanne came more often than Toby to play with Pearl and visit. With my marriage to Paul, she eagerly embraced me as her new sister and, at times, confided more intimately in me than she did in her own blood sister, Toby, and certainly more than she did her mother. One afternoon we sat on the patio and sipped fresh lemonades, watching Mrs. Flemming take Pearl for a little walk through the gardens.

Jeanne had come to Cypress Woods especially to talk to me about her boyfriend, James Pitot, a young attorney. He was a tall, dark-haired, handsome man whose politeness and charm reminded me a bit of Daddy.

"I think we're going to become engaged," Jeanne revealed. I knew from the way she spoke that I was the first to learn of it.

"You think?"

"The thought of such a big yes terrifies me!" she exclaimed. I had to laugh. "It's not funny, Ruby. I lay awake nights just tormenting myself over it."

"No, it isn't funny. You're right. I shouldn't laugh."

"What made you finally decide to marry Paul?" she asked.

If she only knew the truth, she wouldn't be so sisterly, I feared.

"I mean, I don't know what love is, really is. I have had crushes on so many boys, and you remember I used to go with Danny Morgan."

"I remember."

"But he became such an . . . an idiot. James is different. James is . . ."

"What? Tell me," I said.

"Caring and considerate, loving and gentle. We haven't done it yet, you know," she said, blushing. "He wanted to, of course, and so did I, but I just couldn't without being married. I told him that and he understood. He didn't get angry."

"Because he really does care for you and for what makes you happy," I concluded. "That's love or at least the most important part of it. The other things are important, of course, but there doesn't have to be an explosion of bells every time you kiss. What I have learned is that dependability is the soil in which a long and lasting love is planted, Jeanne."

"But surely there was an explosion of bells for you and Paul. The two of you have been in love for so long. I remember when he couldn't wait to finish dinner just so he could get on his motor scooter and ride out to see you, even if it was for just ten minutes. It was like . . . like the sun rose and fell on your face.

"I don't have that intense a feeling for James," she admitted, "so I'm afraid I'm going to make a tragic error if I say yes."

"Some people love too much," I said softly.

"Like Adam loved Eve," she replied, nodding. "He ate of the forbidden fruit after Eve had just so he wouldn't lose her. That's what Father Rush told me once."

"Yes, like Adam, then," I said, smiling.

"But that made the story so romantic for me. I want my marriage to be romantic, as romantic as yours is," she said. "And yours is, isn't it, Ruby?"

I stared at her. Was it only her youth that prevented her from seeing the truth in my eyes or was it my own ability to mask reality? I smiled softly.

"Yes, Jeanne, but it doesn't happen overnight, and from the way you speak of James and from what you tell me of him, it sounds like you will have happiness together."

"Oh, I'm so glad you said that!" she exclaimed. "For I value your opinion more than anyone's, even more than Mother's, and certainly more than Toby's."

"I wish you would speak to your mother first," I said. "I don't want to be the one who convinces you of doing something. You have to convince yourself."

In the back of my mind, I could see Gladys Tate hating me for giving intimate advice to her daughter.

"Don't worry, silly," she said. "I am convinced. I just needed to be sure. You were once just as insecure, weren't you?"

"Yes," I confessed.

"You never talk about your life in New Orleans. Did you have many boyfriends there or when you went to private school?"

"No, not many," I said, and looked away quickly. She was alert enough to catch the shifting of my gaze.

"But there was one?"

"There was . . . no one, really," I said, turning back with a smile. "You know how those rich Creole boys can be. . . . They make you promises just to tempt you to go to bed with them and then they rush off for another conquest."

"Did you?" she asked quickly.

"Did I what?"

"Go to bed with any of them?"

"Jeanne!"

"I'm sorry. I thought I could ask. I thought we could be sisters, better sisters than you and your twin were."

"That wouldn't be hard to do," I said, laughing. I stared at her a moment. "No," I said. "I didn't." I knew if I told her the truth, I would burst into tears myself and this whole wonderful world Paul had created for Pearl and me would come crumbling down around us.

She looked relieved. "Then I'm right to wait until we're married?"

"If it feels right, it's right," I told her. She seemed satisfied for the moment. I was troubled giving advice to anyone when it came to romance and marriage. Who was I to do so?

The next day, Jeanne came over to announce her engagement to James Pitot. They had set a date. Once Paul heard that, he declared the wedding would be at Cypress Woods if she liked. She gazed at me with the expression of a coconspirator and cried her delight.

"Ruby will help me plan the wedding, won't you, Ruby?"

"Of course," I said.

"Oh, Paul," she said, "you did more than marry the woman you always loved and give us a beautiful little niece. You gave me a wonderful new sister."

We hugged and kissed and I hoped I had said the right things and Jeanne was destined for a good and happy marriage. In any case, we had a great family event to plan. It seemed Paul was right: Our lives would be full of excitement and never dull.

That evening Paul knocked on the adjoining door and came into my bedroom as I was sitting in front of my vanity mirror brushing out my hair. I was already in my nightgown. He was in his light blue silk pajamas, one of the birthday presents I had bought for him.

"I just got off the phone with Dad. He says his home now resembles an army command post. They have already drawn up long lists of guests and started to plan the preliminaries. He swears it's like preparing for battle."

I laughed.

"I wish we could have had a grand wedding," he said. "You deserved nothing less than to be treated like some Cajun princess."

"I am treated that way, Paul."

"Yes, but . . ." His eyes fixed on mine in the mirror. "How has it been for you? I mean . . . are you really happy, Ruby?"

"Yes, Paul. I am."

He nodded and then shifted from a deep, pensive look to a soft, gentle smile. "Anyway, thank you for taking my sisters to your heart so quickly and making them your family, too. They adore you, and Mother . . . Mother has learned to do more than simply accept. I know she respects you now."

I wondered how he could make such a statement. Was he blind to the cold, gray look in his mother's eyes whenever she set them on me or was he so determined to be happy that he ignored it and lived in an illusion himself?

"I hope so, Paul," I said, but not with much conviction.

"She does," he insisted. "Well, good night." He stepped up to me and kissed me softly on the neck. He hadn't kissed me like that since we had married. The warmth of his lips radiated in waves over my shoulders and down to my breasts. I closed my eyes and when I opened them again, I saw him still there, his lips inches from my face.

"Good night," I said in a broken whisper.

"Good night." He turned quickly and left my room.

For a moment I just stared after him. I took a deep breath and got ready for bed.

That night I tossed and turned for hours before finally falling into an exhaustion and sleep.

Three days later the happy bubble that had settled over Cypress Woods was shattered with the arrival of Gisselle. She and two of her boyfriends from her ritzy prep school came speeding up our driveway, the horn of their Cadillac convertible blaring. It brought all the servants and myself to the front window. We thought it was some emergency. James looked at me with surprise.

"It's only my twin sister," I said. "Don't bother yourself, James. I'll greet her and show her in."

"Very good, madame," he said, and happily retreated. I went out to the gallery to face them.

It had been some time since Gisselle and I had last set eyes on each other. The two boys she was with were handsome, slim young men, one with dark brown hair and the other quite blond with blue eyes and a very fair complexion. He was the driver. They both wore navy blue blazers with their fraternity emblems embossed in gold on their breast pockets. The dark-haired young man stepped out first and held the door for Gisselle, sweeping himself into a European bow as if she were royalty emerging. The laughter on the lips suggested they had been doing some drinking or maybe smoking pot. I had no reason to expect Gisselle had changed or grown up any since we last saw each other, but I had hoped for some miraculous metamorphosis.

"There she is," she cried as soon as she set her eyes on me. "My dear, darling twin, the mistress of Cypress Woods. I have to admit, sister dear," she said, nodding as she looked around, "you ain't done bad for a Cajun."

The two men laughed, the driver getting out to join them.

"Well, can't you say hello?" Gisselle demanded, her hands on her hips. "We haven't seen each other for a long time. You'd think you'd at least pretend to be pleased."

"Hello, Gisselle," I said dryly.

"What, no sisterly kiss and hug?" She stepped up to me. I shook my head and embraced her. "That's more like it. You should be impressed. We drove all the way up here to visit you and it's a terribly boring ride. Nothing to look at but those shacks on sticks and old shrimp boats rotting along the canals and poor dirty children playing with rusty old tools on their mangy front yards. Right, Darby?" she said, turning to the dark-haired young man. He nodded, his eyes on me.

"Why don't you introduce everyone properly, Gisselle," I said.

She smirked. "Of course, just the way we were taught to do it at Greenwood, huh?" She turned and imitated our etiquette teacher at Greenwood, speaking with nasality. "This is Darby Hennessey, of the filthy rich Hennesseys from the Bank of New Orleans." Darby laughed and bowed. "And this shy, fair-haired young man on my left is Henry Howard. His father is one of Louisiana's most famous and important architects. Either one of these young men wouldn't hesitate to spend his inheritance on me, would you, gentlemen?"

"I'd save a little to keep myself in champagne," Darby quipped, and they all laughed.

"This house . . . I must confess, Ruby," Gisselle said, stepping back, "I had no idea. You are rich even before you inherit your share of our trust. Can you imagine how wealthy my twin sister is going to be, Henry?"

He nodded, gazing around.

"Wealthy," he admitted.

"Brilliant. Henry's working on his doctorate in brain surgery," she said, and Darby laughed. "Well, are you going to show us around or do we have to stand out here all day in the swamp heat?" she demanded.

"Of course, I'll show you around."

"Is it all right to leave the car right here?" Henry asked me.

"Why isn't it?" Gisselle snapped before I had a chance. "What do you think she has, valet parking?" She laughed and threaded her arm through Darby's. "The tour, madame," she said.

"You haven't changed one iota, Gisselle," I said, shaking my head.

"Why should I? I was always perfect. Right, Darby?"

"Right," he said obediently.

I opened the door and led them into the house.

"Daphne would bust a gut if she saw how well you've done for yourself, dear sister," Gisselle said as she gazed at the grand entryway, my paintings and small statues, the long marble floors and grand stairway. She whistled at the elegant furnishings in the living room and den, but her sarcastic attitude dwindled to a quiet look of awe as I took them through the rest of the downstairs and they saw the large pictures, the expensive lamps and chandeliers, the enormous kitchen and dining room with a table that could seat twenty comfortably.

"This beats anything I've seen in the Garden District," Henry confessed.

"You haven't seen everything in the Garden District," Gisselle spit, and he was silent. "How about the bedrooms?" she inquired.

"Right this way."

I showed them the guest rooms first and then Paul's and my bedrooms, skipping the nursery because Pearl was taking her nap.

"Separate but adjoining bedrooms," Gisselle remarked, and smiled licentiously. "How often do we use that doorway?" she whispered. Although I blanched, I didn't reply. She laughed and gazed about. "You don't have an art studio anymore," she said with delight.

"Oh, that's in the attic," I replied nonchalantly.

"The attic?"

"Let me show you," I said, and took them upstairs.

"This is incredible," Darby said, now genuinely impressed. "The place is a palace. Look at the view from this window," he declared, turning to Gisselle. She sulked behind us.

"It's only a view of the swamps," she said.

"Yeah, but . . . it's beautiful. That's a big pool, and those flowers."

"All right," Gisselle said, bursting with frustration. "You have anything to drink? I'm parched."

"Of course. Let's go down to the patio and Molly will bring us some lemonades."

"Lemonades," she ridiculed. "Don't you have anything with a little kick to it?" she asked sharply.

"Whatever you want, Gisselle. Just tell my maid."

"Her maid. Do you hear how my Cajun sister talks? Just tell my maid."

We started out, the young men behind us. Gisselle seized my arm.

"Where's Beau's baby?" she demanded.

"Pearl's asleep and no one knows her as Beau's baby here," I said.

"Of course." She smiled with satisfaction. "And our brother, your husband?" she whispered.

"He's at work in the oil fields right now." My heart began to pound. "If you've come here to make trouble for us . . ."

"Why should I do that? I don't care what you've done, although I know you did it just to spite Beau."

"That's not true, Gisselle."

"Don't you want to hear about him?" she teased. I didn't reply. "He broke up with his fiancée in Europe, so you see, if you hadn't rushed into this sinful arrangement, you might have still won him," she said with great self-satisfaction. I felt the blood rush into my face so quickly, it felt as if it had drained completely out of my legs and I might tumble down the stairs. Then she laughed and put her arm through mine. "But let's not talk of old romances. Let's catch up on other news first. I do have a lot to tell you, a lot you will enjoy and a lot . . . you won't," she suggested with an impish grin.

She paraded me downstairs with her obedient escorts behind us ready at her beck and call.

* * *

"Daphne's wedding," Gisselle began once she had her mint julep in hand, "was an affair to remember. She and Bruce spared no expense. There were hundreds of guests. The church was bursting at the seams. Most people came because they were curious and just wanted to be part of the highlight of the social season. You know she really never had any friends. She just has business acquaintances, but she never cared and still doesn't."

"Are they happy together?"

"Happy? Hardly," she said, and laughed.

"What do you mean?"

"Bruce is still her little gofer. Remember how I used to tease him—Bruce, go for this, Bruce, go for that? Do you know what I discovered listening in on their business conversations one night? She made him sign a prenuptial agreement. He inherits nothing if anything happens to her. Nothing. And he can't divorce her and sue her for any property."

"Why did she marry him?"

"Why?" Gisselle raised her eyes to the sky and then smirked. "Why do you think? . . . To keep his mouth shut. They were embezzling from poor, dear Daddy. But Daphne was shrewd. She kept control of everything and made Bruce dependent upon her.

"She needed an escort, that's all. They don't sleep together. It's like what you have," she said, nodding toward the bedroom windows, "separate bedrooms. Only, they don't even have an adjoining door." She laughed. Then she looked at Darby and Henry, who were sitting there, sipping their drinks, staring and smiling stupidly at her like two infatuated lovebirds. "Why don't you two go look at the oil wells or something. Ruby and I have to talk girl talk," she snapped.

They both rose obediently and walked off.

"They adore me," she said, looking after them, "but they're both unimaginative and boring."

"They why are you with them?"

"Just to amuse myself." She drew closer. "So, Bruce came to my bathroom one day while I was taking a bath."

"What happened?" I asked, wide-eyed.

"What do you think?"

I wasn't sure I should believe her or not, but I did recall the way Bruce used to gaze at me, undressing me with his eyes, and I recalled how I would shrink under his touch.

She jerked her head high, threw back her shoulders, and with an arrogant air bragged, "I've been with many older men. I've even slept with one of my teachers at the school."

"Gisselle!"

"So? How is any of that any worse than what you're doing . . . sleeping with your half brother?" she snapped.

"I'm not. We don't sleep together. We're married, but we're not husband and wife that way. We both agreed."

"Why?" she said, grimacing. "Why get married then?"

"Paul's always loved me, and before we knew what our true relationship is, I was very fond of him. He loves Pearl as much as he would had she been his own daughter. We have a very special relationship now," I said.

"It's special, all right. And boring. You have a lover, then, I assume, some dashing, tall, dark Cajun swamp man who sneaks up to your room at night?"

"No, of course not."

"Of course not, not you, not Miss Goody Two-Shoes." She sat back, her arm dangling over the arm of the chair. "I wrote to Beau and told him of your wedding and how rich you are," she said.

"I bet you couldn't wait."

"Well, you ran away. You should have had the abortion and stayed in New Orleans. Even with all this, you're still living in the swamps."

"The swamps are beautiful. Nature can't be ugly," I said.

She took a long sip of her drink. "Did I tell you about Uncle Jean?" she suddenly asked.

"Uncle Jean? No. What about him?"

"You don't know anything?"

"What is it, Gisselle?"

"He killed himself," she said nonchalantly.

"What?" I gasped. I felt the blood drain from my face and my feet become nailed to the patio.

"One day he stole one of those knives they use to cut clay in their recreation room and cut his wrists. He bled to death before anyone discovered what he had done. Daphne put on a big show, of course, threatening to sue the institution. For all I know, she got some sort of settlement. I wouldn't put it past her. If there's a way to make money in something, she'll find it."

"Uncle Jean . . . killed himself? When?"

"Months ago," she said, shrugging.

I sat back, stunned. The last time I had seen him was when I had gone to him with Beau to tell him about Daddy's death.

"Why didn't anyone write to tell me? Why didn't you?"

"Daphne said you relinquished your relationship to the family when you ran off," she replied. "And you know how I hate writing letters, especially bad news. Unless it's other people's bad news," she added with a slight laugh.

"Poor Uncle Jean. I should never have told him Daddy died. I should have left him thinking he was just not visiting."

"Maybe it is your fault," Gisselle said, enjoying my misery. Then she shrugged again and sipped her drink. "Or maybe you should be congratulated. After all, he's better off."

"How can you say such a terrible thing? No one's better off dead, not even Uncle Jean," I cried back in a choked voice.

"All I know is, I'd rather be dead than live forever in that stuffy institution," she proclaimed.

My eyes filled with tears as I thought about Uncle Jean lost and alone.

"And who do we have here?" we heard, and turned to see Paul come out of the house.

"Well, if it isn't my wealthy brother, or is it brother-in-law?" Gisselle quipped.

Paul turned crimson and shifted his eyes to me. "What's wrong, Ruby?" he asked instantly.

"I just learned that my uncle Jean committed suicide in the institution."

"Oh, I'm sorry."

"Don't I get a kiss hello?" Gisselle asked.

"Sure." He leaned over to kiss her on the cheek, only she turned her face quickly so his lips met hers. Surprised, he stood back. Gisselle laughed.

"When did this suicide happen?" Paul asked.

"Forget about that. I don't want to dwell on bad news," Gisselle said, and twisted her shoulder. "Ruby was just explaining your special marriage arrangement," she teased. Her licentious smile made both Paul and me feel guilty.

"Gisselle, stop it."

"Oh, don't be so sensitive. Besides, what do I care what you two do?" She looked out toward the fields. "Did you see two young, wealthy Creoles wandering about your oil wells?"

"Who?"

"Gisselle's boyfriends," I said dryly.

"Oh. No."

"Maybe they fell into some swamp," she said, and laughed. Then she got up and put her arm through Paul's. "Why don't you show me around your grounds and your oil fields," she said.

"Of course."

"Are you staying for dinner, Gisselle?" I asked.

"How do I know? If I'm bored, I'll leave. If not, I'll stay," she said, winking. "Come along, Mr. Oil Baron."

Paul looked at me helplessly. "You know what I think you would really enjoy, Gisselle, a ride through the swamps. She can get a better view of things that way anyway, can't she, Ruby?"

"What? Oh yes," I said in an empty voice. My mind was still fixed on poor Uncle Jean.

"Not me. I'm not going into the swamps. Where are those idiots?" she said, gazing over the grounds. We saw them walking back from the pool. "Darby, Henry," she shouted. "Get back here."

They broke out in a jog as if she held them on a long, invisible leash. When they arrived, she introduced them to Paul and the three of them started to talk about the oil wells, Paul explaining how one is drilled and capped. Gisselle grew bored quickly.

"Aren't there any places to go around here . . . you know, for dancing or something?"

"There's a lounge nearby that has a great zydeco band," Paul said. "Ruby and I go often to listen."

"I don't think that's for us," Gisselle complained. "How about a clean restaurant?"

"We have a wonderful cook. You're all welcome to stay for dinner," Paul said.

"I don't mind," Henry said.

"Me neither," Darby followed.

"Well, I do. I want to get back to New Orleans so we can go to some nightclubs," Gisselle said. "It's too quiet around here and I can't get that sour smell out of my nose."

"Sour smell?" Paul looked at me, but I just closed and opened my eyes.

"The swamp stench," Gisselle said.

"I don't smell it," Darby said.

"You wouldn't know a skunk if it crawled into bed with you," she snapped. Henry laughed.

"Oh yes he would. He's slept with a few before."

Gisselle laughed and released Paul's arm to take Henry's.

"To the car, James. I've visited my sister and have seen her wealth. Don't worry," she said, "I'll double everything when I describe it to Daphne."

"I don't care what you tell her, Gisselle. She doesn't matter to me anymore," I said.

Disappointed, Gisselle led her boyfriends back to the

house, with Paul and me following. At the patio door, Gisselle suddenly turned on me.

"I would like to see . . . what do you call her . . . Pearl, before I go."

"We can look in on her. She's napping," I said. I took Gisselle upstairs to the nursery. Mrs. Flemming was dozing in the easy chair by the crib. Her eyes snapped open with surprise when she looked upon our duplicate faces.

"My twin sister, Gisselle," I whispered. "Gisselle, Mrs. Flemming."

"How do you do, dear," Mrs. Flemming said, rising. "My, you two are the mirror image of one another. I bet you're often mistaken for each other."

"Not as often as you might think," Gisselle replied sharply. Mrs. Flemming just nodded and then stepped out to go to the bathroom. Gisselle moved to the crib and looked down at Pearl, who slept with her little hand curled under her chin.

"She has Beau's nose and mouth," she said. "And Beau's hair, of course. You know, I'm thinking of spending the remainder of my summer in Europe. I'll see Beau and spend some time with him. Now I'll be able to describe his child to him," she said with a mean little laugh.

Her wide smile of self-satisfaction cut into my heart. I swallowed back my sadness and turned away from her as she marched out of the room. For a moment I stood there gazing at Pearl and thinking of Beau, my heart feeling like a hollowed-out drum. Every beat echoed through my thoughts.

A short while later, it was as if a cool breeze of relief had come blowing through the bayou when Gisselle and her two male friends got back into their car and went tearing away down the drive. I could hear her shrill laughter lingering for a moment after they disappeared around a turn.

Then I charged up the stairs and went to my room to throw myself on my bed, where I sobbed uncontrollably for a few moments. I was so depressed with the news of Uncle Jean's tragic death and Beau, I couldn't keep the tears from streaming down my cheeks, soaking the pillow. Paul knocked softly on my door and came hurrying in when he saw me crying. I felt his hand on my shoulder.

"Ruby," he said softly, and I turned and threw myself into his arms. From the day we were married, we were afraid to touch each other, afraid of what every kiss, every embrace, even holding each other's hand, would mean in light of who and what we were, but when we made promises to each other, we forgot that we would need each other's intimate contact from time to time.

I needed to feel his arms around me; I needed to sense him close and have him hold me and soothe me with his petting my hair and kissing my forehead and cheeks, kissing away the tears and whispering words of solace. I sobbed harder, my shoulders shaking, as he stroked my hair and rocked me softly in his arms.

"It's all right," he said. "It'll be all right."

"Oh, Paul, why did she have to come and bring me all the bad news? I hate her. I do. I hate her," I said.

"She's just so jealous of you. No matter how much she runs down the bayou and the Cajun world, she's still full of green envy. That's a woman who's never going to be happy," Paul said. "You shouldn't hate her; you should pity her."

I sat back and ground back some tears.

"You're right, Paul. She is to be pitied and she won't ever be happy. No matter what she has. But I feel so bad about Uncle Jean. I wanted to go to him soon, bring Pearl along, and maybe . . . maybe find a way to get him out of the institution and even here with us."

"I'm sorry. It would have been nice, but you can't blame yourself. What was destined to happen was decided by events and choices made before your time, Ruby." He reached across the bed to touch my cheek. "I hate to see you unhappy, even for a few minutes. I can't help the way I love you."

I closed my eyes and kept them closed, knowing, sensing, what he was about to do. When his lips touched mine, I wasn't surprised. I let him kiss me and then I lay back on the pillow.

"I'm a little exhausted," I whispered, my heart pounding.

"Rest a bit and let me think of ways to cheer you up," he said. I felt him lift off the bed and heard him walk out. Then I turned over and embraced the pillow.

Beau had broken his engagement. Gisselle was going to see him and tell him about me. What would he think? How would he feel? Far away, across the ocean, he would gaze toward America and the opportunity for a great and lasting love he had lost . . . I had lost.

My heart felt like a twisted rubber band about to snap. I swallowed down my sadness like castor oil. I'm a woman, I thought, a young, vibrant woman, and my needs are greater than I had anticipated.

For the first time since I had taken the vows with Paul, I regretted what I had done and wondered if I had piled one great tragic decision on top of another. Despite the beauty and the splendor of our great home and estate, I felt the walls closing in around me, shutting out the sun, covering me in a dark, deep, depressing blanket of regret from under which I feared I would never escape.

6

Masquerade

After Paul had left me, I lay there on my bed feeling sorry for myself. The late afternoon sun had begun to fall below the willows and cypress trees so that the shadows in the room grew somewhat deeper and darker. When I gazed out through the top of my windows, I saw that the sky had turned a darker turquoise and the scattered clouds were the color of old silver coins. The house was very quiet. It had been so well built that the sounds from downstairs or even from inside rooms across the hall were insulated when doors were closed. How different it was from living in my grandmere Catherine's shack on the bayou, where even from our upstairs bedrooms, we could hear the scurry of a field mouse across the living room floor.

But suddenly I heard the distinct clip-clopping of boots down the corridor outside my doors. I heard what sounded like the rattle of a saber, too. They grew louder and closer. Curious, I sat up just as my door was opened and Paul stepped through, dressed in a Confederate officer's uniform, sword at his hip. He wore a fake sweet-potato red Vandyke beard as well, and he carried a package under his right arm. The costume and the beard fit him so well that for a moment I didn't know who it was. Then I smiled.

"Paul! Where did you get all that?"

"Pardon, madame," he said, and took off his hat to make a sweeping, graceful and elegant bow. "Colonel William Henry Tate at your service." He scowled. "I was just informed that some Yankees had invaded your privacy and caused you some consternation. I'll need a full report before I send my troops after the scoundrels, who, I promise you, will be swinging in the wind under the old oak before sundown.

"Now," he continued, straightening into a formal military posture and running his left forefinger over his mustache, "if you will just be so kind as to give my adjunct their descriptions . . ."

I clapped my hands and laughed.

"Oh, Paul, that's so funny."

He stepped toward me, not cracking a smile.

"Madame, I am William Henry Tate and I am at your service. There is no more distinguished service for a southern gentleman to perform than the service he performs on behalf of a lady, a truly beautiful and elegant daughter of the South."

With that he took my hand and kissed it softly.

"Well, suh," I said, thickening my accent and stepping into his make-believe, "I am flattered. No fina nor more handsome gentleman has come to my aid so quickly before."

"Madame, think of me as your devoted servant." He kissed my hand again. "May I be so bold as to invite you to my tent this evening for dinner. Of course, the service and the victuals won't be up to the standard they should be for a woman of your stature, but we are in the midst of a desperate struggle to keep our way of life survivin', and I'm sure you will understand."

"It's ma contribution to the great effort, suh, to sacrifice, too. You do have linen napkins, however, do you not?" I asked, batting my eyelashes.

"Of course. I didn't mean to imply you would dine like some dirtbag Yankee merchant. And on that note, may I offer you this dress for the occasion. It belonged to ma own sweet departed mother."

He handed me the package under his arm. I set it on my lap and unwrapped it. Within was a brownish pink taffeta dress. I held it up. It had high bodice sleeves that were bell-shaped at the wrists and lavishly embroidered. From these emerged undersleeves made of batiste covered with embroidery. The collar was like the sleeves.

"Why, suh, this is a beautiful dress. I'd be honored to wear such a garment."

"The honor is all mine, madame," he said, stepping back with another sweeping bow. "Shall I stop by . . . say, in twenty minutes and escort you to the dining area?"

"Make that twenty-five minutes, suh. I do want to make special preparations."

"Madame, for you, the clock stops." He stood up and pulled a beautiful, antique gold pocket watch out of his pants pocket and flipped it open. It began to play a sweet tune. "I shall return as you requested."

"Paul," I cried, "where did you get all this?"

"Paul? Madame, my name is William Henry Tate," he said, and with that he pivoted and marched out. I stared after him, the laughter on my lips. Then I looked at the dress again and wondered what I would look like in it.

The dress fit nearly perfectly. I took it in slightly at the waist with safety pins, but the bodice and the sleeves were perfect. Once I had the dress on, the magic of pretending took control and I thought about my hair. Quickly I brushed and pinned it up, making a part down the middle just the way southern women in historical pictures I had seen wore their hair. I stood there gazing at myself in the full-length mirror, wishing for the moment that our make-believe were true and I really was a member of southern aristocracy about to dine with a gentleman officer.

There was a gentle knock at my door. When I opened

it, Paul, in his costume, stepped back with a wide smile over his face, his eyes brightening with pleasure. He had a corsage of white baby roses in his hands.

"Madame, you surpass even my most ambitious expectations. Beauty has no better place to call its home but in your face and fine figure."

I laughed. "Where did you get these words?"

"Madame, please. These are the words of a southern gentleman, and the words of a southern gentleman are never trifling."

"Excuse me, suh." I curtsied.

"May I?" he asked, approaching with the corsage. I stood still as he pinned it on my bodice. When I looked into his face and he looked into mine, it was as if I were looking at the face of a handsome stranger. He smiled and then stepped back and offered me his arm. "Madame."

"Suh," I said, taking it. He escorted me down the corridor and we descended the stairway like the lord and lady of some great manor. Paul had prepared our servants for this costume party, for neither Molly nor James looked surprised. Molly smiled and bit down on her lower lip, but everyone behaved as if this were a perfectly normal evening.

Paul had the lights turned down in the dining room and candles burning in the silver candelabra. He had soft dinner music piped in. After he brought me to my seat, he took his and offered me a glass of wine.

"You set a fine dinner table in the field, suh," I remarked.

"We make do with what we can, madame. These are times to try the souls of gallant men and gallant women. I am not one to diminish the sacrifice made by southern ladies. However, rank has its privileges, and I was able to manage this fine French Chablis." He leaned over, pretending not to want the servants to hear. "Bought it from some smugglers," he said.

"Oh dear. Well, suh, they say the higher the grape, the sweeter the wine."

"Well put, madame. Shall we make a toast?" he said, lifting his glass toward mine. "To the return of better times when the most important thing for a man to do is make the woman of his heart happy."

We clinked glasses and sipped, eyes open and fixed on each other as we did so. Then Paul dabbed his napkin over his lips, taking care not to move his fake Vandyke, and nodded to Molly and James so they could begin to serve our dinner.

I had expected to have little or no appetite this evening, but Paul's elaborate plotting to create these illusions and pleasant distractions was so delightful and romantic, I had to leave my dark and depressing thoughts behind. I had the feeling he had been planning such activity before and had everything ready just in case.

Letty had prepared glazed wild duck as our entrée. And for dessert, with our rich Cajun coffee, we had floating island with strawberries. While we dined, Paul was charming and funny. Apparently he had studied up on the Civil War battles in which his ancestor William Henry Tate had fought. Like an actor who had rehearsed his part for months and months, he kept in character. He sang Civil War ditties, talked about the occupation of New Orleans by the Yankee army and the hated General Butler, whose face was painted on the inside of chamber pots that became known as Butler pots.

He kept me so amused, I had little time to recall Gisselle's visit and the dreadful things she had told me. By the time Paul and I finished dinner, I was giggly and happy and very content. He offered his arm and escorted me to the patio, where we were to have an after-dinner cordial and gaze at the stars.

Over a hundred years ago, I thought, a Confederate officer and his lady looked up at the same night sky dazzled by the same stars. A hundred years wasn't much time to the stars, even less than a second was to us. How small and insignificant we are beneath the celestial firmament, I thought. All our great problems were so tiny.

"A Dixie for your thoughts," Paul said.

"My thoughts that valuable to you?"

"So valuable, it makes no sense to put any monetary offer. That's why I symbolically offer the Dixie."

"I was just thinking how small we are under the stars."

"I beg to differ, madame. You see that one star up there, the one that's blinking brighter than the others?"

"Yes."

"Well, it's blinking that way because it's jealous of the radiance that comes from your face this night. Somewhere on another planet like ours, two people are looking up at their night sky and seeing the brilliance from your eyes, the glow of your lips, and thinking how small their world is."

"Oh, Paul," I said, moved by his words.

"William Henry Tate," he corrected, and leaned over to brush my lips with a kiss. It was so soft and quick, I could have been kissed by the breeze coming up from the Gulf and thought it was Paul's kiss, but when I opened my eyes, his face was still close to mine.

"I can't be happy when you're unhappy, Ruby," he whispered. "Are you a little happier now?"

"Yes, I am," I said. I heard the way my words sounded; I felt the trembling in my body. The cordial, the wine, the wonderful meal, had filled me with a warm glow. The night, the stars, the very air we breathed, all conspired against that part of me that struggled to remind me how close I was to surrendering myself.

"Good," Paul said, and brought his lips to my forehead. He kissed my closed eyes and my nose and brought those warm lips to mine. The tingling that stirred in my breast radiated into my neck, where his lips followed. I moaned and then I pulled away.

"I'm tired," I said quickly. "I think I should go up."

"Of course." He stood up when I did.

"Thank you, suh," I said, smiling, "for a most wonderful evening."

"Perhaps when the war ends, we will do it again," he

replied, "in surroundings more suited to your beauty and stature."

"It was fine, wonderful," I said. He nodded and I turned and walked into the house, my heart pounding. It was as if I really were saying good night to a beau who had been courting me and with whom I had fallen deeper and deeper in love.

Molly had turned down all the lights in the house. Mrs. Flemming had fed and put Pearl to sleep. I hurried up the stairs and to my bedroom, gasping as I entered and falling back against the closed door to catch my breath, my eyes closed, my blood rushing madly through my veins.

After a few moments, I stepped away from the door and went to the vanity table. Slowly I slipped out of the old dress, but I stood there staring at myself in my slip and panties. I unpinned my hair and let the strands fall down my still crimson neck and over my shoulders. I couldn't stop my body from trembling with a longing I had naïvely thought I could subdue at will. My breath quickened as I continued to undress, stepping out of my panties and undoing my bra. Naked, I gazed upon myself in the mirror, imagining a gallant Confederate officer stepping up behind me and placing his hand on my shoulder until I turned to raise my lips to his.

Finally I turned off the lights and crawled under my comforter, luxuriating in the cool touch of the linen on my hot skin. Paul's romantic words lingered in my ears. I lay there thinking about the stars, dreaming. I didn't hear the adjoining door open, nor did I hear him approach my bed. I didn't realize he was beside me until I felt the weight of his body shift the mattress and then felt the warmth of his lips on my neck.

"Paul."

"It's William," he said softly.

"Please, don't . . ." I began, but the words choked in my throat.

"Madame, war makes time a luxury. If we were to have

met and fallen in love before or after, I would spend weeks, months, courting you, but in the morning, I am to lead my troops into a desperate battle from which many will not return."

I spun around and when I did so, his hands cupped my shoulders and he brought my lips to his. It was a long, hot kiss. His chest pressed against my naked breasts and his legs moved between mine until I could feel his manliness probing gently.

I started to shake my head, but his lips went to my throat, and the touch of them pushed back my resistance. I laid my head against the pillow as his lips moved down my neck and grazed the crowns of my breasts, nudging the already erect nipples. Outside my window, I thought I could hear the snorting of horses, impatiently tapping their hooves on the stone.

"I, too, may not return, madame. But if Death is waiting to claim me, he will be disappointed, for on my lips will be your name and in my eyes will be your face."

"No," I said weakly, and then I said, "William . . ."

When he entered me, I gasped and started to cry, but his lips were over mine again. We moved in a gentle rhythm that grew stronger and stronger until we galloped toward an ecstatic explosion that made me moan.

Afterward, we lay beside each other, waiting for our breathing to slow. Then he lifted himself from the bed, turning to say, "God bless you, madame," before he slipped through the darkness to the door and was gone.

I closed my eyes. There was a part of me in turmoil, hysterical, screaming about sin and evil, raging about the curses and the punishments that would rain down over me with hurricane force. But I pressed those voices back and heard only my own thumping heart. I fell asleep to the sound of my blood pumping through my body and didn't wake until the dim light of false dawn played shadows over the walls.

I thought I heard the sound of cannons in the distance and sat up slowly. It sounded like a troop of horses were clip-clopping their way over the yard. I rose from my bed and went to the window. Pulling back my curtain, I looked out. Inflamed swamp gas rolling over the surface of the canals did resemble the flash of cannons. Off in the distance, the silhouetted willows seemed to swallow a company of men on horseback. And then the sun really lifted its first rays over the rim of darkness and sent dreams scurrying back to their havens to wait for another night.

I returned to bed and lay awake until I heard Pearl's first cries and Mrs. Flemming hurrying to her crib. Then I got up and dressed myself to face the reality of another day.

Paul was at the table having coffee and reading his newspaper when I came down with Mrs. Flemming and Pearl. He snapped the pages and folded them quickly and smiled.

"Good morning. Did everyone sleep well?"

"The little one slept through the night," Mrs. Flemming said. "I've never seen such a contented infant. I feel like I'm stealing by taking money from you for caring for such a perfect baby."

Paul laughed and gazed at me. He looked fresh and awake and absolutely glowed with vibrancy. There was not the slightest sign of remorse in his face.

"I thought it was going to rain last night. Did you hear the thunder toward the Gulf?" he asked me.

"Yes," I said. From the way he was smiling and talking, it was as if I had dreamed our entire encounter. Had I?

"I absolutely passed out myself," he said to Mrs. Flemming. "Slept like a log. I guess it was the wine. But I feel well rested. So what are your plans for the day, Ruby?" he asked me.

"Your sister's coming over later to show me some pictures of wedding dresses and bridesmaid gowns. I'm going to be working in my studio most of the day."

"Good. I've got to go to Baton Rouge and won't be

back until dinner. Ah," he cried when Molly began to bring in our eggs and grits, "I'm starving this morning." He beamed a smile at me and we had our breakfast.

Afterward I went up to my studio, and just before he left, Paul came up to say good-bye.

"I'm sorry I've got to be away so much of the day," he said, "but it's oil business that can't wait. Have you any idea how much money I've deposited in our various accounts?"

I shook my head but gazed at my easel instead of him.

"We're millionaires many times over, Ruby. There isn't anything you can't have or can't have for Pearl, and—"

"Paul," I said, turning sharply, "money, no matter how much, can't ease my conscience. I know what you're trying to do, to say, but the fact is, we violated our promises to each other last night. We made our own special vows, remember?"

"What do you mean?" he said, smiling. "I went to bed and passed out last night, just as I described. If you had dreams . . ."

"Oh, Paul . . ."

"Don't," he said. He pleaded with his eyes, and I understood that as long as I went along with the make-believe, he could live with what happened. Then he smiled. "Who knows what's real and what isn't? Last night someone rode a horse over our grounds, right over our newly planted lawn. Go on and look for yourself, if you like. The tracks are still there," he said. Then he leaned over to kiss me on the cheek. "Paint something . . . from your dream," he suggested, and left me.

Could I do what he asked . . . imagine that it had all been a dream? If I couldn't, I couldn't live with my conscience, and Pearl and I would have to leave, I thought. Paul had become so attached to her, and she to him. No matter what sins I might have committed and might yet commit, I had given Pearl a loving and caring father.

I smothered the voices that would haunt me and

turned instead to do just what Paul had suggested . . . paint from the pictures within me. I worked in a frenzy, drawing, constructing and creating an eerie swamp landscape. From out of the moss-hung cypress emerged the shadowy, ghostlike figures of Confederate calvary, their heads bowed. They were returning from some battle, their ranks greatly depleted. The mist curled around the legs of their horses, and on the branches of nearby oak trees, owls peered sadly. Off in the background, the glow of yet-burning fires lingered and turned that part of the inky night sky bloodred.

I became inspired and decided I would create a whole series of pictures depicting this romance. In my next picture, I would have the officer's lady waiting on the balcony of the plantation house, her eyes searching desperately for the sight of him as the men emerged from the night of death and destruction. I was so entranced with my work that I didn't hear Jeanne come up the stairs and couldn't help showing my chagrin at being disturbed.

But she was so excited about her upcoming wedding, I felt terrible about disappointing her.

"You mustn't mind me," I said when her face dropped into glum despondency over my reaction at seeing her. "I get so involved in my painting, I forget time and place. This house could go up in flames and I wouldn't realize it."

She laughed.

"Come, let me see the pictures of the dresses," I said, and we spent the afternoon talking about designs and colors. She had a half dozen friends to serve as bridesmaids. We discussed the little gifts she would get for each of them and their escorts and then she described her mother's plans for the reception.

As we talked and I listened, my regret over not having a wonderful real wedding for myself deepened. Even Jeanne remarked how sorry everyone was that Paul and I had eloped and not given them the same opportunity to plan a grand affair.

"What you should do is get married again," she

suggested excitedly. "I've heard of couples doing that. They have a ceremony for themselves and then an elaborate one for all of the friends and relatives. Wouldn't that be fun?"

"Yes, but for the time being, one elaborate party is enough," I said.

The planning continued as if it were a major campaign. We had dinners at the house after which the family gathered in the living room to discuss the menus, the guest list, the arrangement of flowers, and the location of every part of the ceremony and reception. There were some heated arguments over the music, the girls wanting a more modern band, and Gladys and Octavious wanting a more eloquent orchestra. Every time a disagreement became impossible to solve, Paul would force me to give my opinion.

"I don't see why we can't have both," I suggested. "Let's have an orchestra for the dinner reception and then afterward, bring in a zydeco band or one of those rock bands and let the younger people have their fun, too."

"That's a ridiculous waste of money," Gladys said.

"Money is the least of our worries, Mother," Paul said gently. She fixed her eyes of fire on me for a moment and then gave a little shudder of disgust.

"If you and your father don't care how you throw your money into the swamp, I don't care," she quipped.

"It won't be that much more," Octavious said softly, but Gladys only pressed her lips more firmly together and glared at me. I was happy when these meetings finally came to an end.

Time passed more quickly for me now that I was heavily involved in my series of paintings. I couldn't wait for the day to begin, and some days I got so lost in my work, the sun had started to go down before I realized I had forgotten lunch and it was time to get ready for dinner. I regretted neglecting Pearl, but Mrs. Flemming was more than an adequate nanny. She was really part of the family and took wonderful, loving care of her.

As for Paul, he didn't come into my room at night again, nor did either of us mention the night he had. It soon began to feel like something I had only really dreamed. With the planning of the wedding ceremony, with the satisfaction I was having painting, life at Cypress Woods continued to be fulfilling and exciting. It seemed a day didn't pass without Paul announcing some grand new purchase or development.

One evening after one of our family dinners, I found myself alone with Gladys on the patio having an after-dinner cordial. Paul and his father were still in the house talking, and his sisters had gone to meet some friends. At dinner Octavious revealed he and Gladys had political ambitions for Paul. When I questioned it on the patio, Gladys widened her eyes with surprise.

"People in high places are getting to know about the Tates," she said. "Legislators are already courting Paul. He has all the qualities that could make him governor someday, if he wants."

"Do you think he wants that?" I asked, surprised.

"Why not?" Gladys said. "Of course, he won't do anything if you don't want him to do it," she said with disgust.

"I wouldn't stand in Paul's way if he really wanted something," I said. "I just wonder if it's what he wants or what you want."

"Of course it's what he wants," she fired back. Then she smiled coldly. "What's the matter, can't you see yourself as the first lady of Louisiana? We've got no reason to feel inferior to anyone. Don't you forget it," she added.

Before I could reply, Paul and his father came out and Gladys complained about a headache and asked Octavious to take her home. Nevertheless, I had to smile to myself imagining how my sister would react to such a possibility: me, the first lady of Louisiana? Gisselle would burst with envy.

It had been some time since Gisselle's visit, and I always felt as if a second shoe was going to drop. It came in the form of a postcard she sent to me from France. There was a picture of the Eiffel Tower on the front. I didn't know it then, but I was going to receive one, even two, a week from my darling twin sister, each like a pin stuck into a voodoo doll, each describing the fun she was having with Beau in Paris. *"Chère* Ruby," the first one began . . .

I finally got here and guess who was at the airport waiting for me . . . Beau. You wouldn't recognize him. He has this thin mustache and looks like Rhett Butler in *Gone With the Wind.* He speaks French fluently. He was so happy to see me. He even brought flowers! He is going to show me around Paris, the first sight beginning with his apartment on the Champs-Elysées.

Give my love and kisses to Paul. I'm about to tell Beau all about Pearl.

Amour,
Gisselle

The tears that filled my eyes after reading one of Gisselle's postcards from France lingered for hours, clouding my vision, making drawing and painting difficult, if not impossible. It got so I regretted sorting through the mail and finding one of those picture cards. She would describe the nightclubs they frequented, the cafés, the fine restaurants. With each postcard, the suggestion that more was going on between her and Beau than simply the reunion of school friends grew stronger and stronger.

"Today Beau told me that I have really matured," she wrote. "He said whatever differences there were between you and me have diminished. Isn't that sweet?"

She described the jewelry he bought her and the way they held hands when they walked and talked softly at the banks of the Seine in the evening after one of their wonderful dinners at some romantic café. Always, other lovers walking nearby looked at them enviously.

"I know Beau thinks he can have you by having me and I should be annoyed, but then I think, why not use his love for you to win him back? It's fun."

On the next card, however, she wrote:

"I think I can say with some certainty now that Beau is falling in love with me, not just because I look like you, but because . . . it's me! Isn't that nice?"

A week later she wrote specifically to tell me that Beau no longer asked her questions about me.

He has finally accepted that you are married and gone from his life. But of course, that means nothing now. He has a lot more to look forward to with me at his side again.

Toujours amour,
Your sister Gisselle

I never showed Paul any of these postcards. After reading them, despite my reluctance to read them, I tore them up and threw them away. It always took me hours to recover.

But as the date of Jeanne's wedding grew closer, I had much to occupy my mind anyway. Three hundred guests had been invited. People were coming from as far away as New York and California. Anyone who was important to the cannery and the oil businesses, of course, as well as friends and relatives, was invited.

We had a beautiful day for the wedding. It was warm with bearable humidity and a sky of deep blue with clouds that looked scrubbed clean. Cypress Woods was buzzing with activity from the crack of dawn. I felt like I was queen of the anthill; there were that many people scurrying about, arranging this and that.

Father Rush and the choir arrived early. Most people had not seen Cypress Woods and were very impressed. Paul was beaming with pride and happiness. We all got dressed and began greeting the guests, many of whom arrived in limousines. Before long, our long driveway was lined with automobiles and drivers. The men were dressed in tuxedos, and the women wore gowns of every fashionable design. I thought we might all go blind from the glitter of diamonds and gold in the midday sun.

I gave Jeanne my bedroom suite to use, and Paul gave James his. Of course, the traditions were observed and James did not see his bride until she emerged from the French doors to the patio at the start of "Here Comes the Bride." Before the actual wedding ceremony, Father Rush conducted a service and the choir sang hymns. Under the flower-laden canopy, Jeanne and James took their vows.

How different this ceremony was from mine, I thought sadly. They could take their oaths in the light of day in front of hundreds of people without shame, without fear, without guilt. When they turned and were showered with rice, their faces were full of smiles of anticipation, happiness, and delight. If there were any fears in their hearts, they were well subdued, buried under the weight of great love.

I was filled with a heavy sadness and lowered my eyes. Had this most wonderful part of a woman's life been denied to me or had I denied it to myself? What dark threads of evil had woven their fabric in the bayou and cast it over my destiny?

This was not the time to be melancholy, however. The music started, the waiters and waitresses circulated with their trays of hors d'oeuvres, and the dancing began. We had to gather for family pictures, and my face had to shine with smiles. Only Paul, who had this second sense about me, gazed at me and saw the undercurrent of sadness that ran just below my laughter and grins. Later, when the feast began and the music continued, he and I danced and he brought his lips to my ear to whisper.

"I know what you're thinking," he said. "You wish you had had a wedding like this. I'm sorry."

"It's not your fault. You have no reason to apologize."

"We'll make a wonderful wedding for Pearl," he promised. He kissed me on the cheek and then the music became livelier and we were all doing the Cajun two-step.

The feasting and celebrating went on into the evening, long after Jeanne and James left for their honeymoon. Just before they went to their car, covered with JUST MARRIED signs and cans tied to the back bumper, Jeanne pulled me aside.

"I don't know how to thank you enough, Ruby. You made my wedding wonderful with all of your suggestions and work. But most importantly, with your advice and concern. You are really my sister now," she said, and hugged me.

"Be happy," I said, smiling through my joyful tears. She hurried off to join her impatient new husband.

Finally, in the wee hours of the morning, the last few guests left and the crews of workers completed the cleanup work. Exhausted, I went up to my suite and undressed to collapse in bed. Shortly after I had put out my lights, I heard Paul open the adjoining door. I opened my eyes just enough to see him standing there, silhouetted in his lamplight.

"Ruby?" he whispered. "Are you asleep?"

When I didn't reply, he sighed deeply.

"I wish," he said, "we had had a honeymoon, too. I wish I could love you freely and wholly."

He stood there a moment longer and then he closed the door softly and I shut my eyes before a single tear could find its way to the edge of my lids. Sleep, the best consoler of all, came mercifully quickly and shut away the voices and the regrets.

Two days later I received what was to be my final picture postcard from Gisselle. It had actually arrived after she and Beau had already returned from Paris. She told me about their plans. Beau was returning to New Orleans to attend medical school, and she was going to attend college. Despite her horrible school records, Daphne had somehow arranged it. She promised, or I should rather say, threatened, to come visit me again. Maybe . . . with Beau.

The very thought of such a visit made me tremble. I

couldn't imagine what my first words would be to him if he should ever drive up to Cypress Woods. Of course, I would bring Pearl to him quickly. She was walking now and saying quite a few words. She loved to sit on Mrs. Flemming's lap at the piano and tap the keys. Everyone who heard her said she was musically inclined.

I had completed four of the pictures for my Confederate Romance series. Paul wanted me to show them in a gallery in New Orleans, but I was not yet ready to part with them and actually feared someone buying them. Meanwhile I continued to do landscapes of the bayou and those were sent regularly to Dominique's gallery, the first gallery that had shown and sold my early works.

We learned that they were selling quickly. I no sooner had one completed and there than it was bought. Paul was delighted and had some art critic visit me to discuss my works, take pictures of my studio and of me. A few months later, the photo spread appeared in an art magazine and then in the *New Orleans Times*. That publicity brought a new letter from Gisselle.

> . . . Daphne nearly dropped her coffee cup in her lap when she opened the paper and saw your picture. Bruce was very impressed. I don't know what Beau thought. I didn't mention it to him and he didn't mention it to me. We see each other nearly every day. I think he's on the verge of offering me a ring. You'll be the first to know. It may happen a week from today because we're all going to the horse ranch and Daphne has invited Beau, too.
>
> Anyway, we've only got six months to go and then we inherit our fortunes. It doesn't mean all that much to you now that you are filthy rich through marriage, I know, but having control of my own money will mean a great deal to me. And to Beau.
>
> Anyway, I suppose I should say congratulations.

So . . . congratulations. Why is it you were born
with a talent and I wasn't if we're twins?

Gisselle

I didn't write back, for I had no answer. If she had no
talent at birth, she had no curse on her either. Was it just
a chance thing that she had been born first and delivered
to the Dumas, and I was to remain behind and be the one
who would learn all about our troubled past? I felt like
throwing that in her face, but then I thought about
Grandmere Catherine and how precious she had been to
me. What if I had been the firstborn? I would never have
known her.

Does everything good have to come with something
bad attached? I wondered. Is the world a balance between good and evil? Why weren't there more angels than
devils? Nina Jackson used to tell me there were far more
devils and that was why we needed all the powders and
the chants, the bones and good-luck charms. Even
Grandmere Catherine gazed into the darkness with the
belief that evil lurked within every shadow and she had
to be vigilant and prepared to do battle. Was that my fate,
too . . . to always do battle?

I hated when I fell into these despondent moods, but
that was what Gisselle's letters and cards always did to
me. But nothing she had written or would write would
compare to the phone call I received from her a week
later.

Paul and I were just finishing dinner. Mrs. Flemming
had fed Pearl and taken her to the den to play with her
toys. Molly poured us coffee and went into the kitchen to
bring out the strawberry shortcake Letty had made. We
were both complaining about the weight we had gained
since we had moved into Cypress Woods and had Letty
prepare our meals, but neither of us was willing to put
restrictions on what she prepared. We laughed at our
self-indulgence.

Paul began to tell me about some legislators who were

115

trying to get him to run for office and who would be paying us a visit in a week or so when James suddenly appeared to announce I had a phone call. Neither Paul nor I had heard the phone ring.

"I was standing right beside it and picked it up quickly," James explained.

"Who is it?"

"Your sister. She sounds very excited and demanded I call you to the phone immediately," he said.

I grimaced. I was sure she was going to tell me she and Beau had become formally engaged. That was one bit of news she wanted to deliver personally so she could hear my reaction.

"Excuse me," I said to Paul, and rose.

"Take it in my office," he suggested. I went there quickly, fortifying myself for the announcement.

"Hello, Gisselle," I said. "What's so urgent?"

She didn't respond for a moment.

"Gisselle?"

"There's been an accident," she said breathlessly.

Oh no, I thought. Beau.

"What? Who?"

"It's Daphne," she gasped. "She fell from her horse late this afternoon and struck her head on a rock."

"What happened?" I asked, my heart pounding.

"She died . . . just a little while ago," Gisselle said. "I have no father . . . I have no mother. I have only you."

7

The Ties
That Bind

Paul looked up from his coffee as I slowly reentered the dining room. One gaze at my face told him I had received bad news.

"What happened?" he asked.

"Daphne . . . fell from her horse and struck her head. She's dead," I reported in a lifeless voice. The news had left me stunned.

"*Mon Dieu.* Who phoned?"

"Gisselle."

"How is she taking it?"

"From the tone of her voice and the things she said on the phone, not too well, but I think she's more frightened than anything else. I'll have to go to New Orleans," I said.

"Of course. I'll cancel my meetings in Baton Rouge and go with you," he offered.

"No, you don't have to go right away. The funeral isn't until Wednesday. There's no sense in your hanging around that dreary house all day."

"Are you sure?" he asked. I nodded. "All right. I'll meet you there," he said. "What about Pearl?"

"I think it's better for me to leave her here with Mrs. Flemming."

"Okay. Tragic," Paul said, nodding slowly.

"Yes. I can't help thinking how devastated my father would have been had he been alive when this happened to her. He idolized her. I saw that from the first moment I met them."

"Poor Ruby," Paul said, rising to embrace me. "Even after I've built this little Shangri-La away from everyone, sadness still finds its way to our doors."

"There is no such paradise on earth, Paul. You can pretend and ignore just so much, but the dark clouds won't disappear. I think that's something we both better realize," I warned. He nodded.

"When are you leaving?"

"In the morning," I said numbly. Through my mind flitted all kinds of gloomy thoughts.

"I hate to see any sadness in your face, Ruby." He kissed me on the forehead and hugged me to him, pressing his lips to my hair.

"I better go see to my packing," I whispered, and hurried away, my heart feeling as if it had shrunk in my chest and only tapped a tiny beat.

The following morning, after kissing Pearl good-bye and telling Mrs. Flemming I would call often, I went out to my car. Paul had carried out my things and put them in the trunk. He was waiting for me at the car, his face downcast and troubled. Neither of us had slept well the night before. I heard and saw him come to my door several times, but I didn't let him know I was awake. I was afraid that his comforting kisses and embrace would slip into something else again.

"I really hate to let you go by yourself," he said. "I should accompany you."

"And then do what? Hold my hand? Pace back and forth thinking about all the things you could and should be doing? You would just make me nervous," I told him. He smiled.

"Just like you to always think about someone else's

feelings, even at a time like this." He kissed me on the cheek and hugged me and I got into my car. "Drive carefully," he said. "I'll call you tonight."

"'Bye." With many trepidations, I headed for New Orleans.

I had the top down and wore a white silk kerchief. How much I had changed, I thought. All of the difficulties and troubles during the last year or so had aged and toughened me in ways I was just beginning to understand. A year ago, driving myself to New Orleans would have been the same as taking myself to the moon. Somewhere along this short but difficult journey I had undergone, I had left the little girl behind. I had a woman's work to do now and I had inherited the grit and the strength and the confidence from Grandmere Catherine to do it.

Despite my fears of it happening, I didn't get lost traveling the streets of New Orleans. When I pulled into the circular drive and saw Daddy's old Rolls-Royce parked by the garage, I gazed at the front door and hesitated. It had been years and years since I had entered this house. I took a deep breath and got out of my car. The new butler came to the door quickly. When he set his eyes on me, he blinked rapidly with confusion at first.

"Oh," he said. "You must be Mademoiselle's twin sister."

"That's right. I'm Ruby."

"My name is Stevens, madame," he said with a slight nod. "I'm sorry for your trouble."

"Thank you, Stevens."

"May I bring in your things?" he offered.

"Thank you," I said. I had expected to see many cars in the driveway when I pulled in and dozens of Daphne's friends gathered to console Gisselle and Bruce, but the house was quiet, empty. "Where is my sister?"

"Mademoiselle is upstairs in her suite," he said, stepping back. I entered the great foyer, and for a moment it was as if I had never left, as if all that had happened since had been a dream. I almost expected to see Daphne come out of the office to smirk a greeting at me and question what I was wearing or where I had been. But there was nothing but silence. All of the lights were either low or unlit. The chandeliers hung like drops of ice. The grand stairway was draped in shadows as if Death itself had traipsed through the house and left his tracks over the carpets and floors.

"I'll be staying in the room adjoining my sister's, Stevens," I told the butler.

"Very good, madame." He hurried out to get my suitcase and I started up the stairs. Before I reached the landing, I heard a peal of laughter coming from Gisselle's open doorway. She was on the telephone. When she turned and saw me standing there, her smile quickly faded and she immediately took on the dark look of a bereaved daughter.

"I can't talk anymore, Pauline. My sister has just arrived and we have to discuss all the funeral arrangements and things. Yes, it's just horrible," she said with a deep sigh. "Thank you for being so understanding. Good-bye." She cradled the receiver slowly and then rose to greet me. "I'm so glad you've come, Ruby," she said, and embraced me, kissing both my cheeks. "It's been terrible, a horrible emotional drain. I don't know what's keeping me standing."

"Hello, Gisselle," I said dryly, and gazed around the room. Her clothes were strewn about and there was a tray of empty dishes from breakfast on a nightstand with an opened movie fan magazine beside it.

"I haven't been able to see anyone or do anything," she immediately complained. "It's all fallen on my head."

"What about Bruce?" I inquired.

"Bruce?" She threw her head back with a thin laugh. "What a wet noodle he turned out to be. And don't I know why, too?" she said, her eyes mean and piercing. "He's lost his meal ticket. All he's been doing is going over legal papers, hoping to find a loophole, but I told him in no uncertain terms to forget it."

"But he was her husband."

"I told you before. In name only, and only as a servant. Daphne locked him out of everything. He's going out of here with little more than he came in with. We'll see to that. Beau has spoken with our attorneys and—"

"Beau?"

"Yes, Beau. He's been the only thing keeping me going. He's been an absolute superman. Right from the start. You don't know how horrible it was. You weren't there," she snapped as though it were my fault I wasn't. "She and Bruce went riding and her horse bucked and threw her. Bruce came running back to the house screaming. Beau and I were still in bed," she inserted with a wry smile. "We both heard Bruce shouting and threw on some clothes. We found her sprawled on the ground, a nasty bruise on her temple. Beau, who's had some medical training, told Bruce not to move her, but to send for an ambulance. He checked her eyes and took her pulse and looked up at me and shook his head. 'It looks bad,' he told me.

"I went back to the house to dress in some warmer clothes. The ambulance arrived and they put her on the stretcher and took her to the hospital, but it was a waste of time. She was dead by the time they arrived.

"Bruce went berserk, blaming himself because he let her talk him into taking the more gentle horse. At least, that was what he claimed. My guess is he never volunteered to ride Fury. He wasn't man enough." She smirked.

"Where is Bruce now?"

"Downstairs in the office, drinking himself into a stupor, I imagine. I told him he could stay until after the funeral."

"You mean he doesn't even have any claim on the house?"

"No. It's all complicated, tied up in what is now our estate. According to Beau, our lawyers think they might be able to accelerate our taking more direct control. That was the word he used . . . 'accelerate.' There is a great deal of money, you know. Remember how stingy Daphne was with us after Daddy had died? Well, she can't be so stingy now, can she?

"Have you noticed how long my hair has grown?" she said, shifting topics without pausing to take a breath. "Beau likes it that way." It was nearly the same length as my own hair.

"How is . . . Beau?"

"Wonderful . . . and happy," she added quickly. "So don't say anything or do anything to ruin things for us or . . . or the world might just find out what a sinner you are," she said, shooting a hostile glance at me.

"How can you make threats at a time like this, Gisselle?" I asked, astounded.

"I'm not making threats. I'm just warning you not to spoil my happiness. You've made your decisions and you're happy with your choices. Good. Now I have a right to be happy, too. And so does Beau."

"I didn't come here to ruin anyone's happiness."

"That's nice to hear." She smiled, tilting her head toward the door. "Paul isn't with you?"

"He will be here for the funeral."

"And the baby . . . what's her name?"

"Pearl," I said sharply. I knew she knew her name. "I thought it was better to leave her at home with Mrs. Flemming."

"Good. Then you and I can get right to business."

"Where's . . ."

"Daphne's body? At the funeral home. You don't think I would permit it in the house, do you? Ugh. It was bad enough we had Daddy here afterward. The only thing we'll have here is the wake, and it will be a nice wake, too. I've already called the caterers. Of course, we'll have tons of flowers. People are sending them like crazy, but I'm having them brought right to the funeral home. And I've prepared a list of people to ask."

"What are you talking about? List of people? This isn't supposed to be a party," I said.

"Of course it is," she replied. "It's a party to help us forget the tragedy. Now, don't go around here with a long face and pretend you're devastated. You hated her and she knew it, too. I can't say I cared for her, but I probably have more reason to be sad than you do. She was my stepmother much longer than she was yours."

I stared at her a moment. Maybe Daphne deserved such a daughter. She had certainly sowed the seeds and by example taught Gisselle to be this self-centered. I sighed, anxious now to get the funeral over with and any other arrangements completed and return to Cypress Woods, where life, at least for me, was far less complicated.

Stevens brought my things up to the room.

"Oh, how nice," Gisselle cried when she saw him carrying my suitcase. "We'll be next to each other again. It's times like this that I really appreciate having a sister," she declared, loud enough for Stevens to hear.

"Mrs. Gidot asked me to inform you that she has prepared some lunch, mademoiselle. Do you want it brought up or . . ."

"Oh no. Tell her my sister has arrived and we'll be dining in the dining room, *tout de suite,*" Gisselle replied, and then beamed a smile of pride at me. "I learned quite a bit of French while I was in Paris with Beau," she added.

"*Tres bien,* mademoiselle," Stevens said, and left.

"What did he say?"

"He said very well. Who's Mrs. Gidot?"

"The Frenchwoman Daphne hired to replace Nina Jackson."

"Where is Nina?"

"How would I know where someone like that is? Really, Ruby. Anyway, I hope you're hungry. Mrs. Gidot is a very good cook and will have something delicious for us to eat, I'm sure."

"I'll just freshen up," I said.

"So will I. I've been crying and dragging myself around so much, I'm sure I look terrible. And Beau will be here in a little while," she added.

My heart started to run away with itself. Just the

thought of being face-to-face with Beau again made me tremble. I tried not to let Gisselle see my apprehension.

"Fine," I said, and flashed a smile. Then I hurried out and into the room that had once been so new and wonderful to me, a room in which Beau had first kissed me and in which he had held me and comforted me during Daddy's wake. I smiled when I saw the picture of the little girl and the puppy still on the wall, and then I went to the window and looked out on the tennis courts and the flowers, recalling how I had felt like a princess the first time I had slept here. It had all looked so magical and precious, I could never have imagined the sadness and trouble that loomed above the great house, just waiting to rain down over us all.

I stopped to look into the office before I went to the dining room to join Gisselle for lunch. Just as she had said, Bruce was there thumbing through a stack of papers, an open bottle of bourbon beside them. He wore a jacket and a tie, but the tie was pulled loose. His hair was disheveled and he looked like he hadn't shaved in a week. When he glanced up at me, his first thought was that I was Gisselle, but after he focused, he realized it was I.

"Ruby!" he cried, rising quickly. He bumped into the corner of the desk in his eagerness to embrace me. The stench of whiskey reached me before he did. He hugged me quickly and stepped back. "It's horrible, horrible. I can't believe what's happened."

"Why?" I said sharply. "It happened to my father; it happened to my uncle Jean."

He blinked rapidly and then shook his head.

"Of course, those were terrible tragedies, too, but Daphne . . . Daphne was at the prime of her life. She was more beautiful than ever. She was . . ."

"I know how wonderful you thought she was, Bruce. I am sorry this has happened. I wouldn't wish it on anyone. There is enough sadness in the world without our contributing to it."

"I knew you would think like that," he said, smiling. "Your sister . . ." He shook his head. "She's gone wild, and with that boyfriend of hers . . . they're conspiring against me. I need your help, Ruby."

"My help? You ask for my help?" I nearly laughed aloud.

"You were always the more reasonable one," he said. "And now that you are very well off yourself, you will understand. Daphne and I had certain arrangements," he continued. "Oh, we never put them in writing as such, but we did. She and I discussed what we would do should something happen to one of us, and we agreed that the other should be granted sole power of attorney. If you will have the estate lawyers draw up the papers . . ."

"For years you and Daphne were the conspirators, Bruce," I said with ice in my voice. "The two of you conspired against my father. You embezzled, you deceived. Only apparently you were partners in crime with a much smarter second half who wrote you out of most of your spoils," I said, gazing at the pile of documents. "I feel sorry for you, but I won't lift a finger to help you," I said. "Take what you've stolen successfully and leave," I advised him. His mouth dropped open.

"But . . . La Ruby, you know I always fancied you, and stuck up for you whenever Daphne was too harsh."

"When?" I snapped. "You never had the courage to oppose her, even when you saw her do mean things to me, to my uncle Jean, even to Gisselle. Don't look to me for favors, Bruce."

His eyes narrowed. "You two won't get away with this. I have lawyers also, you know, high-paid, important lawyers and business associates."

"Frankly, I don't care, Bruce. I'm going to leave those battles up to Gisselle."

He smiled wryly. "She stole your boyfriend, you know."

I felt the heat in my face and knew I had turned crimson. "I'm married, Bruce."

His smile widened. "We'll see who gets the last laugh here," he threatened, and returned to the desk.

I went to the dining room and told Gisselle about my conversation with him. She shrugged.

"I'm leaving all that to Beau and our attorneys," she said. "But I was thinking I would buy out your share of this house and the New Orleans properties. You have so much, why should you care?" she added before I could offer any resistance.

"That's fine with me," I said.

She smiled. "I just knew we would get along fine during this difficult time. We have to do what we can to comfort each other, don't we? What are you going to wear to the funeral? Did you bring something appropriate? I have a closet full of new clothing. You can borrow anything. Just look through my racks and racks of garments. You're a little wider than I am in the hips since you gave birth, but most everything should fit," she said.

"I brought something of my own, thank you," I said.

We both turned when Bruce appeared in the doorway. He hugged a bundle of papers in his arms.

"I'm leaving for a while," he said. "Going to the offices of my attorneys."

"Don't think you can destroy any papers, Bruce," Gisselle said. "I know Mother kept copies of everything with Simons and Beauregard, who are now our attorneys."

He spun around angrily and, in doing so, dropped some of his documents. Gisselle laughed as he fumbled and knelt to gather them up. Then, fuming, he pounded his way down the corridor and out the door.

"Good riddance," Gisselle called after him. She smiled at me. "I was thinking of closing the house for a month and traveling. Maybe to London. Aren't these oysters and artichokes delicious? This large pastry shell is called vol-au-vent," she said pedantically.

The food was good, but I wasn't in the mood to enjoy anything. After lunch, Gisselle went to call some friends and I wandered through the house. Little had been changed or added. I sighed deeply and walked on through the house until I came to what was once my studio. Nothing had been taken out of it, but the room had obviously been kept closed. There were layers and layers of dust on everything, and even cobwebs around the windows and in the corners. Paints were dried and brushes hardened. I gazed at some of my aborted drawings and stood by the easel.

The memory of that day with Beau returned, the day he tempted me into drawing him nude. I looked at the sofa and envisioned him there again, that soft, impish smile on his lips and in his eyes. My heart had been pounding the whole time, but somehow, I had managed to get into my art and had drawn a picture so lifelike and realistic that later, when Daphne discovered it, she had no trouble realizing who it was and what had happened.

It was later that day, after I had worked on his picture, that Beau and I first made love. The memory of his kiss, his touch, our passionate embraces, swept over me and even now stole my breath away. Mesmerized by my own recollections, I approached the sofa slowly and gazed at it as if I could see us together again, a replay of those moments of ecstasy, the two of us joining in an act of love so complete, we lost ourselves in each other and pledged a love we thought could never die.

I sat quickly, feeling my legs soften and threaten to give out from under me. For a while I remained there, my eyes closed, my heart thumping against my chest. Then I took a deep breath and turned to gaze out the window at the sprawling oak trees and gardens, recalling how excited I was when I first set out to draw and paint in my own studio.

"Penny for your thoughts," I heard a soft voice say, and turned to see Beau standing in the doorway. His shock of shiny golden hair still fell wildly over his smooth forehead, and his dark complexion still made his blue eyes glimmer that much more. He wore a dark blue blazer and khaki pants with his shirt opened at the collar. His handsome face was so familiar to me: his sensual and perfect mouth, his perfectly straight, Roman nose, and his strong chiseled-looking chin.

I was speechless for a moment, unable to move under the radiance of his warm and attractive smile, which quickly turned into a soft laugh.

"You look like you're gazing at a ghost," he said. He came to me quickly and took my hands, guiding me to my feet. We embraced and then he stepped back and held my hands up to look at me.

"You haven't changed, except to look more beautiful," he said. "Well?" he said. "Say something."

"Hello, Beau."

We laughed and then he gathered himself into a more serious demeanor, pulling his shoulders back and tightening his lips.

"I'm glad I've found you alone. I wanted to explain what happened, why I left so quickly when your pregnancy was discovered," he began.

"I don't demand explanations," I said, turning away.

"It wasn't the act of a southern gentleman . . . to leave the woman he loved in the lurch. I was a coward, short and simple. My parents were overwrought. My mother was on the verge of a nervous breakdown. She thought everyone in New Orleans would learn of the scandal and their lives would be ruined. I never saw my father that low.

"Then they met with Daphne and she assured them she would take care of the problem if they would have me sent off immediately. I tried to call you before I left, but I couldn't get through. I was practically led off in shackles. In hours they arranged for the transportation, the air tickets, the school, my Paris apartment.

"I had nothing of my own at the time. I was completely dependent upon my parents. If I had defied them, they would have surely disowned me, and what could I have done for you, for us and a baby?

"I admit, I was afraid. Before I knew what I was doing and what was happening to me, I was over the Atlantic Ocean. My parents forbade me to have anything more to do with you, but I sent you letters in the beginning. Did you receive any?"

"No," I said, shooting a quick glance at him. "I was no longer here, and Daphne wouldn't have made any effort to save them or have them forwarded to me."

"I never ran out on any of my responsibilities before," he said. "Everyone, my parents, Daphne, everyone assured me that things would be all right with you."

I looked at him. "All right?" I almost laughed, remembering.

Pain flashed in his eyes. "What did happen?" he asked softly.

"Daphne sent me to have an abortion in some backroom clinic. Once I set eyes on the place, I realized what I was doing and ran off, back to the bayou."

"Where you gave birth to . . ."

"Pearl. She's a beautiful child, Beau."

"And where you got married?"

"Yes."

He lowered his eyes. "When I heard you had married, I decided to stay on in Europe. The truth was, I didn't want to ever come home again. But," he said with a sigh, "that wasn't realistic. Then Gisselle arrived." He smiled. "She's changed, hasn't she?" he asked, hoping for my agreement. "I think she's finally growing up, maturing. Terrible events like this drag you kicking and screaming out of childhood. She knows she's got to be a responsible person now. She has a fortune to oversee, business interests."

"I understand you've been a great help so far," I said.

"I'm doing what I can. Have you seen Bruce?" he asked.

"Yes. Whatever happens to him is only just," I said.

"Don't worry. I'll make sure he doesn't get a penny more than he's supposed to get," he promised.

"Money isn't that important to me anymore, Beau. Actually, it never was as important to me as it was to Gisselle."

"I know. I saw the write-up on you in the paper. Do you have a studio like this?"

"Yes, but with magnificent views of the canals. It's in the attic of our house," I said.

"It sounds wonderful. Gisselle has kept me up-to-date on everything, and from the way she describes . . . what do you call it, Cypress Woods?" I nodded. "From the way she describes it, it sounds like utopia."

"I was always happier in the bayou, surrounded by natural things. That was all too much a part of me, of who and what I was, for me to ever give them up."

"Even for me?" he asked softly. His eyes shone brilliantly with unused tears.

"Beau . . ."

"It's all right. I'm being unfair. I have no right to ask or demand anything from you. You have a right to despise me for leaving you. Nothing that's happened to me or will happen is undeserved," he said.

"We were both at fault, Beau, and both victims of a cruel fate," I replied softly. We stared into each other's eyes, drawing each other closer.

"Ruby," he whispered. He started to reach for me when Gisselle burst into the studio.

"So here you are," she shrilled. "I should have known you would find her. Stevens told me you had come, and when I couldn't find you in the office or living room, I just asked myself, where would he go?"

"Hi, Gisselle," he said. She lunged at him and kissed him fully on the lips, her eyes opened and turned toward me as she did so. "I missed you this morning," she said after she pulled her mouth from his. "When did you leave?"

Beau blushed. "Early. You knew I had to meet with your attorneys."

"Oh. Right. My brain is like a bowl of scrambled eggs today. Well, you might as well tell us what you discussed and what we have to do," she said. "Let's all go to the office and talk." She took Beau's hand and, very full of herself, smiled at me. "All right, Ruby?"

"Fine," I said, and followed them out.

Back at the office, we listened as Beau reviewed what our attorneys believed. How Daphne had gotten Bruce to sign documents excluding himself from her fortune and ours before he married her was a puzzle, but sign them, he did, and the attorneys felt they were ironclad.

"Whatever legal maneuvering he tries will be an exercise in futility," Beau said. "Now, there is a short time left before you take control of everything, but with the attorneys acting as executors, you will have control immediately."

"Then we can spend whatever we want? Buy whatever we want?" Gisselle asked excitedly.

"Yes."

"No more restrictions! The first thing I want is my own sports car. Daphne wouldn't let me have it," she whined, and then turned to me. "You should go through the house and decide what you want to take back to the swamps with you now. I might just have someone come and auction things off," she threatened. "And there is the question of the ranch, our apartment buildings . . ."

"Gisselle, must we discuss this now?"

"I don't care when we discuss it or if we never discuss it. If you want to, just send your attorney around one day to talk to our estate attorneys, right, Beau?"

He gazed at me. "If that's what she wants," he said.

"Let's leave it at that for now," I said. The emotional weight of returning to the house, reviving memories, and then meeting Beau again was overwhelming. I felt like I could sleep a week. "I'd like to just rest for a while," I said. "I think I'll go up to my room. I've got to call home and check on Pearl, too."

Beau shifted his eyes from me to Gisselle and then down to the documents.

"So go take a rest," she said. "I'm not the least bit tired now. In fact, I want to get out of here for a few hours. I feel like I'm suffocating under all this dreariness. Beau, take me down to Jackson Square for coffee and beignets," she commanded.

"If that's what you want to do," he said.

"I do. Thank you, Beau." She beamed a wide smile of self-satisfaction at me.

Beau looked very reluctant to leave, but he did so. I phoned Mrs. Flemming and heard that everything was fine at home. Then I went up to what had once been my own room and lay down on the bed in which I had dreamed often of Beau and myself together, happy. I closed my eyes and in moments, I was asleep.

I woke up to the sound of laughter rising from the base of the stairway and listened.

"Come by in an hour to take us to the wake," I heard Gisselle call out, and then I heard her pound up the stairs. She stopped in my doorway and I sat up, grinding the drowsiness out of my eyes.

"Hi," she said. "We had such a nice time. There was a wonderful breeze at the Riverwalk and we sat and watched the tourists and the artists. You should have come along. Are you well rested? Because we have to go to the funeral parlor for the wake. I'm not having people at the house until after the funeral," she said.

"Yes."

"Then get dressed," she sang. "Beau's coming for us in an hour."

She hurried off and I wondered how even she could be in such a party mood on such a dark occasion. But at the wake she behaved properly, producing tears whenever she wanted them. Despite the role he had played in the little conspiracies against my father, I couldn't help but feel some pity for Bruce, who stood alone in a corner most of the time. Apparently the truth about his relationship with Daphne was no secret, and now that Daphne was gone, everyone understood Bruce had little power and relatively little wealth.

All of Daphne's social friends and many of her business associates stopped by to greet us. Our attorneys were there to introduce them. I sensed that Gisselle was becoming impatient and tired of the somber atmosphere. After an hour or so, she was ready to leave. But Beau was at her side imploring her to stay a little longer. Mourners were still arriving. When she gave in, I realized how strong and good an influence he was on her and smiled to myself.

Periodically I would shift my eyes toward him. He and I would gaze at each other and I would feel my heart start to pitter-patter. I was afraid that someone else would see in my face the warm feelings that still flowed through my body whenever I was close to him or he spoke to me, so I tried to avoid him. But it was like trying to avoid a tall glass of cold water after spending days in the dry desert. I couldn't keep my eyes from shifting in his direction, and every time I heard his voice, I stopped speaking and listening to anyone else. It was still music to my ears, but it was difficult for us to spend any time alone, and the next morning, Paul arrived early to accompany me to the funeral.

I knew we were a great curiosity to many people who had heard about my marriage and new life in the bayou. When Daphne's coffin was slid into the Dumas family vault, my thoughts went to Daddy. In my heart I believed he would have rather been laid to rest beside my real mother. I hoped that spiritually, wherever souls went to spend eternity, they had found each other again, and Daphne . . . would be delivered to another place.

After the funeral most of Gisselle's old friends returned with us to the house. The first hour was quiet, but I saw how heavily Bruce was drinking and how angrily he was muttering to his few friends while he eyed Gisselle and me with a growing fury. I had explained the reason to Paul.

Suddenly Bruce dropped the glass in his hand and it shattered on the floor. The crowd of mourners stopped talking. He smiled and wobbled forward.

"What are you all looking at?" he demanded. "You don't have to whisper behind my back anymore. I know what you're thinking. I served my purpose and now I'm to be discarded, is that it?"

"Bruce," I said, stepping forward. "This isn't the time."

"No, La Ruby, this isn't the time. But if you and your sister have your way, there'll never be the time, will there? Well, all right. Enjoy what you've got now, because you won't have it forever. I've got my rights. I know I do, no matter what your high-paid attorneys say," he assured us. Everyone was speechless. Then he smiled and bowed.

"I will take my leave of this fine, upper-class gathering, for I have been informed that I am persona non grata. In short, my presence is no longer appreciated. Not that it ever was. So be it," he said, "for now." He pivoted so sharply, he almost toppled, and then started for the door, followed by two of his associates who took his arms quickly.

The chatter started again. I looked at Gisselle.

"Good riddance to him," she flared, her face red and very angry. "I don't know what he's complaining about. He got more than he deserves anyway. Beau," she suddenly cried weakly. He rushed to her side. "Wasn't that just awful?"

"Yes," he said. "He's just drunk."

"This on top of everything else. I can't stand a moment more. Please, Beau. Help me to my room," she pleaded, and he guided her out, her head on his shoulder as she muttered her apologizes to the people who had stopped by. After that, people began to leave.

"I want to go home tonight, Paul," I declared suddenly.

"Really? But I thought . . ."

"I don't care about any financial arrangements, anything. I just want to go home."

He nodded. He had flown into New Orleans from Baton Rouge, so we would drive back in my car. I went up to my room to pack my suitcase. While I was doing so, I heard a gentle knock on the partially opened door.

"Yes?"

Beau stepped in. "You're going home tonight?"

"Yes, Beau. I can't stay here any longer. It's the longest I've been away from Pearl," I added.

"I'm sorry that I haven't asked you more about her. I just felt . . . like I had no right to ask," he said.

"She *is* your daughter," I reminded him.

He nodded. "I know. Paul seems to have accepted everything completely. I mean, from the short conversations we've been able to have, I think so."

"He loves Pearl, yes."

"And he loves you," Beau said.

I looked down at my suitcase without replying for a moment. "Gisselle tries to be different when she's with you. I can see that," I said. "Maybe you are good for her."

"Ruby," he said, coming closer. "The only reason I started with her again was that when I looked at her, I could pretend, imagine, I was looking at you. I have this dream that I can make her into you, but it's a foolish dream. There can't be another you and I can't stand the thought that I've lost you and the life we might have had together."

Tears came to my eyes, but I didn't turn around so he could see them. I swallowed down the throat lump and completed my packing, only muttering, "Don't, Beau. Please."

"I can't help it, Ruby. I'll never stop loving you, and if it means I have to live forever with an illusion, then that's what I'll do."

"Beau, illusions die quickly and leave us far worse off than if we had faced reality," I warned.

"I can't face a reality without you, Ruby. I know that now."

We heard footsteps on the stairway. I snapped my suitcase closed just as Paul came to the door.

"The car's ready," he said, looking suspiciously from Beau to me.

"Good. Good-bye, Beau. You must try to come to the bayou soon."

"Yes, I will."

"I'll just say good-bye to Gisselle, Paul."

"Fine," he said, and took my suitcase.

"I'll go down with you, Paul," Beau said. As the two of them headed for the stairway, I went to Gisselle's room. She was lying on the bed with a damp washcloth over her forehead.

"I'm leaving now, Gisselle," I said.

Her eyes fluttered open as if she weren't sure she had heard a real voice. "What? Is that you, Ruby?"

"Yes. I'm leaving for Cypress Woods tonight."

"Why?" she asked sitting up, suddenly rejuvenated. "We'll have a big breakfast tomorrow and maybe the four of us will do something that's fun for a change."

"I've got to get back to Pearl, and Paul has a lot of business to tend to," I said.

"Oh, pooh on all that. You just want to run away from all this sadness and ugliness with Bruce," she accused.

"Yes, that, too," I admitted.

Her expression softened and then her lips quivered. "What will become of me?" she cried.

"You have Beau now," I said. "You will do just fine."

"Yes," she said, pulling her face into a full, gleeful smile. "I guess I will."

I turned and hurried away, my heart pounding. How she enjoyed reminding me I had lost Beau again.

8

From Bad to Worse

During our ride back to the bayou, Paul tried to make small talk and then he tried to get me excited about some new things that were happening not only in our business, but also in politics. I listened with half an ear, filling every silence between us with the sound of Beau's voice, and filling every dark mile along the way with the images of Beau smiling, talking, gazing at me with that look of anguish in his eyes and yes, that look of love.

I tried to keep myself busy and not think about him during the days immediately following our New Orleans trip, but for the first few days I couldn't get myself to draw a line. I would just stare at the blank paper and think about my studio in New Orleans and Beau. I tried sketching and painting animals, flowers, trees, everything and anything but people, for I knew that every man I would envision would be a man who had Beau's hair, Beau's eyes, Beau's mouth.

What made it even worse was gazing at Pearl, who had developed more distinct facial features and had begun to look more like Beau. Maybe it was just that I was seeing him everywhere since the funeral, but when Pearl laughed and smiled, I heard Beau's laugh and saw his smile.

One afternoon a few weeks after we had returned from Daphne's funeral, I sat on the patio and tried to read a book while Mrs. Flemming played with Pearl on the grass. It was one of those rare days in the bayou when there was barely a breeze and the clouds looked pasted against the soft blue sky. It made everyone feel lazy. Even the birds barely flitted from tree to tree. They sat quietly on branches, looking more like stuffed animals. From off in the distance, I could hear the dull thump, thump, thump of one of our oil drills and occasionally the voices of the men shouting things to each other. But other than that, it was very quiet so that Pearl's laughter rippled over the grass toward the canals, a tiny tinkle of a laugh, making me feel we were all in a toy world.

Suddenly James came rushing out of the house carrying a large envelope.

"This was just brought special delivery for you, madame," he said excitedly, and handed it to me.

"Thank you, James."

He nodded and left while I undid the fastener and pulled a newspaper out of the envelope. Mrs. Flemming gazed at me curiously and I shrugged.

"It's just a New Orleans newspaper, two days old," I said. I gazed at it, wondering why it had been sent special delivery, when I saw that an inside page had been marked with a bright red clip. I opened to the page and gazed at a circled story. It was a wedding announcement, describing the marriage of Beau Andreas to Gisselle Dumas. They had eloped.

I reread the story to confirm that the words actually said what I thought they said, and for a moment it felt as if the air around me had been sucked away. I couldn't breathe; I couldn't swallow, and I was afraid if I tried too hard, I would gag and turn blue. My heart seemed to sink deeper into my chest, making me feel empty and cold inside.

"Something not unpleasant, I hope," Mrs. Flemming said.

I stared at her for a moment and then found my voice. "My sister . . . she eloped," I said.

"Oh. With a nice young man?"

"Yes. A very nice young man," I said. "I have to go upstairs for a moment," I added, and rose quickly so I could turn and walk away before any tears showed themselves on my cheeks. I charged through the house and up the stairs and threw myself on my bed, where I buried my face in my pillow. Of course, I knew that this might happen, but I had lived with the wish that Beau would come to his senses and not succumb. Now some of his last words spoken to me returned, words that had suggested otherwise.

I can't help it, Ruby. I'll never stop loving you, and if it means I have to live forever with an illusion, then that's what I'll do.

Apparently he had decided to do it. Could I be happy knowing that every time he kissed my sister's lips, he closed his eyes and made himself believe he was kissing mine? That every time he woke in the morning and gazed at her face, he convinced himself he was gazing at me? He was in love with me; he would always be in love with me. I knew that Gisselle thought she had achieved some sort of victory by winning him back and getting him to marry her, although in her heart she must know that it was a shallow victory, and that he was using her like some magic mirror into which he could gaze and see the woman he really loved.

But Gisselle didn't care. She didn't care about anything but making me unhappy even if it meant marrying someone she didn't really love, not that she could love anyone but herself, I thought. I tried to be more angry than sad, but my broken heart wouldn't permit it. I cried so hard, my ribs ached and my tears soaked my pillow. When I heard a knock on my doorjamb, I choked back my sobs and turned to see Paul standing there, his face dark and troubled.

"What is it?" he asked.

"Nothing. I'll be fine," I said, and quickly wiped the tears away with the back of my hand. He stood there staring.

"It was this, wasn't it?" he said, bringing the newspaper around from behind his back. "I found it where you dropped it in the hallway. You don't have to answer," he followed quickly, his face red with frustration and fury. "I know how much you still love him."

"Paul . . ."

"No, I realize it's not something I can make disappear with my money. I can build you a house twice as big as this one on twice as much acreage and fill it with things ten times as expensive and you will still mope about, dreaming of Beau Andreas." He sighed, his shoulders lifting and falling. "I thought I could substitute devotion and security for romantic love, but I was a fool to think so. Mother was right after all," he moaned.

"I'm over it, Paul," I said determinedly. "He's married my sister and that's that."

His face brightened. "That's the way you should feel," he said, nodding. "He didn't come for you and the baby while you were living here in your grandmere's shack, did he?"

"No," I said sadly.

"And he never even inquired about your well-being afterward. He's just as self-centered as your sister. They belong together. I'm right, aren't I?"

I nodded reluctantly.

He smirked. "But that doesn't mean you don't love him, does it?" he asked in a tired and defeated tone of voice.

"Love is something . . . you can't control sometimes," I said.

"I know," he replied. "I'm glad you think so, too."

We stared at each other for a moment. Then he put the newspaper on the dresser and left.

I sat by my window thinking that Paul and I had more in common now than ever before. Both of us were in love with people we couldn't love the way we wanted to, the way we should love. I sighed just as deeply as he had sighed and then I took the newspaper and threw it in the nearest garbage can.

Despite Paul's and my desperate attempts to cheer each other up, a pall fell over Cypress Woods during the days that followed. The shadows seemed darker and longer, and the rain more persistent, heavier, gloomier than ever. I retreated to my work. I wanted to leave the real world and live in the world I was creating with my paintings. I continued painting the series of pictures of the Confederate soldier and his lover, but my next painting was a very melancholy one. In it I depicted the soldier being carried out of the wooded battlefield on a stretcher. He looked like Beau, of course, and on his lips one could almost read his call for me . . . Ruby. He had that far-off, dreamy look in his eyes, the eyes of a man who had focused on the woman he loved with all his strength, knowing that in moments the light would go out and he would lose her face, her voice, the scent of her hair and the touch of her lips, in the darkness forever and ever.

I actually sobbed while I painted, the tears dripping off my cheeks, and when I was finished, I sat in the window seat and gazed out at the canals, embracing myself and crying like a baby.

My next picture depicted his lover getting the terrible news. Her face was twisted with agony, her hands wrenching a handkerchief in them while a pocket watch he had given her dangled from her fingers. The messenger looked just as sad as she did, with his head bowed and his shoulders slumped.

I did both pictures in darker shades and had the Spanish-moss-laden cypress either in the background or off to the side. I decided to paint the outline of gleeful Death in the cobweblike strands.

When Paul saw the pictures the first time, he said nothing. His eyes narrowed and then he walked to the window and gazed out over our beautifully landscaped gardens and hedges toward the canals where we used to pole in a pirogue together and talk about the sort of man and woman we wanted to be when we were adults living on our own.

"I've put you in a different sort of prison," he said sadly. "I've done a terrible thing."

"No you haven't, Paul. You've only tried to do the best things for Pearl and me. Don't blame yourself for anything. I won't hear of it."

He turned around, his face darker and more despondent than I had ever seen it.

"I wanted only for you to be happy, Ruby."

"I know that," I said, smiling.

"But I feel like the man who captured the beautiful mockingbird and put it in a cage in his house, giving it the best things to eat and the most loving attention he could. Even so, he woke up one morning and found it had died of a broken heart, its eyes turned toward the window and the freedom it had known and needed. It's true, you can love too much."

"I don't mind being loved too much," I said. "Please, Paul, I don't want you to be sad because of anything I say or do. I'll throw these pictures away."

"Oh no. They are some of your best work. Don't you dare!" he exclaimed. "You're going to become famous because of this series."

"It's almost more important to you than it is to me that I become a well-known artist, isn't it?" I asked.

"Of course. 'Wild Cajun artist captures the minds and imaginations of the sophisticated art world,'" he announced, and drew the headlines in the air.

I laughed.

"Let's have a nice dinner tonight, a special dinner, and then go listen to some zydeco music. We haven't done that for quite a while," he suggested.

"Fine."

"Oh," he said on the way out, "did I tell you? I bought some more property this morning."

"What property?"

"All the land south of us to the canals. We're now the biggest landowners in all Terrebone Parish. Not bad for two swamp rats, huh?" he said proudly. He laughed and went down to tell Letty to do something special for us for dinner. Just before I went down to dinner, however, I received a phone call from Gisselle.

"I've been waiting for you to call me," she began, "to congratulate me on my marriage."

"Congratulations," I said.

"Sounds like sour grapes."

"It's not. If Beau wanted to marry you and you wanted to marry him, then I wish you both health and happiness."

"We're the most exciting couple in New Orleans again, you know. Everyone's inviting us to dinner parties, and when we walk into restaurants, everyone stops eating to watch us take our seats. We're a very handsome couple and quite famous. Our names and pictures are always in the society pages. Beau says we should attend as many charity functions as we can. It looks good and he feels he's doing something important. I don't mind, although I can't remember one from the other, so don't ask me."

"What is Beau doing?" I asked as casually as I could.

"Doing? What do you mean?"

"With his life. He once wanted to be a doctor, remember?"

"Oh, he's too busy looking after my affairs now. He's a businessman and he'll make more money than he would being a doctor anyway. And don't say he's too young. Look at how well Paul has done," she added quickly.

"He used to talk about helping people, healing people, and how rewarding he thought that might be," I said sadly.

"So? Now he's helping and healing me, and that's quite rewarding for him, too," Gisselle responded. "Well, I've got to go. We have so many affairs to attend, I'm running out of clothes to wear. I have an appointment with a designer later. I think I should be wearing originals, don't you? Of course, you're lucky. The only place you have to go is some shack bar and restaurant, so you don't have to worry about looking stylish. Say hello to Paul. 'Bye," she sang, and hung up the phone.

I felt like smashing my receiver against the wall, but swallowed back the knot of frustration in my throat and hung up gently. Then I took a deep breath and went to join Paul, driving Gisselle's voice and words as far down into the basement of my thoughts as I could.

But a week later, Paul came up to my studio to tell me Beau had just phoned.

"He says your attorneys have completed all the work on the estate and he would like to meet with us to go over everything. I thought it would be convenient to have them come here."

"Here? You invited them to Cypress Woods?"

"Yes. Why? Are you upset about it?"

"No, I'm not upset. I . . . Wait until he mentions it to Gisselle," I said. "He'll be calling back," I assured him.

But Beau didn't call back. He and Gisselle were coming and Beau would finally set eyes on his own daughter.

They drove up in Daddy's Rolls-Royce. I was pruning in the rose garden, doing everything and anything I could to keep busy and keep from thinking. Mrs. Flemming was on the other side of the house with Pearl. I had made sure that Pearl was dressed in one of her prettiest outfits and her hair was brushed and tied with a little pink bow. Of course, Mrs. Flemming didn't know who Beau really was, but she could tell from my excitement and nervousness that he was a special visitor.

Paul had gone to the cannery for what he promised was only a short visit, but he had not yet returned when I heard the car horn and turned to see the familiar luxurious automobile make its way up our long driveway. I took off my gloves and walked out to greet them.

"Where are your servants?" Gisselle demanded haughtily. "They should be right here when a guest arrives."

"Things aren't as formal in the bayou, Gisselle," I said. I turned to Beau. "Hello, Beau, how are you?"

"Fine," he said. "This is . . . magnificent. Gisselle's descriptions didn't do it justice," he added, looking around and nodding. "It's one of those places you have to see for yourself to really appreciate. I can see why you're happy here, Ruby," he added.

"Of course she's happy. She has a modern home and yet she lives in her beloved swamp," Gisselle said. James appeared in the doorway. "That's your butler, right? What's his name?"

"James," I said.

"James," she called immediately. "Will you get our bags from the trunk? I need to freshen up as soon as possible. The long ride and the swamp heat has turned my hair into steel wool."

James gazed at me and I nodded.

"Very well, madame," he said. I had already told him which guest room they would be using.

"I can't wait to be shown around," Beau said, his eyes fixed on me.

"I've seen the place," Gisselle said. "So I'll go right to our suite. We do have a suite, don't we?"

"Of course," I said. "Right this way."

"We'll be here just one night. Beau has brought all the paperwork and documents for you to sign, right, Beau?"

"Yes," he said, his eyes still fixed on me.

"I want to get it over with as soon as possible so I don't have to make any more trips out to the swamps," she added, reprimanding Beau with a sharp look.

"We'll do whatever we have to do to move things along to everyone's satisfaction, I'm sure," I said.

"You sound just like Daphne. Doesn't she, Beau? Don't become a snobby rich woman, dear sister," she warned, and then threw her head back to laugh. I looked at Beau, who smiled softly and shook his head.

"All right, James. Lead the way," Gisselle commanded, and we all walked into the house.

Beau exclaimed his awe at the size of the foyer, the woodwork and the chandeliers. The more he complimented me on the house, the more irritated Gisselle grew.

"You have been in finer houses in the Garden District, Beau. I don't know why you're pretending to be so impressed."

"I'm not pretending, *chérie,*" he said softly. "You must give Ruby and Paul credit for building a very dramatic house in the bayou."

"Don't you just love it when he uses French?" Gisselle squealed. "All right. I'll admit this is quite a shack," she said, and laughed. "James? Where is he?"

"Waiting for you with your things at the top of the stairway, Gisselle," I said, nodding toward it.

"Oh. Don't you have a maid, too?"

"All of my servants will be at your beck and call," I assured her. She smirked and started up the stairway.

"It is a beautiful house in a beautiful location," Beau said.

We stared at each other for a moment, silence thicker than fog coming between us.

"Let me bring you to . . . Pearl," I said softly. His eyes brightened with anticipation. I led him out to the patio, where Mrs. Flemming had Pearl playing in a playpen.

"Mrs. Flemming, this is my brother-in-law, Beau Andreas," I said quickly.

"How do you do?" Beau extended his hand, his eyes really riveted on Pearl.

"Pleased to meet you," Mrs. Flemming said.

"And this is Pearl," I murmured. He was already moving toward her. He knelt down by the playpen, and she stopped fiddling with her toy to look into his face. Could one so tiny and young recognize her true father? Did she see something in his eyes, something of herself instantly? Unlike her curious look at other people that usually died in a flash, she studied Beau and formed a tiny smile on her diminutive lips, and when he reached over to lift her out of the playpen, she didn't cry. He kissed her cheek and hair, and she reached out to touch his hair and his face as if she wanted to be sure he wasn't a dream.

I couldn't keep the tears from filling my eyes, but I blinked them back before they could spill over my lids. Beau turned toward me, his face radiant.

"She's beautiful," he whispered. I bit down on my lower lip and nodded. Then I gazed at Mrs. Flemming, who was staring with great interest, a faint smile in her face. Her age and her wisdom were giving her signals that confused and intrigued her, I was sure.

"She likes you a great deal, monsieur," Mrs. Flemming said.

"I have a way with young women," Beau teased, and put Pearl back into her playpen. She began to cry instantly, which brought a look of astonishment to Mrs. Flemming's face.

"Now, behave, Pearl," I chastised gently. "I want to show Uncle Beau the house."

Without another word I led him toward the pool and the cabana.

"Ruby," he said after we were sufficiently away. "You did such a wonderful thing. She's more precious than I ever could have imagined. No wonder Paul is so taken with her. She looks just like you."

"No, she has more of your features," I insisted. "Here, as you can see, is our pool. Paul wants to build a tennis court over there next month. We have a dock on the canal over there," I said, pointing. Only by talking and concentrating on other things could I keep myself from bursting out in tears. But Beau wasn't listening.

"Why didn't I battle with my parents? Why didn't I run away, too? I should have fled to the bayou with you and started a new life."

"Beau, don't talk foolishness. What would you have

done? Sat on the roadside and sold handicrafts with me?"

"I would have gotten an honest man's work. Maybe I would have ended up working for Paul's family or a shrimp fisherman or . . ."

"When there is a baby, a real, live infant, you can't live in a fantasy world," I said, perhaps too harshly and cruelly. Beau swallowed back his dream words and nodded.

"Yes, you're right. Of course."

"Do you want to see my studio here?" I asked quickly.

"Very much. Please."

I led him around to the stairway. As we ascended, I rattled on an on about Paul's businesses, the way some state politicians had been courting him, not only for contributions but for a possible political office someday.

"You're very proud of Paul, aren't you?" Beau said at the entrance to my studio.

"Yes, Beau. He was always a very mature young man, years ahead of others his age, and he is an astute businessman. Most importantly, he is devoted to Pearl and me and would do anything to make us happy," I said as I opened the door to my studio.

"I've been buying some of your paintings, you know. I keep them in what is now my office," he said. "I start every day gazing at something of yours."

"As you can see," I said, ignoring his words, "I have a wonderful view of the canals and the grounds from up here."

He looked out the window and nodded. "Now that I see what you look out on every day, I will be able to conjure you more vividly every morning."

"This is my newest series of work," I said, pretending I didn't hear these words either. "My Confederate soldier series."

Beau studied the pictures. "They're magnificent," he said. "I must have them. The whole series. How much?"

I laughed. "I'm not finished yet, Beau, and I have no

idea what they're going to be worth. Probably a lot less than we imagine."

"Probably a lot more. When will you take them to New Orleans?"

"Within the month," I replied.

"Ruby," he said with such force and emotion, I had to turn to look into his eyes this time. He seized my hands and held them in his. "I must explain why I married Gisselle. I had to find a way to stay close to you although I had lost you. Despite the way she behaves, she has her quiet, intimate moments when she resembles you more than you can imagine. She's a very frightened and lonely girl who tries to cover it up by acting snobby and by being selfish. But she's selfish only because she's afraid she will have nothing, no one to love her.

"When she's like that, I think of you. I feel I am holding you in my arms, comforting you, kissing the tears off your cheeks and kissing your closed eyelids. I've even gotten her to wear your favorite perfumes so when I close my eyes, I see only you in my thoughts."

"Beau, that's wrong."

"I know it is. Now I know," he agreed. "She's not stupid. She senses it, too, but she has been willing to put up with it. Until recently, that is. She's . . . reverting to her old self quickly, throwing off the finer things she has learned and the better habits and behavior as if it were spare weight on a sinking ship. She's started drinking excessively again, inviting her old, degenerate friends back for late night parties. . . ." He shook his head. "It's not what I thought it would be. I can't make her into you," he confessed, and then he lifted his eyes to me, "but maybe I don't have to anymore."

"What do you mean, Beau?"

"I've taken an apartment off Dumaine Street in the French Quarter. Gisselle knows nothing about it. I want you to meet me there when you come into New Orleans."

"Beau!" I said, pulling my hands from his and stepping back in astonishment.

"I'm not suggesting anything horrible, not even sinful, Ruby. We love each other. I know we do, and do completely. I know what sort of arrangement you have with Paul. It's half a marriage, and I'm telling you the truth about my marriage to Gisselle. We can't leave this part of our lives so empty. We can't live with such longing unanswered. Please, Ruby, please come to me," he pleaded.

For a moment I was speechless. The images his proposal generated in my own imagination were overwhelming. I felt the heat rush to my face. To go to him and throw myself into his arms, to cling to his body and feel his lips on mine, to hear his soft words of love and listen to the beating of his heart, to reach the ecstasy we had known again, had seemed beyond possibility, even beyond dreams.

"I can't," I whispered. "Paul would be . . ."

"No one has to know. We'll make perfect arrangements. No one will be hurt, Ruby. I've been planning this for days. It's consumed my thoughts. Yesterday, when I took the flat in the French Quarter, I knew we could do it and I knew we had to do it. Will you come? Will you?"

"No," I said, stepping toward the door. "We can't." I shook my head. "Let's go down. Paul must have arrived by now," I said.

"Ruby!"

I walked out of the studio and started down the stairs, fleeing from my own temptations. Beau finally came after me. I waited for him at the bottom of the stairs.

"Ruby," he said again, in a quiet, reasonable tone of voice, "if—"

"There you are," we heard, and saw Paul and Gisselle coming from the patio.

"I was just showing Beau my studio," I said quickly.

"Oh," Paul said, his eyes narrowing as he gazed at Beau. He kissed me on the cheek. "Did you see her new series?" he asked, his eyes shifting to me and turning dark.

"It's fantastic," Beau said. "I've already offered to buy the entire thing, but she cleverly said it's too soon to set a price," he added with a laugh.

"You paid too much for the ones you have," Gisselle reprimanded. "It's not like she's a famous artist or anything."

"Oh, but she will be," Paul assured her. "And you're going to be very proud of her, as proud of her as I am," he added, looking at me.

"Let's get down to some business," Gisselle said impatiently. "I don't need another tour of the swamps."

"Ah, but you've never really had a tour of the swamps, Gisselle," Paul said. "Please permit me to take you in the motorboat and show you the beauty of the canals."

"What? You mean go into that?" she said, nodding toward the swamp. "I'll be eaten alive."

"We have something to put on your face and arms that will keep all bugs away," Paul promised. "You must be a tourist, just for a short while. I insist on impressing you."

"I would really like to do it," Beau said.

"Then it's settled. Right after lunch, we all go for a spin through the canals. In the meantime let's go to my office and begin to unravel the legal work."

"Fine," Beau said. He moved forward and took Gisselle's arm in his. Pleased, she started for the house, and Paul gazed at me.

"You all right?" he asked softly.

"Yes. Everything's fine," I said.

"Good." He took my hand and we followed.

Gisselle began our meeting by declaring that she thought everything in New Orleans should go to her. "Beau and I are willing to trade other properties and assets that are of . . . what was the word, Beau?"

"Comparable value," he offered.

"Yes, comparable value."

"Ruby?" Paul said.

"I have no problem with that. I have no interest in owning anything in New Orleans right now."

"Daddy, or I should say, Daphne, had bought apartment buildings in other places. We're big landlords, right, Beau?"

"Rather impressive portfolio," he said, presenting the first pages of the documents. "All of the properties are listed here with their appraised values. This land on Lake Pontchartrain is like gold."

Paul leaned over and studied the list. Soon it became a conversation between the two of them. Gisselle took out an emery board and began doing her nails as we talked. I had no interest in being a landlord and was more than willing to sell commercial holdings.

"What about Bruce?" I asked after a while.

"We haven't heard a word from him or his lawyer since his lawyer spoke with ours. I think he realizes that he would only be throwing away in wasted legal fees whatever money he's been able to get."

"Is he still in New Orleans?"

"Yes. He has an apartment building of his own and a few other holdings, but nothing like the fortune he might have inherited had Daphne not foreseen the possibilities and blocked them with her lawyers."

"Why, though?" I wondered aloud. "She certainly didn't want the money and the property to go to us," I said, looking at Gisselle for agreement.

"That's for sure," she said.

"Maybe . . . she was afraid of Bruce," Beau suggested.

"Afraid? How do you mean that?" Paul asked.

"Afraid that if he could get such wealth at her death, he might . . . what should I say, accelerate her death?"

Everyone was quiet for a moment, even Gisselle, as we pondered what Beau was saying.

"She knew what kind of man she had married and the things he was capable of doing," Beau continued. "We came across some of their shenanigans together before Pierre died. There were documents forged, false papers created . . . a trail of deceit."

"Then Bruce isn't getting anything he doesn't deserve," Paul concluded.

Beau and he continued to go through the details of the holdings. Gisselle, who had demanded the meeting take place immediately, grew more fidgety. Finally we decided to adjourn for lunch.

We ate on the patio. Paul kept Beau intrigued with his talk of politics and oil, and Gisselle rambled on about some of her old friends, the things they bought, the places they had been. When Mrs. Flemming brought Pearl to see us, I held my breath, expecting Gisselle to make some embarrassing comment, but she held her tongue and performed like the perfect aunt, suddenly taking delight in her niece.

"I'm going to wait to have children," she declared. "I know what it can do to your figure and I'm not ready for that yet. Beau and I are completely agreed about it, right, Beau?"

"What? Oh, sure, *chérie.*"

"Say something romantic in French, Beau. Just like you used to when we walked along the banks of the Seine. Please."

He looked at me and then he said, "Whenever you come into a room, *mon coeur battait la chamade.*"

"Oh, isn't that beautiful. What does it mean, Beau?"

His eyes fell on me for an instant again and then he smiled at Gisselle and said, "Whenever you come into a room, my heart goes bumpety bump."

"You Cajuns have any French expressions of love?" she asked.

"A few," Paul said. "But our accent is so different, you'd probably not understand. Well, how about our tour of the swamp. Ready?"

"I'll never be ready for that," Gisselle complained.

"You're going to be fascinated, despite yourself," Paul promised.

"I don't have anything to wear. I don't want to get any of the clothes I have with me spotted with swamp mud and grease."

"I have some old pants that will fit you, Gisselle," I said. "And some old shirts. Come on. Let's get ready."

She whined and complained all the way up the stairs, in the room changing, and back down again. Paul had some bug repellent for her to smear on her face and exposed arms and neck.

"What if I break into a rash from this?" she whined.

"You won't. It's an old Cajun recipe."

"What's in it?" she demanded.

"It's better if you don't know," Paul wisely replied.

"It stinks."

"So the bugs will stay away from you," Beau said.

"As well as everyone else."

We laughed and, after Gisselle was properly smeared, went down to the boat. Beau sat between Gisselle and me.

"Laissez les bon temps rouler!" Paul cried. "Let the good times roll!"

Gisselle screamed when we pulled away from the dock, but in minutes, she grew calm and interested. Paul pointed out the ropes of green snakes, the movement of alligators, the nutrias, the birds, and the beautiful honeysuckle covering the banks of the canals. He was a wonderful guide, his voice filled with his love of the swamp, his admiration for the life that fed and dwelt within the canals. He cut the engine and we floated over shallow brackish lakes, observing the muskrats busily building their dried domes of grass. He pointed out a cottonmouth sunning itself on a rock, its triangular head the color of an old penny.

The flutter of wood ducks over the surface of the water caught our attention, and moments later, a large, old alligator raised its head and peered at us, dragonflies circling just above him. We floated through islands of lily pads and under the sprawling weeping willows. Beau asked Paul question after question about the vegetation, the animals, the way to read the canals and know what to anticipate.

Gisselle was forced to admit she had enjoyed the tour.

"It was like floating though a zoo or something," she

said. "But I can't wait to take a bath and get this gook off."

Afterward, we dressed for dinner. We had cocktails in the library, where Paul and Beau discussed New Orleans politics, and Gisselle described the new fashions and the original designs she had commissioned for herself. Letty prepared one of her gourmet meals, and Beau continually expressed his admiration. We all drank too much wine and talked incessantly, Paul, Beau, and myself filling every silent moment out of nervousness more than anything else, I thought. Only Gisselle seemed relaxed and comfortable.

After dinner we had cordials in the living room. The wine, the good food, the endless stream of conversation, and the emotional tension exhausted us. Even Gisselle was yawning.

"We should go to sleep and get up early," she suggested.

"Early?" Beau said, amazed. "You?"

"Well, as early as possible so we can finish the paperwork and get back to New Orleans. We have that performing arts ball tomorrow night. It's black tie," she said. "You ever go to a black-tie affair, Paul?"

Paul blushed. "Well, only in Baton Rouge at the governor's mansion," he said.

"Oh." Gisselle's face drooped. "I'm tired, Beau. I ate too much."

"We'll go right up. Thank you for a lovely day and a lovely evening," he said. He took Gisselle's arm. She did wobble a bit.

"Nighty-night, you two," she sang, and let Beau guide her to the stairway. Paul shook his head and laughed. Then he sat down again.

"Are you happy with these decisions? I didn't mean to interfere in your business," he said.

"My business is your business, Paul. I'm completely depending on you for this sort of thing. I'm sure you made the right choices."

He smiled. "If Beau thought he was coming here to deal with some dumb Cajun, he got a big surprise. Believe me, we came out better than they did," he said with uncharacteristic arrogance. "I was hoping he would be more . . ." He smiled at me. "Of a challenge. So," he said, sitting back, "what is it like for you two now?"

"Paul, please, don't."

"An accident of birth," he muttered. "A curse. If my father hadn't wandered into the swamp, hadn't betrayed my mother . . ."

"Paul . . ."

"I know. I'm sorry. It just seems so unfair. We should have a say in all this, huh? As spirits before we were born, we should have a say. And don't laugh at that, Ruby," he warned. "Your grandmére Catherine believed the spirit was there even before the body."

"I'm not laughing, Paul. I just don't want you to agonize. I'm okay. We've all had too much to drink. Let's go to sleep, too."

He nodded.

"Go ahead up," he said. "I want to finish something in the office."

"Paul . . ."

"I'll go up soon. I promise." He kissed me on the cheek and held me tightly to him for a long moment. Then he sighed, turned away, and left quickly.

With a heavy heart I went upstairs. I checked on Pearl and then I went to my bedroom to go to sleep, knowing that in the rooms beside me there were two men who longed to be at my side. I felt like forbidden fruit, sealed away by ethical, religious, and written law. Years ago my parents listened only to the dictates of their hearts. Despite the prohibitions and the heavy weight of the sins they would commit, they went to each other, thinking about the touch of each other's fingers, the softness of each other's lips.

Was I built from stronger moral timber? More important, did I want to be, really, deep down want to be? Or did I want to throw myself into my lover's arms and become so drunk on love that no morning after, no days that followed, no nights filled with haunting voices, could ever matter?

It wasn't our fault; it couldn't be our fault that we were in love and events had made that love sinful. It was the events that were sinful, I told myself. But that didn't make it any easier to face the break of day and the longing that would inevitably follow.

9

Forbidden Fruit

Although Gisselle had whined about her desire to wake up early, complete our business, and be on her way back to New Orleans, Paul, Beau, and I were already seated at the table having coffee when she finally floated in, moaning and groaning about her restless night's sleep.

"I kept having nightmares that some of those swamp creatures we saw were getting into the house, slithering up the stairs and right into my room and into my bed! I knew I shouldn't have gone on that boat trip through the canals. Now it will take months to get those pictures out of my head. Ugh," she said, and shook herself free of a chill.

Paul laughed. "Really Gisselle, I'd think you would have more to worry about living in a city with all that street crime. At least our creatures are predictable. If you try to pet a cottonmouth snake, he'll give you his opinion quickly."

Beau laughed, too.

"Well, it might be funny to you men, but women are more dainty, more fragile. At least women in New

Orleans," she said, eyeing me when I didn't come to her defense.

Then she disclosed that she was too tired to eat very much. "I'll just have some coffee," she said.

The rest of us ate a hearty breakfast, after which we went into the office and completed the paperwork. I signed whatever documents had to be signed, and Beau promised he would keep us up-to-date on all the proceedings.

Beau quietly asked to see Pearl before he left, so I took him to the nursery. Mrs. Flemming had just changed her, brushed her hair, and tied a little pink ribbon in it. The moment Pearl set eyes on Beau, she brightened. Without a word, Beau lifted Pearl into his arms and kissed her curls. She was intrigued with his hair and wanted to run her fingers over it.

"She's very bright," he said, his eyes fixed on her when he spoke. "You can see from the way she gazes at things—how they hold her attention."

"I agree," Mrs. Flemming said.

"Take her down with us, Beau. She'll say good-bye along with Paul and me," I told him. He nodded and we walked out and down the stairs. Gisselle was already moving through the front door, warning James to be careful with her suitcase.

On the gallery, Beau handed Pearl to me and shook Paul's hand. "Thanks for inviting us. It was a very interesting day. I must admit, I learned a lot about the bayou and have grown to respect it a great deal more."

"You're quite welcome," Paul said, gazing quickly at me, too, a tight smile on his lips.

"Beau! Are we going to stand here forever saying good-bye? It's getting muggy and hot and the bugs are stampeding from the swamp to the house," Gisselle cried from the car.

"I'd better be going," he said to us. Paul nodded and went down to kiss Gisselle good-bye.

"Thank you for a lovely time," Beau said to me. He

took my hand in his and leaned over to kiss my cheek, but brushed his lips over mine instead. When he pulled his hand away, there was a small piece of paper left in mine. I was about to ask what it was when his eyes told me. For a moment it felt like I was holding a lit match in my palm. I shot a glance toward Paul and Gisselle and then shoved the tiny note into the pocket of my blouse. Beau kissed Pearl on the cheek and hurried down the stairs and got into the car.

"Thanks again," he called.

"'Bye. Come visit us in civilization when you get a chance," Gisselle called. "Home, James," she said, waving toward the highway, and laughed. Beau shook his head, smiled back at us, and put the car into gear.

"Your sister is a piece of work," Paul said. "I don't envy Beau one bit when it comes to living with her. When it comes to other things, I envy him more than he'll ever know." He stared at me a moment, but I shifted my eyes away guiltily. "Well, I've got to get to work," he said. He kissed Pearl and me and then hurried to his own car.

Mrs. Flemming took Pearl from me when I went inside. I didn't feel much like painting, but the quiet solitude I found in my studio was very attractive to me now. I hurried upstairs and closed the door. I stood there for a moment against the door with my eyes closed, reliving the moment downstairs when Beau brought his lips to mine for a quick good-bye kiss. I saw his eyes and felt his love.

My heart was pounding as I plucked the note out of my pocket and unwrapped it. There was simply an address on it and a date and time. The day was Tuesday of next week. I crushed the note in my fist and went to throw it in the wastebasket under the easel, but it was as if the paper had glue on it now. It wouldn't leave my hand.

I shoved it back into the breast pocket of my blouse and tried to push it out of my mind when I began to work, but every few minutes I imagined it grew warm and sent a tingle of anticipation down one breast and around the other. It was as if Beau's fingers were there,

Beau's lips were there. My heart raced, shortening my breath. I couldn't work; I couldn't concentrate on anything else.

Finally I gave up and went to the window seat. I sat for nearly an hour just staring at the canals, watching the herons fly in and out. With trembling fingers I took Beau's note out of my pocket again and studied the address, committing it and the date to memory. Then I put the note in a drawer in my art supply cabinet. I just couldn't get myself to throw it away.

Paul didn't return home for lunch. I did a little work, but most of the time I listened to the competing voices in my mind. One voice was softer, pleading, tempting, trying to convince me that I deserved Beau's love and that our love was too good and pure a feeling to be dirty or evil.

But the second voice was harsher, biting, cutting, reminding me of the pain I could bring to Paul, whose devotion to Pearl and me was unwavering and complete. Look at the sacrifices he's making for your happiness, the voice said.

But that's only more reason to keep my rendezvous with Beau secret, my softer voice retorted.

Deceit!

No, it's not deceitful if you're doing it to protect someone you love and prevent him from suffering any pain.

But you're being sneaky and you're lying and hiding. Would Paul do that to you?

No, but you and Paul did agree that neither of you would stand in the way of the other if one of you found someone else to love. Paul is upset and frustrated, but he is understanding and he doesn't want to do anything to make you unhappy or prevent you from becoming happy.

But . . .

Oh, stop the but's and the if's, I screamed at myself. I threw down my brush and left the studio, where the solitude only encouraged my two selves to argue. I took a walk around the house and grounds and then, impulsively, I went inside, found Pearl and Mrs. Flemming, and told Mrs. Flemming I was taking Pearl for a ride with me.

I put her in her car seat beside me and drove to Grandmere Catherine's old shack. It was a mostly overcast day now with the breeze from the southwest threatening to blow in darker rain clouds.

"Do you remember this place, Pearl?" I asked as I took her out and carried her toward the sloping gallery. The weeds were high and there were spiderwebs all over my roadside stand. I could hear field mice in the house scurrying in every direction looking for places to hide when they sensed my approach and heard my footsteps on the gallery planks. The screen door groaned on its rusted hinges as I opened it and entered what now looked like so tiny a room to me. Funny, I thought, when I was growing up here, this was my whole world, and to me it was tremendous. Now I had closets bigger than the living room, and Letty had a pantry bigger than this kitchen.

I walked through the house, hoping that my return would draw Grandmere Catherine's spirit and I would get some advice from her. If only there were a sign, an omen, I thought. But the shack was empty and hollow, my footsteps echoing. It was a grave site from which the bodies had long fled. Even my memories seemed uncomfortable here, for there was no longer any warmth, no music, no aromas of gumbo and jambalaya, no voices, nothing but the sound of the wind slapping loose boards against each other and skimming over the tin roof, making it sound as if a flock of mockingbirds or blue jays were nervously pacing from one end to the other.

I went out back and gazed at the canal.

"Mommy used to play down there, Pearl. Mommy used to walk along that bank and see the animals and the fish, even the alligators and turtles. Sometimes the deer would come right up to the back here to graze and they would lift their heads and look at me with sad eyes."

Pearl just gazed at everything with wonder in her eyes. She appeared to sense my pensive feelings and was quieter than usual. Then, as if she had heard my words, a small doe stepped out from behind some bushes and raised her head to gaze at us. Pearl's eyes widened with interest. The beautiful deer was as still as a statue, only its long ears flicking occasionally. Even when Pearl cried out, it only scrutinized us with more curiosity, no fear. After a few more moments, just as casually as it had appeared, it turned and disappeared like an apparition.

This was a world that did have pure and innocent things in it, and if they were left alone, they would remain that way, I thought; but they were rarely left alone. I walked about the shack for a while but left concluding that there was only one place to look for an answer to my dilemma, and that place was in my own heart.

A few days later at dinner Paul told me of his need to go to Dallas, Texas.

"I'll have to be away three days," he said. "I'd like Pearl and you to come along. You can bring Mrs. Flemming, too, of course. Unless you have other plans, that is," he said.

"Well, I was planning on bringing the Confederate series to New Orleans. I've already spoken to Dominique about it and my other works, and he thinks it's time to arrange for an art show. He wants to invite some of his best customers, do lots of advertising."

"That's wonderful, Ruby."

"I don't think I'm ready for such exposure, but . . ."

"You'll never think you're ready, but if Dominique does, then why not give it a shot?"

I nodded and played with my napkin for a moment.

"So what I think I'll do is go into New Orleans while you're in Dallas," I said. "I'll just stay a night."

"Will you stay with Gisselle?" he asked.

"I'd rather not," I said. "I'll probably stay at the Fairmont."

"Good."

We gazed at each other. Did Paul know what was really in my heart? It had always been hard to hide my true feelings and thoughts from him. If he knew, he chose not

to speak. He smiled and turned to Pearl. I hated doing
something I considered deceitful, but my softer voice had
won out when it said I was doing something to prevent
Paul from suffering any pain.

He had to leave early the day he went to Dallas. After I
rose, I packed my things and went down to breakfast.
James helped me pack my paintings in the trunk of the
car carefully and then Mrs. Flemming brought Pearl out
to wave as I drove off.

I gazed in my rearview mirror and saw them standing
there . . . Mrs. Flemming and Beau's and my beautiful
daughter. Surely a love that produced her couldn't be
evil, I thought, and that thought propelled me forward.
Moments after I pulled onto the main highway and
accelerated, I took the ribbon out of my hair and let the
wind lift the strands, making me feel free and alive and
full of excitement.

"I'm coming, Beau," I whispered. "Everything else be
damned. I'm coming."

It was a delightful day in New Orleans. The clouds and
rain that had swept in the night before were long gone
and replaced with a vast, soft blue sky spotted with small,
fluffy milk white clouds. As soon as I pulled up in front of
the hotel and the doorman shot out to greet me, I felt the
increased tempo I always sensed in the inner city. That,
along with my heightened nervousness, made me sensitive to every sound and every new scent. When I entered
the hotel, I thought everyone was looking at me and that
my heels clicked too hard on the marble floors. I had
everything brought up to my room and then I sat at the
vanity table and brushed out my hair. I freshened my
lipstick and then decided to brush my teeth.

I had to laugh at myself. I was behaving like a teenager
about to go on her first date, but the rhythm of my
heartbeat never slowed and the flush that had entered my
cheeks planted itself there firmly. I saw the frantic and
frightened look in my eyes and wondered if anyone else
who gazed at me could tell that I was a woman tottering

on an emotional tightrope, a married woman about to meet her former lover. I kept checking the clock. I changed three times before deciding that the outfit I had first worn was the best. Finally it was time to go. My fingers trembled around the doorknob. I took a deep breath and pulled it open and then walked quickly to the elevator.

I had decided I would walk all the way to our rendezvous. Canal Street was as busy and as crowded as ever, but losing myself in the clumps of people who crossed it and walked quickly toward the French Quarter helped. It was as if they kept me moving, kept me standing. I turned down Burborn Street and walked toward Dumaine.

The barkers were already out in full force, crying the bargains, urging the tourists to come into their restaurants or bars. I caught whiffs of the crawfish étoufée, the freshly baked bread, and the strong coffee. Vendors had their fruits and vegetables for sale on the sidewalks. At a corner where the restaurant was wide open to the street, I smelled the sautéed shrimp and my stomach churned. I had not eaten much of a breakfast and had been too nervous to have any lunch. From one café came the sounds of a jazz band, and when I looked through the open doorway of another, I saw four men dressed in straw hats playing a guitar, a mandolin, a fiddle, and an accordion.

There was always excitement in the air here. It was as if one great and perpetual party were being held. People had a sense of abandon. They would eat too much, drink too much, dance and sing too long and too late. It was as if I had crossed over from the world of responsibility and obligations into a world without restraints or laws and rules. Anything went as long as it was pleasing. No wonder Beau had chosen the French Quarter, I thought.

Finally I came to the address he had written on the little note. The apartment was in a two-story stucco building with a flagstone courtyard. All the apartments had small, scrolled iron balconies looking down on the street. I smelled the aroma of the spearmint growing

165

against the walls. It was a quiet building, just far enough off the other streets and yet steps away when the inhabitants wanted to indulge in the music and the food. I hesitated.

Maybe he wouldn't be in there. Maybe he had thought twice about it, too. I saw no signs of anyone in the windows. The curtains didn't move. I took a deep breath and looked back. If I did retreat, would I be happier or would I always wonder what it would have been like had I gone into the apartment building and met Beau? Maybe we would just talk, I thought. Maybe we would both come to our senses. I closed my eyes like someone about to dive into a pool and I entered the courtyard. Then I opened them and walked to the front door. I checked the numbers on the directory and walked up the small stairway to a narrow landing. When I found the door, I paused, took another deep breath, and knocked.

For a few moments, I heard nothing and I began to think he wasn't there. He had indeed changed his mind. I felt a mixture of relief and disappointment. That part of me that had tried to keep me away urged me to turn and flee, to actually run back up the street and return to the hotel; but the other part of me, the part that longed for complete love, filled me with such despondency, I thought my heart would turn to stone and crumble in my chest.

I started to turn away when the door was pulled open and I saw Beau standing there. He wore a soft white cotton shirt and trousers of the finest dark blue wool. His eyes blinked rapidly as if trying to focus and convince himself I was really standing there.

"Ruby," he said softly, "I'm sorry. I must have fallen asleep in my chair dreaming about you. I thought you wouldn't come."

"I almost didn't, even when I found the address," I said.

"But you're here. You did come. Come in. Please." He stepped back and I entered the small apartment. It was a one-bedroom with a tiny kitchen and a living room that had French doors opening to the balcony. The furniture and the decor were very simple, modern with that slightly worn look found in hotels or motels. The walls were practically bare, only a small print depicting fruits and flowers here and there.

"It's not much," he said, gazing around with me. "Just a quiet hideaway."

"It's quaint. It just needs some warmth."

He laughed. "I just knew you'd apply your artist's eye instantly. Sit down," he said, indicating the small sofa. "Did you have an easy ride into the city?"

"Yes. I'm becoming a sophisticated traveler," I said. It was funny how we were both acting as if we were meeting for the very first time, and he . . . he was the father of my child. But time, distance, and events had made us strangers to each other.

"You're here alone?" he asked cautiously.

"Yes. I checked into the Fairmont. I'm going to bring my new series over to Dominique. He has been talking about this art show he wants to do with me."

"Great. But I warn you, I'm not going to let anyone else buy those pictures. No matter what the cost, I'll get them," he vowed. I laughed. "Would you like something cold to drink? I have some chilled white wine."

"Please," I said. He went out to the kitchen.

"So Paul knows you've come to New Orleans?" he asked while he poured the wine.

"Oh yes. He's gone to Dallas for some meetings."

"And the baby?" Beau asked, returning.

"With Mrs. Flemming. She's wonderful with Pearl."

"I saw that. You're lucky to get someone like that nowadays." He handed me my glass of wine and I sipped some while he sipped his, both of us peering over our glasses at each other. "You never looked more beautiful, Ruby," he said softly. "Motherhood has made you blossom."

"I've been lucky, Beau. I could have been the fallen woman scrounging out a meager living in the bayou . . . until my trust came through, that is."

"I know," he said. "Ruby, is there any way I can make things up to you? Is there any apology that would sound right?"

"I told you before, Beau. I don't blame you for anything."

"Well, you should. I nearly destroyed both our lives," he said. He sipped some more of his wine and then he sat beside me.

"Where's Gisselle?" I asked.

"Partying with some of her old friends by now, I'm sure. She was different for a while, especially when she came to France. She had me convinced she had grown up because of all the trouble and hardship in the family. She was vulnerable, sweet, and, believe it or not, considerate. The truth is, she conned me, or maybe I . . . maybe I let her. I was very lonely and depressed after you got married. I realized I had let the one person who could make me feel complete slip through my fingers. I felt like a little boy who had lost grip of his kite string and was chasing after it in vain. I could see it drifting away, only it was your face being carried from me in the wind.

"I drank more, partied harder, tried to forget. And then Gisselle appeared on the scene and there was your beautiful face before me . . . your hair, your eyes, your nose, though Gisselle to this day believes her nose is smaller and her eyes are brighter.

"Actually," he continued, gazing down at his glass, "a friend of mine in school in Paris who was studying psychology told me most men fall in love with someone who reminds them of their true love, their first love, someone who impressed them at an early age, someone they couldn't have, but someone they spend a lifetime trying to win. It made sense and I let myself get close to Gisselle again.

"That's my story," he said, smiling. "What's yours?"

"Mine's simpler, Beau. I was alone with a baby, afraid. Paul was always there, helping. Everyone in the bayou knew we were once very fond of each other. Everyone believed Pearl was his child. Paul is devoted to me and,

despite my protests, is willing to sacrifice for me. I don't
want to hurt him, if I can help it."

"Of course not," Beau said. "He's a very nice man. I
enjoyed being with him. I just envy him."

I laughed.

"What?"

"That was what he said to me about you."

"Why?"

I stared into his eyes, falling back through time.
"Because he knows how much I love you, how much I've
always loved you, and how much I always will," I said.

It was enough to shatter the wall of nervousness and
tension between us. His eyes brightened and he put down
his glass so he could embrace me. Our first passionate
kiss after so long a span of time was like a first kiss, full of
fresh excitement.

"Oh, Ruby, my Ruby, I thought I had lost you forever."
He brought his lips to my hair, my eyes, my nose. He
kissed my neck and the tip of my chin, one kiss following
immediately upon another as if he were starved for love,
as starved as I was, and as if he were afraid that I was an
illusion and I would pop out of his mind any moment.

"Beau," I whispered. His name was all I wanted to say.
The sound of it from my lips restored me, filled me with
pleasure, assuring me I, too, was really here, in his arms.

He stood up, holding my hand, and I stood up and
followed him into the small but cozy bedroom. The
afternoon sun poured through the sheer cotton curtains,
filling the room with brightness and warmth. I kept my
eyes closed while he undressed me. Moments later we
were beside each other in the bed, our bodies clinging
together magnetically. We moaned, we whispered words
of love and promises that went from now to eternity.

At first our caresses were frenzied, but gradually we
became calmer, softer. He pressed his lips to my breasts
and traced a line of kisses from them to the small of my
stomach. I dropped my head to the pillow and felt my
body sinking into the soft mattress as Beau brought his
body over mine, covering me with his chest and bringing

his hard manliness to me. I cried out when he entered me and he soothed me with his petting and his soft words.

Then we moved against each other, drawing love from each other, touching passionate heights time after time until we both reached deeply into our minds and bodies and exploded in an ecstatic crescendo that made everything else but his lips, his voice, his body, disappear. I felt like we were drifting in space.

"Ruby," he said. "Ruby. Are you all right?"

Wherever our lovemaking had taken us was a place I didn't want to leave. I clung to it like someone in a wonderfully pleasing dream refusing to regain consciousness. But my peaceful aftermath frightened him and he raised his voice. "Ruby!"

My eyes fluttered open and I looked up at his concerned face.

"I'm fine, Beau. I was just drifting."

He smiled. "I love you," he said, "and I won't stop."

"I know, Beau. I won't stop loving you either."

"This will be our love nest, our paradise," he said, turning over in the bed to lie beside me. He held my hand and we stared up at the ceiling. "You can dress it up any way you want. We'll go shopping today and find things to put in it, okay? And I'll buy some of your paintings for the walls. We'll get new linens and a rug and—"

I couldn't help laughing.

"What?" he said indignantly. "You think I'm foolish?"

"No, never, dear Beau. I'm laughing at your exuberance. You're sweeping me off and into your dreams so rapidly, I can barely catch my breath."

"So? I don't care. I don't care about anything else." He turned and propped himself on his elbow to gaze down at me. "Maybe you can bring Pearl into New Orleans next time, too, and the three of us can enjoy the day together."

"Maybe," I said, but not confidently.

"What's wrong?"

"I just don't want to confuse her. She believes Paul is her father right now."

Beau's bright smile faded and his face darkened. He

nodded and fell back on his pillow. He was silent for a minute.

"You're right," he finally said. "Let's take it an inch at a time. I have to learn to control my excitement."

"I'm sorry, Beau. I didn't mean . . ."

"No, you're right. It's okay. I shouldn't be greedy. I have no right to ask for any more. I have no right to ask for this." He turned to kiss me softly and we smiled at each other again. "Hungry?"

"Starving. I forgot to eat lunch."

"Great. I know a wonderful little café close to here where they make the best po'boy sandwiches in New Orleans."

"Afterward, I do have to see Dominique," I said.

"Of course. I'll go with you, if you want."

"I think I should just go myself. Dominique has met Paul and . . ."

"I understand," Beau said quickly. "Let's get dressed and go eat."

Beau was right about the po'boy sandwiches. I had one with the works: sautéed shrimp, cheese, fried oysters, sliced tomatoes and onions. We sat out on a patio where we ate and watched the tourists with their cameras parading by and gawking at the architecture, the novelty shops and restaurants. Afterward, we went for a walk and I returned to the hotel to call home to see how Pearl was doing. Mrs. Flemming told me everything was fine. I called for my car and brought the Confederate series over to Dominique, who thought the pictures were wonderful.

"There is no question you are ready to be formally introduced to the New Orleans art world," he told me, and we began to plan my art show. Afterward, I returned to the hotel to shower and change to meet Beau for dinner. I had a message from Paul waiting, telling me how to reach him.

"How is it going?" he asked when I phoned.

"Fine. You were right. Dominique thinks I should have a show. We're setting it up," I said, making it seem as if that was all I was doing in New Orleans.

"That's wonderful."

"And your meetings?"

"Going better than I expected, but I'm sorry I'm not with you," he said.

"I'm all right. I'm going home tomorrow sometime in the late morning. Dominique and I are having breakfast together," I said. The lie nearly got stuck on my tongue. Paul was silent.

"Good," he said after a moment. "Have a safe trip back."

"You, too, Paul."

"See you soon. 'Bye."

"'Bye."

The receiver felt like a stone in my hand. My eyes glistened with tears and my chest ached. Grandmere Catherine used to say that deceit was a garden in which only the blackest weeds grew, and those who sowed their seeds in it reaped disaster. I hoped this wasn't something I had planted in Paul's future. There was no one I would want to hurt less than him.

Beau knew a quaint little French restaurant close to Jackson Square. I took a cab to our love nest and from there we walked. We had a wonderful meal of quail in wine followed by cups of rich coffee and orange crème brûlée. Afterward, I insisted we take a long walk.

"I'm stuffed," I moaned.

We held hands and walked slowly through the French Quarter, which was bustling with its nightlife. There was a different sort of excitement in the Quarter after the sun went down. The women who stood in the doorways and alleyways were more scantily dressed and heavily made-up. The music had a deeper wail, some singers sounding mournful, full of blues and tears. In other places where younger tourists flocked, there was upbeat jazz and the shrieks, shouts, and laughter of people letting down their hair, looking for the ultimate excitement, whatever that might be. All the novelty shops and souvenir shops were brightly lit. Drifters, poor musicians, lined the sidewalks. There was someone at every corner pleading for a handout, but no one resented them. It was as if they were meant to be there, part of what made the Quarter unique. Scam artists hovered about, searching for easy prey.

"'Scuse me, sir, but I bet I can tell where you come from exactly. If I don't, I'll give you ten bucks; if I do, you give me twenty. Here's my ten. What'dya say?"

"No, thank you. We know where we come from," Beau responded with a smile.

It was exciting walking here with him and I thought, yes, I could have another life, a secret life with him here. We would make our love nest comfortable and we would enjoy the city, the food and its people, and we would cheat Fate.

We circled until we returned to the small apartment, where I made an impulsive decision to spend the night with him. We made love again, this time turning to each other the moment we closed the door behind us. Before we reached the bedroom, we were both naked. He lifted me in his arms and put me down gently on the bed and then he knelt beside the bed and began kissing me from my toes up. I closed my eyes and waited for him to reach my lips, which by that time were burning with desire.

As we made love, we heard the music and the murmuring sounds of people talking in the street outside, a constant flow of voices and laughter. It was intoxicating and I held Beau close to me, whispering his name, whispering my undying love, actually coming to tears when we reached our sweet climax and lay beside each other, pleasantly exhausted.

In the morning we rose early and went to the Café du Monde for coffee and beignets. Then he walked me back to my hotel. We had planned to meet again in a week's time when I returned to complete the arrangements for the art show and bring Dominique some more of my work. I kissed him good-bye and hurried into the hotel to get my things.

I was afraid I would find a message indicating Paul had tried to reach me the night before, but there was nothing. I was in and out of the hotel quickly, and in minutes, back on the highway that would take me home. I felt full of life, restored, blossoming, just as Beau had said. But my elation was to be short-lived. It ended the moment I drove up to the house.

The dark expression on James's face when he came down the front steps to help me with my things told me immediately that something terrible was wrong. My first thoughts went to Pearl.

"What is it, James? What's happened?"

"Oh, it's Mrs. Flemming, madame. She's had some bad news, I'm afraid."

"Where is she?"

"Upstairs, waiting for you in Pearl's nursery."

I hurried into the house, practically charging up the stairway to find Mrs. Flemming sitting in the rocking chair, her face white, her lips pale. Pearl was asleep in her crib.

"What is it, Mrs. Flemming?"

She lifted her hands, seeming to wipe away invisible cobwebs, and pressed her lips together. Then she nodded toward Pearl and got up quietly to join me in the hallway.

"My daughter in England," she said, finally finding the strength to speak. "She was in a car accident and she is very badly hurt. I have to go."

"Of course," I said. "How dreadful. I'll help you with the arrangements."

"I've already taken care of most of it, madame. I was just waiting for your return."

"Oh, Mrs. Flemming. I'm so sorry," I said.

"Thank you, dear. I hate to leave, you know. You've made me feel like part of the family. I know you're very excited about your artistic career and need me to help with Pearl."

"Nonsense. You must go. I'll pray for you and your daughter," I said.

She pressed her lips together and nodded, the tears streaming down her face. "It's sad how it takes bad things to bring loved ones closer," she said. I hugged her and kissed her cheek.

When James brought my things up, he brought hers down. She had a taxicab on order.

"Kiss the little one for me every morning," she said.

"I know she'll miss you terribly. Please, let us know how things go and what we can do for you, Mrs. Flemming."

She promised and then left. It was as if a hurricane had come and blown my happy home apart. I couldn't help wondering if capricious Fate had decided to punish those close to me for any sins I might commit.

Nina Jackson, the Dumas cook, used to tell me that maybe a long time ago someone burned a black candle against us. Grandmere Catherine, being a spiritual healer, kept the evil away, but after she died, the devil, Papa La Bas, started coming around again, peeping in on my life, waiting for an opportunity.

Had I just given him one?

10

Picture Perfect

Paul phoned that night from Baton Rouge and I told him about Mrs. Flemming.

"I'll come right home," he said.

"You don't have to, Paul. We're all right. I'm just very sad for her and for her daughter."

"I like to be with you when you're sad, Ruby. I don't like your being alone at times like this," he said.

"You can't protect me from every little storm that befalls me, Paul. Besides, I didn't have a nanny helping me when I lived in the shack and things were twice as difficult, did I?" I replied, my tone of voice harder than I had intended.

"I'm sorry. I didn't mean to suggest you couldn't do everything for Pearl yourself," he said in a small voice.

"You don't have to be sorry, Paul. I'm not angry. I'm just . . . upset about Mrs. Flemming."

"Which is why I should be home," he insisted.

"Paul, do what you have to do and then come home. I'll be all right. Really," I said.

"Okay. I should be able to leave here before lunch

tomorrow anyway," he said. There was a short pause and then he asked how things went in New Orleans.

"Fine. Dominique and I made all the arrangements, but I think I'll postpone it until things get calmer around here."

"We'll begin a search for a new nanny as soon as I come home," he said. "There's no need to postpone your show, Ruby."

"Let's not talk about it now, Paul. Suddenly that's not as important to me anyway. And I don't want to go out and get a new nanny just yet. Let's wait and see what happens with Mrs. Flemming and her daughter."

"Whatever you want."

"Besides, I think I can be a full-time mother and an artist at the same time."

"Okay," he said. "I'll be home as soon as I can."

"Don't speed, Paul," I warned. "We don't need another car accident."

"I won't," he promised. "See you soon. 'Bye."

"Good-bye, Paul."

The day's ride on an emotional roller coaster exhausted me. After I put Pearl to sleep, I crawled into bed myself. I lay there for a while with my eyes open debating about calling Beau. I just dreaded the thought that Gisselle would find out I was calling, however, and I decided against it. I would wait for him to call me. I shut my eyes, but despite my fatigue, I tossed and turned, fretting in and out of nightmares, some of which had terrible things happening to Paul and some had terrible things happening to Beau. How fragile our lives were, I thought. In seconds, everything we had, everything we learned, everything we built, could become dust. It made me question what were really the most important things and what were not.

I knew Paul must have driven fast despite his promises, because he was at Cypress Woods very early in the afternoon the next day. When I accused him of it, he swore he had been able to end his meetings earlier than anticipated. I was just finishing my lunch and having coffee on the patio. Pearl was beside me in her playpen, sitting comfortably and coloring with her crayons. She couldn't stay within the lines, but she was content smearing the colors over the faces and figures, pretending she was doing what Mommy did. Occasionally she would stop and raise her eyes to see if I was watching and admiring her work.

"Another artist in the family," Paul declared when he sat down.

"She thinks she is. Did your meetings go well, then?"

"I signed a new contract. I don't want to tell you the numbers. You'll tell me they're obscene, just like you did the last time."

"They are. I can't help feeling guilty about making so much money when there are so many people in need of the simple, basic things."

"True, but our industrious work and clever arrangements will create hundreds of new jobs and provide employment, opportunities, and money for many people, Ruby."

"You're beginning to sound like a big businessman, all right," I said, and he laughed.

"I suppose in my heart I always was. Remember when I was only ten and I had my roadside stand, selling my Cajun peanuts, the dried shrimp, from my father's cannery?"

"Yes. You were very cute, dressing yourself neatly in your shirt and little tie, having your cigar box of change."

He smiled at his memories. "I never wanted to charge you and your grandmere Catherine when you walked by and stopped, but she wouldn't take it for nothing. 'You can't stay in business that way,' she told me."

I nodded, remembering.

Paul gazed at Pearl for a moment and then turned back to me. There was a deep dark look in his blue eyes. I could see the hesitation, too.

"What is it, Paul?"

"I don't want you to think I was checking up on you. I just called to see how you were."

"Called? When? Where?"

"The night before last, when you were at the hotel in New Orleans," he said.

My heart throbbed in triple time as I held my breath.

"What time?" I asked softly.

"After eleven. I didn't want to call too late for fear I might wake you, but . . ."

I turned away.

"As I said," he continued, "don't think I was checking up on you. You don't owe me any explanations, Ruby," he added quickly.

Over the cypress trees that walled the swamps, I saw a marsh hawk lift itself and float downward, probably to pluck some unwary prey. It caused a half dozen rice birds to scatter. Beyond the trees, a ceiling of bruised clouds made its slow but determined journey in our direction, promising torrents of rain before the day ended. I felt a cloud burst within me, releasing drops of ice over my heart. They streamed down into my stomach and into my legs, filling me with a cold numbness.

"I wasn't in the hotel, Paul," I said slowly. "I was with Beau."

I turned quickly to catch the confirmation in his face. He was caught in a tug-of-war of emotions. He had known, but I knew he didn't want to know; and yet he did. He wanted to face reality, but he was hoping it wasn't the reality he dreaded. Pain flashed in his eyes. I shrank into a tighter ball.

"How could you do that? How could you be with that man after the way he deserted you?"

"Paul . . ."

"No, I'd like to know. Don't you have any self-respect? He left you to have his baby while he went off and enjoyed Paris and who knows how many Frenchwomen. Then he married your sister and inherited half your wealth. Now you go running back to him, sneaking in the night."

179

"Paul, I didn't mean to be deceitful. Really . . ."

He turned quickly to me. "That was your real purpose for going to New Orleans, wasn't it? It wasn't the paintings, your art career. It was to run to his arms again. Have you planned other sneaky rendezvous?"

"I was going to tell you," I said. "Eventually."

"Sure," he said. He sat back and pulled up his shoulders. "What have you two decided to do?"

"Decided to do?"

"Is he going to divorce Gisselle?"

"No such proposal was discussed," I said. "Except we both know what our religious beliefs are and how divorce is not an acceptable option, especially to his family. Besides, I can't imagine Gisselle being cooperative, can you?"

"Hardly," Paul said.

"Just the opposite would happen. She would feed on the scandal. She would help write the headline: One Twin Steals the Other's Husband. You can just imagine what it would do to Beau and his family in New Orleans, and . . . it wouldn't be fair to you, Paul. These people here . . ."

"Really?" he said with a smirk.

"Paul, please. I feel dreadful about this. There's no one I want to hurt less than you."

He looked away so I wouldn't see the tears and anger in his face. "It's nothing I haven't brought on myself," he muttered. "Mother said it would happen eventually." He was silent.

"Don't just sit there like that, Paul. Scream at me. Throw me out."

He turned slowly. The pain in his face was like a sword in my heart. "You know I won't do that, Ruby. I can't stop myself from loving you."

"I know," I said sadly. "I wish you didn't. I wish you could hate me," I said.

He smiled. "You might as well wish for the earth to stop spinning, the sun to stop coming up in the morning and going down at night."

We gazed at each other and I thought how cruel it was for Fate to cause him to have such unrequited passion for me. Fate had turned him into a thirsty man forever hovering above cool, clear water, but forbidding him to drink. If only there were a way to get him to hate me, I thought with irony. It would be painful for me, but it would be so much better for him. Between us, like a raw wound that refused to heal, lingered our regrets and sadness.

"Well," he said finally, "let's not speak of unhappy things right now. We have too many other problems at the moment. You're certain about us not seeking another nanny?"

"For the time being, yes."

"Okay, but I hate to see you put your career on hold. I'm supposed to be married to a famous Cajun artist. I did a great deal of bragging in Baton Rouge. There are at least a dozen rich oil men eager to buy one of your paintings."

"Oh, Paul, you shouldn't do that. I'm not that good."

"Yes you are," he insisted, and rose. "I have to stop at the cannery and speak to my father, but I'll be home early."

"Good, because I invited Jeanne and James to dinner. She called earlier and sounded like she wanted to see us very much," I said.

"Oh? Fine." He leaned over to kiss me, but he was much more tentative about it and his kiss was much more perfunctory: a quick snap of his lips against my cheek, the way he would kiss his sister or his mother. A new wall had fallen between us, and there was no telling how thick it might become in the days and months to follow.

After he had left I sat there on the verge of tears. Although I was sure it wasn't his intention, the more he demonstrated his love for me, the more guilty I felt for loving and being with Beau. I told myself I had warned Paul. I told myself I had never made the same sort of vows he had made, marrying myself to some pure and religious idea of a relationship that rivaled a priest or a nun's marriage to the church. I told myself I was a full-blooded woman whose passions raged through her veins with just as much intensity as any other woman's and I could not quiet them down nor shut them away.

What's more, I didn't want to. Even at this moment, I longed to be in Beau's arms again, and I longed for his lips on mine. Filled with frustration, I sucked in my breath and swallowed back my tears. It wasn't the time to weaken and sob on pillows. It was the time to be strong and face whatever challenges malicious Fate threw my way.

I could use some good gris-gris, I thought. I could use one of Nina Jackson's fast-luck powders or Dragon Blood Sticks. Some time ago, she had given me a dime to wear around my ankle. It was to bring me good luck. I had taken it off and put it away, but I remembered where it was, and when I took Pearl up for her afternoon nap, I found it and fastened it around my ankle again.

I knew many would laugh at me, but they had never seen Grandmere Catherine lay her hands on a fevered child and cause his or her temperature to go down. They had never felt an evil spirit fly by in the night, fleeing from Grandmere Catherine's words and elixirs. And they had never heard the mumbo jumbo of a Voodoo Mama and then saw the results. It was a world filled with many mysteries, peopled by many spirits, both good and bad, and whatever magic one could conjure to find health and happiness was fine with me, no matter who laughed or who ridiculed it. Most of the time, they were people who believed in nothing anyway, people like my sister who believed only in their own happiness. And I, better than most people my age, already knew how vulnerable and how fleeting that happiness could be.

That night I saw how eager Paul was for us to have an enjoyable dinner with his sister and her husband. He wanted to do all that he could to drive away the dark shadows that had fallen between us and lingered in the secret corners of our hearts. He stopped by the kitchen and asked Letty to make something extra special and he served our most expensive wines, both he and James drinking quite a bit. At dinner our conversation was light and punctuated by many moments of laughter, but I could see Jeanne was troubled and wanted to have a private talk. So as soon as dinner ended and Paul suggested we all go into the living room, I said I wanted to show Jeanne a new dress I had bought in New Orleans.

"We'll be right down," I promised.

"You just want to skip our political talk, that's all," Paul accused playfully. But when he looked at me closer, he saw why I wanted to take Jeanne upstairs and he put his arm around James and led him away.

Jeanne burst into tears the moment we were alone.

"What is it?" I asked, embracing her. I led her to the settee and handed her a handkerchief.

"Oh, Ruby, I'm so unhappy. I thought I would have a marriage as wonderful as yours, but it's been disappointing. Not the first two weeks, of course," she added between sobs, "but afterward, when we settled down, the romance just seemed to die. All he cares about is his career and his work. Sometimes he doesn't come home until ten or eleven o'clock and I have to eat dinner all alone, and then when he does arrive, he's usually so exhausted, he wants to go right to sleep."

"Did you tell him how you feel about it?" I asked, sitting beside her.

"Yes." She sucked in her gasps and stopped sobbing. "But all he says is he's just starting his career and I have to be understanding. One night he snapped at me and said, 'I'm not as lucky as your brother. I wasn't born with a silver spoon in my mouth so I would inherit oil-rich land. I've got to work for a living.'

"I told him Paul works for a living. I don't know anyone who works harder. He doesn't take anything for granted, right, Ruby?"

"Paul thinks there are twenty-five hours in every day, not twenty-four," I said, smiling.

"Yet somehow he manages to keep the romance in your marriage, doesn't he? A person would just have to look at you two together and he or she would see how devoted you are to each other and how much you care about each other's feelings. No matter how hard Paul works, he always has time for you, doesn't he? And you don't mind his being away so much, right?"

I shifted my eyes away quickly so she couldn't read the truth in them and then I folded my arms across my chest in Grandmere Catherine's way and filled my face with deep thought. She waited anxiously for my reply, her hands twisting in her lap.

"Yes," I finally replied, "but maybe that's because I'm so involved in my art."

She nodded and sighed.

"That's what James said. He said I should find something to do so I don't dote upon him so much, but I wanted to dote on him and our marriage. That's why I got married!" she exclaimed. "The truth is," she continued, dabbing at her cheeks with the handkerchief, "the passion is already gone."

"Oh, Jeanne, I'm sure that's not so."

"We haven't made love for two straight weeks," she revealed. "That's a long time for a husband and wife, right?" she followed, fixing her eyes on me for my reaction.

"Well . . ." I looked down and smoothed out my skirt so she wouldn't see my face again. Grandmere Catherine used to say my thoughts were as obvious as a secret written in a book with a glass cover. "I don't think there's any set time or rate of lovemaking, even for married people. Besides," I replied, now thinking about Beau, "it's something that both have to want spontaneously, impulsively."

"James," she said, gazing at her entwined fingers, "believes in the rhythm method because he's such a devout Catholic. I have to take my temperature before we make love. You don't do that, do you?"

I shook my head. I knew that a woman's body temperature was supposed to reflect when she was most apt to become pregnant, and that was considered an acceptable method of birth control, but I had to admit, taking your temperature before sleeping together would diminish the romance.

"So you see why I'm so unhappy?" she concluded.

"Doesn't he know just how deeply unhappy you are?" I asked. She shrugged. "You should talk to him more about it, Jeanne. No one else can help you two but you two."

"But if there's no passion . . ."

"Yes, I agree. There must be passion, but there must be compromise, too. That's what marriage is," I continued, realizing how true it was for Paul and me, "compromise —two people sacrificing willingly for the good of each other. They must care as much for each other as they do for themselves. But it works only if both do it," I said, thinking about Daddy and his devotion to Daphne.

"I don't think James wants to be like that," Jeanne worried.

"I'm sure he does, but it doesn't happen overnight. It takes time to build a relationship."

She nodded, slightly encouraged. "Paul and you have certainly spent a long time together. Is that why your marriage is so perfect?" she asked.

A strange aching began in my heart. I hated how one lie led to another and then another, building one upon the other until we were buried under a mountain of deceit.

"Nothing is perfect, Jeanne."

"Paul and you are as close as can be. Look how the two of you were toward each other from the first day you two met. The truth is," she said sadly, "I was hoping James would worship me as much as Paul worships you. I suppose I shouldn't compare him to my brother."

"No one should worship anyone, Jeanne," I said softly, but the way she viewed Paul and me and the way others saw us made me feel ever so guilty for loving Beau on the side. What a shock it would be if the truth were to be known, I thought, and how devastating it would be to Paul.

Talking like this with Jeanne made me realize that my relationship with Beau would go nowhere. It might even destroy Paul little by little. I had made my choice, accepted his kindness and devotion, and now I had to live with that choice. I couldn't be selfish enough to do anything else.

"Maybe I will have another long talk with James," Jeanne said. "Maybe you're right—maybe it takes time."

"Anything worthwhile does," I said softly.

She was so involved with her own problems, she couldn't see the longing in my eyes. She seized my hands in hers. "Thank you, Ruby. Thank you for listening and caring."

We hugged and she smiled. Why was it so easy to help other people feel happy, but so hard to help myself? I wondered.

"There really is a new dress to show you," I said, and took her to my closet. Afterward, we joined Paul and James in the living room and had some after-dinner cordials. Jeanne smiled at me when James put his arm around her and kissed her on the cheek. He whispered something in her ear and she turned crimson. Then they announced they were tired and had to go home. At the doorway, Jeanne leaned over to thank me again. From the look in her eyes, I saw she was excited and happy. Paul and I remained on the gallery and watched them go to their car and drive away.

It was a rather clear evening, so that we could look up at the star-studded sky and see constellations from one horizon to the other. Paul took my hand.

"Want to sit outside awhile?" he asked. I nodded and we went to the bench. The night was filled with the monotonous symphony of cicadas interrupted by the occasional hoot of an owl.

"Jeanne wanted some big-sister advice tonight, didn't she?" he asked.

"Yes, but I'm not sure I'm the one she should have been asking."

"Of course you are." After a pause he added, "James asked me for advice, too. Made me feel older than I am." He turned to me in the darkness, his face cloaked in the shadows. "They think we're Mr. and Mrs. Perfect."

"I know."

"I wish we were." He took my hand again. "So what are we going to do?"

"Let's not try to come up with all the answers tonight, Paul. I'm tired and confused myself."

"Whatever you say." He leaned over to kiss me on the cheek. "Don't hate me for loving you so much," he whispered. I wanted to hug him, to kiss him, to soothe his troubled soul, but all I could do was shed some tears and stare into the night with my heart feeling like a lump of lead.

Finally we both went in and up to our separate bedrooms. After I put out my light, I stood by my window and gazed into the evening sky. I thought about Jeanne and James hurrying home after a wonderful meal, wine, and conversation, excited about each other, eager to hold each other and cap the evening with their lovemaking.

While in his room, Paul embraced a pillow, and in mine, I embraced my memories of Beau.

Shortly after Paul left for work the next morning, Beau called. He was so excited about our next rendezvous, barely squeezing in a breath as he described his plans for our day and evening, that at first I couldn't get in a word.

"You don't know how this has changed my life," he said. "You've given me something to look forward to, something to cheer me through the most dreary days and nights."

"Beau, I have some bad news," I finally inserted, and told him about Mrs. Flemming's daughter. "I'm afraid I'm going to have to postpone things."

"Why? Just come in with Pearl," he pleaded.

"No. I can't," I said.

"It's more than that, isn't it?" he asked after a pause.

"Yes," I admitted, and told him about Paul.

"Then he knows about us?"

"Yes, Beau."

"Gisselle has been very suspicious lately, too," he confessed. "She's even uttered some veiled threats and some not so veiled threats."

"Then maybe it's best we cool things down," I suggested. "We must think of all the people we might hurt, Beau."

"Yes," he said in a cracked voice.

If words had weight, the telephone lines between New Orleans and Cypress Woods would sag and tear apart, I thought.

"I'm sorry, Beau."

I heard him sigh deeply. "Well, Gisselle keeps asking to go to the ranch for a few days. I guess I'll take her next week. The truth is, I hate living in this house without you, Ruby. There are too many memories of us together here. Every time I walk past your room, I stop and stare at the door and remember."

"Talk Gisselle into selling the house, Beau. Start new somewhere else," I suggested.

"She doesn't care. Nothing bothers her. What have we done to each other, Ruby?" he asked.

I swallowed back the throat lumps, but fugitive tears trickled down my cheeks. For a moment I couldn't find my voice.

"We fell in love, Beau. That's all. We fell in love."

"Ruby . . ."

"I've got to go, Beau. Please."

"Don't say good-bye. Just hang up," he told me, and I did so, but I sat at the phone and sobbed until I heard Pearl wake from her nap and call to me. Then I wiped my eyes, took a deep breath, and went on to fill my days and nights with as much work as I could find, so I wouldn't think and I wouldn't regret.

A quiet resignation fell over me. I began to feel like a

nun, spending much of my time in quiet meditation, painting, reading, and listening to music. Caring for Pearl was a full-time job now, too. She was very active and curious about everything. I had to go about and make the house child-proof, placing valuable knick-knacks out of her reach, being sure she couldn't get into anything dangerous. Occasionally Molly would look after her for me for a few hours while I shopped or had some quiet time alone.

Paul was busier than ever; deliberately so, I thought. He was up at the crack of dawn and gone some days before I came down for breakfast. Sometimes he couldn't get back in time for dinner. He told me his father was doing less and less at the cannery, and talking about retirement.

"Maybe you should hire a manager, then," I suggested. "You can't do it all."

"I'll see," he promised, but I saw that he enjoyed being occupied. Just like me, he hated leisure because leisure made him reflect on what his life was really like now.

I thought it would go on like this forever until we were both old and gray, rocking side by side on the gallery and looking out at the bayou, wondering what life would have been like had we not made some of the decisions we had made when we were young and impulsive. But one night after dinner toward the end of the month, the phone rang. Paul had already settled himself in his favorite easy chair and had the journal opened to the business pages. Pearl was asleep and I was reading a novel. James appeared in the doorway.

"It's for Madame," he announced. Paul looked up curiously. I shrugged and rose.

"Maybe it's Jeanne," I suggested. He nodded. But it was Beau, who sounded like a voice without a body . . . a wisp of himself, so soft and stunned, I questioned whether it was really he.

"Beau? What is it?"

"It's Gisselle. We're at the ranch. We've been here for more than a week now."

"Oh," I said. "She knows about us, then?"

"No, that's not it," he replied.

I held my breath. "What then, Beau?"

"She was bitten by mosquitoes. We thought nothing of it. She complained like crazy, of course, but I rubbed alcohol on her and forgot it. Then . . ."

"Yes?" My legs felt as if they might turn to air and float out from under me.

"She started to have these severe headaches. Nothing I gave her helped. She took nearly a bottle of aspirin. She had a fever, too. Last night the fever went way up and she was hallucinating. I had to call the doctor from the village. By the time he arrived, she was paralyzed."

"Paralyzed!"

"And she was babbling incoherently. She couldn't remember anything, not even who I was," he said, amazed.

"What did the doctor say?"

"He knew what it was immediately. Gisselle has contracted St. Louis encephalitis, an inflammation of the brain caused by a virus mosquitoes transmit to people."

"Mon Dieu," I said, my heart thumping. "Is she in the hospital?"

"No," he said quickly.

"No? Why not, Beau?"

"The doctor said the prognosis is not good. There is no known treatment of the disease when it is transmitted by viral infections other than the herpes simplex virus. Those are his exact words."

"What does this mean? What will happen to her?"

"She can remain in this condition for some time," he said in a voice devoid of any feeling, a voice drained and lost. And then he added, "But no one back in New Orleans knows about it yet. In fact, only this doctor and some servants here are aware of what's happened, and they can be persuaded not to talk about it."

I held my breath. "What are you suggesting, Beau?"

"It came to me just a little while ago while I stood by her bedside and watched her sleep. When she's asleep, she looks so much like you, Ruby. No one would question it."

My heart stopped and then began to pound so hard, I thought I would lose my breath and consciousness. I shifted the receiver to my other ear and took a deep breath. I knew what he was suggesting.

"Beau . . . you want me to assume her identity?"

"And become my wife now and forever," he said. "Don't you see what an opportunity this is?" he asked quickly. "None of the secrets of the past have to be revealed and no one has to be hurt."

"Except Paul," I said.

"What good is it if we're all unhappy?"

Could we do this? I wondered, my excitement building. Would it be wrong?

"What will happen to Gisselle?"

"We'll have to institutionalize her, secretly, of course. But it won't be hard to do."

"That's terrible. You remember when Daphne tried to do that to me," I said.

"That was different, Ruby. You were alive and well and had your whole life ahead of you. What difference will it make to Gisselle? She has accidentally given us a gift, repaired so many wrongs she has committed. Fate wouldn't hand us this opportunity if Fate didn't want to right the wrongs, too. Come to me," he pleaded. "With you I can restore my troubled soul and become someone I can respect again. Please, Ruby. We can't waste a moment of this chance."

"I don't know. I have to think." I turned and looked toward the study. "I have to talk it over with Paul."

"Of course, but do it right away and call me back," he said, and gave me the telephone number. "Ruby, I love you and you love me and we should be together. Destiny has come to realize that, too. Who knows? Maybe your grandmere Catherine's at work someplace in the hereafter or maybe Nina Jackson's cast a spell for us."

"I don't know, Beau. It's all happening so fast. It's complicated."

"Talk it over with Paul. It's right; it's good. It's what was meant to be, finally," he said.

After we hung up, I stood there, my heart still pounding very hard and quickly. The possibilities loomed before me as well as the dangers. I would have to assume my sister's identity, become Gisselle, but we were so unalike, really. Could I do it well enough to fool people and be with Beau forever? Love, if it's strong enough, I thought, gives you the power to do things beyond your imagination. Maybe this was true for us now.

I took a deep breath and then returned to the study and told Paul what had happened and what Beau had proposed. He sat there with amazing calm and listened as I gushed the story and the fantastic proposal. Then he got up and went to the window. He stood there for the longest time.

"You'll never stop loving him," he muttered bitterly. "I was a fool to think otherwise. If I only had listened to my mother . . ." He sighed deeply and turned.

"I can't help the way I feel about him, Paul."

He nodded and looked very thoughtful for a moment. "Maybe you have to live with him to see what sort of a man he really is. Maybe then you'll understand the difference between him and me."

"Paul, I love you for what you've done for Pearl and me and your devotion to me, but we've been living only half a marriage. Besides, we once agreed that if either of us could have someone else, someone we loved and could have a full relationship with, the other would not prevent it."

He nodded. "What a dreamer I was when I made those vows with you on your grandmere Catherine's gallery. "Oh well," he continued with a wry smile, "I'll finally be able to do something that will make you truly happy." His eyes suddenly brightened with an additional thought. "Even more than you and Beau would expect." He paused, his face tight with determination.

"What?" I asked, breathlessly.

"When you call Beau, tell him we'll bring Gisselle here," he said.

"What?"

"He's right. What difference will anything make to her now? You and I will go to the ranch after lunch tomorrow. I have some important business to conduct. We'll pretend we're going for a short holiday and then I will return with Gisselle and give out the story that it is you who have suffered the encephalitis. I'll fix a comfortable place for her upstairs and we'll have nurses around the clock. Since she has lapses of memory and is confused and semiconscious most of the time, it won't be difficult."

"You would do that for me?" I asked, incredulous.

He smiled. "I love you that much, Ruby. Maybe now you'll really understand."

"But I can't do this to you, Paul. It would be too hard and unfair."

"It's nothing. In this big house, I wouldn't even notice the arrangements," he said.

"I don't mean only that. You have a life to live, too," I insisted.

"And I will. In my own way. Go on, call Beau."

He had such a strange look in his eyes. I sensed that he believed this would somehow bring me back to him someday. Whatever his reasons, it certainly made our switch of identities far more possible.

I turned to call Beau and then stopped, realizing the biggest problem of all.

"We can't do this, Paul. It's impossible."

"Why?"

"Pearl!" I said. "If I'm Gisselle, what happens to her?"

Paul thought a moment and then nodded. "With you supposedly seriously ill and with our nanny gone to care for her own family, I will take her to live with her aunt and uncle until the ordeal at Cypress Woods ends. For the time being, it will serve as a good cover story."

I was overwhelmed with his quick thinking. "Oh, Paul,

193

I don't deserve this kindness and sacrifice. I really don't," I cried.

He smiled coolly. "You'll come visit your sick sister from time to time, won't you?" he asked, and I understood that in this strange way, he hoped to keep me tied to him.

"Of course, although Gisselle wouldn't care."

"Be careful," he warned with another grin. "Don't be too nice or people will say . . . what's come over her? She's not herself these days."

"Yes," I said, realizing how great the challenge ahead of me was. I had very little confidence in myself. For now, I would have to be happy with only desire, the desire to be with Beau as his wife forever. Maybe that was enough. For Pearl's sake and mine, I prayed it was.

Book
Two

11

Nothing Ventured

Beau was very excited and happy about Paul's proposal, but I was troubled by Paul's willingness to be part of this. What was he thinking? What was he hoping would happen as a result? I tossed and turned all night, haunted by the things that could go wrong and expose our deception. Once that happened, people would want to know more, and then the truth about Paul and me with all the sins of the past would be revealed. Not only would Pearl and I be disgraced, but the Tates would be devastated. The risks were enormous. I was sure Paul understood them as well as I did, but he was determined to remain tied to me, even in this bizarre fashion.

When I awoke in the morning, I thought it had all been a dream until Paul knocked on my door and poked his head in to tell me we would leave for the Dumas country home a little after two. He estimated the ride to the ranch would take us close to three hours. A ripple of apprehension shot down my spine. I rose and started to make preparations. My body actually trembled as I moved about, thinking about what I would and wouldn't take.

Since my taste in clothing and Gisselle's was different, I realized I had to leave most of my things behind, but I decided to take the jewelry and the mementoes that were most precious to me. I packed as many of Pearl's things as I could without drawing any suspicions. After all, we were supposed to be going away for only a few days.

As I folded Pearl's things into her small suitcase, I thought how strange it was going to be for me to pretend I was only her aunt and not her mother. Fortunately, Pearl was still young enough so that when she called me Mommy, people would only assume she was confused. I would say that it was easier to let her do so for now. What I dreaded was later when she was old enough to understand it all, because then I would have to tell her the truth as to why her father and I had done this and why I took my sister's name. I couldn't help worrying about how it might change the way she thought of us.

I spent the morning wandering about Cypress Woods with Pearl, drinking it all in as though I would never see any of it again. I knew whenever I did return, it would look different to me since I had to think of it no longer as my home, but as my sister's home, a place to visit and a place I supposedly disliked. I would have to behave as though the bayou were as foreign as China to me, for that was the way Gisselle reacted to it.

I thought that would be the hardest thing to do: pretend to hate the bayou. No matter how I practiced, I was sure I couldn't be very convincing about that. Surely my heart would not permit me to mock and complain about the world in which I had grown and the world I had loved all my life.

While Pearl was taking her nap, I went up to my studio to store the things I wanted to protect from time and inattention. As my sister, Gisselle, I would have to do any drawing and painting secretly. Once the news got out that Ruby was an invalid, semiconscious and mentally impaired, the new paintings could no longer be delivered to the art gallery, but I took solace in the fact that I wasn't doing them so much for the fame and money as I was for my own inner satisfaction.

Paul returned home for lunch, which was hard for both of us. Neither of us came right out and said it, but we knew this was the last meal we would sit down to as man and wife. It was important that we didn't act too differently in front of our servants. Nevertheless, every other moment it seemed we were both gazing across the table at each other as if we had just met and neither knew how to begin a sentence. Tension made us overly polite toward each other. Twice we started simultaneously.

"Go on," he said again.

"No, you go on this time," I insisted.

"I wanted to assure you I would see that the studio is kept clean. Maybe you and Beau will vacation here and you can slip up there and do some work, if you like. I'll just say the work was completed before Ruby became so sick."

I nodded, although I didn't think that would ever happen. Despite the fact that it was Gisselle who had contracted St. Louis encephalitis and not me, it made me feel strange to talk about myself as the one who was seriously ill. I quickly envisioned everyone's initial reactions, reactions I wouldn't see because I would be already gone. I expected Paul's sisters would be very upset. His mother would probably be overjoyed, but I did think his father would be sad, for we had gotten along quite well despite Gladys Tate's feelings toward me. The servants would take it hard. I was sure there would be tears.

As soon as the news was spread throughout the bayou, all the people who knew me would feel terrible. Many of Grandmere Catherine's friends would go to church and light a candle for me. As I imagined these scenes, one after the other, I felt a sense of guilt for causing all this sorrow based on a grand deception and I began to wilt in my seat.

"Are you all right?" Paul asked after our dishes were cleared away.

"Yes," I said, but the tears burned under my eyelids and I felt one hot flush after another. Suddenly the room was like an oven. "I'll be right back," I cried, and got up abruptly.

"Ruby!"

I ran out of the dining room and into a bathroom to throw cold water on my cheeks and forehead. When I gazed at myself in the mirror, I saw how the blood had drained from my face, leaving me looking white as fresh milk.

"You're going to be punished for doing this," I warned my reflection. "Maybe someday you will become seriously ill, too."

My mind was in turmoil. Should I put a stop to it before it was too late?

There was a gentle knock on the door.

"Ruby. Beau's on the phone," Paul said. "Are you all right?"

"Yes. I'll be right there, Paul. Thank you."

I dabbed my face with more cold water, quickly wiped it dry, and then went into the office for privacy.

"Hello."

"Paul said you weren't doing so well. Are you all right?"

"No."

"You still want to go through with it, don't you?" he asked, his voice cracking with fear of disappointment. I took a deep breath. "Everything's set," he added before I could reply. "I have the station wagon prepared like an ambulance so we can drive her back to Cypress Woods, pretending it's you. I'll follow in Paul's car and help get her into the house. He's still willing to go through with it all, isn't he?"

"Yes, but . . . Beau . . . what if I can't do this?"

"You can. You must. Ruby, I love you and you love me and we have a daughter to bring up together. It's what was meant to be. We have a chance to defeat Fate. Let's not throw it away. I promise. I'll be at your side constantly. I'll make sure it works."

Strengthened by his words, I felt myself regain composure. The blood returned to my face and my heart stopped pounding.

"All right, Beau. We'll be there."

"Good. I love you," he said, and hung up. I heard another click and realized Paul had been listening in on our conversation, but I wasn't going to embarrass him by letting him know I knew. He left to complete some last-minute errands and I fetched Pearl after her nap and fed her lunch. Afterward, I took her up to my room to wait. My small suitcase and my pocketbook looked pathetic beside the vanity table. I was taking so little with me, but when I had first returned to the bayou, I had brought even less, I reminded myself.

I became very fidgety. The minutes seemed more like hours. When I gazed out the window, I saw clouds moving in from the southwest. They were growing thicker and longer. The wind became stronger and I realized a storm was brewing. A bad omen, I thought. I trembled and embraced myself. Was Nature, the bayou, conspiring to keep me from doing this? I knew Grandmere Catherine might say something just like that if she were at my side now. Lightning flashed and there was a roar of thunder that seemed to shake the house.

Just a little after two o'clock, Paul came to my door and peered in. "Ready?"

I looked around one final time and nodded. My knees were knocking together and my abdomen felt like a hollowed-out cave, but I lifted Pearl into my arms and leaned over to get my bag.

"I'll get it," he said, and picked it up before I could. He gazed into my eyes, searching for my true inner feelings, but I looked away quickly.

"You're going to miss it here, Ruby," he said, piercing me with his diamond-hard glare. "No matter how much you tell yourself you won't, you will. The bayou is as much a part of you as it is a part of me. That's why you returned to it when you were in trouble," he said.

"It's not like I won't ever return, Paul."

"Once we make the switch and we go through the performances, it will be impossible for you to return as Ruby, though," he reminded me sharply.

"I know," I said.

"You must really love him to do all this to be with him," he said, his voice dripping with envy. When I didn't reply, he sighed and gazed out the windows at the canals for a moment. Poor Paul, I thought. A part of him wanted to vent rage and anger at both Beau and me, but that part of him that loved me prevented it and left him filled with frustration.

"Disregard what I just said," he muttered. "If he abuses you or betrays you, or something unexpected happens, I will find a way for you to return," he promised, and turned to look at me intently. "I'd turn the world topsy-turvy to get you back at my side," he added.

Was this why he was being so cooperative? I wondered. Because he wanted to be there for me should something go wrong? Deep in my heart I knew, no matter what he said or did, Paul would never give me up.

He went into Pearl's room to get the suitcase of things I had packed for her and then we all descended the stairs quickly.

The rain had started, so we had to ride with the windshield wipers wagging monotonously. As we left the long drive, I turned back once to look at the great house. Our lives are filled with so many different sorts of good-byes, I thought. We can say good-bye to the people we love, or the people we've known most of our lives, but we can say good-bye to places, too, especially the places that had become a part of who and what we were. I had said good-bye to the bayou before, once thinking I would never come back, but I always believed that if I had, it would still be what it had been to me. In a strange way, I felt as if I were betraying it, too, this time, and I wondered if a place could be as reluctant to forgive you as could people.

The rain came down in a solid sheet. Despite the humidity, I had a wintry feeling rush through my body, and shuddered. I checked Pearl, but she seemed quite comfortable and content.

"Isn't it funny how far we will go to be with someone we think we love," Paul suddenly said, speaking softly. "A grown man will behave like a young boy, a young boy will do everything he can to appear like a grown man. We'll risk our reputations, sacrifice our worldly possessions, defy our parents, even our religious beliefs. We'll do illogical and foolish things, things that are impractical, wasteful, just for a moment of what we think is ecstasy on earth."

"Yes," I said. "Everything you say is true, but knowing it's true doesn't keep us from doing these things."

"I know," he replied bitterly. "I understand better than you think I do. I know you could never fully understand me and why I wanted to be with you so much, but I have a feeling you appreciate my feelings for you now."

"I do," I said.

"Good. Because you know what, Ruby?" He looked at me with icy eyes. "Someday you're going to come back." He said it with such assurance, I felt a chill in my heart. Then we turned onto the main highway and sped up, shooting into my new destiny with a fury that took my breath away.

Pearl fell asleep during the ride. She usually did fall asleep in the car. Two hours after we had started, the rain began to move off and some sunlight pierced through the layer of lighter clouds. Paul studied the directions Beau had given him earlier, and less than an hour later, we found the road to the ranch.

The main building of what Daphne used to refer to as her ranch was châteauesque. It had a steeply pitched hipped roof with spires, pinnacle, turrets, gables, and two shaped chimneys. The ornamental metal cresting along the roof's ridges had elaborate moldings. Both the windows and the doorway were arched. To the right were two small cottages for the servants and caretakers, and to the right of that, some thousand yards or so away, were the stables with the riding horses and a barn. The property had rambling fields with patches of wooded areas and a stream cutting across its north end.

Like some château in the French countryside, it had beautiful gardens and two gazebos on the front lawn, as well as benches and chairs and stone fountains. When we arrived, the caretakers were busily at work trimming hedges and weeding. They were an elderly couple and looked up for only one curious moment before turning back to their work so fast, it was as if someone had snapped a whip.

Beau was in the doorway before we had parked our car. He gestured for us to come in quickly. Pearl was still asleep, her eyelids barely fluttering when I lifted her into my arms to follow Paul to the house. Beau stepped back, smiling softly at me.

"Are you all right?" he asked.

"Yes," I said, even though a paralyzing numbness gripped me.

Paul and Beau looked at each other a moment and then Beau became very serious, his eyes narrowing and darkening.

"We'd better hurry," he said.

"Lead the way," Paul replied sharply.

We entered the château. It had a short foyer decorated with drapes and large scenic paintings. The furnishings were a mixture of modern and some of the same French Provincial found in the New Orleans house. The lights were low, the curtains closed on the windows. Shadows fell everywhere, especially over the stairway. We hurried up.

"Let's get Pearl settled in first," Beau suggested, and took us immediately to a nursery. "That was Gisselle's old crib," he said. "Apparently Daphne had guests with children from time to time. She loved being the hostess with the mostest," he said, smirking at me.

Pearl moaned when I placed her in the crib. I waited a moment to see if she would wake, but she just sighed and turned on her side. Then Beau turned to Paul.

"I managed to get a folding gurney for us to use. No one knows or suspects anything," he assured me. "Money stops curiosity."

"It doesn't solve every problem," Paul said pointedly, shifting his eyes to me, too. I looked down and Beau nodded without a reply and ushered us out. We followed him to the master suite. Gisselle looked tiny in the king-size canopy bed with the quilt up to her chin. Her hair was strewn out over the pillow and her complexion was pasty white.

"She goes in and out of coma now," Beau explained.

"Oh, Beau. She really belongs in a hospital," I moaned.

"Paul can have her put in one if his doctor so advises. Mine didn't think it would matter much as long as she had good nursing care."

"I'll take care of it," Paul said, his eyes fixed on Gisselle. "She'll get the best possible attention."

"Then let's get started," Beau said, obviously anxious to begin before any of us changed his or her mind. Paul nodded and went around to the side of the bed to help move Gisselle to the waiting gurney. Beau leaned in and scooped under her arms. Her eyelids fluttered but didn't open as he lifted and slid her toward the edge of the bed. Then he nodded at Paul, who took hold of her legs. They placed her on the gurney. She was in a white cotton nightgown with frilly sleeves and a blue flower pattern over the bodice. I was sure Beau had picked it out, knowing it was something I would wear.

He put a blanket over her and then looked at me. "We have to exchange the wedding rings," he said. "I've already taken hers off."

He handed it to me. It felt hot in my fingers. I looked at Paul, who stared with an expression of curiosity. It was as if he were studying my every move to see just what I would do and how I would feel about what I did. I turned around and twisted at my ring. My finger was a bit swollen and it wouldn't come right off.

"Run some cold water over it," Beau advised. He nodded toward the bathroom. I looked at Paul again. He seemed happy about the difficulty I was having symbolically separating from him.

Water helped and the ring came off. Beau quickly worked it onto Gisselle's finger.

"Any other rings?" he asked me.

"No, nothing I wear all the time."

"She changed her jewelry so often, no one would remember anything she wore, except her wedding ring." He started to wheel the gurney toward the door and stopped.

"I'll bring the station wagon to the front. I'll back right up to the front steps. Wait right here." He hurried out and down.

Paul gazed at Gisselle a moment and then sighed deeply and looked at me. "Well, here we are, doing it," he said.

My heart was tripping along so fast, I couldn't catch my breath. "Do whatever the doctor says, Paul," I told him.

"You don't have to say it. Of course I will." He hesitated a moment and then added, "I've already spoken to a doctor about this condition."

"You have?"

"Yes, someone in Baton Rouge this morning."

"And?"

"She could recover," he said, and fixed his eyes on me. Now I understood. This was his hope: Gisselle's return to health forcing me to return to Cypress Woods.

It was on the tip of my tongue to put an end to our exchange of identities.

"Stay with her a moment," he said before I could comment. He left to go down to speak with Beau. Alone with my sick twin sister, I stepped up to the gurney and took her cold hand into mine.

"Gisselle," I whispered. "I don't know if you can hear me, if it's only your eyes that are shut and not your mind, but I want you to know that I never did anything to hurt you and I'm not doing anything to hurt you now. Even you, in your sick state, must realize Fate has taken over and decided our destinies. I'm sorry you are so ill. I did nothing to bring it about unless you want to say my love for Beau is so great, I must have stirred the spirits to decide we belong together. In your secret, most put-away heart, I know you believe we belong together, too."

I leaned over and kissed her on the forehead. A moment later I heard Beau and Paul come up the stairs.

"Just wheel her to the top of the stairway there," Beau instructed. "Then I'll fold the gurney's legs up and we'll carry her down."

"Be careful," I warned.

The two of them did struggle on the steps, but they managed to get her down quickly. Beau released the legs and the wheels again and they rolled her to the doorway. I started after them and followed them out, watching them load the gurney into the back of the wagon. Beau closed the door and then the two of them looked back at me. After a moment Paul stepped up.

"I guess this is good-bye . . . for now," he said. He leaned forward to kiss me. I watched him stroll back to the station wagon.

"I'll be back as soon as I can," Beau promised.

"Beau." I seized his hand. "He thinks she will make a full recuperation and we'll have to return to our true identities someday."

Beau shook his head. "My doctor has assured me that won't happen."

"But . . ."

"Ruby, it's too late to turn back," he said. "But don't worry. It's meant to be." He, too, kissed me and then went to Paul's car. Then he hurriedly returned to me. I held my breath, expecting he had decided not to go through with it. But that wasn't it.

"I almost forgot. Just in case," he said, "the caretakers' names are Gerhart and Anna Lenggenhager. They both have such thick German accents, you probably won't understand them half the time, but don't worry. Gisselle would never talk to them unless it was to shout an order at them. She had no patience when it came to trying to understand them. But they're very nice people. Also, the maid's name is Jill and the cook's name is Dorothea. I've left instructions for your dinner to be brought to the suite. No one will think anything of it. Gisselle often ate in the suite."

"What about Pearl?"

"Just tell Jill what you want brought up for her. They know our niece was coming. And don't worry. No one will ask any questions. Everything's been taken care of," he assured me. Then he kissed me again and returned to the car.

I stood there, watching them drive away. When I gazed to the left, I saw Gerhart and Anna looking at me. They turned away quickly and went to their cottage. With my heart thumping, I entered the house again. I thought about exploring, but decided to go up to Pearl instead and be sure she hadn't woken to find herself in a strange room. I knew it would frighten her. It frightened me to realize I was here.

From the look in Jill's eyes when she came up for her instructions a little while later, I knew she feared Gisselle. Pearl had woken and I had her with me in the suite. Jill knocked so softly on the door, I didn't hear her the first time.

"Yes?" I called. She opened the door slowly and stepped only a few inches into the room. She was a tall, thin girl with a birdlike face, her mouth small, her nose long, and her dark eyes set back in her head. Her dark brown hair was snipped short.

"Dorothea would like to know if Madame wants anything special this evening."

I hesitated a moment, realizing this would be the first time I would speak to anyone as my sister, Gisselle. I envisioned her first, recalling the way she always smirked with annoyance when a servant made an inquiry or request.

"I'd like a light meal. Just some chicken and rice with a

little salad and ice water," I replied as matter-of-factly as I could. I looked away quickly.

"And the child?"

I gave her instructions for Pearl's meal just as firmly and she nodded, quickly retreating, seemingly happy to hear nothing else. What an ogre Gisselle had been, I thought. Surely I was not capable of performing exactly like her.

Later, when she brought up our food and set the table, Jill risked smiling at Pearl, who was gazing at her with great interest. Immediately after, however, she shot a fearful glance at me, expecting to be reprimanded for taking too much time or permitting herself to be distracted. It was all I could do to remain silent rather than try to be nasty.

"Will there be anything else, madame?" she asked.

"Not at the moment." I started to say thank you and then stopped, recalling that was an expression Gisselle rarely used, except sarcastically. Jill didn't expect it either. She was already turned and marching out.

I didn't think I would have much of an appetite, but I was so nervous, my stomach felt like it had a small bird trapped inside, flapping its wings. I thought it would be best to put something in it. Even though the food was delicious, I ate mechanically, unable to do anything but wonder what was happening, how Paul and Beau managed the delivery of Gisselle. I thought about the shock on everyone's face when Paul said something had happened and they had decided to bring me back quickly. I was on pins and needles until I heard footsteps on the stairway hours and hours later, and opened the door to see Beau rushing up the stairs, taking two steps at a time. He smiled at the sight of me.

"It's all right," he said quickly, catching his breath. "It went well. Your servants bought it hook, line, and sinker." He took my hands into his. "Welcome to your new life, Mrs. Andreas, the life that was meant to be."

I looked into his eyes and thought, yes, I'm Mrs. Andreas, Mrs. Beau Andreas.

He embraced me and held me tightly to him for a moment before kissing me on the forehead, and then moving down my face to kiss me firmly on the lips.

Our first night together as man and wife was not as romantic as either of us had anticipated. Despite his bravado, Beau was just as emotionally drained by the ordeal as I was. After we lay together in bed for a while, holding and kissing each other, he revealed how tense he had been and how nervous about the exchange.

"I wasn't sure what Paul was going to do," he said. "To be honest, I half expected he was going to sabotage it all deliberately. Especially after what you had told me on the front steps. I began to realize how much he didn't want to lose you," he said.

"Before you took Gisselle down to the car, he went out to talk to you. What did he say?" I asked.

"More like warn and threaten me, you mean."

"Why? What did he say?"

"He said he was going through with this only because he was convinced it was what you wanted and what you thought would make you happy, but if he heard just one negative thing about our relationship, if I did anything to make you unhappy, he would expose the exchange and reveal our deception. He assured me he didn't care about his own reputation or what the consequences might be for him. I believe him, so don't you ever tell him anything bad," Beau said, half smiling.

"There won't be anything bad to tell him, Beau."

"No. There won't," he promised. He kissed me again and started to caress me, but I was exhausted and still too nervous.

"Let's save our honeymoon nights for New Orleans," he decided.

I nodded and we fell asleep in each other's arms.

Our plan was to return immediately to New Orleans, explaining that something terrible had happened to my sister, Ruby, and we had to care for her child in the interim. No one seemed particularly upset about our leaving the château so abruptly. On the contrary, I thought I saw a look of relief on Gerhart and Anna's faces, and genuine happiness on Jill's.

On the way back to New Orleans, Beau revealed he had let go of all of the servants in the House of Dumas.

"Oh no," I said, feeling sorry for them.

"It's all right." He smiled. "They weren't exactly in love with serving Gisselle, and I gave each and every one of them six months' severance salary. It's better that we start with new people. It will make it so much easier for you," he said. I had to agree with that.

For me, returning to the House of Dumas was perhaps the most difficult part of our deception. It was a partly cloudy day in New Orleans, with the sun only teasing the world from time to time with slim rays of sunshine. The shadows cast by the heavy clouds made the streets under the long canopies of spreading oaks darker, and even the beautiful Garden District with its rich, fine homes and extravagant gardens looked sad and depressed to me.

All of the windows in the grand house were dark, the shades drawn in the ivory mansion that had once been my father's happy home. Absent of any activity in and around it, the property looked so deserted and lonely, it made my heart feel as heavy as a lump of lead in my chest. As we drove up to the front gallery, I half expected my stepmother, Daphne, to appear in the doorway and demand to know what we were doing here. But no one appeared; nothing moved except an occasional gray squirrel whose curiosity had been tickled by our arrival.

"We're home," Beau declared. I nodded, my eyes fixed on the tile stairway and front door. "Relax," he said, taking my hand and shaking it as if he could shake the nervousness out of my body. "We're going to do just fine."

I forced a smile and looked hopefully into his summer blue eyes, bright with excitement. How far we had come from that first day when I had arrived secretly from the bayou and he had met me standing in front of the great house, gaping with wonder and filled with trepidation about meeting my real father for the first time. Now it seemed even more ironic and perhaps even prophetic that Beau had mistaken me for Gisselle back then, thinking she had disguised herself as a poor girl for the Mardi Gras costume ball.

Beau gathered our things and I took Pearl into my arms. She gazed at everything with curiosity. I kissed her cheek.

"This is going to be your new home, honey. I hope it has better luck for you than it did for me."

"It will," Beau promised. He marched ahead of us to the front door and unlocked it. He quickly turned on the chandeliers, for the dismal sky made the great foyer cold and dark. The lights made the peach marble floor glitter and illuminated the ceiling mural, the paintings, and the enormous tapestry depicting a grand French palace and gardens. Pearl's eyes were wide with astonishment. She gazed quickly at everything, but she clung to me tightly.

"Right this way, madame," Beau called. His voice echoed through the empty mansion. As he proceeded before us, he turned on whatever lamp or hall light he could. I followed quickly to the beautiful curved stairway with its soft carpeted steps and shiny mahogany balustrade.

Despite its plush antique furniture, its expensive wall hangings, its vast rooms, the grand house had never been a home to me. I was a stranger from a strange land when I came here to live, and at the moment, I felt even more alien. When I had first set eyes on the inside of the mansion, I thought it was more of a museum than it was a house. Now, with the bitter and sad memories still clinging to the walls of my mind, I knew it would take even more of an effort to make it cozy and warm and feel welcome and secure here.

"I thought you might want to make your old room into Pearl's nursery," Beau suggested. He opened the door of what had been my room and stood back, grimacing like a satisfied cat.

"What?"

I gazed in. There was a crib similar to the one Pearl had at Cypress Woods, with a matching dresser and a little desk and chair. My mouth fell open in astonishment.

"How?"

"I came back into New Orleans right after we had our conversation and paid a furniture dealer twice the price to get everything set up for her," he said. "Then I rushed back to the ranch."

I shook my head in amazement.

"I want this to work," he said softly but determinedly. "For all of us."

"Oh, Beau." Tears came to my eyes. Pearl did seem happy and was eager to explore her new surroundings.

"I'll make some phone calls and start the ball rolling for us to get some new servants. The agency will send candidates for butler and maid and cook."

"What will people think once they hear about all the servants leaving?" I asked.

"Nothing. It wouldn't be anything unexpected. I'm sure they were all mumbling complaints about Gisselle anyway. After Daphne's death and Bruce's departure from the house, she became so oppressive and demanding, I felt sorry for them. The fact is, I had to plead and beg with them not to quit." He paused. "Gisselle and I took Daphne and Pierre's suite," he said. "Might as well make yourself at home," he suggested.

I took Pearl into my arms again and followed him across the hall. Very little had been changed in the suite. It still had its great canopy bed and elaborate velvet drapes over the windows. However, the vanity table was a mess and there were some garments tossed over the love seat.

"Gisselle wasn't the neatest woman. She didn't respect her possessions because she replaced them so often. We were always arguing about that," Beau said. The closet door was open and I could see her vast array of dresses, skirts, and blouses, some dangling from their hangers precariously, some actually on the floor of the closet.

"Gisselle's going to have some remarkable character changes," I said.

Beau laughed. "Not too quickly, however," he warned.

The phone rang and we both looked at it.

"We don't have to answer it," he said.

"It might be Paul. I've got to start sometime; it might as well be immediately, Beau. If I can't pull this off, we'd better know right away."

He nodded and looked apprehensive as I started toward the phone.

"Wait," he said. "If it's one of her friends, I'll know which one." He picked up the receiver. "Hello." He listened. "Yes, she's right here. It's Pauline," he told me, and held out the receiver. "She can be very bitchy," he whispered.

I nodded and took the phone into my trembling fingers. "Hello."

"Gisselle? I called the ranch and they said you had left for New Orleans. I thought you were staying another week. I got Peter to agree to go. I thought we were going to have a party," she whined. "It's just lucky I decided to call first. I might have driven all the way out there for nothing. What happened? Why didn't you call me?" she demanded angrily.

I took a deep breath, recalled how my sister spoke on the phone, and replied. "What happened?" I said. "Only a disaster."

"What?" Pauline exclaimed.

"My sister came to visit and was bitten by mosquitoes," I explained as if it were my sister's fault.

"That's a disaster?"

"She came down with . . . Beau, what was that stupid disease again?"

He smiled at me.

"Encepha something," I said after pretending to listen.

"She's in a coma and I had to take the baby home with me."

"Baby?"

"My sister's baby."

"You're taking care of a baby?" she asked, astonished.

"Until I hire someone," I said petulantly. "Why?"

"Nothing, except I know what you think of children."

"You don't know everything about me, Pauline," I snapped in my best Gisselle tone of voice.

"Excuse me?"

"You're excused."

"I just meant . . ."

"I know what you meant. Look, I don't have time to waste on the phone with stupid gossip right now. I have some major responsibilities."

"I'm sorry. I won't bother you."

"Fine. 'Bye," I said, and cradled the receiver.

"That was incredible," Beau said. "For a moment I thought you were Gisselle and I had really taken Ruby back to Cypress Woods."

Even Pearl was looking up at me with an expression of confusion.

I breathed relief. Maybe, I thought, this wouldn't be as hard as I had imagined. In fact, Beau was so impressed with my performance, he decided we should go to one of the fine restaurants he and Gisselle often frequented and let the New Orleans social community learn the story as soon as possible.

Butterflies beat small wings of panic in my stomach.

"Beau, should we? Maybe it's too soon."

"Nonsense," he said with confidence. "You settle in, choose something to wear, something Gisselle," he added pointedly, "and I'll take care of some business. Welcome home, darling," he said, kissing me softly on the lips. My heart fluttered as he hurried out and I turned to look at my sister's wardrobe.

12

Body Double

Our first evening out as Beau and Gisselle Andreas was a great success. I wore one of Gisselle's strapless outfits with a tight-fitting bodice. Beau laughed at my reaction to my image in the mirror. Almost all of her dresses had the same low necklines, so they revealed more cleavage than I would have liked.

"Your sister always pushed to the limits when it came to what was and was not socially acceptable," Beau said. "I think she enjoyed outraging high society."

"Well, I don't."

"Still, you look enchanting," he said, stepping back with a sensual smile painted on his face. He laughed. "There was nothing Gisselle liked more than walking into a fancy, expensive restaurant and having heads turn her way in astonishment."

"I'll be blushing so badly, everyone will know who I really am!"

"They'll just think it's Gisselle's way of flirting," Beau replied.

Heads did turn when we entered the restaurant. Beau carried Pearl, who looked adorable in the little sailor girl outfit we had bought her. I tried to imagine Gisselle's arrogance and swagger, but when people's eyes met mine, faces smeared into one giant blur and I instinctively looked down. However, none of the people we met who were acquaintances of Beau and Gisselle's displayed any suspicions. Whatever nervousness or uncharacteristic behavior they saw in me, they attributed to the current tragic situation. Gisselle was always willing to let people know how much she suffered. Nevertheless, I noticed that most people showed their sympathy more to Beau than to me, and I realized quickly that those who were friends with Beau and Gisselle were friends with them mainly because of him.

Beau cleverly announced anyone's name in greeting before I had to say anything.

"Marcus, Lorraine, how are you?" he would cry as they approached the table.

"Whose lovely child is this?" almost everyone asked.

"My sister's," I replied with a smirk. "But for now and maybe forever, she's my responsibility."

"Oh?"

That would lead to Beau providing the explanation. If anyone did show sympathy to me, it was solely because of the new burden I was to bear.

"As you can see," Beau told me on the way home, "most of Gisselle's friendships are thin and artificial. I used to notice how they never really listened to each other or cared that much about what each other said."

"'Snakes of the same color are drawn to each other,' Grandmere used to say," I told him.

"Exactly."

We were both so buoyed by my premier performances in the role of my sister, our hearts felt light and gay when we returned to the house. Beau had arranged for interviews the next day, hoping to hire new servants as soon as possible. I put Pearl to sleep in her new crib and new room, thinking to myself how wonderful it was that she was to have the room that had been mine. My father had been so proud of it and so happy with my elated reaction to it and the views of our gardens and property. To me it was the doorway to a wonderland. Hopefully it would become that for Pearl, too.

Beau came up behind me and put his hands on my shoulders and his lips on my neck.

"Feeling better?" he asked softly.

"Yes."

"A little happy?"

"A little," I offered.

He laughed and turned me to him for a long and passionate kiss. Then a small smile played about his beautifully shaped lips. "You know, you did look very sexy tonight."

"Not in front of the baby," I chastised gently when his fingers found the snaps on my dress and he began to lower it off my shoulders. He laughed and scooped me up to carry me to our suite. After he placed me gently on the bed, he stepped back and smiled strangely.

"What?" I asked.

"Let's pretend this is really our first night together as man and wife, our honeymoon night. We've never made love with each other before. We've touched each other, kissed each other hard and long, but I have always respected you when I courted you and you always said, let's wait. Well, now we're married; now it's time," he declared.

"Oh, Beau . . ."

He knelt down and put his fingers on my lips. "Don't speak," he said. "Words are too clumsy now."

I sat quietly as he gracefully peeled my dress down my arms. He kissed my shoulders, now gleaming in the soft light of the three-quarter moon streaming through our bedroom window. He unfastened my bra and drew it off me. For a moment all he did was gaze at me. My heart pounded so hard, I thought he could see the hammering under my breast. Slowly he brought his hands to me, caressing me. I moaned and lay back on the plush, fluffy pillows. I closed my eyes and just listened to the rustling of his clothing. I remained still, quiet, as he completed undressing me and moments later brought his naked body to mine.

Funny the power our illusions had over us, I thought, because we did make love as if it were for the first time. Each kiss was a new kiss, each touch a new touch. We made discoveries about each other, listened to each other's moans and heavy breathing as if we both heard things we had never before heard. Our passion was so great and so deep, it drove me to tears of ecstasy. If we declared our love once, we declared it a hundred times as we stroked the deepest part of ourselves repeatedly.

It was exhausting, but ecstatically so, leaving us both tired but content. All the problems and difficulties ahead of us became insignificant. Our lovemaking left us feeling invulnerable, for surely a romance this great was blessed and protected. It was immortal, indestructible, invincible. We fell asleep in each other's arms, blanketed by confidence, and my dreams took off on wings of fancy.

The phone's ringing early in the morning, even before Pearl woke, startled us. Beau groaned. For a few moments I forgot where I was. I blinked in confusion and waited for my memory to catch up with my senses. Beau groped for the phone and struggled to sit up.

"Hello," he said in a raspy voice. He listened so long without speaking, my curiosity was aroused and I ground the sleep from my eyes and sat up beside him.

"Who is it?" I whispered.

He put his hand over the mouthpiece. "Paul," he replied, and listened again. "Fine. You did the right thing. Just keep us up-to-date. No. She's still asleep," he added, fixing his gaze on me with wider eyes. "I'll tell her. Right. Thanks." He cradled the phone.

"What?"

"He said his doctor advised putting Gisselle into the hospital for tests, a CAT scan. His doctor had the same initial diagnosis as mine did, but he's not as pessimistic as my doctor was about the outcome."

"How did she spend the night?" I asked.

"Paul said she had a few periods of consciousness, but

her babbling was so incoherent, no one suspected anything."

"What's going to happen, Beau?"

"I don't know. My doctor was so definite about her condition." He thought a moment and shook his head. "I don't think anything will come of this."

"I don't want to have to wish for her to be sick and die, Beau. I couldn't be happy knowing my happiness was based on that wish."

"I know. It doesn't matter what you wish. Believe me," he said assuredly. "It's beyond what any one of us wants, even Paul," he added. "Might as well get up and start the day." He rose, but I sat there.

Mornings always had a way of sobering us up, I thought. Reality rode in on the back of the sunlight, erasing the magic we experienced under the stars and in the moonlight. I heard Pearl's cry and rose myself, that tentative feeling returning.

It had been a while since I had been in a kitchen, but cooking and baking for me was like riding a bike. The moment I began, everything came back to me and I not only prepared our breakfast, but began a gumbo for our lunch as well. Beau wasn't sure he could get back for lunch.

"Since the settlement and Bruce's departure, I've been running the Dumas Enterprises," he explained. "Of course, Gisselle did little more than cash checks and spend money. She was always bored with business."

"Paul conducted all of our business," I said, "but I wouldn't mind getting involved and being a real partner for you."

He shook his head.

"Why not?" I asked.

"Everyone working for us knows how Gisselle is."

"Tell them I've had a sudden change of heart and mind because of what happened to my sister. Tell them . . . I've got religion."

"Religion? Gisselle? No way anyone would believe that, *mon chère.*"

"Well then tell them a voodoo spell was cast over me," I suggested, half-seriously.

Beau laughed. "All right. We'll figure something out to explain your new interests. We'll have to ease you into things slowly, though, so as not to arouse suspicions. In the meantime, I'll do what has to be done. I have three interviews set up beginning at two this afternoon: a candidate for butler, maid, and cook."

"I could do all of our cooking," I said.

"Gisselle couldn't boil water without burning it," he reminded me. I felt like a graceful dancer who had to suddenly appear clumsy. All my talents had to remain hidden. Beau kissed me on the cheek, kissed Pearl, and hurried off to the office.

After he left I took Pearl around the house to show her our new home. She loved our patios, fountains, and gardens, but was especially excited when I brought her to my old studio. The familiar sight of easels, frames, drawing tables, paints, oils, and clay brought laughter to her lips. She clapped her hands and I put her down on the floor and gave her a set of colored pencils and some paper with which to amuse herself while I began to reorganize my studio.

I was so lost in the work and my memories of pictures I had done here that I didn't hear the tapping on the windowpane for a few moments after it had begun. It grew louder and I turned to see a curly-haired young man smiling in at me. He was dressed in a short-sleeve blue shirt and jeans, the shirt opened down his chest to reveal a gold chain and medallion. He was a slim man about six feet tall with a dark face, light brown eyes, and very light brown hair, and I didn't think he was much older than twenty-four or -five.

"Open the window," he cried.

I walked toward him slowly and undid the latch.

"Pauline told me you were back. Why didn't you call?" he asked, and started to crawl in through the window. I stepped back amazed, but too shocked and confused to speak. As soon as he was in, he reached out to take my shoulders and bring me to him to kiss me passionately on the lips, twisting and turning his head and jetting out his tongue. I gasped and pulled out of his grip.

"What's wrong?" he demanded. He smirked. "Did Pauline tell you something? Because if she did, it wasn't true. Helaine Delmarco was here for only a couple of days, and her parents and my parents are like relatives. I think of her the way you would think of your sister."

"Pauline didn't tell me anything," I said.

"Oh." He heard Pearl mumble some of her baby gibberish and looked around the corner of the settee to see her seated on the floor. "Who's that?"

"My sister's child. It's the reason we returned so quickly. My sister became very sick. She's in the hospital. I'm looking after her baby."

"No kidding? You? Volunteered?"

"I didn't exactly volunteer."

"No," he said, laughing. "I guess you wouldn't. So that's it. All right. I forgive you, then." He started toward me again. "What's wrong?" he asked when I retreated a step. He smiled. "I watched and waited to be sure Beau was gone for a while. Where did he go, to the office?"

"No, he's coming back soon," I said.

"Oh. Too bad," he muttered with disappointment. "I thought we'd make up for lost time, especially in here. We had a good time in here once, didn't we?" he said, gazing around with a lascivious smile washed across his face. "On this very sofa," he added. "I still don't know why it was so important we do it in here," he added. "In fact, as I recall, it was a little uncomfortable. Not that I'm complaining," he said.

His revelation so amazed me that the expression on my face intrigued him.

"What's the matter? You don't remember? You make love so often in so many places, you forgot?"

"I didn't forget anything," I said sullenly.

He nodded and gazed at Pearl again. "So when will I see you? Can you come up to my apartment later?"

"No," I said quickly, perhaps too quickly. He squinted and continued to study me curiously. My pounding heart brought a hot flush to my face. I knew my cheeks were crimson.

"You're not yourself, for some reason."

"Well, would you be if your twin sister came down with a fatal illness and you were left caring for her child because her husband was too overwhelmed?"

"Fatal? I'm sorry. I didn't realize it was that serious."

"Well, it is," I snapped.

"Why don't you just hire someone to watch her for you?" he asked after a moment.

"I intend to, but not right away. I've got to pretend I care at least," I said.

"She's a pretty little girl," he said, gazing at Pearl again. "But little kids are little kids." He stepped toward me again, his eyes soft, demanding, his lips folded into a impish smile. "I missed you. Didn't you miss me?"

"I miss my freedom," I replied.

He didn't like the response and grimaced. "You weren't so indifferent the night before you left. You were moaning so loud, I thought I'd have problems with my neighbors."

"Is that so?" I said indignantly. "Well, you don't have to worry about the neighbors anymore. I'll do my moaning at home," I added with my hands on my hips in Gisselle's way and my head wagging.

"What?"

"You heard me." My voice took on the steely edge of a razor. "Now, leave before Beau comes back and you have to explain your injuries to your parents."

"Huh?" He shook his head. "Looks like you're the one with the fatal illness, not your sister."

"Would you get out of here?" I demanded, and pointed to the window.

He stood there and then smiled at me. "You'll change your mind. You'll get bored and call. I know you will."

"Don't hold your breath."

My reaction confused him. I could see him struggling to understand. A theory flashed. "You're seeing someone else on the side, aren't you?" he accused. "Who is it? Kurt Peters? No, you wouldn't sleep with Kurt. He's not wild enough for you. I know, Henry Martin, right?"

"No."

"It's Henry, isn't it?" He nodded, convincing himself. "I should have realized that would happen when you told me you thought he was cute. How is he? Is he as exciting in bed as I am?"

"I'm not sleeping with anyone but Beau," I said, and he threw his head back and laughed.

"You? Stay with only one man? Don't make me laugh. Oh well," he said, shrugging with an air of indifference. "We had a good fling. Carey Littlefield told me not to expect too much for too long. So, as you see, dear Gisselle, your reputation precedes you. The only one who seems oblivious about it is your darling Beau Andreas. Or maybe . . . he's not as oblivious as you think. Maybe he, too, has found other distractions."

"Get out!" I shouted, and pointed to the window.

"I'm going. Don't worry." He looked at Pearl again. She was staring up with confusion and some fear in her face because I had raised my voice. "You better get someone to take care of that child soon, before you ruin her," he said, and headed for the window. *Au revoir,* Gisselle. I shall never forget the way you squealed when I kissed that little beauty mark under your breast," he added, and laughed as he crawled out the window. He waved and was off as quickly as he had appeared. Only then did I release the air I had been holding in my lungs. I reached back to find the settee and sat hard.

My sister had been having affairs with other men after she had married Beau. Apparently he didn't know, because he hadn't said anything to me. How many more men would come sneaking around the house or calling? I had been lucky this time, but the next man might be more perceptive.

I should have realized Gisselle would have been involved with other men, I thought. She married Beau only as a way to get at me, to flaunt him. Even when she was going with him in high school, she was seeing other boys on the side. Whoever that man was who had just been here, he was right. One man was never enough for Gisselle. She was always thinking about what she was missing.

I could never be like that, I thought. Her friends would soon be chattering about how different she had suddenly become. I hoped they weren't smart enough to figure out why.

I regained my composure and continued to work on my studio. A little more than an hour later, Beau called to say he would be returning for lunch after all.

"Good," I said. He heard the tension in my voice.

"Anything wrong?"

"I had a visitor."

"Oh? Who?"

"One of Gisselle's secret lovers," I revealed. He was silent a moment.

"I should have prepared you for that," he admitted.

"You knew?"

"Let's say I had some strong suspicions."

"Then why didn't you tell me, prepare me?" I demanded. His silence reconfirmed my theory. "You were worried I wouldn't go through with doing this, weren't you?"

"A little."

"You should have told me, Beau. It could have been a big problem."

"I know. I'm sorry. What did you do? How did it go? You didn't . . ."

"Of course not. I acted annoyed about everything and drove him off. He accused me of sleeping with someone else. I don't even know his name."

"What did he look like?"

I described him quickly and Beau laughed.

"George Denning. No wonder he was so nice to me all the time." He laughed again. "I would have thought she would have chosen someone better-looking."

"Doesn't it bother you to learn this now, Beau, and confirm your suspicions?"

"No," he said. "Because now that I have you, there is no longer any past. There is only the present and the future," he said.

"Beau," I asked before he could end the conversation, "were you seeing other women, too?"

"Yes," he admitted. "You. Remember?"

"I meant . . . other women."

"No. My mind, my eyes, my soul, were fixed only on you, Ruby."

"Come home, Beau. I'm a bit shaken."

"All right. I'll hurry," he said, and hung up.

We had met all the challenges and tests so far, I thought, but I was sure they would continue to come at me hard and heavy. I threw myself back into my work and kept busy so as not to worry, but at lunch Beau revealed we had to prepare for the biggest challenge of all.

"My parents," he announced. "They're returning from their European holiday trip in two days. We'll have to go there for dinner."

"Oh, Beau, they'll surely see the differences and know, and you remember how much they disliked me, thanks to Daphne," I reminded him.

"They won't be any more perceptive than anyone else," he assured me. "The fact is, they didn't see much of us after we were married. Gisselle wasn't very fond of my mother, and my father was too serious and too proper for her. They made her uncomfortable. I could count on my fingers how many times we were together. Whenever we were together, Gisselle was usually sullen and quiet. And we won't have to see them that often," he added, but I was still quite nervous about meeting them as Gisselle.

That afternoon we met with the candidates for butler, maid, and cook. The butler was a proper Englishman, about five feet seven with thin, gray hair and hazel eyes. He wore thick-rimmed glasses, which kept falling down the bridge of his bony nose, but he was a pleasant man who had obviously worked for many fine families. His name was Aubrey Renner and he had a warm, friendly smile.

The maid's name was Sally Petersen. She was a tall, thin woman in her mid-forties with a long face that had eyes as big as half dollars and a thin nose that dipped over her pencil-thin mouth. I saw that being a maid was a profession to her, not a job. She appeared to me to be a very responsible person, a bit hard, but efficient.

Our cook was a light-skinned quadroon woman who said she was sixty, but I thought was closer to seventy. She called herself Mrs. Swann and said she rarely bothered to tell people her first name these days because it made her sound too rich, Delphinia. She was a short woman, not more than four feet five, with rolling-pin arms and a chubby face. But I imagined she was once a very pretty young lady. She had full, dark liquid eyes, coral lips, and teeth of pearl. She had worked in the homes of two wealthy Creole families most of her life. I had the feeling that she had retired and then become bored.

Once the servants were hired, Beau thought we should look into the nanny for Pearl; but I was reluctant about throwing another person at Pearl so soon.

"It's something Gisselle would do immediately," Beau reminded me.

As luck would have it, a friend of his knew of a Frenchwoman who had worked as a private tutor as well as a nanny, and was now unemployed. Her name was Edith Ferrier. Beau had her come to the house the next day. During the interview I found out she had been married, but for only a short time. Her husband had died in a train accident, and the traumatic effect had left her terrified of forming another romantic relationship.

She was a soft-spoken woman of fifty-four with short, black hair streaked with gray, a soft, gentle mouth, and warm, almost sad brown eyes that brightened at the sight of Pearl. Caring and nurturing other people's children had become her whole life, every one of them replacing the children she never had. Pearl was a little suspicious of her at first, but Mrs. Ferrier's soothing voice and happy tones perked up her interest, and in a short time she was letting Mrs. Ferrier show her how to do a new picture puzzle.

Beau had met with all of these candidates before I had and he had explained the situation to them: how we were caring for my sister's child. Few questions were asked, and since none of them had ever known my sister, I didn't have to put on any performances. Beau emphasized with each of them that confidentiality about the family and its affairs was of primary importance. Anyone who talked out of school would be released immediately.

Both of us were happy about the people we had hired. Establishing our new lives seemed well under way, but before I could take a breath and relax, Beau reminded me that his parents had arrived and our dinner was arranged for the following evening.

I had never really gotten to know Beau's parents when I lived in New Orleans. Right from the beginning, because of my stepmother, Daphne, they treated me like common trash. They were people who were quite in love with their own place in high society, the sort who constantly had their names in the society columns and their pictures in the newspapers for attending or sponsoring charity balls and other affairs.

"You can choose something to wear that is more in your character, if you like," Beau told me. "Gisselle knew how my parents were and at least made some small effort not to antagonize them by wearing one of her outrageously sexy outfits. She would wear some of Daphne's jewelry, too. And she would be a little less heavy-handed with the makeup."

"I'd rather wear my own. Your parents won't know the difference." I didn't want to touch anything that had once belonged to my dreadful stepmother, even though her things were expensive and quite chic.

We decided it would be easier for us if we left Pearl at home. My knees were practically knocking together when we drove up to the Andreas mansion on Chestnut Street, which was one of the famous old houses, dating back to the 1850s. It was a classic example of Greek Revival architecture and had double front balconies with Ionic columns below and Corinthian above. Beau emphasized how proud his father was of their home, never missing an opportunity to describe its historical significance to the Garden District.

"Gisselle showed little interest in his lectures, once even yawning while he spoke about the 'dep' windows," Beau said.

"What are they? If I don't remember . . ."

"I wouldn't worry about that. Gisselle barely listened to our conversations, and my parents knew it. Dep windows serve as doorways when a wood panel beneath them is opened. Don't worry. My father won't show you around. He showed Gisselle around and was disappointed in her reactions."

"Then they didn't like Gisselle any more than they liked me, did they?"

"Not much," he said, smiling. He was amused, but all this made me even more nervous. How was I to behave knowing his parents weren't happy he had married me?

The butler let us in and we walked down the long corridor to the sitting room where his parents waited. His father, after whom Beau took the most, had grayed considerably in the temples since I last saw him. Beau had inherited his father's Roman nose and sharp jawline. He was an inch or so taller than his father, who kept his figure quite trim for a man of his age. Tonight he wore a white dinner jacket and a black silk ascot. He had color in his face, which brought out his deep blue eyes.

Beau's mother, a woman almost as tall as Beau's father, had gained some weight since I had seen her last.

Her hair was still that bleached light brown shade and she kept it styled and lacquered. She never let herself get even slightly tanned, coming from that generation of upper-class people who believed a tan made a person look common, like a street worker who was in the sun most of the time. Her best feature was her emerald eyes, which gave her tight, firm face some radiance.

"You're late," his father said, folding his paper and standing.

"Sorry. Hello, Mother," Beau said, and went to kiss her. She turned her face so he could press his lips to her cheek. "Father." He shook his father's hand.

"It was the baby," I said suddenly. "Otherwise, we would have been on time."

"Didn't you say you hired a nanny for her?" his mother asked Beau.

"We did, but . . ."

"She's a spoiled little girl and I had to help calm her down," I said. It was swallowing castor oil, but it was something that one might have expected Gisselle to say.

Beau's father raised his eyebrows. "You did? Well now, maybe the two of you will be thinking of having your own children soon. I'm expecting a grandson."

"If all children are like my sister's, I think I'll check into a nunnery," I said. It was almost as if Gisselle had crawled inside me to make these remarks. Beau formed a smile around his lips and his eyes danced with impish delight.

"Yes, well, I think we should go into the dining room. Our dinner is ready," his father said.

"What exactly happened to this Cajun girl?" Beau's mother asked as we walked to the dining room. Beau explained as much of it as he could.

"And you don't expect she will recover?" his father asked.

Beau shot a glance at me before replying. "It doesn't look promising," he replied.

"Well, what do you intend to do with the child? Why

don't you just send her back to her father?" his mother suggested. "It was bad enough Daphne and Pierre tried to keep a Cajun girl in their home before."

"He's in a pretty bad way emotionally at the moment, Mother."

"Isn't there any Cajun family to look after her? Really, Beau, you and Gisselle will have your own family someday and—"

"For the time being, it's all right. Isn't it, Gisselle?"

"For the time being," I said. Beau's mother seemed to like that.

"Tell us about your European trip," Beau said, and most of the evening was filled with their descriptions of sight-seeing. Before the evening ended, Beau and his father got into a business discussion and his mother asked if I would like to see some of the things she had bought in Europe.

"Okay," I said with little enthusiasm. If they weren't things bought for Gisselle, she wouldn't care about them. I followed his mother to the master suite, where she showed me the elegant new gowns she had bought in Paris, the hats and the shoes. She told me proudly how she had bought things that were only going to come into fashion here in New Orleans this year and then she handed me a present.

"I thought you might like this," she said. "We got it for you in Amsterdam. It's the best place to buy something like that."

I found a diamond tennis bracelet in the box. It was exquisite and I knew quite expensive, but I remembered that Gisselle never really appreciated how expensive these things were and took most everything for granted.

"It's nice," I said, putting it over my wrist.

"Nice?"

"I mean . . . beautiful. Thank you, Mother," I said. Her eyes widened. Apparently Gisselle had never referred to her as Mother. She stared at me curiously. I swallowed hard, my nerve ends twanging.

"Yes, well, I'm glad you approve," she finally said.

"Let's go show Beau," I said, eager not to be alone with her too long. Goose bumps had come and chicken-skinned my arms.

"That's very beautiful!" Beau exclaimed with proper enthusiasm. His father nodded and his mother looked more satisfied.

I felt relieved when the evening finally ended and we left to go home.

"I think I made a faux pas upstairs," I told Beau immediately. "I called your mother 'Mother,' after she gave me the bracelet."

"Yes. Gisselle never called her anything but Madame Andreas or Edith. My mother isn't the type of woman who warms up to other women easily, and Gisselle made no effort to be a real daughter-in-law. But I think you did very well."

"I hardly said a word at dinner."

"Which was the way Gisselle behaved. My father's very old-fashioned. He doesn't mind quiet women, with one exception. . . . He didn't mind Daphne because she was so astute about business. Actually, he was quite taken with her. I think my mother was a little jealous."

I didn't want to say it, but I thought Daphne and Beau's father would have made a good pair.

"Anyway," Beau said. "Another test passed." He squeezed my hand, his eyes happy and shining.

He was right: We were getting away with it. But when we arrived home, we had a message waiting to call Paul.

"He said it was urgent, madame," Aubrey explained.

"Thank you, Aubrey. Let me check on Pearl first, Beau." I ran upstairs and found her fast asleep. Mrs. Ferrier came out of the adjoining room to tell me everything was fine. Then I went down to the office and called Paul while Beau sat on the sofa.

"It's worse than we thought," he said in a voice so low and dejected, I thought I was listening to a stranger. His words were a little distorted, too, suggesting he had been drinking. "My doctor says it's the worse case he's ever encountered. She went into severe epileptic seizures and now she's in a deep coma."

"Oh no, Paul. What does the doctor say now?"

"He told me that if she did live, he's almost certain she would have permanent brain damage and, most likely, persistent epilepsy."

"How horrible. What do you want to do?"

"What is there for me to do? For any of us to do? It's what you and Beau hoped for, isn't it?" he said with an uncharacteristic note of bitterness.

"No," I said in a small voice.

"What do you mean, no? Didn't you tell me how you once went to a Voodoo Mama to get a spell cast on her?" he said. Why did he have to remind me?

"That was a long time ago, Paul, and I regretted it immediately afterward."

"Well, apparently that spell is still working. I'm happy for the two of you," he said.

"Paul . . ."

"I have to go now. I have something to do," he said, and hung up before I could say another word.

"What is it?" Beau asked, seeing me holding the phone and staring. My heart was pounding and I felt as if the blood had drained from my face.

I told him what Paul had said about Gisselle's condition.

"I don't understand. It's not any different than I first described to him."

"He didn't believe it. I know he was hoping he would get her cured and thus bring me back," I said.

"What's he going to do?" Beau asked.

"I don't know. He sounded so strange to me, Beau, not like Paul. I think he'd been drinking."

"He made a commitment to us," Beau said firmly. "I'm going to hold him to it."

He got up quickly to embrace me, and I laid my head on his shoulder. He kissed my hair and stroked it gently as he kissed me again, whispering soothing words into my ear.

"It will be all right. Everything's going fine. It's meant to be," he insisted, but Paul's words had made my blood run cold and drain down to my ankles.

"I can't get rid of this sick feeling in the base of my stomach, Beau. I love you and I want to be with you and I want Pearl to be with you, but it's like a dark cloud hovers above us always, no matter how blue the sky."

"That feeling will pass," he promised. "Just give yourself a chance."

"I think we better go see Paul next week, Beau. We would bring Pearl back to see him anyway, wouldn't we?"

"I suppose," he said, but I saw he didn't like the idea.

Every day for the next few days, I called Paul to see how things were. Most of the time, he was not at home. The servants told me he was at the hospital holding vigil. At first he didn't return any of my calls, and then, when he did, he sounded stranger and stranger. I almost didn't recognize his voice the last time we spoke.

"She remains in a deep coma. There's talk now of putting her on a machine to breathe," he said in a voice that seemed devoid of feeling, the voice of someone who had had all the emotion drained out of him until he was just the shell of his former self.

"Paul, you're wearing yourself down. James told me you're hardly ever home anymore. You spend day and night at the hospital."

"A man should be at his wife's side at times like these, don't you think?" he asked, followed by a chilling little laugh. "He should be at her bedside, holding her hand, talking softly to her, pleading, begging, encouraging her to snap out of the coma, if not for his sake, for the sake of their child. Everyone at the hospital understands. They all feel so sorry for me. The nurse even cried herself today. I saw her wiping the tears away," he said.

For a moment it was as if I were the one who couldn't breathe. I felt my chest turn to stone, my heart freeze within. I tried to swallow and to speak, but I couldn't. I heard him sigh.

"You never understood, did you? Not really, I mean.

You're married, but what's marriage to you? A convenient union serving your own selfish purposes?" he said, his voice coming almost like the hiss of a snake.

"Paul, please . . ."

"You should see how small she's getting, Gisselle. She's wilting like a flower in that bed, her beauty decomposing right before my eyes."

"What? What did you call me?"

"You know what I tell people? I tell them the angels were jealous. They looked down on us and saw how perfect our love was. Even heaven was not as perfect and so they conspired out of envy to cause this tragedy. Too romantic for you, Gisselle? You were never very romantic, were you? What was a man to you . . . a partner in bed, someone to tease and torment. You were jealous of your sister because she had the capacity to love and you didn't, right?

"Oh, what a miserable thing jealousy is. It rots you from inside. You'll see, Gisselle. You'll see. I feel sorry for you and for all the women of the world who don't have the capacity to love as Ruby had."

A numb kind of sensation in my chest made me feel unreal. "Paul, why are you talking like this? Is there someone standing near you? Why are you saying these things?"

"Why? Because . . . because I'm sick to death of the good suffering and the bad enjoying all the pleasure and happiness in this world. That's why. Anyway, thanks for calling. You did your duty. You can ease your conscience and go back to your pursuit of pleasures."

"Paul!"

"I'm tired. I need to get a drink and then try to get a little sleep. Good night, Gisselle. Oh, say hello to your dashing, debonair husband. I'm sure he feels lucky his wife isn't the sick-to-death one."

"Paul!" I cried as the phone went silent. I stood there holding the receiver in my hand as if it were a dead bird. Then I ran to find Beau. He was in the office going over some business documents, and looked up with surprise.

"What's wrong?" he asked immediately.

I told him about Paul and what he had been doing all week.

Beau thought a moment and then shrugged. "Just sounds like he's taken the responsibility of his role in all this seriously and he's putting in a good performance. We should be grateful."

"No, Beau. You don't understand. You don't know Paul. He wouldn't say the things he said to me. He's not well. I want to go to Cypress Woods tomorrow. We have to go, Beau. Don't try to talk me out of it!"

"All right. We'll do it," he said. "Calm down. Are you sure he's not just playing to your feelings, taking advantage of them?"

"I don't think so. You don't know how strange he sounded. Beau," I said, looking up with my eyes wide and full of anxiety. "He called me Gisselle and spoke about her as Ruby."

"So? That was the idea."

"But I don't think anyone was listening in. He had no reason to call me Gisselle."

Beau thought a moment. "Maybe he was just drunk," he said. "Confused."

"It put a chill through me," I said, embracing myself. "What have we done? Beau, what have we done?"

"Stop it," Beau cried, springing up from his seat. He took my shoulders into his hands, his fingers feeling like steel through the thin fabric of my blouse. "Just stop this now, Ruby. You're going to get yourself all worked up for nothing. He's upset that you're with me now and he's not taking that well. He'll get used to it and this will all end as we expected it would. Gisselle's condition isn't our fault. It happened and we just took advantage of the opportunity. Paul agreed to it, helped make it possible. Now he's feeling sorry for himself. Well, I'm sorry about that, but it's too late to turn back, and he's going to have to realize it and get hold of himself. Just as you must," he added sternly.

I pulled back my tears and nodded. "Yes, Beau. I'm sure you're right. I'm sorry I got a little hysterical."

"Hey. You've been doing fantastically. I understand the pressure you've been under and I appreciate it, but you can't lose it now."

I nodded again. "Okay, Beau. I'm all right."

"Sure?"

"Yes."

He kissed me on the forehead and held me to him tightly, kissing my cheeks and stroking my hair. When he looked at me, his soft eyes caressed me.

"I won't let anything happen and I certainly won't ever lose you again, Ruby. I love you more than anything." We kissed and then he put his arm around my shoulders and walked me out. We kissed again at the foot of the stairway. I started up, pausing to look down at him. He gave me a big smile. I took a deep breath and told myself he was right. Tomorrow we would go see Paul and we would calm him down, too.

It's all meant to be, I chanted, as I continued up the stairs. It's all meant to be.

13

Almost Caught

Late the following morning after Beau had returned from the office, we set out for Cypress Woods. I was in deep thought and silent for most of the journey. Beau tried to distract me by discussing some of the Dumas business enterprises, and then just before we arrived, he revealed that Bruce Bristow had been calling and making new threats concerning what he would reveal about Daphne's past shady deals if he didn't receive a better settlement.

"What did you tell him?" I asked.

"I told him to do whatever he wanted, called his bluff. The word on the street is, he's not doing so well. He's been gambling and lost most of what he had managed to get from the estate. Now the bank is threatening to foreclose on his apartment building," Beau said.

"He'll be trouble, Beau, like a pebble in your shoe. You think you shook it out, but after you start walking again, it's still there."

Beau laughed. "Don't worry. I'll shake him out," he replied. "He's not much of a challenge."

I was a little surprised at Beau's arrogance. I feared he had been around Gisselle too long.

The sky had turned completed gray and overcast by the time we pulled into Cypress Woods. The dreary feeling it imposed on me was thickened by the lack of activity around the great house. Where were the gardeners, the grounds staff? Cypress Woods always looked like a bee-hive to anyone, buzzing with bustle and hustle. Paul was so proud of our property, he wouldn't tolerate a weed in the garden. Both Beau and I noticed that some of the oil wells were not being worked as efficiently. The pall that had fallen over the bayou mansion and its spectacular surroundings was as heavy as the humidity and almost as oppressive.

"Looks deserted," Beau mumbled. My heart tripped and then began to pound as we stopped in front of the house. Pearl had fallen asleep in her seat. "I'll get her," Beau said.

The fear I had had about returning to Cypress Woods as Gisselle proved valid. Suddenly I was a stranger in what had been my own precious home. I would have to ring the doorbell and wait, and those who greeted me would greet me as an outsider. My heart would burst with the desire to cry out the truth. Beau sensed my anxiety and, with Pearl asleep on his shoulder, squeezed my hand and smiled reassuringly.

"Take it easy. You'll do just fine," he said, but uneasiness pervaded my entire being.

We walked up to the front door and rang. Moments later, James greeted us.

I could see from the expression on his face, the way his eyes had darkened and the lines had deepened, that he was very distraught and cheerless. Our servants were always so involved with us and so close that our moods affected them.

"Hello, James," I said, unable to effect the conde-scending tone Gisselle usually had when she addressed servants, whether they be her servants or someone else's. James gazed at me with dull, empty eyes. He didn't appear to hear my true self in my voice, having no reason to think I was other than my sister, Gisselle, whom I knew he didn't particularly care for anyway.

"Good afternoon, madame. Monsieur," he said, bowing his head slightly. Then he saw Pearl and his eyes brightened some. "And how is the little one?"

"Fine," I said.

"Is Monsieur Tate at home?" Beau asked.

"He returned from the hospital just a short while ago," James said, stepping back. "Mademoiselle Tate and Madame Pitot are with him in the study," he added. I glanced at Beau. It would be the first time Paul's sisters would see me as Gisselle.

James led us down the corridor. How strange it felt to walk through the house now and look at the things that had been mine. I gazed up the stairway toward what had been my suite. Beau and I exchanged another glance, and I saw he was deeply worried about me now that I was actually in the house. I could feel the flush in my face. My heart was pounding, but I took a deep breath and nodded.

"I'm all right," I whispered.

James paused at the doorway of the study. "Monsieur and Madame Andreas," he announced, and stepped back.

Paul was on the sofa, slouched down in the corner, a glass of bourbon in his hand. His hair was disheveled and he looked like he had slept in his clothes. Jeanne sat across from him, her eyes bloodshot from crying, and Toby sat on the other end of the sofa, looking dour, her hands folded in her lap.

But Jeanne's eyes brightened when she set eyes on us, and for a moment, my heart skipped. Did she know it was me and not my sister? I almost wished she did. However, that wasn't what had lifted the gloom for her. It was the sight of Pearl.

"The baby!" she cried, and got up. "How is she doing?"

"Just fine," Beau said.

Pearl, realizing we had stopped moving, lifted her head and squinted as she tweaked her nose like a rabbit.

"Oh, darling, sweet Pearl," Jeanne cried. "Let me hold her."

Beau handed her to Jeanne, whom Pearl immediately recognized. She smiled and Jeanne flooded her cheeks with kisses, squeezing her lovingly to her.

"Well now," Paul said, "this is an unexpected honor, Monsieur and Madame Andreas in the flesh." His lips moved to twist into a grotesque mockery.

"Anything new, Paul?" I asked quickly, ignoring his sarcasm.

"New?" He looked at Toby, pretending we had asked the simplest nonchalant question. "Anything new, Toby?"

"There's no change for the better," Toby said sadly. "In fact, this morning they decided to put her on a breathing apparatus."

"Care for a drink, Beau?" Paul said, lifting his glass.

"No, none for me, thanks."

"Too early in the day for you Creoles?" he quipped.

"Paul," Jeanne snapped. "Why don't you say hello to your child?"

Paul gazed at Pearl a moment and then nodded.

"Bring her to me," he asked. Jeanne did so. Paul didn't take her from Jeanne, but he reached up and stroked Pearl's hair before kissing her cheek. Then he sat back and sighed so deeply, I thought his heart had shattered in his chest.

"I'll take the baby for a little walk and get her something to eat," Jeanne said quickly.

"Good idea," Toby said. "I'll go speak to Letty and see about getting you something to eat, too."

"Don't trouble anyone," Beau said.

"Trouble anyone?" Paul lifted his eyes and laughed. "Anyone here troubled?"

Toby paused in front of us and smirked. "He's been drinking heavily ever since Ruby was taken to the hospital," she explained. "He's stopped looking after his business and just sits around now wallowing in self-pity. My parents are at their wits' end, especially my mother. She doesn't eat; she doesn't sleep worrying about him. See if you can do anything with him," she whispered. "I'm sorry."

"It's all right," Beau said.

"What's that?" Paul cried. "Did someone say it's all right?"

After Toby left, I crossed the room and stood in front of Paul and folded my arms across my chest to glare down at him sternly.

"What are you trying to prove, Paul? What are you doing to yourself?"

"Nothing. I'm not proving anything." He lifted his arms and shrugged. "Just accepting what Fate has decided will be my destiny. Right from the beginning, I was chasing a dream. Every time I thought I had turned it to reality, Fate came busting in to splatter the dream over the bayou like so much swamp mud." He paused to gaze up at me and his eyes narrowed in the strangest dark way.

"You didn't know her, but Ruby's grandmere Catherine used to say if you swim against the tide, you'll drown," he said. It was as if he had poked a stick in my ribs.

"Stop it, Paul. Stop this overacting. The three of us know the truth. There's no need to pretend like this in front of ourselves."

"Truth? Did you mention the truth? Funny word coming from your lips, or anyone's lips for that matter," he added, and then looked up again. "What is the truth? Is it that love is really a cruel sword we turn on ourselves, exquisite torment? Or is it that only the chosen, the lucky few," he said, gazing up at Beau, "are meant to be happy on this earth? Under what star were you born that you should realize such happiness, Monsieur Beau Andreas?"

"I don't know the answer to that, Paul," Beau said softly. "But I do know that what you promised to Ruby must be kept."

"Oh, I always keep my promises," he said, eyeing me now. "I'm not the sort who doesn't."

"Paul, please . . ."

"It's all right," he muttered. He finished his drink in a gulp. "I have to lie down awhile." He struggled to stand, falling back and then pulling himself up again. "You two make yourselves at home. My sisters will look after you."

I looked at Beau desperately.

"Hey, Paul, listen," Beau said in a reasonable tone of voice, "let us help you with this burden now. We realize you took on too much. Let's move Gisselle to a hospital in New Orleans and—"

"Move her to a hospital in New Orleans just to ease my burden?" He shook his right forefinger in Beau's face. "You're speaking about the woman I love," Paul said, swaying. He smiled. "I pledged to have and to hold, through sickness and through health, until death do us part."

"Paul . . ."

He pushed me aside. "I've got to lie down," he said, and stumbled his way out of the room.

"Let him get some sleep," Beau said. "Later he'll sober up and be more sensible."

I nodded, but a moment later, we heard Paul fall on the stairway. We ran out and found he had rolled down a few steps and was sprawled at the base. James was already at his side, trying to get him up.

"Paul!" I cried.

Beau helped James get him to his feet. They each took an arm around their shoulders and carried him up the stairs, his head bobbing. I sat down on a hall bench and buried my face in my hands.

"He's all right," Beau assured me when he returned. "James and I got him to bed."

"This is horrible, Beau. We should have never let him become such an intricate part of this. I don't know what I was thinking."

"He wanted to do it; it made it all easier. We can't blame ourselves for the way he's acting. He might very well have become this way once you left anyway, Ruby. After a while he'll come to his senses. You'll see."

"I don't know, Beau," I moaned. I was ready to throw up my hands and reveal our elaborate deception.

"We have no other choice now but to see this thing through. Be strong," Beau said firmly. Then he straightened up and smiled at the sight of Jeanne and Pearl approaching.

"She's been calling for her mother. It's so sad, I can't stand it," Jeanne moaned.

"Let me take her," I said.

"You know," Jeanne said as she handed Pearl back to me, "I think she believes you're Ruby. I can't imagine why or how a child would make such a mistake."

Beau and I gazed at each other a moment and then Beau smiled.

"She's just in a state of confusion because of the rapid turn of events, the traveling, the new home," Beau said.

"That's why I was going to suggest you leave her with me. I know what a burden a baby is, but—"

"Oh no," I said sharply. "She's no burden. We have already hired a nanny to help."

"Really?" She grimaced. "Toby said you would."

"Well, why shouldn't we?" Beau said quickly.

"Oh, I didn't mean you shouldn't. I probably would, too, if I . . ."

"Everything's set. We can eat out on the patio, if that's all right with you," Toby said, coming up behind Jeanne.

"Fine," Beau said. "Gisselle?" He looked at me and I sighed. The tension and the emotional weight of seeing Paul this way were the real reason, but Paul's sisters thought I was just being my petulant self as Gisselle. They glanced at each other and tried to hide a smirk.

"It's all right," I said with great effort. "Not that I'm that hungry. Long rides always ruin my appetite," I complained. Ironically, it was a relief to fall back into Gisselle's personality. At least I didn't have the burden of conscience on my heart.

For the first time it occurred to me that this was why

Gisselle had been the way she was; and for the moment, at least, I understood and even envied her for being so self-centered. She never felt sorrow over someone else's pain. To Gisselle, the world had been a great playground, a land of magic and pleasure, and anything that threatened that world was either ignored or avoided. Maybe she wasn't so stupid after all.

Except I remembered something Grandmere Catherine once said. "The loneliest people of all are those who were so selfish, they had no one with them in the autumn of their lives."

I wondered if Gisselle, falling down that dark tunnel of unconsciousness, drifting away, realized that now, if she realized anything anymore.

After lunch we let Pearl take a nap. Beau and I sat outside with Paul's sisters drinking café au lait and listening to them complain about Paul's behavior and how their mother was so beside herself because of it, she wasn't seeing anyone or leaving the house.

"Has she been to the hospital to see Ruby?" I asked, very curious.

"Mother hates hospitals," Toby said. "She had Paul at home because she hated being around sick people, and it was a difficult birth. Daddy had to plead with her into going there for our births."

Beau and I exchanged knowing glances, understanding this was part of the fabrication Paul's parents had created to cover up Paul's real mother's identity.

"Are you two going to the hospital to see Ruby?" Jeanne asked.

I thought how Gisselle would respond to such a question first and then replied, "What for? She's always sleeping, isn't she?"

Toby and Jeanne glanced at each other.

"She's still your sister . . . dying," Jeanne said, and then burst into tears. "I'm sorry. I can't help it. I really loved Ruby."

Toby threw her arms around her, rocking and comforting her and shooting glances of reproach my way.

"Maybe we should go to the hospital, Beau," I said quickly, and rose from my chair. I couldn't sit out there with them any longer and pretend to be insensitive, nor could I stand their sorrow over what they thought was my demise.

Beau followed me into the house. He caught up with me in the study, where I, too, had burst into tears that fell scalding on my cheeks.

"Oh, Beau, we shouldn't have come here. I can't stand all this sorrow. I feel it's my fault."

"That's ridiculous. How can it be your fault? You didn't cause Gisselle to get sick, did you? Well . . . did you?"

I ground my eyes dry and took a deep breath. "Paul reminded me of the time I once went with Nina Jackson to see a Voodoo Mama, who put a spell on Gisselle. Maybe that spell never stopped."

"Now, Ruby, you don't seriously believe—"

"I do, Beau. I always have believed in the spiritual powers some people have. My grandmere Catherine had them. I saw her heal people, comfort them, give them hope, with merely a laying on of her hands."

Beau grimaced skeptically. "So what do you want to do? Do you want to go to the hospital?"

"Yes, I have to go."

"All right, we'll go. Do you want to wait for Pearl to wake up or—"

"No. We'll ask Jeanne and Toby to look after her until we return."

"Fine," Beau said.

"I'll be right down. I've got to get something," I said, and started out.

"What?"

"Something," I said firmly. I hurried upstairs to what had been my suite and slipped in without anyone seeing or hearing me. I went to the dresser and opened the bottom drawer where I had the pouch of five-finger grass

Nina Jackson had once given me to ward off evil and the dime with the string through it to wear around my ankle for good luck.

Then I went to the adjoining door and opened it slightly to peek in on Paul. He was fast asleep in his bed, hugging his pillow to him. Over his headboard, hanging like a religious icon, was my picture in a silver frame. The pathetic sight brought hot tears to my eyes again and made my chest ache with the weight of such sadness, I couldn't breathe. I felt as if I had thrown myself into the pot and it was up to me to keep from being boiled.

I closed the door softly and left the suite. Beau was waiting at the foot of the stairs.

"I've already spoken to Jeanne and Toby," he said. "They'll look in on Pearl until we return."

"Good," I said. Beau didn't ask what I had gone upstairs to get. We drove to the hospital and inquired at the nurses' station for directions to Gisselle's private room. The nurse Paul had hired was sitting in a chair near the bed crocheting. She looked up with surprise, her mouth agape.

"Mr. Tate told me his wife had a twin sister, but I've never seen so identical a set of twins," she said, regaining her composure.

"We're not so identical," I said sternly. Gisselle would have said something like that and would have made her feel uncomfortable. The nurse was happy to excuse herself while we visited. I wanted her out of the room anyway.

As soon as she left, I went to Gisselle's bedside. She had the oxygen tubes in her nose and the IV bag connected to her arm. Her eyes were closed and she looked even smaller and paler than when I had last seen her. Even her hair had grown dull. Her skin had the pallor of the underbelly of dead fish. Beau stood back as I held Gisselle's hand and stared down at her. I don't know what I expected, but there was no sign that she had any awareness whatsoever. Finally, after a sigh, I took out the pouch of five-finger grass and put it under her pillow.

"What's that?" Beau asked.

"Something Nina Jackson once gave me. Inside the bag is a plant with a leaf that is divided into five segments. It brings restful sleep and wards off any evil that five fingers can bring."

"What? You're not serious."

"Each segment has a significance: luck, money, wisdom, power, and love."

"You really believe in this stuff?" he asked.

"Yes," I said. Then I lifted the cover and quickly tied my good-luck dime around Gisselle's ankle.

"What are you doing?"

"This, too, brings good luck and wards off evil," I told him.

"Ruby, what do you think they'll say when they find this stuff?"

"They'll probably think one of my grandmere's friends came around and did it," I said.

"I hope so. Gisselle would certainly never bring anything like this. She made fun of these things," he reminded me.

"Still, I had to do it, Beau."

"All right. Let's not stay too long, Ruby," he said nervously. "We should return to New Orleans before it gets too late."

I held Gisselle's hand for a moment, said a silent prayer, and touched her forehead. I thought her eyelids fluttered, but maybe that was my hope or my imagination.

"Good-bye, Gisselle. I'm sorry we were never real sisters." I felt a tear on my cheek and touched it with the tip of my right forefinger. Then I brought it to her cheek and touched her with the wetness. Maybe now, maybe finally now, she's crying inside for me, too, I thought, and turned quickly to run out of the room and rush away from the sight of my dying sister.

Paul had still not risen when we returned, but Pearl was up and playing with Jeanne and Toby in the study. Her eyes brightened with happiness when she saw it was me. I wanted to rush to her and hold her dearly in my arms, but Gisselle wouldn't have done that, I told myself, and I kept a check on my emotions.

"We've got to get back to New Orleans," I said abruptly.

"What was it like at the hospital?" Toby asked.

"Like talking to yourself," I said. Ironically, that was the truth.

The two sisters nodded with identically melancholy faces.

"You can leave the baby with me," Jeanne suggested. "I don't mind."

"Oh no. We couldn't do that," I said. "I promised my sister I would look after her."

"You? Promised Ruby?"

"At a weak moment," I said, "but I have to keep the promise."

"Why? You're not crazy about children, are you?" Toby asked disdainfully.

I looked at Beau for help.

"We've already hired a nanny," he said. "Everything's arranged and in place."

"An aunt is better suited to look after her than a nanny, isn't she?" Jeanne retorted.

"What do you think I am, chopped onions?" I snapped. When it came to holding on to Pearl, I could be as firm and as stinging as my sister.

"Well, I just meant . . . it's no problem for me."

"And it's no problem for me," I retorted. "Pearl." I held out my arms and she ran to me. "Tell Paul we'll call him later," I said.

I hurried out with Pearl in my arms and Beau at my side before there could be any further discussion. My face was flushed, my eyes wide with near hysteria.

"Take it easy," Beau said when we were all in the car. "You did fine. Everything's all right."

I didn't calm down until we were well on our way. The rain that had hovered in the clouds all day kept its promise and fell in a constant downpour during the whole trip back to New Orleans. The sky over the city was ripped with seams of lightning and the thunder rolled so loud and hard, it shook us even in the car. I was happy when we finally arrived at the house. Aubrey greeted us with a list of phone calls and we saw that Bruce Bristow had called frequently.

"I see I'm going to have to get tough with him to get him off our backs," Beau said, and crumpled the messages in his fist angrily. At the moment I couldn't care less about those problems. Pearl was too groggy from the ride to eat anything, and I was emotionally exhausted. I put her to bed and then took a hot bath and crawled into bed myself. Hours later, I heard Beau come up, but I barely acknowledged him when he crawled into bed beside me, and minutes later, he was asleep, too.

I was filled with nervous tension and great anxiety during the next few days. For me the hours were like days and the days like months. I would stop myself and gaze at the clock, shocked that only minutes had ticked by. Every time the phone rang, I jumped and my heart skipped beats and pounded, but it was usually one or another of Gisselle's friends calling. I was short with all of them, and soon most of them stopped bothering to call. One afternoon Pauline phoned to tell me I was losing all my friends, driving them away one by one.

"Everyone says you've become more stuck-up than ever," she informed me. "They say you think you're too good to speak to them on the phone and you haven't invited anyone to the house."

"I have more important things to worry about right now," I snapped.

"Don't you care if you lose all your friends?"

"They weren't really my friends anyway. All they care about is what they can get from me," I told her.

"Does that include me?" she asked petulantly.

"If the shoe fits, wear it," I said.

"Good-bye, Gisselle. I hope you're happy in your own world," she said with disgust.

In weeks I had driven away most of Gisselle's friends,

people I never liked anyway, and I had done it in character so no one thought anything unusual about it. Beau was amused and happy. It was practically the only bright spot in the gloomy days that followed our visit to Cypress Woods.

Whenever I called, either Toby or Jeanne came to the phone. Paul was always unavailable. They were very short with me, too. Gisselle's condition remained unchanged. Toby, who could be more caustic than Jeanne, said, "It's only a matter of time. I hope your sister's death doesn't interfere with anything you've scheduled. I know how important your social calendar is to you."

I thought to myself that Gisselle deserved such reprimands, and kept my lips sealed, but it hurt nevertheless. At the end of the last call, she said, "I don't know why my brother doesn't insist you bring Pearl home, where she belongs, but I think you should."

How could I tell her that Paul couldn't ask me to bring home the child who wasn't his?

"Worry about yourself, Toby. It seems to me you have enough there to occupy you," I snapped, and ended the conversation. I felt absolutely dreadful about it, and when I told Beau he nodded sadly.

"It's the way things have to be for now," he offered, but that wasn't enough.

"Sometimes I feel like I've put myself into a spider's web, Beau. The more I twist and struggle, the more I entrap myself."

"It will come to an end soon and we'll go on with our lives. You'll see," he assured me; however, I didn't have his confidence. Life had clearly shown me that it could take twists and turns when we least expected it.

Two days later one of those twists occurred. I had been doing well in my role as my sister mainly because I had driven away her friends and her boyfriends and stayed away from her usual haunts. Few, if any, were astute enough to see the differences. None expected such a switch of identities, of course. In their hearts they probably thought, who would want to be Gisselle?

My hope was that after a time, I would transform my sister's personality until it resembled my own, and Beau and I would even move to another location, perhaps another city, and start our lives over with far less deceit.

I was in my studio just dabbling with a picture when Aubrey knocked on my door to tell me I had a visitor. Before I could ask who it was, Bruce Bristow appeared behind him. My stepmother's husband looked like he had aged decades since I had last set eyes on him. His dark brown hair was flecked with gray, the temples all gray, and their were dark sacks under his eyes. He had lost considerable weight, too, his face gaunt, those flirtatious eyes now dim orbs. He slouched a bit and wore a creased jacket and slacks, the tie stained and his shirt open at the frayed collar. There was a scuff mark of some sort on his left cheekbone. He smiled coyly and entered. The moment he did, the stench of gin invaded the air.

"What are you doin' in here, tryin' to be your sista?" He laughed. Now that he was closer, I saw how bloodshot his eyes were and understood why he was slurring his words.

"You're drunk, Bruce. Get out of here, this instant," I ordered.

"Not sooo fass," he said. He closed and opened his eyes, swaying for a moment. "You and your hushbun might think you're smoothies, but you better hear me out before you make a decision you'll regret."

"Getting you out of our lives can't be a decision I'd ever regret," I said, and because I meant it, I was able to be as vicious about it as Gisselle would have been.

He snapped his head back, but he smiled again. "Sooo, what are you doin' in here?" He gazed at the canvas. "You can't draw or paint. You're the sista without talent, remember?" He laughed sharply and steadied himself by taking hold of the back of a chair.

"I remember how much I despised you," I said. "You were like a leech, swimming in here when my father died and attaching yourself to the family to suck whatever you could out of it. But that's all over now, and nothing you say, no matter how outrageous it might seem, will get you back. Now, go before Beau returns."

His smile widened and some drool leaked out of the corners of his mouth. "You weren't always so eager to send me away," he said, moving closer. I stepped to the side, the paintbrush still in my hand. I was holding it like a sword between us. He stared at me a moment, his eyes opening and closing with his attempts to focus sharply. And then he looked at the canvas again.

"You don't sheem too upset 'bout your sista bein' in a bad way," he said.

"Why should I? Would she be upset if it was me in the hospital?"

"You know she would," he replied softly, and closed his eyes for a moment. Then he snapped them open as if a thought had just made its way into his clogged brain. "Ya don't sound like yourself either." He looked at the canvas again. "Thass too good for you ta have done. Was it here before?"

"Yes."

"I thawt show. I mean, I thought so." He smiled again and then he grew as serious as he could, trying to straighten his tie as he corrected his posture. "I want you ta help me convince Beau he should be a little more reasonable about this family fortune. I know some of the shady tax schemes Daphne did and I'm willing ta go to the government and expose them," he threatened.

"So go. You didn't have your hands clean either, did you? You'd only be exposing yourself for what you were and what you probably still are."

He smiled with confidence and more sobriety. "Yeah, but you know how it is when someone turns state's evidence. He gets leniency. I can see to it that this estate gets some terrific fines. How would you and your high-society husband do then, huh?"

"We'll be all right. Get out, Bruce, before I have Aubrey call the police."

He raked his eyes over me scornfully. "What if I told your husband about the time I came to see you while you were taking your bubble bath? Remember how I washed your back and gave you that massage and then—"

"I've already told him," I blurted.

He stared at me a moment. "I don't believe you."

"So don't. I don't care. Just get out."

My determination and lack of fear annoyed and confused him. "I took some papers out of here. I'm warning you two. I can prove my accusations."

"Then go prove them."

"You're crazy. Both of you are crazy." He stared at me a moment longer and then looked at the canvas again. One of his eyebrows jerked up quizzically. My resistance had sobered him quickly and gotten him thinking.

"That's not an old picture. The paint's still wet. How did you do that? You can't do that." His eyes narrowed into slits that reminded me of snake's eyes. "Something's not right here." His words had the impact of bullets.

"Get out!" I screamed. "Get out!"

His eyes brightened with a possibility. "La Ruby," he said. "You're La Ruby. What's going on?"

"Get out!" I charged at him and he put his arms up. Just then, Beau appeared in the doorway. He lunged into the room and seized Bruce by the back of the neck and turned him roughly toward the door.

"What are you doing in our house! I told you not to come here, didn't I?" He pushed him toward the door. Bruce regained his balance and looked back at us. His face was magenta with rage.

"What are you two up to, huh? This isn't Gisselle. I know Gisselle. She has a harder look in her eyes."

"You're ridiculous," Beau said, but not with enough confidence. Bruce was buoyed. He smiled.

"This is some sort of scam to get you two more money or something, isn't it? I'll tell everyone."

"Go ahead," Beau said. "Everyone will believe the words of a drunken, pathetic gambler. The whole city's talking about you and the way you've degenerated. You have as much credibility as a convicted serial killer."

Bruce nodded. "All right. I'll get proof, that's what I'll

do. Unless you two get sensible and cut me in on what is rightly mine anyway. I'll call you in a couple of days and see if you want to be smart or greedy," he said.

"Get out of here before I break your neck," Beau said, moving toward him. Bruce backed away and started down the corridor. Beau followed him all the way to the front entrance, opening it and pushing him out. Bruce voiced one final threat before the doors closed.

"The whole city is going to know what you're up to!" he cried, shaking his fist.

Beau slammed the door in his face. "It's all right, Aubrey," he said. "Everything is under control."

"Very good, sir." Aubrey retreated and Beau followed me into the living room.

"Don't worry yourself about him," he told me after I sat. My heart was pounding and I felt the blood rushing into my face. "I mean it, no one will give one word he says any credibility. You should hear some of the things they're saying about him now."

"How could Daphne had brought such a person into her life after being married to my father?" I wondered aloud.

"You said yourself she used people and then discarded them like so much baggage," Beau replied. He came to my side and sat beside me to take my hand. "You can't let him get to you, Ruby."

"But how did he know? Of all the people to look at me and know . . . a drunken man?" I looked at Beau and answered my own question. "He was intimate with Gisselle. She toyed with him, I'm sure."

"Probably," Beau said.

"He was always flirting with me, coming right up to me and taking my hands and looking into my eyes. I hated it; he always had some onions or something on his breath and I had to be polite but firm. And it was my painting . . . I shouldn't have let him see my painting. That, more than anything, gave it away."

"What difference does it make what he knows and doesn't know, what he did and didn't do? He's a man who's lost respect, and in this town, when you have no respect, you don't have a voice. Believe me, I'll be able to handle him," Beau promised.

"It's no good, Beau," I said, shaking my head. "If a shack's built on weak legs, the first bad flood will wash it away. We're trying to build a new life with a foundation of lies. It's going to come back and haunt us."

"Only if we let it," he insisted. He put his arm around me. "Come on, take a rest. Later you'll feel better. We'll go out to one of the finer restaurants and have a spectacular dinner, okay?"

"I don't know, Beau," I said with a deep sigh.

"Well, I do. The doctor's prescribing," he said, sighing, and helped me to my feet.

Above the marble fireplace, Daphne's portrait still hung, the beautiful ivory face peering down at me with an expression of arrogance and self-satisfaction. My father worshiped that beauty and loved having replicas of her everywhere in the mansion.

Remember, child, the devil in all his forms fascinates us, Grandmere Catherine had warned. *We're drawn to him like a child is drawn to the wonder of a candle flame and is tempted to put the tip of his finger into the light, only to get burned.*

How I hoped and prayed Beau and I had not put our fingers into the candle's flame.

14

Shadows from the Past

Beau was apparently right about what would happen in regards to Bruce and anything he might do or say. Bruce had lost all his credibility in the business world, and the bank did foreclose on his one major means of making money, his apartment building. Somehow he continued to find money for his drinking, but anything he did tell anyone was considered a pathetic attempt at getting back at the Dumas family. Those who knew him when he was married to Daphne remembered how disdainfully she had treated him. They referred to him as just another ornament on her arm, another piece of jewelry.

Finally, one day Beau called to tell me he had heard that Bruce had moved to Baton Rouge, where he had gotten a job through one of his few friends as the manager of a small hotel.

"So we're rid of him," Beau said, but somehow I thought Bruce Bristow was like a swarm of swamp mosquitoes: One day they were gone, but you knew they would return to pester you again someday.

Meanwhile, the situation at Cypress Woods remained

at status quo. Gisselle lingered in her comatose state; Paul had his good days when he did some work and was sensible, but according to Toby and Jeanne, he still spent most of his time wallowing in self-pity. Jeanne told me he even visited Grandmere Catherine's old shack.

"The shack! Why would he go there?" I asked, feeling myself slide into the abyss of yesterdays.

"It's become something of a shrine to him," she said in her small, sad voice one afternoon on the telephone.

"What do you mean?"

"He doesn't care if the gardens and the landscaping are looked after here at Cypress Woods, but he brings some of his men down to the shack and has them cut the grass, plant new grass, and even repair the shack." She paused. "He has even spent evenings there."

"Evenings?" I felt my ever-present anxiety slip into a knot.

"Slept there," she revealed.

My heart stopped beating and then pounded. "Slept at the shack?"

Jeanne mistook the shock in my voice for disgust. "I know how revolting that must sound to you, Gisselle. He doesn't admit to it. It's almost as if he really does forget the things he does," she continued, "but my husband and I drove down there one night and we saw the dim light of a single oil lamp. We spied on him," she admitted.

"What do you see?"

"He was curled up on the floor at the foot of that old settee, sleeping like a baby. We didn't have the heart to wake him. It's so sad."

I didn't speak. I couldn't speak. My own tears were falling inside me. I crumpled like a rag in the chair. Paul's pain was far more intense than I ever imagined it might be. He wasn't, as Beau expected, coming to terms with the way things were and would be. He was falling back in time, clinging to happier memories, destroying himself with his return to the past.

"I know you don't care, but he's getting worse and worse, and if he doesn't get hold of himself soon, how

will he ever be able to be a father to his child again?"
Jeanne said, because she thought that was the one thing
that would disturb and worry Gisselle.

"He'll get hold of himself. One day he'll just wake up
and realize that what has to be done, has to be done," I
said in as cold a voice as I could muster, but it was a voice
without any confidence in what it was saying, and Jeanne
heard it.

"Sure. I believe that as much as you do." After a pause
she asked, "Do you intend to visit your sister again?"

"It upsets me too much," I said. Gisselle would say
that, although it would upset me, I thought. It was just
that as Ruby, I wouldn't be thinking of myself as much
and I would go.

"It doesn't exactly make the rest of us ecstatic, but we
go," Jeanne said dryly.

"It's easier for you. You don't have to make the trip to
the bayou," I complained.

"Right, that enormous trip. How is the baby?"

"She's doing fine."

"Doesn't she ask for her father and mother all the
time? You don't even talk about her."

"She's all right," I insisted. "Just do what you can for
your brother."

"I think if he had Pearl here with him, he would do
better," she said. "Toby thinks so, too."

"We have to think about what's best for the baby," I
insisted, perhaps too strongly for Gisselle.

"Being with her father is best," Jeanne replied. A
flutter of panic crossed my stomach and sent a chill up to
my heart. Then Jeanne added, "But Mother seems to
agree with you for the time being, and Paul . . . Paul
won't discuss it."

"Then leave it alone," I warned.

"Who'd have thought you of all people would want an
infant roaming about her house, as big as it is," Jeanne
said.

"Maybe you don't know me as well as you think you
do, Jeanne."

259

"Maybe I don't." She sighed. "Maybe some of your sister's goodness is in you after all. I know I'm just sick to my stomach over all this. It's so unfair. They were the most perfect couple in the world, the two people who were living the fantasy romance all of us wish to live."

"Maybe it was a fantasy," I said softly.

"You would say that."

"This conversation isn't going anywhere important," I snapped in my best Gisselle tone of voice. "I'll call you tomorrow."

"Why do you call so much? Is Beau making you do it?"

"There's no reason to be insolent, Jeanne."

She was quiet a moment. "Sorry," she said. "You're right. I'm just overwrought myself these days. I'll talk to you tomorrow."

Now that my conversations with Jeanne were a strain, it was becoming harder and harder to keep in contact with Cypress Woods and learn what was happening there. Beau's advice was to let things go for a while.

"It's more in Gisselle's character anyway, Ruby. None of them are in the mood to be particularly nice to you as it is."

I nodded, but not calling to see how Paul was and what, if anything, was new about Gisselle was very difficult. I didn't have all that much to distract me now that we had servants looking after the house.

Ever since my confrontation with Bruce in the studio, I was hesitant about returning and starting a painting. Keeping my talent a secret stifled the creative impulse, but I didn't want to hover around Mrs. Ferrier all day and give her the impression I didn't trust her with Pearl. So I would spend hours sitting in the studio, staring at an empty canvas, waiting for the inspiration that appeared to be clouded by my darker thoughts.

One morning after breakfast, just before I was preparing to go into the studio, the doorbell rang and Aubrey came to tell me I had a gentleman visitor.

"A Monsieur Turnbull," he said, handing me the man's card. For a few seconds the name didn't register.

Then I looked at the card and saw it read "Louis Turnbull."

"Louis," I said aloud, a wave of ecstatic joy coming over me. It was Louis, Mrs. Clairborne's grandson, the blind young man I had met and become friends with at the Greenwood School for girls, the private school in Baton Rouge to which Daphne had sent Gisselle and me.

The school's chief benefactor was a widow, Mrs. Clairborne, who lived in a mansion on the school grounds with her grandson Louis. Louis, a man in his twenties, had become blind when he was still a young boy after he had suffered the traumatic experience of seeing his father kill his mother, smother her to death with a pillow. His blindness lingered and handicapped him even after dozens and dozens of sessions with a psychiatrist.

However, he was a talented pianist and composer who put all of his feelings into his music. I met him accidentally when I had attended a tea at the mansion with the other new students from our dormitory. Drawn by the sound of his music, I wandered into the study, and Louis and I became close friends. Louis claimed my friendship helped him start to regain his sight. He came to my rescue when I was nearly expelled from Greenwood because of something Gisselle had done. His testimony provided an alibi for me and ended the incident.

Louis had gone to Europe to get further treatment for his condition and study at the musical conservatory. We had lost contact, and now, seemingly out of the blue, here he was on my doorstep.

"Show him in," I told Aubrey, and waited anxiously for our meeting when suddenly it occurred to me: I couldn't greet him as Ruby. I was Gisselle! It stopped me cold in my tracks.

Aubrey brought him to the study. Louis had grown a bit heavier since I had last seen him, but his face had matured, his cheeks and chin somewhat leaner. He wore his dark brown hair longer and swept back on the sides. He was still quite a handsome man with a strong, sensuous mouth and a perfectly straight Roman nose. The only real change was, he wore a pair of glasses with the thickest lenses I'd ever seen.

"Thank you for seeing me, Madame Andreas," he said. I approached him and gave him my hand in greeting. "I don't know if you remember me or not. I was very friendly with your sister, Ruby," he said, and I realized he had heard the news and thought I was Gisselle.

"Yes, I know. Please, have a seat, Mr. Turnbull."

"Just call me Louis," he said, and went to the settee across from my chair. I sat and gazed at him for a moment, wondering if I could just blurt out the truth. I felt my stomach churn with frustration. It was as if hundreds of soap bubbles were popping inside.

"I have just returned from Europe," he explained, "where I studied music and performed."

"Performed?"

"Yes, in some of the finest concert halls," he said. "As soon as I arrived in New Orleans, I made some inquiries and was told the dreadful story about your sister. The fact is, I'm going to perform here in New Orleans this coming Saturday at the Theater of the Performing Arts in Louis Armstrong Park on St. Ann Street. I had been hoping your sister would be in the audience." He paused.

"I'm sorry," I said. "I know how much she would have wanted to be there."

"Do you?" He studied me a moment and then added, "I brought along a couple of tickets for you and Monsieur Andreas, should you wish to attend." He took them out and laid them on the table.

"Thank you."

"Now," he said, his face turning glum, "please be so kind as to tell me about your sister. What dreadful thing has happened?"

"She was infected with a virus that causes a severe form of encephalitis," I said. "She is in a hospital in a coma, and I'm afraid the outlook is bleak."

He nodded. I had confirmed what he knew and feared.

"I see your eyesight has been completely restored. My sister told me about you," I added quickly.

"My vision is now as good as it would have been had I suffered no problems, but as you can tell from these glasses, I wasn't born to have the best eyesight anyway. As long as I can see the pages and write my notes, I'm fine," he added, and smiled. "That's what I'm doing here Saturday night, you know, playing original compositions. I think you might be very interested in one. I wrote it for your sister. It's Ruby's Symphony."

"Yes," I said. A lump came to choke my throat and a tiny tear trickled from my right eye and then one from my left. I wondered if his eyes permitted him to see something as small. He fixed his gaze on me for a moment without speaking.

"Pardon, madame, I mean no disrespect, but Monsieur Andreas," he said, "was he not your sister's boyfriend?"

"Once," I said softly.

"I knew she was quite in love with him. You see, I was in love with her and she made sure to let me know her heart already belonged to another and nothing I could do or say would ever change that. Such a strong love is rare, I thought, but I understand she married someone else?"

"Yes." My eyes skipped guiltily away. Like a raging river against a dam, my story longed to gush forward.

"And had a child, a daughter?" he continued.

"Yes. Her name is Pearl. She is living here with me now."

"Ruby's husband is quite distraught, I imagine."

I nodded. "How is your grandmother, Madame Clairborne?" I asked.

"My grandmother passed away three months ago."

"Oh, I'm sorry."

"Yes. She suffered more than anyone knew. Her life, despite her wealth, was not a happy life. But she lived to see me regain my sight and play in great concert halls."

"That must have made her very happy. And your

cousin, the Iron Lady who ran Greenwood? Is she still lording it over all the young women?"

He smiled. "No. My cousin retired shortly after my grandmother's passing and was replaced by a much gentler and kinder woman, Mrs. Waverly." He smiled. "Your family doesn't have to be afraid of sending Pearl there someday."

"That's good," I said.

He took out a pen and a pad. "Perhaps you would be so kind as to give me the name and address of the hospital where your sister is being treated. I would like to send some flowers."

I told him and he jotted it down.

"Well, I don't want to take up any more of your time. This is a trying period for you and your family." He stood up and I rose slowly. He picked up the tickets and brought them to me, placing them in my hands. "I hope you and your husband will be able to attend the concert," he said. He held on to my fingers and fixed his dark brown eyes on mine with such intensity, I had to look down. When I looked up again, he was smiling. "You will recognize the piece, I'm sure," he whispered.

"Louis . . ."

"I ask no questions, madame. I hope only that you will be in the audience."

"I will."

"Very good then."

I walked him to the front door, where Aubrey gave him his hat. Then Louis turned to me.

"I want you to know that your sister was a major influence on my life. She touched me deeply and restored my desire not only to live, but to continue my music. Her sweet, innocent nature, her pure outlook on things, restored my own faith in life and has given me the inspiration to write what I hope people will consider significant music. You should be very proud of her."

"I am," I said.

"We'll all pray for her, then."

"Yes, we'll all pray," I said. The tears were trickling

down my cheeks, but I made no attempt to wipe them away. "God bless you," I whispered, and Louis nodded and left. My heart sunk in my chest like a rock in the swamp canal. I finally wiped away my tears.

One lie spawns another, Grandmere Catherine used to say. *And then the lies feed upon each other like snakes feasting on their young.*

How many more lies would I have to tell? How much deeper did my deceptions have to go before I could live in peace with the man I loved? Louis knew the truth, discerned who I was. It made perfect sense. He had known me mostly through my voice, my touch. He had gone beneath the surface because the surface was dark to him, so he recognized me instantly. And yet he understood there were reasons for the switch of identities and he didn't challenge or do anything to jeopardize the intricate illusion Beau and I had conceived and performed. Louis cared for me too much to ask embarrassing questions.

When Beau returned home that day, I told him about Louis's visit.

"I remember him, remember you talking about him all the time. Do you think he'll keep what he knows to himself?"

"Oh yes, Beau. Absolutely."

"Perhaps we shouldn't attend that concert," Beau suggested.

"I must go. He expects me to and I want to go." I spoke so firmly that Beau raised his eyebrows. He thought a moment.

"It's not the sort of thing Gisselle would attend," he warned.

"I'm tired of doing only the things Gisselle would do; tired of thinking only the thoughts she would think and saying only the things she would say. I feel like a prisoner trapped in my sister's identity!" I cried.

"All right, Ruby."

"I keep myself locked up in this house most of the time out of fear that I might go out and say the wrong thing or do the wrong thing without you at my side," I continued, my voice shrill.

"I understand."

"No, you don't. It's torture," I insisted.

"We'll go to the concert. If anyone asks, you're doing it for me, that's all," he concluded.

"Sure. I'm the stupid, crass, and insensitive one, a lump of . . . upper-class, spoiled flesh and bones," I moaned. Beau laughed. "Well?"

"You're right. You've just described what Gisselle was."

"Then how did you convince yourself to marry her?" I demanded, far more sharply than I had intended.

I saw him wince. "I explained all that to you once, Ruby. The reasons haven't changed. I love you; I've loved only you," he said, and lowered his head before he turned to walk away.

I stood there feeling absolutely dreadful. It seemed there was no one I wouldn't hurt in this state of mind. Everyone I loved was in emotional pain as well as myself. My mind did flip-flops. How did I get all of us into this twisted and painful situation? I was drowning, drowning in that old familiar pool of hopeless despair.

Of course, I realized it wasn't entirely my fault. Beau shouldn't have deserted me and driven me to the point where I believed there was no hope for myself and my baby if I didn't marry Paul, and Paul shouldn't have pleaded and persuaded and worn me down with his temptations of a rich comfortable life. Most of all, Gisselle shouldn't have taken advantage and married Beau just to hurt me. I had already learned she didn't really love him; she had been unfaithful to him, who knew how many times? We're all guilty of something that brought us to this point, I thought, but that didn't make me feel better nor diminish my own sense of blame.

Still, what good did it do to bite at each other now? What good did it do to add to the turmoil that already existed and may never end? I thought. I went after him and found him standing in the study, gazing out the window.

"I'm sorry, Beau," I said. "I didn't mean to explode like that."

He turned slowly and smiled. "It's all right. You have a right to explode now and again. You are under a great deal of pressure. It's much easier for me. I just have to be myself and I can occupy myself with the business. I should be more understanding and more sensitive to your needs. I'm sorry."

"Let's not argue about it, then," I said.

He came to me and took my shoulders into his hands. "I can't imagine ever getting angry at you, Ruby. If I do, I will hate myself more for it afterward. I promise you that," he said, and then we kissed and held each other and walked out to the patio together to see how Pearl was doing with Mrs. Ferrier.

I decided that nothing Gisselle had in her wardrobe was right for Louis's concert, and so I went out and purchased an elegant ankle-length black velvet gown. When Beau saw me in it, he was quiet for a long moment. Then he shook his head.

"What?" I demanded.

"Only the most insensitive clod wouldn't see the difference between you and your sister and realize who you really are," he said.

"That's because you know me so well, Beau. On the surface Gisselle wouldn't look all that different from me if she wore something like this, too. She was just not interested in looking like a mature woman. She thought that wasn't sexy."

"Perhaps you're right," he said. "In any case, she was wrong if she thought sophisticated wasn't sexy. You take my breath away." He thought a moment and then nodded. "I think tonight you should wear one of Daphne's diamond necklaces. Gisselle would," he added pointedly.

I sighed, looked at myself in the mirror, and agreed I could use something to dress my neck.

"Besides," Beau continued, chasing away my hesitation, "why hold it against the jewelry? The diamonds couldn't choose who would be their owner, could they?"

I laughed and went to Daphne's jewel box.

"I'm sure they never looked as good on her," Beau said, beaming, after I put on the necklace I recalled my father had bought her.

"No, they did, Beau. As bad as she was and as cruel as she could be to us, she was still a beautiful woman, an enchantress who captured my father's heart and love and then twisted and tormented him because of it."

"And his brother, too," Beau reminded me.

"Yes, and his brother, too," I said, thinking about poor Uncle Jean.

It was good to crawl out from under my dark, heavy thoughts and get out for an elegant evening. The richest and most renowned people in New Orleans were attending Louis's concert. It filled my heart with joy to see his name in lights and his picture on the billboards. We followed the parade of expensive automobiles and limousines to the front of the theater, where drivers and doormen leapt to open the doors for women in designer gowns and men in tuxedos. When we stepped out into the lights, I felt as if all eyes were on me, watching my every move, listening to my every word. Recalling what Beau had said about Gisselle's attending such an affair, I tried to appear unhappy and uncomfortable. The uncomfortable part wasn't hard because I was so nervous.

Those who approached us to talk all asked about Ruby's condition. "Unchanged," was Beau's stock response. They looked sympathetic for a moment and then went on quickly to discuss other things. Most of the people who attended held season tickets and followed all the concerts. I was surprised at how many knew about Louis, how he had composed music while he was blind and then, as he regained his vision, began performing throughout Europe.

Since none of Gisselle's friends would attend such a concert, I had no problem dealing with their surprise at seeing me dressed this way. Nevertheless, I was happy when we finally were seated and the audience grew quiet. The conductor walked out to the sound of applause and then Louis entered to an even greater ovation. He took his seat at the piano, the hall grew absolutely still, and the music began.

As Louis played concerto after concerto, I closed my eyes and recalled those nights at his grandmother's mansion. Memories flooded back. I saw him sitting at his piano, his eyes shut in darkness, but his fingers bringing him light and putting a glow in his face. I remembered the way we would sit together on the stool as he played, and I remembered his touching me and kissing me. Then I recalled his great outburst of tears and emotion in his room when he finally told me the dreadful story of his parents, his mother's obsession with him and his father's anger.

Like the rainbow after the storm, Louis had risen out of this turmoil and pain to become a world-class pianist. It filled my heart with not only warmth and joy, but hope for Beau, Pearl, and myself. Our storm would end soon, too, I thought, and we would have a quiet, sweet aftermath.

Finally, before the concert ended, Louis got up and addressed the audience. "This last piece, as your program explains, is entitled Ruby's Symphony. It's a piece inspired by a wonderful young lady who came into my life briefly and helped me to find hope and self-confidence again. You might say she showed me the light at the end of the tunnel. So it is with particular pleasure that I play this for you tonight," he said. Only a few people in the audience suspected it was actually me, Ruby Dumas, for whom the music had been written and to whom it had been dedicated.

Beau held my hand but said nothing. I tried not to cry, for fear people would notice, but holding back these tears was a feat beyond Samson. My cheeks were soaked by the time the music ended; however, the audience had been enraptured and everyone rose to his feet to applaud. Beau and I did, too. Louis took his bows and left the stage in glorious success.

"I just have to go backstage to see and congratulate him, Beau," I said.

"Of course," he said.

Louis's dressing room was packed with people complimenting him. Champagne bottles were popping open all over the place. I thought we wouldn't get within five feet of him, but he spotted me in the back of the crowd and beckoned us forward, asking people to step aside. Naturally all eyes were on us, people wondering, who were these special guests?

"It was wonderful, Louis," I said. "I'm so glad we were able to attend."

"Yes, spectacular," Beau added.

"Thank you. I'm so happy I could bring a little joy into your lives at this particularly trying time, Madame Andreas." He kissed my hand.

"I wish Gisselle's sister could have been here herself," Beau said quickly, and loudly enough for everyone in the room to hear. My heart paused in the silence that followed. Louis's smile widened.

"Yes, don't we all?" he said. "But of course, in a real sense, she was," he added with a soft smile. We gazed at each other for a moment and then another champagne bottle was popped and Louis's attention was drawn away long enough for Beau and me to effect a graceful retreat.

My heart felt like a twisted ball of Spanish moss in my chest. Even with the car window wide open and my face practically in the breeze, I couldn't get enough air.

"I'm happy you talked me into going to that concert," Beau said. "He really was spectacular. I'm not just saying it. When he played, the music had a life of its own and melodies I had heard before suddenly became as beautiful as I imagine they were meant to be."

"Yes, he has an extraordinary talent."

"You should be proud you helped him regain his purpose in life," Beau said.

"I don't know how much I really had to do with it."

"One look in his eyes told me you had all to do with it," Beau said. "But I'm not jealous," he added quickly with a smile. "You passed through his life like some angel of mercy, touched him and went on. But you are my life."

He drew me to his side and kissed me quickly. I snuggled against him and felt truly safe and happy for the first time since our arrival in New Orleans as man and wife. That night we made love gently, gracefully, sweetly, and fell asleep in each other's arms. Both of us slept longer than usual. Not even the sunlight streaming in through the windows woke us, and Beau had disconnected our telephone at the bed so we wouldn't be disturbed.

I was the first to hear Aubrey's footsteps and gentle knock. At first I thought I was dreaming. Then I opened my eyes and listened again. Beau groaned when I stirred.

"Just a moment," I called, and got up to put on my robe. Beau turned over in bed and closed his eyes again.

"I'm sorry to disturb you, madame, but Madame Pitot is on the phone and she is rather distraught. She insisted I bring you to the phone immediately."

"Thank you, Aubrey," I said. I went to the night table and plugged in our telephone, my hands already shaking badly in anticipation of bad news.

"What is it?" Beau asked, wiping his eyes with the palms of his hands.

"It's Jeanne," I said, and lifted the receiver. "Hello, Jeanne."

"She's dead," she said in a voice that sounded like it belonged to a corpse itself. "She died early this morning. Paul was there, holding her hand."

"What?"

"Ruby's gone. They told me to call you. No one else wanted to do it. I'm sorry if I woke you up. You can go back to sleep," she added.

271

"Jeanne, when? How?"

"What do you mean, when, how? It wasn't exactly unexpected, was it? But you have a way of avoiding unpleasant things, ignoring them, don't you, Gisselle? Well, the Grim Reaper doesn't tolerate being ignored, even by rich, high-society Creoles from New Orleans."

"How's Paul?" I asked quickly, ignoring her bitter sarcasm.

"He won't leave her side. He's following the body every step of the way, even to the undertaker's parlor. He won't listen to my parents. He's uttered only one sensible sentence, and to me because he knew I was calling you."

"What was that?"

"He told me to tell you not to bring the baby to the funeral. He doesn't want her seeing any of it. That is, if you attend the funeral."

"Of course we'll be at the funeral," I said. "She was my sister."

"Yes, she was your sister," Jeanne said dryly. "I'm sorry. I can't talk anymore. You can call later and ask James for the details about the funeral."

After I cradled the phone, I sat back on the bed. I felt as if all my blood had drained down to my feet. I chocked back a sob.

Beau knew but asked anyway. "What happened?"

"She died this morning."

He shook his head and released a deep sigh. I felt his hand on my shoulder. We both sat silently for a moment, digesting the reality of what had happened.

"At least it's over," he said. "Finally."

I turned to him. "Oh, Beau, it's so strange."

"What?"

"Their thinking it's me who died. I couldn't bear the sadness and the anger in Jeanne's voice."

"Yes, but this seals it forever. You and I, just as I told you, as I promised. We've defeated Fate."

I shook my head. These were words that should be making me happy, but all they did was fill my heart with heavy dread. I had felt Fate's surprising and unexpected stings before. I didn't have Beau's confidence and probably never would have.

Despite all the terrible things Gisselle had done to me in the past, and despite her jealousy and her way of looking down at me because I had been brought up in the bayou, a Cajun, I couldn't help but recall the softer moments when I would look at her and see her desire to be loved and to be a real sister. I know Beau would tell me I had a heart so soft it must be made of marshmallow, but I couldn't help shedding tears for the Gisselle I saw longing to be wanted.

Later in the afternoon, I called and spoke to James. He was very polite, but cold, too. I couldn't think of anything stranger than attending my own memorial service and burial. When we arrived at Cypress Woods on the day of the funeral, we found the pallor of death and gloom had settled over the grand house and grounds. The leaden sky had grown swollen and turgid, the thick overcast stretching from one horizon to another. The darkness stole the blush from the petals of flowers and put shadows everywhere I looked. Grounds staff, the bereaving, everyone looked weighted down by the tragedy. People whispered, glided, touched and hugged each other as if to join in a circle to keep the melancholy at bay. I thought the servants looked the saddest, their eyes bloodshot, their shoulders slumped.

It was hard, if not impossible, for me to accept expressions of condolence and sympathy. I felt horrible about deceiving people in grief and turned and walked away as quickly as I could. But once again, people mistook my feelings for Gisselle's indifference and selfishness.

Paul's parents, his sisters, Toby and Jeanne, and Jeanne's husband stationed themselves in the living room, where they greeted people. I felt Gladys Tate's eyes fix on me with a cold glare the moment I entered, and then I thought I saw a sneer in her knife-sliced mouth when I greeted her. She made me feel so uncomfortable, I left the room as quickly as I could.

Paul kept himself secluded most of the time. We understood he was drinking heavily. The only people he would see were his immediate family, mainly his mother. He even shut his door to Beau and me. Toby, who went up to inform him that I was there, returned to tell me he said it was too painful for him to gaze at me since I resembled Ruby so much. Beau and I looked at each other with surprise.

"He's really overdoing it now," Beau admitted in a whisper.

I was very worried and went up to his suite anyway. I knocked on the door and waited, but he didn't respond. I tried the handle, but the door was locked.

"Paul, it's me. Open the door. We have to talk. Please," I begged. Beau stood back to be sure no one overheard my pleas.

"It's no use," he said. "He doesn't want to see you. Wait until later."

But I didn't see him until it was time to attend the services. Despair had washed the radiant color from his face until it resembled a death mask. He gazed at me with vacant eyes and moved like someone in a trance. I squeezed Beau's hand and shot him a troubled glance and he nodded. He tried to approach Paul before me and speak to him, but Paul didn't acknowledge him. He barely acknowledged his own parents, and with people all around him continuously, it was difficult for me to say the things I wanted to say to him.

The church was filled to capacity, not only because of the people the Tates knew and did business with, but because of the people who knew and remembered my grandmere Catherine. My heart nearly burst when I saw their faces. Beau and I sat up front in the pew behind Paul and his family and listened to the priest deliver the eulogy. Every time I heard my name, I winced and gazed around. There wasn't a dry eye in the church. Paul's sisters were crying openly, but Paul was like one of Nina Jackson's zombies, his body stiff, his eyes so empty, they sent chills down my spine. Who in his or her right mind would look at him and not believe it was really Ruby in that coffin? I thought. It gave me a sick, empty feeling in the base of my stomach.

I'm watching people cry over me, listening to a priest talk about me, and gazing at a coffin that is supposed to have my body in it, I thought. It made me feel absolutely ghoulish. It was all I could do to keep myself from fainting.

It was worse at the cemetery. It was I who was supposedly being lowered into the ground; it was I over whose coffin the priest was saying the final words and giving the last rites. My name, my identity, was about to be buried. I thought to myself that this was the final chance, the last time for me to cry out and say, "No, that's not Ruby in the coffin. That's Gisselle. I'm here. I'm not dead!"

For a moment I thought I had actually spoken, but the words died on my lips. My actions had made them forbidden. The truth had to be buried here and now, I realized.

The rain started and fell relentlessly, colder than usual. Umbrellas sprouted. Paul didn't seem to notice. His father and Jeanne's husband, James, had to hold his arms and keep him standing. When the coffin was lowered and the priest cast the holy water, Paul's legs folded. He had to be carried back to the limousine and given some cold water. His mother gave me a scathing glance and followed quickly.

"He's going to win the Academy Award for this," Beau said, shaking his head. Even he was beyond amazement; he was in awe and, from the look in his face, as frightened by Paul's behavior as I was.

"You're right," he whispered to me as we walked back to our vehicle. "He was so disturbed about losing you, he went a bit mad and accepted the illusion as reality. The only way he could accept the fact that you had left him was to believe it was you who was sick and now you who died," Beau theorized, and shook his head.

"I know, Beau. I'm so worried."

"Maybe now that it's over, that she's gone, he'll snap out of it," Beau suggested, but neither of us was filled with any confidence.

We returned to Cypress Woods, mainly to see how Paul was. The doctor went up to the suite to examine him, and when he came down, he told us he had given Paul something to help him sleep.

"It will take time," he said. "These things take time. Unfortunately, we have no drug, no medicine, no treatment, to cure grief." He pressed Gladys's hand between his, kissed her on the cheek, and left. She turned and glared at me in the strangest way, shooting icicles out of her eyes. Then she went upstairs to be with Paul.

Toby and Jeanne went off in a corner to comfort each other. People began to leave, anxious to put this dreadful sadness behind them. Paul's mother remained in the suite with him, so I couldn't get to see him even if I had wanted. Octavious came down to speak to us. He directed himself at Beau as if he, too, couldn't fix his eyes on my face.

"Gladys is as bad as Paul is," he muttered. "It's the way she is about him. Whenever he was sick, even as a child, she was sick. If he was unhappy, so was she. Dreadful, dreadful thing, this," he added, shaking his head and walking off. "Dreadful."

"We should leave now," Beau said softly. "Give him a day or two and then call. After he comes back to himself somewhat, we'll invite him to New Orleans and work out everything sensibly."

I nodded. I wanted to say good-bye to Jeanne and Toby, but they were like two clams who had closed their shell of grief tightly around themselves. They wouldn't look at or talk to anyone. And so Beau and I started out. I paused at the door. James was holding it open, waiting impatiently, but I wanted to gaze around at the grand house once more before leaving. I was filled with a sense of termination. This was the end of so many things. But it wasn't until late in the afternoon of the next day that I was to discover just how many.

15

Farewell to
My First Love

Early in the evening of the following day, just as Beau and I were about to take our seats for dinner, Aubrey appeared in the dining room doorway, his face pale, to inform me I had a phone call. Since returning from the funeral and Cypress Woods, both Beau and I had been moving like two sleepwalkers, eating little, doing little, talking in low voices. The clouds of gloom that hovered over the bayou followed us back to New Orleans and now lay over us like a ceiling of oppression, darkening every room, filling our very souls with shadows. It had rained all the way back from Cypress Woods. I fell asleep to the monotonous wagging of the wipers on the windshield and woke with a chill that a pile of blankets and a dozen sweaters couldn't chase from my bones.

"Who is it?" I asked. I was in no mood to talk to any of Gisselle's friends, who I imagined had heard about my death and wanted to gossip, and I had left instructions with Aubrey to tell any of them who did call that I was unavailable.

"She wouldn't say, madame. She's speaking in a coarse

whisper, however, and she is very insistent," he explained. From the way he couched his words and shifted his eyes, I understood that whoever it was, she had spoken to him roughly. I was positive now that it was one of Gisselle's bitchy, spoiled girlfriends who wouldn't take no as an answer from a servant.

"Do you want me to take it?" Beau asked.

"No. I'll take care of it," I said. "Thank you, Aubrey. I'm sorry," I added, apologizing for the ugliness he had to experience.

I went into the study and seized the receiver, my heart pumping, my face flush with anger.

"Who is this?" I demanded. For a moment there was no reply. "Hello?"

"He's gone," a raspy voice replied. "He's gone away and we can't find him and it's all because of you."

"What? Who is this? Who's gone?" I asked with machine-gun speed. The voice had sent an icicle down my spine and nailed my feet to the floor.

"He's gone into the canals. He went there last night and he hasn't returned and no one has been able to find him. My Paul," she sobbed, and I knew it was Gladys Tate.

"Paul . . . went into the canals last night?"

"Yes, yes, yes," she cried. "You did this to him. You did all this."

"Madame Tate . . ."

"Stop!" she screamed. "Stop your pretending," she said, and lowered her voice into that scratchy old witch's voice again. "I know who you really are and I know what you and your . . . lover did. I know how you broke my poor Paul's heart, shattered it until there was nothing left for him to feel. I know how you made him pretend and be part of your horrible scheme."

I felt as if I had stepped into ice water and sunk down to my knees in it. For a moment I couldn't speak. My throat closed and all the words jammed up in my chest, making it feel as if it would burst.

"You don't understand," I finally said, my voice cracking.

"Oh, I understand, all right. I understand better than you know. You see," she said, her voice now full of arrogance, "my son confided in me far more than you ever knew. There were never secrets between us, never. I knew the first time he paid a visit to you and your grandmere. I knew what he thought of you, how he was falling head over heels in love with you. I knew how sad and troubled he was when you left to live with your upper-class New Orleans Creole parents, and I knew how happy he was when you returned.

"But I warned him. I warned him you would break his heart. I tried. I did all that I could," she said, and sobbed. "You enchanted him. Just as I told you that day, you and your witch mother put a spell on my husband and then my son, my Paul. He's gone, gone," she said, her voice faltering, her hatred running out of steam.

"Mother Tate, I'm sorry about Paul. I . . . We'll come right out and help find him."

"Help find him." She laughed a chilling laugh. "I'd rather ask the devil for help. I just want you to know that I know why my son is so brokenhearted and I will not sit by and let him suffer without you suffering twice as much."

"But . . ."

The phone went dead. I sat there, my heart going thump, thump, thump, my mind reeling. I felt as if I were in a pirogue that had been caught in a current and was spinning furiously. The room did twirl. I closed my eyes and moaned and the phone fell from my hand and bounced on the floor. Beau was at my side to catch me as I started to lean too far.

"What is it? Ruby!" He turned and shouted for Sally. "Hurry, bring me a cold, wet washcloth," he ordered. He put his arm around me and knelt down. My eyes fluttered open. "What happened? Who was on the phone, Ruby?"

"It was Paul's mother, Gladys," I gasped.

"What did she say?"

"She said Paul's disappeared. He went into the swamps last night and still hasn't returned. Oh, Beau," I moaned.

Sally came running with the cloth. He took it from her and put it on my head.

"Just relax. She'll be all right now, Sally. *Merci,*" Beau said, dismissing her.

I took some deep breaths and felt the blood returning to my cheeks.

"Paul's disappeared? That's what she said?"

"Yes, Beau. But she said more. She said she knew about us, knew what we had done. Paul told her everything. I never knew he had, but now that I think of the way she glared at me at the funeral . . ." I sat up. "She never liked me, Beau." I gazed into his wide eyes. "Oh, Beau, she threatened me."

"What? Threatened. How?"

"She said I would suffer twice as much as Paul's suffered."

He shook his head. "She's just hysterical right now. Paul's got them all in a frenzy."

"He went into the swamps, Beau, and he didn't come back. I want to go right out there and help find him. We must, Beau. We must."

"I don't know what we can do. They must have all their workers looking."

"Beau, please. If something should happen to him . . ."

"All right," he relented. "Let's change our clothes. You were right," he said with an underlying current of bitterness in his voice, "we shouldn't have involved him as much as we did. I jumped at the opportunity to make things easier for us, but I should have given it more thought."

My legs trembled, but I followed him out and upstairs to change my clothes and tell Mrs. Ferrier we would be leaving the house and might not return until very late or even the next day. Then we got into our car and drove through the night, making the trip in record time.

There were dozens of cars and pickup trucks along the driveway at Cypress Woods. As we pulled up to the house, I looked toward the dock and saw the torches being carried by men who were going in pirogues and motorboats to search for Paul. We could hear the shouts echoing over the bayou.

Inside the house Paul's sisters sat in the study, Toby looking as cold as a statue, her skin alabaster, and Jeanne twisting a silk handkerchief in her hands and gritting her teeth. They both looked up with surprise when we entered.

"What are you doing here?" Toby asked. From the expressions on their faces and their astonishment, I guessed that Gladys Tate hadn't told her daughters the truth. They still thought of me as Gisselle.

"We heard about Paul and came to see what we could do to help," Beau said quickly.

"You could go down and join the search party, I suppose," Toby said.

"Where's your mother?" I asked.

"She's upstairs in Paul's suite, lying down," Jeanne said. "The doctor was here, but she refused to take anything. She doesn't want to be asleep if . . . when . . ." Her lips trembled and the tears rushed over her eyelids.

"Get hold of yourself," Toby chastised. "Mother needs us to be strong."

"How do they know for sure that he went into the swamps? Maybe he's in some zydeco bar," Beau said.

"First of all, my brother wouldn't go off to a bar the day after he buried his wife, and second, some of the workers saw him heading toward the dock," Toby replied.

"And carrying a bottle of whiskey clutched in his hand," Jeanne added mournfully.

A dead silence fell between us.

"I'm sure they'll find him," Beau finally said.

Toby turned to him slowly and fixed her eyes on him in

a cold glare. "Have either of you ever been in the swamps? Do either of you know what it could be like? You make a turn and find yourself floating through overhanging vines and cypress branches and soon you forget how you got there and have no idea how to get out. It's a maze full of poisonous copperhead snakes, alligators, and snapping turtles, not to mention the insects and vermin."

"It's not that bad," I said.

"Oh really. Well then, march on out of here with your husband and join the search party," Toby retorted with a bitterness that shot through my brain like a laser beam.

"I plan on doing just that. Come on, Beau," I said, spinning around and marching out. Beau was at my side, but he wasn't enthusiastic.

"You really think we should go into the swamps, Ruby? I mean, if all these people who live here can't find him . . ."

"I'll find him," I said firmly. "I know where to look."

Jeanne's husband, James, was at the dock when we arrived. He shook his head and lifted his arms in frustration.

"It's impossible," he said. "If Paul doesn't want to be found, he won't be found. He knows these swamps better than he knows the back of his hand. He grew up in them. We're giving up for tonight."

"No, we're not," I said sharply.

He looked up, surprised. "We?"

"Is that your boat?" I asked, nodding toward a dinghy with a small outboard engine.

"Yes, but . . ."

"Please, just take us into the swamps."

"I just came back, and I assure you—"

"I know what I'm doing, James. If you don't want to go along, let us just borrow your boat," I insisted.

"You two? In the swamps?" He smiled, sighed, and then shook his head. "All right. I'll give it one more sweep. Get in," he said.

Beau, looking very uncomfortable, stepped into the dinghy after me and sat down. James handed us torches. Then we saw Octavious arriving with another group. His head was down like a flag of defeat.

"Paul's father is taking it very hard," James said, shaking his head.

"Just start the engine, please," I said. "Please . . ."

"What do you expect to be able to do that all these other people, some of whom fish and hunt in here, couldn't do?"

I stared. "I think I know where he might be," I said softly. "Ruby once told me about a hideaway she and Paul shared. She described it so well, I'm sure I could find it."

James shook his head skeptically but started the engine. "All right, but I'm afraid we're just wasting our time. We should wait for daylight."

We pulled away from the dock and headed into the canal. The swamps could be intimidating at night, even to men who had lived and worked them all their lives. There wasn't enough of a moon to give much illumination, and the Spanish moss seemed to thicken and blacken to form walls and block off other canals. The twisted cyprus branches looked like gnarled old witches, and the water took on an inky thickness, hiding tree roots, dead logs, and, of course, alligators. Our movement and the torches kept the mosquitoes at bay, but Beau looked very uncomfortable and even frightened. He nearly jumped out of the dinghy when an owl swooped alongside.

"Go to the right, James, and then, just as you come around the bend, bear left sharply."

"I can't believe Ruby gave you such explicit directions," he mumbled.

"She loved this spot because she and Paul spent so much time there," I said. "It's like another world. She said," I added quickly.

James followed my directions. Behind us, the torches

of other searches dimmed and were lost. A sheet of darkness fell between us and the house. Soon we could no longer hear the voices of men in the search party.

"Slower, James," I said. "There's something I have to look for and it's not easy at night."

"Especially when you've never been here before," James commented. "This is futile. If we just wait until morning—"

"There," I said, pointing. "You see where that cypress tree bends over like an old lady plucking a four-leaf clover?"

"Old lady? Four-leaf clover?" James said.

"That's what Paul told Ruby all the time." Neither James nor Beau could see the smile on my face. "Just turn right sharply under the lower branch."

"We might not fit under that," he warned.

"We will if we bend down," I said. "Slowly."

"Are you sure? We'll just get hung up on a rock or a mound of roots or—"

"I'm sure. Do it. Please."

Reluctantly he turned the dinghy. We dipped our heads and slipped under the branch.

"I'll be darned," James said. "Now where?"

"You see that thick wall of Spanish moss that reaches the water?"

"Yeah."

"Just go through it. It's the secret doorway."

"Secret doorway. Damn. No one would know that."

"That's what I meant by it being another world," I said. "You can cut the engine. We'll float on through and we'll be there."

He did so and I held my breath as the dinghy pierced the moss, which parted like a curtain to permit us to enter the small pond. Once we were completely through, I raised my torch and Beau did the same.

"Just paddle in a circle slowly," I said. The glow of our torches lifted the darkness, uncovering the pond. Snakes or turtles slithered beneath the surface, creating ripples. We saw the bream feeding on the mosquitoes. An alligator lifted its head, its teeth gleaming in our light, and then it dove. I heard Beau gulp. Somewhere to the right, a hawk screeched. On the shore of the pond, a half dozen or so nutrias scrambled for cover.

"Wait, what's that?" James said. He stood up and poked into the water with his oar to draw a bottle closer to the dinghy. Then he reached in to pluck it out of the water. It was an empty bottle of rum. "He was here," James said, looking around harder. *"Paul!"* he screamed.

"Paul!" Beau followed.

For a moment I couldn't form his name on my lips. Then I cried out, too. *"Paul, please, if you're here, answer us."*

Nothing but the sound of the swamp animals could be heard. Over to the right a deer rustled through the bushes. Terror jumped into my heart, flooded my eyes.

"Just keep rowing around the pond, James," I said, and sat back, but held my torch high to the right while Beau held his to the left. The water lapped against the dinghy. There was barely a breeze and mosquitoes began to sense our presence with delight. Suddenly the round bottom of a pirogue became visible. At first it looked like an alligator, but as we drew closer, it became clear that it was Paul's canoe. No one spoke. James poked it with his oar.

"It's his, all right," he said. *"Paul!"*

"Over there. Is that something?" Beau asked, leaning with his torch. James turned the dinghy in the direction Beau was pointing, and I brought my torchlight to bear as well. Slumped over a large rock, his *chatlin* hair matted and muddied by the water, Paul lay facedown. He looked like he had dragged himself up and collapsed. James turned the dinghy so he and Beau could stand up and reach Paul's body. I started to step toward him, too, when Beau turned sharply.

"Don't!" he ordered. He seized me at the elbows to hold me back and get me to sit. "It's not pretty and he's gone," he said.

I slapped my palms over my face and screamed. My

shrill cry pierced the darkest corners and shadows in the swamp, sending birds flapping, animals scurrying, and fish diving. It echoed over the water and was finally stopped by the wall of dark silence that waits out there for all of us.

The doctor said Paul's lungs were so full of water, he had no idea how Paul had managed to drag himself up the rock a few inches, much less enough to get his entire body up. There he took his last gasps and passed away. Miraculously, no alligator got to him, but the death by drowning had distorted him and Beau was right to keep me from looking.

Cypress Woods was already a house in mourning, so it just continued under the dark cloud of more grief. Servants who had cried so hard over what they thought was my death now had to find another well of tears from which to draw. Paul's sisters, especially Toby, had anticipated bad news, but were devastated nevertheless and retreated with James into the privacy of the study, while Octavious went upstairs to be with Gladys.

I felt so weak all over, my body so light, I thought I would get caught up in the wind and be carried into the night. Beau clutched my hand and put his arm around my shoulders. I leaned against him and watched them bring Paul's body up from the dock. Beau wanted us to return immediately to New Orleans. He was insistent and I had no strength to resist, no words to offer in argument. I let him lead me to our car and slumped down in the seat as he drove us away. I had cried dry that bottomless pit of tears.

When I closed my eyes, I saw Paul as a young boy riding his motor scooter up to Grandmere Catherine's front gallery. I saw the brightness in his eyes when he set them on me. Both our voices were full of excitement then. The world seemed so innocent and precious. Every color, every shape, every scent, was richer. When we were together, exploring our young feelings, we were like the first couple on earth discovering things we couldn't imagine others discovering before us. No one ever adequately explains the wonder born in your heart when you undress your new feelings in front of someone who is undressing his, too. That trust, that childhood faith, is so pure and good, you can't imagine any betrayals. Surely all the trouble and misery you know and hear about in the world around you will be walled out by these powerful new feelings woven into an impenetrable fabric. You can make promises, expose your dreams, and dream new things together. Nothing seems impossible and the last thing you can imagine is that some malicious Fate has been toying with you, leading you down a highway that will bring you to these tragic, dark moments.

I wanted to be angry and bitter and blame someone or something else, but in the end I could think of no one to blame but myself. The weight of that guilt was so heavy, I couldn't bear it. I was crushed, defeated, and so tired, I didn't open my eyes again until Beau said we were home. I let him help me out of the car, but my legs wouldn't support me. He carried me into the house and up the stairway and lowered me to our bed, where I curled up, embraced myself, and fell unconscious.

When I woke up, Beau was already dressed. I turned, but the ache in my bones was so deep, I could barely stretch out my legs and lift myself. My head felt like it had turned to stone.

"I'm so tired," I said. "So weak."

"Stay in bed today," he advised. "I'll have Sally bring your breakfast up to the suite. I have some things I must tend to at the office and then I'll come home to be with you."

"Beau," I moaned. "It is my fault. Gladys Tate is right to hate me."

"Of course it isn't your fault. You didn't break any promises, and anything he did, he did willingly, knowing what the consequences might be. If it's anyone's fault, it's mine. I shouldn't have let him become so involved. I should have forced you to make a clean, clear break with him so he would have realized he should go on with his life and not mourn over things that couldn't be, that weren't supposed to be.

"But, Ruby," Beau said, coming to my side and taking my hand in his, "we are meant to be. No two people could love each other as much as we do and not be meant to be. That is the faith you must have, the faith you must cling to when you mourn Paul. If we fail each other now, then everything he did was even more in vain.

"Somewhere, deep inside himself, he must have also realized you belonged with me. Maybe he couldn't face that in the end and maybe it overwhelmed him, but he did realize it as a greater truth and a greater reality.

"We must hold on to what we now have. I love you," he said, and kissed me softly on the lips. He lowered his head to my bosom and I held him against me for a long moment before he rose, took a deep breath, and smiled. "I'll send Sally around and then tell Mrs. Ferrier to bring Pearl in later, okay?"

"Yes, Beau. Whatever you say. I can't think for myself anymore."

"That's all right. I'll think for the two of us." He threw me a kiss and left.

I gazed out the window. The sky was overcast, but the clouds looked light and thin. There would be hazy sunshine and the day would be hot and muggy. After breakfast, I would take a bath and get back on my feet. The prospect of attending Paul's funeral seemed overwhelming to me now. I couldn't imagine mustering the strength, but as it turned out, that was to be the least of my problems.

Late in the morning, after I had had some breakfast and taken my bath, I brushed out my hair and dressed myself. Mrs. Ferrier brought Pearl in to watch and I let her play with my brushes and combs. She sat beside me, mimicking my every move. Her hair had grown down to her shoulders and it was turning a brighter, richer golden shade every day. Her blue eyes were full of curiosity. As soon as she learned what one thing was, she was asking about another, touching something else. Her bountiful energy and excitement brought some joy and relief to my aching heart. How lucky I was to have her, I thought. I was determined to devote myself to her, to make certain that her life was smoother, happier, and fuller than mine. I would protect her, advise her, guide her, so she would avoid the pitfalls and treacherous turns I had taken. It was in our children, I realized, that our hope and purpose lay. They were the promise and the only real antidote for grief.

Beau called to say he would be home shortly. Mrs. Ferrier took Pearl out to play in the garden, and I decided to go down so that Beau and I could have lunch on the patio when he returned. I had just rounded the base of the stairway when the phones rang. Aubrey announced it was Toby Tate and I hurried to a receiver.

"Toby," I cried. "I'm sorry we left so quickly, but—"

"No one was concerned here about that," she said coldly. "I'm certainly not calling to complain about your behavior. Frankly, I can't imagine any of us caring." The hard, formal tone in her voice set my heart racing. "In fact, Mother asked me to call to tell you she would rather you don't attend Paul's funeral."

"Not attend? But—"

"We're sending a car with a nanny we're hiring to pick up Pearl and bring her home," she added firmly.

"What?"

"Mother says Paul and Ruby's daughter belongs with her grandpere and grandmere and not with her self-centered aunt, so your obligations, your promises, are all over. You can go back to your life of pleasure and not worry. Those were Mother's exact words. Please have Pearl ready by three o'clock."

My throat wouldn't open to let me form any words. I couldn't swallow. My heart felt as if it had slid down into my stomach and a wave of heat rose from the base of my spine to the base of my head, where it circled around my neck like the long, thin fingers of a witch, choking me.

"Do you understand?" Toby demanded.

"You . . ."

"Yes?"

"Can't . . . take . . . Pearl," I said. I fought to open my lungs and suck in some air. "Your mother knows you can't."

"What sort of nonsense is this? Of course we can. Don't you think a grandmere has more claim to a grandchild than an aunt?"

"No!" I shouted. "I won't let you take Pearl."

"I don't see where you have much to say about it, Gisselle. I hope you won't add any unpleasantness and ugliness to our tragedy right now. If there is anyone left out there who doesn't despise you, he or she will soon do just that."

"Your mother knows she can't do this. She knows. Tell her. Tell her!" I screamed.

"Well, I'll tell her what you said, but the car will be there at three o'clock. Good-bye," Toby snapped and the phone went dead.

"No!" I screamed into the receiver anyway. I quickly hung up and then lifted the receiver to dial Beau.

"I'm coming right home," he said after I gasped and poured out what Toby had told me Gladys Tate demanded.

"This is what she meant by my suffering twice as much as Paul, Beau. This is her way of getting vengeance."

"Stay calm. I'll be right there," he said.

I hung up, but I couldn't stay calm. I went into the study and paced back and forth, my mind reeling with the possibilities. It seemed hours before Beau finally arrived, even though it was only a few minutes. He came rushing into the study to embrace me and sit me down. I couldn't stop trembling. My teeth were actually chattering.

"It's going to be all right," he assured me. "She's bluffing. She's just trying to upset you because she is so upset right now. She'll realize what she's doing and she'll stop it."

"But, Beau . . . everyone thinks I'm Gisselle. They buried me!"

"It'll be fine," he said, but not with as much confidence as before.

"We were born in the swamps in a shack. It's not like here in New Orleans in a hospital where babies' footprints are taken so they can be easily identified later. Paul was my husband and he told the world I was sick and dying. He attended my funeral and killed himself, whether purposely or accidentally, because of my death," I rattled, each realization like another nail in the coffin of truth. I seized Beau's hands in mine and fixed my eyes on his.

"You yourself said that I've done such a good job of pretending to be Gisselle, everyone thinks I am. Even your parents!"

"If it comes down to whether or not we keep Pearl, we'll confess the truth and tell the authorities what we have done. I promise," he said. "No one will take our child from us. No one. Especially not Gladys Tate," he assured me. He squeezed my hands and made his face tight with determination. It slowed down my runaway heart and eased some of my trepidation.

"Toby said a car is arriving here at three with a nurse."

"I'll handle it," he said. "Don't you even come near the front door."

I nodded. "Pearl," I said suddenly. "Where is she?"

"Take it easy. Where could she be but with Mrs. Ferrier? Don't frighten her," he warned, seizing my wrist. "Ruby."

"Yes, you're right. I mustn't frighten the child. But I want her upstairs now. I don't want her outside when they come."

"All right, but do it gently, calmly," he ordered. "Will you?"

"I will." I took a deep breath and went out to find Mrs. Ferrier and Pearl. Without going into any detail why, I asked her to bring the baby in and keep her up in her room. Then I went to join Beau in the dining room, but not only couldn't I eat any lunch with Beau, I couldn't bring a morsel of food near my lips. I could barely swallow water. My stomach was that nervous. A little after two, he told me to go upstairs and stay with Pearl and Mrs. Ferrier. My heart was thumping madly. I thought I could easily pass out from fear, but I fought down my trepidation and occupied myself with Pearl.

Just before three o'clock, I heard the door chimes and my heart jumped in my chest. I couldn't keep myself from going to the top of the stairway and listening. Beau had already told Aubrey he would answer the door. I didn't want Beau to know I was looking and listening in, so I backed into the shadows when he turned and looked up the stairway just before opening the door.

A man in a suit and a nurse in uniform were there.

"Yes?" Beau said as nonchalantly as he could.

"My name is Martin Bell," the man in the suit said. "I am an attorney representing the Tates. We have been sent by Monsieur and Madame Tate to pick up their granddaughter," he said.

"Their granddaughter is not going anywhere today or any day," Beau said firmly. "She is home where she belongs and where she will stay."

"Are you refusing to turn their granddaughter over to them?" Martin Bell asked with some astonishment. Apparently he had been led to believe this was a simple assignment. He probably thought he was making easy money.

"I am refusing to turn our daughter over to them, yes," Beau said.

"Pardon. Your daughter? I'm confused here," Martin Bell said, glancing at the nurse, who looked just as confused. "Is the little girl the daughter of Paul and Ruby Tate?"

"No," Beau said, "and Gladys Tate knows that. I'm afraid she's wasted your time, but be sure you bill for it," Beau added. "Good day," he said, and closed the door on their bewildered faces. For a moment he stood there waiting. Then he went to the window and gazed out to be sure they drove away. When he turned, he saw me standing at the top of the stairway.

"Were you there the whole time?" he asked.

"Yes, Beau."

"So you heard. I did what I promised. I told the truth and I've sent them back. When Gladys hears what I said, she'll back off and leave us alone," he assured me. "Relax. It's over. It's all over."

I nodded and smiled hopefully. Beau came up the stairs to embrace me. Then the two of us went to look in on Pearl. She was sitting contentedly on the floor of what had once been my room and coloring animals in a coloring book called "A Visit to the Zoo."

"Look, Mommy." She pointed and then growled like a tiger. Mrs. Ferrier laughed.

"She imitates all the animals," she said. "I've never seen such a good little mimic."

Beau tightened his embrace around my shoulders and I leaned against him. It felt good to be surrounded by his strength and feel his firmness. He was my rock now, my pillar of steel, and it deepened my love for him and filled me with confidence. Gradually, as the day wore on, my nervousness diminished and my stomach stabilized. I realized I was ravishingly hungry when we sat down at dinner.

Later that night in bed, we talked for nearly an hour before closing our eyes.

"I regret not being able to go to Paul's funeral," I said.

"I know, but under the circumstances, it's better that we don't attend. Gladys Tate would only make an unpleasant situation even more miserable. She would create an ugly scene."

"Even so, someday after sufficient time has passed, I would like to visit the grave, Beau."

"Of course."

We talked on, Beau suggesting plans for the future now. "If we want, we can build a new house on a piece of real estate we own just outside of the city."

"Maybe we should," I said.

"Of course, there are things we could do to this house to change it as well. In either case, we'll want new memories," he explained. I couldn't agree more. His descriptions of what was possible for us now filled me with renewed hope and I was able to shut my eyelids and drift off, emotionally exhausted and tired down to my very soul.

I wasn't refreshed when I woke in the morning, but I had regained enough strength to start a new day. I made plans to begin painting again and I thought I would start to buy a new wardrobe, one that fit my personality more. Now that I had driven away all of Gisselle's friends and we were talking about a new beginning, I thought I had the freedom to ease back into my true self and eventually put Gisselle to rest. Those prospects buoyed me.

We had a good breakfast with an animated conversation. Beau had so many plans for business and for our changes, my mind felt stuffed. I could see where we would both become so busy shortly, there wouldn't be much time to dwell on sadness. Grandmere Catherine always said that the only real antidote for grief and sadness was busy hands.

After breakfast Beau went upstairs to the bathroom and I went into the kitchen to talk to Mrs. Swann about dinner. I sat listening to her describe how to prepare chicken Rochambeau.

"You start with preparing the gravy," she began, and went through the ingredients. Just listening to her talk about the recipe made my mouth water. How lucky we were to have a cook with so much experience, I thought.

Mrs. Swann was clanking dishes and pans as she spoke and walked around the kitchen, so I didn't hear the door chimes and was surprised when Aubrey arrived to tell me there were two gentlemen at the door.

"And there's a policeman, too," he added.

"What? Policeman?"

"Yes, madame."

My chest felt hot and heavy as I rose.

"Where's Pearl?" I asked quickly.

"She's in her nursery with Mrs. Ferrier, madame. They just went upstairs."

"And Monsieur Andreas?"

"I think he's still upstairs, madame."

"Please fetch him for me, Aubrey. Quickly," I said.

"Very well, madame," he said, and hurried out. I looked at Mrs. Swann, who stared at me with curious eyes.

"Troubles?" she asked.

"I don't know. I don't know," I mumbled, and let my feet carry me slowly toward the foyer. Beau appeared on the stairway just as I arrived in the foyer and saw the attorney Martin Bell and another man at the door.

"What's this?" Beau cried, hurrying down the remaining steps.

"Monsieur and Madame Andreas?" the taller of the two men in suits inquired. Beau stepped forward rapidly so he would be at the door before me. I saw the nurse who had come the day before standing behind them and my heart sunk.

"Yes?"

"I'm William Rogers, senior partner of Rogers, Bell and Stanley. As you know from Mr. Bell's previous visit, we represent Monsieur and Madame Octavious Tate of Terrebonne Parish. We're here under court order to take the infant Pearl Tate back to her grandparents," he said, and handed Beau a document. "It's been signed by the judge and must be carried out."

"Beau," I said. He waved me off for a moment while he read.

"This is not true," he said, looking up and attempting to hand the document back. "Madame Tate is not the child's grandmere."

"I'm afraid that's for a court to decide, sir. In the interim this court action," he said, nodding at the document, "will be enforced. She has primary legal rights to custody."

"But we're not the uncle and aunt. We're the mother and father," Beau said.

"The court understands otherwise. The child's parents are both deceased and the grandparents are the primary legal guardians, therefore," Mr. Rogers insisted. "I hope this doesn't become unpleasant," he added. "For the child's sake."

As soon as he said that, the policeman moved up beside him. Beau gazed from one face to the other and then looked at me.

"Ruby . . ."

"No!" I screamed, backing away. "They can't take her. They can't!"

"They have a court order, but it will only be temporary," Beau said. "I promise. I'll call our attorneys right now. We have the best, highest-paid attorneys in New Orleans."

"This court action will be conducted in Terrebonne Parish," William Rogers said. "The child's legal residence. But if you have the highest-paid, best attorneys, they would know that anyway," he added, enjoying his sarcasm.

"Beau," I said, my lips trembling, my face crumpling. He started toward me to embrace me, but I backed farther away. "No," I said, shaking my head. "No."

"Madame, I assure you," Mr. Rogers said, "this court order will be carried out. If you truly have any concern for the child, you'd better adhere to the order smoothly."

"Ruby . . ."

"Beau, you promised! *No,"* I screamed. I struck him in the chest with my small fists, pummeling him. He grabbed my wrists and embraced me tightly.

"We'll get her back. We will," he said.

"I can't," I said, shaking my head. "I can't." My legs gave out and Beau held me up.

"Please," he said, turning to the lawyers, the policeman, and the nurse, "give us ten minutes to prepare the baby."

Mr. Rogers nodded and Beau literally carried me along, up the stairs, whispering assurances in my ear.

"It will be ugly," he said, "if we physically resist. Once we explain who we are, it will all end quickly. You'll see."

"But, Beau, you said this wouldn't happen."

"How did I know she would be this vicious? She must be crazy. What sort of a man is she married to for him to let her do this?"

"A guilty man," I said, and sniffed back my tears. I looked toward Pearl's nursery door. "Oh, Beau, she'll be terrified."

"Only until she gets to Cypress Woods. She knows all the servants and—"

"But they're not taking her to Cypress Woods. They're taking her to the Tates."

Beau nodded, the realizations deepening in him, too. He sighed deeply and shook his head. "I could kill her," he said. "I could put my hands around her neck and choke the life out of her."

"It's already been choked out of her," I said, nodding. "When Paul died. We're dealing with a woman who's lost every feeling but one, the desire for revenge. And my child has to go into that household."

"Do you want me to do this?" he asked, looking at the nursery.

"No. I'll do it with you so we can comfort her as much as possible."

We went in and explained to Mrs. Ferrier that the baby had to go to her grandparents. Beau thought that was best for now. Pearl knew the Tates as her grandparents, so I sucked back my sorrow and hid my tears. Smiling, I told her she had to go see her grandmere Gladys and grandpere Octavious.

"There's a nice lady to take you to them," I continued.

Pearl gazed at me curiously. It was almost as if she were wise enough to see through the deception. She put up no resistance until we carried her down and actually placed her in the backseat of the limousine with the nurse. When I backed away from the door, she realized I wasn't coming and started to scream for me. The nurse attempted to comfort her.

"Let's get moving," Mr. Rogers told the driver. The two lawyers got into the car and slammed the doors shut, but I could still hear Pearl's screams. As the limousine pulled away from the house, the baby broke loose from the nurse and pressed her little face against the back window. I could see the fear and the torment in her and I could hear her screaming my name. The moment the car disappeared, my legs went out from under me and I folded too quickly for Beau to stop me from crashing to the tile and the comfort of darkness.

16

All Is Lost

"Well," Monsieur Polk said after he heard Beau describe our story, "this is a rather complicated matter. Very," he added, and nodded emphatically, jiggling his jowls and his loose double chin. He sat back in his oversize black leather desk chair and pressed his palms against his bear-size chest with his fingers intertwined, the large gold pinky ring with a black onyx oval stone glittering in the afternoon sunlight that came pouring through the thin, white blinds.

Beau sat beside me and held my hand. My other hand clutched the mahogany arm of the chair as if I thought I might be toppled out and onto the dark brown carpet in Monsieur Polk's plush office. It was on the seventh floor of the building, and the large windows behind Monsieur Polk's desk looked out on the river with a vast view of the boats and ships navigating in and out of New Orleans harbor.

I bit down on my lower lip and held my breath as our attorney pondered. His large, watery hazel eyes gazed down and he was so still, I feared he had fallen asleep.

The only sound in the office was the ticktock of the miniature grandfather clock on the shelf to our left.

"No birth certificates, you say?" he finally asked, just raising his eyes. The rest of him, all two hundred forty pounds, remained settled in the chair, his suit jacket folded and creased in the shoulders. He wore a dark brown tie with lemon dots.

"No. As I said, the twins were born in swamp country, no doctor, no hospital."

"My grandmere was a *traiteur,* better than any doctor," I said.

"Traiteur?"

"Cajun faith healer," Beau explained.

Monsieur Polk nodded and shifted his eyes toward me and stared a moment. Then he sat forward and clasped his hands on his desk.

"We'll move quickly for a custody hearing. It will be conducted like a trial in this situation. The first order of business will be to find a legal way to establish you as Ruby. Once that is accomplished, you will testify to being the father of your child, which you will own up to," he said to Beau.

"Of course." Beau squeezed my hand and smiled.

"Now let's look at the face of this," Monsieur Polk said. He reached over to a dark cherry wood cigar box and flicked up the cover to pluck a fat Havana cigar out of it. "You," he said, pointing at me with the cigar, "and your twin sister, Gisselle, were apparently so identical in looks, you could pull off this switch of identities, correct?"

"Down to the dimples in their cheeks," Beau said.

"Eye color, hair color, complexion, height, weight?" Monsieur Polk listed. Beau and I nodded after each item.

"There might have been a few pounds difference between them, but nothing very noticeable," Beau said.

"Scars?" Monsieur Polk asked, raising his eyebrows hopefully.

I shook my head.

"I have none and my sister had none, even though she

was in a bad car accident and was crippled for a time," I said.

"Bad car accident?" I nodded. "Here in New Orleans?"

"Yes."

"Then she was in the hospital for a time. Good. There'll be a medical history with records about her blood. Maybe you two had a different blood type. If so, that would settle it immediately. A friend of mine," he continued, taking out his lighter, "tells me that in years to come, from blood tests, using DNA, they'll be able to identify who is the parent of a child. But we're a number of years away from that."

"And by then it would be too late!" I complained.

He nodded and lit his cigar, leaning back to blow the puffs of smoke toward the ceiling.

"Maybe some X rays were taken. Did she break any bones in the accident?"

"No," I said. "She was bruised and the shock of it did something to her spine, affecting the nerves, but that healed and she was able to walk again."

"Um," Monsieur Polk said. "I don't know if there would be anything discernible by X ray. We'd have to have X rays done of you and then find a medical expert to testify that there should be some residual evidence of the trauma."

I brightened. "I'll go right to the hospital for X rays."

"Right," Beau said.

Monsieur Polk shook his head. "They might very well locate an expert who would claim X rays wouldn't pick up any residual damage if the problem was cured," he said. "Let me research the medical records at the hospital and get one of my doctor friends to give me an opinion about it first."

"Ruby had a child; Gisselle did not," Beau said. "Surely an examination . . ."

"Can you establish Gisselle did not beyond a doubt?" Monsieur Polk asked.

"Pardon?"

"Gisselle is dead and buried. How can we examine her? You'd have to have the body exhumed, and what if Gisselle had been pregnant sometime and had had an abortion?"

"He's right, Beau. I would never swear about that," I said.

"This is very bizarre. Very bizarre," Monsieur Polk muttered. "You worked at convincing people you were your twin sister and did it so well, everyone who knew her believed it, right?"

"As far as we know."

"And the family, Paul Tate's family, believed it and believed they buried Ruby Tate?"

"Yes," I said.

"There was actually a death certificate issued in your name?"

"Yes," I said, swallowing hard. The vivid memories of attending my own funeral came rushing back over me.

Monsieur Polk shook his head and thought a moment. "What about the doctor who first treated Gisselle for encephalitis?" he asked with some visible excitement. "He knew he was treating Gisselle and not Ruby, right?"

"I'm afraid we can't call on him," Beau said, deflating our balloon of hope. "I made an arrangement with him, and anyway, it would ruin him, wouldn't it? His being a part of this?"

"I'm afraid that's very true," Monsieur Polk said. "He put his name to fraud. Any of the servants we can call upon?"

"Well . . . the way we worked it, the doctor and myself . . ."

"They didn't know what was happening exactly, is that it?"

"Yes. They wouldn't make the best witnesses anyway. The German couple don't speak English too well and my cook saw nothing. The maid is a timid woman who wouldn't be able to swear to anything."

"That's not an avenue to pursue, then." Monsieur Polk

nodded. "Let me think. Bizarre, very bizarre. Dental records," he cried. "How are your teeth?"

"Perfect. I've never had a cavity or a tooth pulled."

"And Gisselle?"

"As far as I know," Beau said, "she was the same. She had remarkable health for someone with her lifestyle."

"Good genes," Monsieur Polk said. "But both of you had the benefit of the same genetic advantages."

Was there no way to determine our identities to the satisfaction of a judge? I wondered frantically.

"What about our signatures?" I asked.

"Yes," Beau said. "Ruby always had a nicer handwriting."

"Handwriting is an exhibit to use," Monsieur Polk said with a bit of official-sounding nasality, "but it's not conclusive. We'll have to rely on the opinions of experts, and they might bring in their own expert who would develop the effectiveness of forgery. I've seen that happen before. Also," he said after another puff of his cigar, "people are inclined to believe that twins can imitate each other better. I'd like to have something more."

"What about Louis?" Beau asked me. "You said he recognized you."

"Louis?" Monsieur Polk asked.

"Louis was someone I met when Gisselle and I attended a private girls' school in Baton Rouge. He's a musician who recently had a concert here in New Orleans."

"I see."

"When I knew him, he was blind. But he sees now," I added, hopefully.

"What? Blind, you say? Really, monsieur," he said, turning to Beau. "You want me to put a man who was blind on the stand to testify he can tell the difference."

"But he can!" I said.

"Maybe to your satisfaction, but to a judge's?"

Another balloon deflated. My heart was thumping. Tears of frustration had begun to sting my eyes. Defeat seemed all around me.

"Look," Beau said, squeezing my hand again, "what possible motive could we have for Ruby pretending to be Ruby? First, we will be exposing our deception to the world, and besides, everyone who knew Gisselle knew how self-centered she was. She wouldn't want to win custody of a child and be responsible for the child's upbringing."

Monsieur Polk thought a moment. He turned his chair and gazed out the window.

"I'll play the devil's advocate," he said, continuing to gaze down at the river. Then he turned sharply back to us and pointed at me with his cigar again. "You said your husband, Paul, inherited oil-rich land in the bayou?"

"Yes."

"And built you a mansion with beautiful grounds, an estate?"

"Yes, but—"

"And has wells pumping up oil, creating a large fortune?"

I couldn't swallow. I couldn't nod. Beau and I gazed at each other.

"But, monsieur, we are far from paupers. Ruby inherited a tidy sum and a profitable business and—"

"Monsieur Andreas, you have at your fingertips the possibility of inheriting a major fortune, a continually growing major fortune. We're not talking now about just being well-to-do."

"What about the child?" Beau threw out in desperation. "She knows her mother."

"She's an infant. I wouldn't think of putting her on a witness stand in a courtroom. She would be terrified, I'm sure."

"No, we can't do that, Beau," I said. "Never."

Monsieur Polk sat back. "Let me look into the hospital records, talk to some doctors. I'll get back to you."

"How long will this take?"

"It can't be done overnight, madame," he said frankly.

"But my baby . . . Oh, Beau."

"Did you consider going to see Madame Tate and

talking it out with her? Perhaps this was an impulsive angry act and now she's had some time to reconsider," Monsieur Polk suggested. "It would simplify the problem."

"I don't say this is her motive," he added, leaning forward, "but you might offer to sign over any oil rights, et cetera."

"Yes," I said, hope springing in my heart.

Beau nodded. "It could be driving her mad that Ruby would inherit Cypress Woods and all the oil on the land," Beau agreed. "Let's drive out there and see if she will speak with us. But in the meantime . . ."

"I'll go forward with my research in the matter," Monsieur Polk said. He stood up and put his cigar in the ashtray before leaning over to shake Beau's hand. "You know," he said softly, "what a field day our gossip columnists in the newspapers will have with this?"

"We know." Beau looked at me. "We're prepared for all that as long as we get Pearl back."

"Very well. Good luck with Madame Tate," Monsieur Polk said, and we left.

"I feel so weak, Beau, so weak and afraid," I said as we left the building for our car.

"You can't present yourself to that woman while you're in this state of mind, Ruby. Let's stop for something to eat to build your strength. Let's be optimistic and strong. Lean on me whenever you have to," he said, his face dark, his eyes down. "This is really all my fault," he murmured. "It was my idea, my doing."

"You can't blame yourself solely, Beau. I knew what I was doing and I wanted to do it. I should have known better than to think we could splash water in the face of Destiny."

He hugged me to him and we got into our car and started for the bayou. As we rode, I rehearsed the things I would say. I had no appetite when we stopped to eat, but Beau insisted I put something in my stomach.

The late afternoon grew darker and darker as the sun took a fugitive position behind some long, feather-brushed storm clouds. All the blue sky seemed to fall behind us as we drove on toward the bayou and the confrontation that awaited. As familiar places and sights began to appear, my apprehension grew. I took deep breaths and hoped that I would be able to talk without bursting into tears.

I directed Beau to the Tate residence. It was one of the larger homes in the Houma area, a two-and-a-half-story Greek Revival with six fluted Ionic columns set on pilastered bases a little out from the edge of the gallery. It had fourteen rooms and a large drawing room. Gladys Tate was proud of the decor in her home and her art, and until Paul had built the mansion for me, she had the finest house in our area.

By the time we drove up, the sky had turned ashen and the air was so thick with humidity, I thought I could see droplets forming before my eyes. The bayou was still, almost as still as it could be in the eye of a storm. Leaves hung limply on the branches of trees, and even the birds were depressed and settled in some shadowy corners.

The windows were bleak with their curtains drawn closed or their shades down. The glass reflected the oppressive darkness that loomed over the swamps. Nothing stirred. It was a house draped in mourning, its inhabitants well cloistered in their private misery. My heart felt so heavy; my fingers trembled as I opened the car door. Beau reached over to squeeze my arm with reassurance.

"Let's be calm," he advised. I nodded and tried to swallow, but a lump stuck in my throat like swamp mud on a shoe. We walked up the stairs and Beau dropped the brass knocker against the plate. The hollow thump seemed to be directed into my chest rather than into the house. A few moments later, the door was thrust open with such an angry force, it was as if a wind had blown it. Toby stood before us. She was dressed in black and had her hair pinned back severely. Her face was wan and pale.

"What do you want?" she demanded.

"We've come to speak with your mother and father," Beau said.

"They're not exactly in the mood to talk to you," she spit back at us. "In the midst of our mourning, you two had to make problems."

"There are some terrible misunderstandings we must try to fix," Beau insisted, and then added, "for the sake of the baby more than anyone."

Toby gazed at me. Something in my face confused her and she relaxed her shoulders.

"How's Pearl?" I asked quickly.

"Fine. She's doing just fine. She's with Jeanne," she added.

"She's not here?"

"No, but she will be here," she said firmly.

"Please," Beau pleaded. "We must have a few minutes with your parents."

Toby considered a moment and then stepped back. "I'll go see if they want to talk to you. Wait in the study," she ordered, and marched down the hallway to the stairs.

Beau and I entered the study. There was only a single lamp lit in a corner, and with the dismal sky, the room reeked of gloom. I snapped on a Tiffany lamp beside the settee and sat quickly, for fear my legs would give out from under me.

"Let me begin our conversation with Madame Tate," Beau advised. He stood to the side, his hands behind his back, and we both waited and listened, our eyes glued to the entrance. Nothing happened for so long, I let my eyes wander and my gaze stopped dead on the portrait above the mantel. It was a portrait I had done of Paul some time ago. Gladys Tate had hung it in place of the portrait of herself and Octavious. I had done too good a job, I thought. Paul looked so lifelike, his blue eyes animated, that soft smile captured around his mouth. Now he looked like he was smiling with impish satisfaction, defiant, vengeful. I couldn't look at the picture without my heart pounding.

We heard footsteps and a moment later Toby appeared alone. My hope sunk. Gladys wasn't going to give us an audience.

"Mother will be down," she said, "but my father is not able to see anyone at the moment. You might as well sit," she told Beau. "It will be a while. She's not exactly prepared for visitors right now," she added bitterly. Beau took a seat beside me obediently. Toby stared at us a moment.

"Why were you so obstinate? If there was ever a time my mother needed the baby around her, it was now. How cruel of you two to make it difficult and force us to go to a judge." She glared at me and then turned directly to Beau. "I might have expected something like this from her, but I thought you were more compassionate, more mature."

"Toby," I said. "I'm not who you think I am."

She smirked. "I know exactly who you are. Don't you think we have people like you here, selfish, vain people who couldn't care less about anyone else?"

"But . . ."

Beau put his hand on my arm. I looked at him and saw him plead for silence with his eyes. I swallowed back my words and closed my eyes. Toby turned and left us.

"She'll understand afterward," Beau said softly. A good ten minutes later, we heard Gladys Tate's heels clicking down the stairway, each click like a gunshot aimed at my heart. Our eyes fixed with anticipation on the doorway until she appeared. She loomed before us, taller, darker in her black mourning dress, her hair pinned back as severely as Toby's. Her lips were pale, her cheeks pallid, but her eyes were bright and feverish.

"What do you want?" she demanded, shooting me a stabbing glance.

Beau rose. "Madame Tate, we've come to try to reason with you, to get you to understand why we did what we did," he said.

"Humph," she retorted. "Understand?" She smiled coldly with ridicule. "It's simple to understand. You're the type who care only about themselves, and if you inflict terrible pain and suffering on someone in your pursuit of happiness, so what?" She whipped her eyes to me and flared them with hate before she turned to sit in the high-back chair like a queen, her hands clasped on her lap, her neck and shoulders stiff.

"Much of this is my fault, not Ruby's," Beau continued. "You see," he said, turning to me, "a few years ago we . . . I made Ruby pregnant with Pearl, but I was cowardly and permitted my parents to send me to Europe. Ruby's stepmother tried to have the baby aborted in a run-down clinic so it would all be kept secret, but Ruby ran off and returned to the bayou."

"How I wish she hadn't," Gladys Tate spit, her hating eyes trying to wish me into extinction.

"Yes, but she did," Beau continued, undaunted by her venom. "For better or for worse, your son offered to make a home for Ruby and Pearl."

"It was for worse. Look at where he is now," she said. Ice water trickled down my spine.

"As you know," Beau said softly, patiently, "theirs was not a true marriage. Time passed. I grew up and realized my errors, but it was too late. In the interim, I renewed my relationship with Ruby's twin sister, who I thought had matured, too. I was mistaken about that, but that's another story."

Gladys smirked.

"Your son knew how much Ruby and I still cared for each other, and he knew Pearl was our child, my child. He was a good man and he wanted Ruby to be happy."

"And she took advantage of that goodness," Gladys accused, stabbing the air between us with her long forefinger.

"No, Mother Tate, I—"

"Don't sit there and try to deny what you did to my son." Her lips trembled. "My son," she moaned. "Once, I was the apple of his eye. The sun rose and fell on my happiness, not yours. Even when you were enchanting him here in the bayou, he would love to sit and talk with me, love to be with me. We had a remarkable relationship and a remarkable love between us," she said. "But you were relentless and you charmed him away from me," she charged, and I realized there was no hate such as that born out of love betrayed. This was why her brain was screaming out for revenge.

"I didn't do those things, Mother Tate," I said quietly. "I tried to discourage our relationship. I even told him the truth about us," I said.

"Yes, you did and viciously drove a wedge between him and me. He knew that I wasn't his real mother. Don't you think that changed things?"

"I didn't want to tell him. It wasn't my place to tell him," I cried, recalling Grandmere Catherine's warnings about causing any sort of split between a Cajun mother and her child. "But you can't build a house of love on a foundation of lies. You and your husband should have been the ones to tell him the truth."

She winced. "What truth? I was his mother until you came along. He loved me," she whined. "That was all the truth we needed . . . love."

A pall fell among us for a moment. Gladys sucked in her anger and closed her eyes.

Beau decided to proceed. "Your son, realizing the love between Ruby and myself, agreed to help us be together. When Gisselle became seriously ill, he volunteered to take her in and pretend she was Ruby so that Ruby could become Gisselle and we could be man and wife."

She opened her eyes and laughed in a way that chilled my blood. "I know all that, but I also know he had little choice. She probably threatened to tell the world he wasn't my son," she said, her flinty eyes aimed at me.

"I would never . . ."

"You'd say anything now, so don't try," she advised.

"Madame," Beau said, stepping forward. "What's done is done. Paul did help. He intended for us to live with our daughter and be happy. What you're doing now is defeating what Paul himself tried to accomplish."

She stared up at Beau for a moment, and as she did so,

the gossamer strands of sanity seemed to shred before they snapped behind her eyes. "My poor granddaughter has no parents now. Her mother was buried and her father will be interred beside her."

"Madame Tate, why force us to go to court over this and put everyone through the misery again? Surely you want peace and quiet at this point, and your family—"

She turned her dark, blistering eyes toward Paul's portrait, and those eyes softened. "I'm doing this for my son," she said, gazing up at him with more than a mother's love. "Look how he smiles, how beautiful he is and how happy he is. Pearl will grow up here, under that portrait. At least he'll have that. You," she said, pointing her long, thin finger at me again, "took everything else from him, even his life."

Beau looked at me desperately and then turned back to her. "Madame Tate," he said, "if it's a matter of the inheritance, we're prepared to sign any document."

"What?" She sprang up. "You think this is all a matter of money? Money? My son is dead." She pulled up her shoulders and pursed her lips. "This discussion is over. I want you out of my house and out of our lives."

"You won't succeed with this. A judge—"

"I have lawyers. Talk to them." She smiled at me so coldly, it made my blood curdle. "You put on your sister's face and body and you crawled into her heart. Now live there," she cursed, and left the room.

Right down to my feet, I ached, and my heart became a hollow ball shooting pains through my chest. "Beau!"

"Let's go," he said, shaking his head. "She's gone mad. The judge will realize that. Come on, Ruby." He reached for me. I felt like I floated to my feet.

Just before we left the room, I gazed back at Paul's portrait. His expression of satisfaction put a darkness in my heart that a thousand days of sunshine couldn't nudge away.

After the funeral drive back to New Orleans, I collapsed with emotional exhaustion and slept into the late morning. Beau woke me to tell me Monsieur Polk had just called.

"And?" I sat up quickly, my heart pounding.

"I'm afraid it's not good news. The experts tell him everything is identical with identical twins, blood type, even organ size. The doctor who treated Gisselle doesn't think anything would show in an X ray. We can't rely on the medical data to clearly establish identities.

"As far as my being the father of Pearl . . . a blood group test will only confirm that I couldn't be, not that I could. As Monsieur Polk said, those sorts of tests aren't perfected yet."

"What will we do?" I moaned.

"He has already petitioned for a hearing and we have a court date," Beau said. "We'll tell our story, use the handwriting samples. He wants to also make use of your art talent. Monsieur Polk has documents prepared for us to sign so that we willingly surrender any claim to Paul's estate, thus eliminating a motive. Maybe it will be enough."

"Beau, what if it isn't?"

"Let's not think of the worst," he urged.

The worst was the waiting. Beau tried to occupy himself with work, but I could do nothing but sleep and wander from room to room, sometimes spending hours just sitting in Pearl's nursery, staring at her stuffed animals and dolls. Not more than forty-eight hours after Monsieur Polk had filed our petition with the court, we began to get phone calls from newspaper reporters. None would reveal his or her sources, but it seemed obvious to both Beau and me that Gladys Tate's thirst for vengeance was insatiable and she had deliberately had the story leaked to the press. It made headlines.

TWIN CLAIMS SISTER BURIED IN HER GRAVE!
CUSTODY BATTLE LOOMS.

Aubrey was given instructions to say we were unavailable to anyone who called. We would see no visitors, answer no questions. Until the court hearing, I was a virtual prisoner in my own home.

On that day, my legs trembling, I clung to Beau's arm as we descended the stairway to get into our car and drive to the Terrebone Parish courthouse. It was one of those mostly cloudy days when the sun plays peekaboo, teasing us with a few bright rays and then sliding behind a wall of clouds to leave the world dark and dreary. It reflected my mood swings, which went from hopeful and optimistic to depressed and pessimistic.

Monsieur Polk was already at the courthouse, waiting, when we arrived. The story had stirred the curious in the bayou as well as in New Orleans. I gazed quickly at the crowd of observers and saw some of Grandmere Catherine's friends. I smiled at them, but they were confused and unsure and afraid to smile back. I felt like a stranger. How would I ever explain to them why I had switched identities with Gisselle? How would they ever understand?

We took our seats first, and then, with obvious fanfare, milking the situation as much as she could, Gladys Tate entered. She still wore her clothes of mourning. She hung on Octavious's arm, stepping with great difficulty to show the world we had dragged her into this horrible hearing at a most unfortunate time. She wore no makeup, so she looked pale and sick, the weaker of the two of us in the judge's eyes. Octavious kept his gaze down, his head bowed, and didn't look our way once.

Toby and Jeanne and her husband, James, walked behind Gladys and Octavious Tate, scowling at us. Their attorneys, William Rogers and Martin Bell, led them to their seats. They looked formidable with their heavy briefcases and dark suits. The judge entered and everyone took his seat.

The judge's name was Hilliard Barrow, and Monsieur Polk had found out that he had a reputation for being caustic, impatient, and firm. He was a tall, lean man with hard facial features: deep-set dark eyes, thick eyebrows, a long, bony nose, and a thin mouth that looked like a slash when he pressed his lips together. He had gray and dark brown hair with a deeply receding hairline so that the top of his skull shone under the courtroom lights. Two long hands with bony fingers jutted out from the sleeves of his black judicial robe.

"Normally," he began, "this courtroom is relatively empty during such proceedings. I want to warn those observing that I won't tolerate any talking, any sounds displaying approval or disapproval. A child's welfare is at stake here, and not the selling of newspapers and gossip magazines to the society people in New Orleans." He paused to scour the crowd to see if there was even the hint of insubordination in anyone's eyes. My heart sunk. He seemed a man void of any emotion, except prejudices against rich New Orleans people.

The clerk read our petition and then Judge Barrow turned his sharp, hard gaze on Monsieur Polk.

"You have a case to make," he said.

"Yes, Your Honor. I would like to begin by calling Monsieur Beau Andreas to the stand."

The judge nodded, and Beau squeezed my hand and stood up. Everyone's eyes were fixed on him as he strutted confidently to the witness seat. He was sworn in and sat quickly.

"Monsieur Andreas, as a preamble to our presentation, would you tell the court in your own words why, how, and when you and Ruby Tate effected the switching of identities between Ruby and Gisselle Andreas, who was your wife at the time."

"Objection, Your Honor," Monsieur Williams said. "Whether or not this woman is Ruby Tate is something for the court to decide."

The judge grimaced. "Monsieur Williams. There isn't a jury to impress. I think I'm capable of understanding the question at hand without being influenced by innuendo. Please, sir. Let's make this as fast as possible."

"Yes, Your Honor," Monsieur Williams said, and sat down.

My eyes widened. Perhaps we would get a fair shake after all, I thought.

Beau began our story. Not a sound was heard through his relating of it. No one so much as coughed or cleared his throat, and when he was finished, an even deeper hush came over the crowd. It was as if everyone had been stunned. Now, when I turned and looked around, I saw all eyes were on me. Beau had done such a good job of telling our story, many were beginning to wonder if it couldn't be so. I felt my hopes rise to the surface of my troubled thoughts.

Monsieur Williams rose. "Just a few questions, if I may, Your Honor."

"Go on," the judge said.

"Monsieur Andreas. You said your wife was diagnosed with St. Louis encephalitis while you were at your country estate. A doctor made the diagnosis?"

"Yes."

"Didn't this doctor know he was diagnosing your wife, Gisselle?" Beau looked toward Monsieur Polk. "If so, why didn't you bring him here to testify that it was Gisselle and not Ruby?" Monsieur Williams hammered. Beau didn't respond.

"Monsieur Andreas?" the judge said.

"I . . ."

"Your honor," Monsieur Polk said. "Since the twins are so identical, we didn't think the doctor would be able to testify beyond a doubt as to which twin he examined. I have researched the medical history of the twins, as much as could be researched, and we are willing to admit that identical twins share so many physiological characteristics, it is virtually impossible to use medical data to identify them."

"You have no medical records to enter into the record?" Judge Barrow asked.

"No, sir."

"Then what hard evidence to you intend to enter into the record to substantiate this fantastic story, sir?" the judge asked, getting right to the point.

"We are prepared at this time," Monsieur Polk said, approaching the judge, "to present handwriting samples that you will quickly be able to see distinguish one twin from the other. These come from school records and legal documents," Monsieur Polk said, and presented the exhibits.

Judge Barrow gazed at them. "I'd have to have an expert analyze them, of course."

"We would like to reserve the right to bring them to our experts, Your Honor," Monsieur Williams said.

"Of course," the judge said. He put the exhibits aside. "Are there any more questions for Monsieur Andreas?"

"Yes," Monsieur Williams said, and stood his ground between Beau and us. He smiled skeptically. "Sir, you claim Paul Tate, once hearing of this fantastic scheme, volunteered to take the sick twin into his home and pretend she was his wife?"

"That's correct," Beau said.

"Can you tell the court why he would do such a thing?"

"Paul Tate was devoted to Ruby and wanted to see her happy. He knew Pearl was my child and he wanted to see us with our child," Beau added.

Gladys Tate groaned so loud, everyone paused to see. She had closed her eyes and fallen back against Octavious's shoulder.

"Monsieur?" the judge asked. Octavious whispered something in Gladys's ear and her eyelids fluttered open. With great effort, she sat up again. Then she nodded she was all right.

"And so," Monsieur Williams continued, "you are telling the court that Paul Tate willingly took in his sister-in-law and then pretended she was his wife to the extent that when she died, he fell into a deep depression which caused his own untimely death? He did all this to make sure Ruby Tate was happy living with another man? Is that what you want this court to believe?"

"It's true," Beau said.

Monsieur Williams widened his smile. "No further

questions, Your Honor," he said. The judge told Beau he was excused. He looked very dark and troubled as he returned to his seat beside me.

"Ruby," Monsieur Polk said. I nodded and he called me to the stand. I took a deep breath and with my eyes nearly closed, walked to the witness chair. After I was sworn in, I took another deep breath and told myself to be strong for Pearl's sake.

"Please state your real name," Monsieur Polk said.

"My legal name is Ruby Tate."

"You have heard Monsieur Andreas's story. Is there anything with which you wish to disagree?"

"No. It's all true."

"Did you discuss this switching of identities with your husband, Paul, and did he indeed agree to the plan?"

"Yes. I didn't want him to be so involved," I added, "but he insisted."

"Describe the birth of your child," he said, and stood back.

I told the story, how Paul had been there during the storm to help with Pearl's birth. Monsieur Polk then took me through many of the highlights of my life, events at the Greenwood School, the people I had known and things I had accomplished. After I finished with that, he nodded toward the rear and an assistant brought in an easel, some drawing pencils, and a drawing pad.

Monsieur Williams shot up out of his seat as soon as it was obvious what Monsieur Polk wanted to demonstrate. "I object to this, Your Honor," Monsieur Williams cried.

"Monsieur Polk, what do you plan to enter into the record here?" the judge asked.

"There were many differences between the twins, Your Honor, many we recognize will be hard to substantiate, but one is possible, and that is Ruby's ability to draw and paint. She has had paintings in galleries in New Orleans and—"

"Your Honor," Monsieur Williams said, "whether this

317

woman can draw a straight line or not is irrelevant. It was never established that Gisselle Andreas could not."

"I'm afraid he has a point, Monsieur Polk. All you will show here is that this woman can perform artistically."

"Monsieur Polk sighed with frustration. "But, Your Honor, never in Gisselle Andreas's history has there ever been any evidence . . ."

The judge shook his head. "It's a waste of the court's time, monsieur. Please continue with your witness or enter new exhibits or call another witness." Monsieur Polk shook his head. "Are you finished with this witness?"

With deep disappointment, Monsieur Polk replied, "Yes, Your Honor."

"Monsieur Williams?"

"A few minor questions," he said, dripping with sarcasm. "Madame Andreas. You claim you were married to Paul Tate even though you were still in love with Beau Andreas. Why did you marry Monsieur Tate, then?"

"I . . . was alone and he wanted to provide a home for me and my child."

"Most husbands want to provide homes for their wives and children. Did he love you?"

"Oh yes."

"Did you love him?"

"I . . ."

"Well, did you?"

"Yes, but . . ."

"But what, madame?"

"But it was a different sort of love, a friendship, a . . ." I wanted to say "sisterly," but when I looked at Gladys and Octavious, I couldn't do it. "A different sort of love."

"You were man and wife, were you not? You were married in a church, you said."

"Yes."

He narrowed his eyes. "Did you see Monsieur Andreas romantically while you were married to Monsieur Tate?"

"Yes," I said, and some in the audience gasped and shook their heads.

"And according to your tale, your husband was aware of this?"

"Yes."

"He was aware of this and he tolerated it? Not only did he tolerate it, but he was willing to take in your dying sister and pretend it was you so you would be happy." He spun around as he continued, directing himself to the audience as much as he directed himself to the judge. "And then he became so depressed over her death that he drowned in the swamp? This is the story you and Monsieur Andreas want everyone to accept?"

"Yes," I cried. "It's true. All of it."

Monsieur Williams gazed at the judge and twisted the corner of his mouth until it cut into his cheek.

"No further questions, Your Honor."

The judge nodded. "You may step down, madame," he said, but I couldn't stand. My legs were like wet straw and my back felt as if it had turned to jelly. I closed my eyes.

"Ruby," Beau called.

"Are you all right, madame?" the judge asked.

I shook my head. My heart was pounding so hard, I couldn't catch my breath. I felt the blood drain from my face. When I opened my eyes, Beau was holding my hand. Someone had brought up a wet cloth for my forehead and I realized I had fainted.

"Can you walk, Ruby?" Beau asked.

I nodded.

"We'll have a short recess," the judge said, and slammed his gavel down. I felt as if he had slammed it down on my heart.

17

Thicker Than Water

During the recess Beau and I were shown to a waiting room in which there was a small sofa. Beau had me lie down and keep the wet cloth on my forehead while Monsieur Polk went to make a phone call to his office. He looked glum and disturbed. In fact, I thought he seemed angry at us for bringing him into the situation.

"Beau, we looked foolish in there, didn't we?" I asked mournfully. "After we told our story, the Tates' attorney made us look like liars."

"No," Beau encouraged. "People believed us. I saw it in their faces. And besides, once your handwriting is compared to Gisselle's and analyzed . . ."

"They will find an expert to discount it. You know they will. She's so determined to hurt us, Beau. She won't spare any cost. She would use Paul's entire fortune to defeat us!"

"Take it easy, Ruby. Please. We have to go back and—"

We both turned when the door opened and Jeanne entered. For a moment no one spoke. She held the door partially opened behind her as if she might change her mind and bolt out of the room any moment.

"Jeanne," I said, sitting up. "Please, come in."

She stared at me, her eyes watery. "I don't know what to believe anymore," she said, shaking her head. "Mother swears you and Beau are just good liars."

"No, Jeanne. We're not lying. Remember when you came to me and we had that nice talk before you got married? Remember how you weren't sure you should marry James?"

Her eyes widened and then narrowed. "Ruby could have told you."

I shook my head. "No. Listen . . ."

"But even if you are Ruby, I don't know how you could have hurt my brother like you did."

"Jeanne, you don't understand everything. I never meant to hurt Paul, never. I did love him."

"How can you say that with him right here?" she asked, nodding at Beau.

"Paul and I had a different sort of love, Jeanne."

She studied me with such intensity, I felt her eyes inside me. "I don't know. I just don't know what to believe," she said. And then her eyes turned crystal-hard. "But I came here to tell you that if you are Ruby and you did all this, I feel sorry for you."

"Jeanne!"

She turned and left quickly.

"You see," Beau said, smiling. "She has doubts now. She knows in her heart you are Ruby."

"I hope so," I said. "But I feel so terrible. I should have realized how many people I would hurt."

Beau held me tightly and I took a deep breath. He got me a glass of water, and as I was drinking it, Monsieur Polk returned, looking even more despondent.

"What is it?" Beau asked.

"I've just gotten some bad news," he said. "They have a surprise witness."

"What? Who?" I asked, my mind searching through the possibilities.

"I don't know who it is yet," he said. "But I was told he could nail it down for them. Is there anything else you two haven't told me?"

"No, Monsieur," Beau said. "Absolutely nothing has been deliberately withheld. And everything we've told you is the truth."

He nodded, skeptically. "It's time to return," he said.

It was even more difficult to return to the courtroom than it was to first enter it. I felt like a specimen under a microscope. Everyone's gaze followed me down to the front of the courtroom, and people near us covered their mouths to whisper. It made me flush with a wave of heat that rose up my legs and over my face. Every old friend of Grandmere Catherine's was studying my every move, searching gestures for evidence to confirm my identity. The air was thick with their questions. Were Beau and I trying to pull off some scam? Or was our tale the truth?

We took our seats. Gladys Tate was already seated, steely-faced. Octavious sat staring blankly ahead. Jeanne whispered something to Toby, and Paul's sisters gazed at me angrily. A few moments later, Judge Barrow returned and the courtroom grew still.

"Monsieur Polk," he said. "Are you ready to continue?"

"Yes, Your Honor." Our attorney rose with the documents he had prepared for us to sign concerning the inheritance.

"Your Honor. My clients recognize that their motives for trying to regain custody of Pearl Tate might be misinterpreted. In order to alleviate such misinterpretations, we are prepared to offer the surrender of any and all rights to any spousal inheritance concerning the estate of Paul Marcus Tate." He stepped forward and brought the documents to the judge, who gazed down at them and then nodded at Monsieur Williams to come forward, too. He looked at the papers.

"We'd have to study these, of course, Your Honor, but," he said with the confidence of someone who had anticipated our move, "even if these do prove satisfactory, this doesn't eliminate the possibility of these two impostors getting their clutches on the Tate fortune. The child whom they are trying to get custody of would inherit, and they would naturally be the trustees of that enormous inheritance."

The judge turned to Monsieur Tate.

"Your Honor, it is the contention of my clients that Pearl Tate's natural father is Beau Andreas. She would have no claims to Monsieur Tate's estate."

The judge nodded. It was like watching a game of chess being played with real people on the board instead of figurines of knights and queens, pawns and kings. We were the pawns, and to the victor went my darling Pearl.

"Do you have any further exhibits to enter, Monsieur Polk, or any further witnesses?"

"No, Your Honor."

"Monsieur Williams?"

"We do, Your Honor."

The judge sat back. Monsieur Polk returned to his seat beside us, and Monsieur Williams went to his desk to confer with his associate for a moment before turning and calling out his witness's name.

"We would like to call Monsieur Bruce Bristow to the stand."

"Bruce!" I exclaimed. Beau shook his head in astonishment.

"Is this not your stepmother's husband?" Monsieur Polk asked.

"Yes, but . . . we have nothing to do with him anymore," Beau explained.

The doors opened in the rear and Bruce came sauntering down the aisle, a Cheshire cat's grin on his lips when he gazed our way.

"She must have made him an offer, bought his testimony," I told Monsieur Polk.

"What sort of testimony can this man give?" he wondered aloud.

"He'll say anything, even under oath," Beau said, eyeing Bruce angrily.

323

Bruce was sworn in and sat in the witness chair. Monsieur Williams approached him.

"Please state your name, sir."

"I'm Bruce Bristow."

"And were you married to the now-deceased step-mother of Ruby and Gisselle Dumas?"

"I was."

"How long have you known the twins?"

"Quite a long time," he said, gazing at me and smiling. "Years. I was employed by Monsieur and Madame Dumas for about eight years before Monsieur Dumas's death."

"After which you married Daphne Dumas and became, for all practical purposes, the stepfather to the twins Gisselle and Ruby?"

"Yes, that's true."

"So you knew them well?"

"Very well. Intimately," he added.

"As the only living parent of the twins, can you assure the court you can distinguish between them?"

"Of course. Gisselle," he said, looking at me again, "has a completely different personality, a more, shall we say, sophisticated awareness. Ruby was more of an innocent, shy, soft-spoken."

"Are you now, and have you recently been, involved in some legal problems with the current owners of the Dumas Enterprises, Beau and Gisselle Andreas?" Monsieur Williams asked.

"Yes, sir. They threw me out of the business," he said, glaring at us. "After years of dedicated service, they decided to enforce a foolish prenuptial agreement between me and my deceased wife. They manipulated me out of my rightful position and drove me into the streets, turning me into a pauper."

"He's lying," Beau whispered to Monsieur Polk.

"You should have told me all about him," he replied. "I asked you if there was anything else."

"Who knew Gladys Tate would find him?"

"More likely, he found her, Beau," I said. "For revenge. They fit together like a hand in a glove."

"This woman who you see sitting before you, sir," Monsieur Williams said, turning to me. "Was she a party to all this, directly?"

"Yes, she was. I went back to plead with her recently and she literally had me thrown out of what had been my own house," he said.

"So," Monsieur Williams concluded with a smile of satisfaction, "this was no shy, innocent woman."

"Hardly," Bruce said, widening his own smile and looking at the judge, who turned his scrutinizing eyes on me.

"Still, sir, it is possible, I imagine, for an identical twin to fool someone into believing she is her sister," Monsieur Williams said. "She could have performed a well-prepared script and said all the right things to convince you she was her sister."

"I suppose," Bruce said. Why was Monsieur Williams giving us that benefit of doubt? I wondered, but it was like hearing the first shoe drop. I cringed inside and clutched my hands so hard, my fingers went numb.

"Then how can you be so sure you were in an argument with Gisselle and not Ruby recently?"

"I'm ashamed to say," Bruce replied, looking down.

"I'm afraid I have to ask you nevertheless, sir. A child's future is in the balance, not to mention a major fortune."

Bruce nodded, took a deep breath, and looked up as if he were concentrating on an angel in the ceiling. "I once let myself be seduced by my stepdaughter Gisselle."

The audience gave one simultaneous gasp.

"As I said, she was very sophisticated and worldly," he added.

"Did anyone else know about this, monsieur?"

"No," Bruce said. "I wasn't very proud of it."

"But this woman indicated to you that she knew?" Monsieur Williams asked, pointing to me.

"Yes. She brought it up during our argument and threatened to use it against me should I put up any resistance to her and her husband's effort to drive me out of my rightful position. Under the circumstances I thought it was better to effect a quick retreat and start my life anew.

"However," he said, looking at Madame Tate, "when I heard what they were up to now, I had to step forward and do my duty regardless of the consequences to my reputation."

"So you are telling the court under oath that this woman who has presented herself as Ruby Tate knew intimate details between you and Gisselle, details only Gisselle would have known?"

"That is correct," Bruce said, and sat back contented.

"The only reason he is doing this," Beau whispered to Monsieur Polk, "is because we forced him to leave the business. He and Daphne did some very shaky financial dealings."

"Are you prepared to open up all that?" Monsieur Polk asked.

Beau looked at me. "Yes. We'll do anything." Beau began to write some questions for Monsieur Polk quickly.

"I have no further questions for the witness, Your Honor," Monsieur Williams said, and returned to his table, where Gladys Tate sat looking stronger. She gazed my way and smiled coldly, sending chills down my spine.

"Monsieur Polk. Do you wish to question this witness?"

"I do, Your Honor. If I may have one moment," he added while Beau completed his notes. Monsieur Polk perused them and then stood up.

"Monsieur Bristow, why didn't you contest the actions taken against you to remove you from Dumas Enterprises?"

"I've already said . . . there was an unfortunate prenuptial agreement and I was blackmailed by my stepdaughter Gisselle."

"Are you sure your reluctance to take counteraction

had nothing to do with the financial activities you and Daphne Dumas conducted?"

"No."

"You are willing to have those dealings scrutinized by this court?"

Bruce squirmed a bit. "I didn't do anything wrong."

"Aren't you here to get revenge for being pushed out of the business?"

"No. I'm here to tell the truth," Bruce said firmly.

"Did you not recently lose a commercial property in New Orleans through foreclosure?"

"Yes."

"You've lost quite a comfortable income and lifestyle, haven't you?"

"I have a good job now," Bruce insisted.

"Not paying you a quarter of what you made before you were asked to leave Dumas Enterprises, correct?"

"Money isn't everything," Bruce quipped.

"Have you gotten over your problem with alcohol?" Monsieur Polk pursued.

"Objection, Your Honor," Monsieur Williams said, rising. "Monsieur Bristow's personal problems have nothing to do with this testimony."

"They have everything to do with it if he hopes to gain financially and he is an alcoholic who needs money for his disease," Monsieur Polk said.

"Are you accusing my clients of bribing this man?" Monsieur Williams cried, pointing at Bruce.

"That will be enough," the judge said. "Objection sustained. Monsieur Polk, have you any more questions pertaining to the issue?"

Monsieur Polk thought a moment and then shook his head. "No, Your Honor."

"Fine. Thank you, Monsieur Bristow. You may step down. Monsieur Williams?"

"I would like to call Madame Tate to the stand, Your Honor."

Gladys Tate rose slowly as if she were battling against

an enormous weight on her shoulders. She dabbed at her eyes with a beige silk handkerchief and then sighed loudly before stepping around the table to walk toward the stand. I looked at Octavious. He'd had his head down most of the time and had it down now, too.

After she was sworn in, Gladys settled into the witness chair like someone easing herself into a hot bath. She closed her eyes and pressed her right hand against her heart. Monsieur Williams stood waiting for her to become calm enough to speak. When I gazed at the people in the audience, I saw how most felt sorry for her. Their eyes were filled with compassion and sympathy.

"You are Gladys Tate, mother of the recently deceased Paul Marcus Tate?" Monsieur Williams asked. She closed her eyes again. "I'm sorry, Madame Tate. I know how fresh your sorrow is, but I have to ask."

"Yes," she said. "I am Paul Tate's mother." She didn't look at me.

"Were you very close with your son, madame?"

"Very," she said. "Before Paul was married, I don't think a day passed when we didn't see or speak to each other. We had more than a mother-son relationship. We were good friends," she added.

"And so your son confided in you?"

"Oh, absolutely. We had no secrets from each other, ever," she said.

"That's a lie," I whispered. Monsieur Polk raised his eyebrows. Beau turned to me. His eyes told me that he wanted me to tell Monsieur Polk the truth. I had hoped I wouldn't have to do it. It seemed like such a betrayal of Paul.

"Did he ever discuss with you this elaborate plan to switch his wife with Monsieur Andreas's wife after she was stricken with encephalitis?"

"No. Paul loved Ruby dearly and he was a very proud young man, as well as religious. He wouldn't give away the woman he loved just so another man could be happy living in sin," she said disdainfully. "He married Ruby in church after he realized it was the proper thing to do. I

328

remember when he told me he was going to do it. I was unhappy he had fathered a child out of wedlock, of course, but I was happy he wanted to do what was morally right."

"She wasn't happy," I murmured. "She made him miserable. She—"

"Shh," Monsieur Polk said. He looked like he was as fascinated as everyone else with her story and didn't want to miss a detail.

"And in fact, after they were married, you and your husband and your daughters accepted Ruby and Pearl as your family, correct?"

"Yes. We had family dinners. I even helped her design and decorate her home. I would do anything to keep my son happy and close to me," she said. "What he wanted for himself, I wanted for him. And he doted on the child. Oh, how he worshiped our precious granddaughter. She has his face, his eyes, his hair. To see them walking together in the garden or to see him take her for a pirogue ride in the canals filled my heart with joy."

"So there is no doubt in your mind that Pearl is his child?"

"None whatsoever."

"And he never told you anything to the contrary?"

"No. Why would he marry a woman with someone else's child?" she asked.

Heads bobbed in agreement.

"During Ruby Tate's illness, you had many opportunities to visit their home?"

"Yes."

"And did he ever give you an indication he was worrying about his wife's sister and not his wife?" Monsieur Williams pursued.

"No. On the contrary, and as anyone here who had seen my son during this trying period can testify, he mourned so hard, he became a shell of himself. He neglected his work and began drinking. He was in a constant depression. It broke my heart."

"Why didn't he just put his wife into a hospital?"

"He couldn't bear being away from her. He was at her side constantly," Madame Tate said. "Hardly how he would be were it not Ruby," she added, gazing scornfully at me.

"Why did you ask the court to grant an order for you to retrieve your granddaughter?"

"These people," Gladys Tate said, spitting her words toward us, "refused to give Pearl back to me. They turned my attorney and a nurse away from the door. And all this," she moaned, "while I was mourning the horrible death of my son, my little boy . . ."

She burst into tears. Monsieur Williams stepped forward quickly with his handkerchief.

"I'm sorry," she wailed.

"That's all right. Take your time, madame."

Gladys wiped her cheeks and then sniffled and sucked in her breath.

"Are you all right, Madame Tate?" Judge Barrow asked.

"Yes," she said in a small voice. Judge Barrow nodded to Monsieur Williams, who stepped forward to continue.

"Recently Monsieur and Madame Andreas came to your home, did they not?" he asked.

She glared at us. "Yes, they did."

"And what did they want?"

"They wanted to make a deal," she said. "They offered fifty percent of my son's estate if I didn't force this court hearing and just gave them Pearl."

"What?" Beau stammered.

"She's lying!" I cried.

The judge rapped his gavel. "I warned you. No outbursts," he reprimanded.

"But . . ."

"Be still," Monsieur Polk ordered.

I cowered back, shrinking in my chair with rage burning my cheeks. Was there no limit to how far she would go to satisfy her thirst for vengeance?

"What happened then, madame?" Monsieur Williams asked.

"I refused, of course, and they threatened to take me to court, which they have done."

"No further questions, Your Honor," Monsieur Williams said.

The judge looked at Monsieur Polk with hard eyes. "Do you have any questions for this witness?"

"No, Your Honor."

"What? Make her take back these lies," I urged.

"No. It's better to get rid of her. She has everyone's sympathy. Even the judge's," Monsieur Polk advised.

Monsieur Williams helped Madame Tate out of the seat and escorted her back to her chair. Some people in the audience were openly crying for her.

"You won't get the child back today, if you ever do," Monsieur Polk muttered, half under his breath.

"Oh, Beau," I wailed. "She's winning. She'll be a terrible grandmother. She doesn't love Pearl. She knows Pearl's not Paul's child."

"Monsieur Williams?" the judge said.

"No further witnesses or exhibits, Your Honor," he said confidently.

Monsieur Polk sat back, his hands on his stomach, his face dour. I looked across the courtroom at Gladys, who was preparing to leave in victory. Octavious still had his eyes fixed on the table.

"Call one more witness, Monsieur Polk," I said in desperation.

"What's that?"

Beau took my hand. We gazed into each other's eyes and he nodded. I turned back to our attorney.

"Call one more witness. I'll tell you just what to ask," I said. "Call Octavious Tate to the stand."

"Do it!" Beau ordered firmly.

Monsieur Polk rose slowly from his seat, unsure, tentative, and reluctant.

"Monsieur Polk?" the judge said.

"We have one more witness, Your Honor," he said.

The judge looked displeased. "Very well," he said.

"Let's conclude this matter. Call your final witness," he added, emphasizing the word "final."

"We call Monsieur Tate to the stand."

A ripple of astonishment moved through the audience. I wrote feverishly on a piece of paper. The judge rapped his gavel and glared at the crowd of people, who immediately grew still. No one wanted to be removed from this courtroom now. Octavious, stunned by the sound of his name, lifted his head slowly and gazed around as if he just realized where he was. Monsieur Williams leaned over to whisper some strategy to him before he stood up. I handed my questions to Monsieur Polk, who perused them quickly and then looked at me sharply.

"Madame," he warned, "you could lose any sympathetic ear you might have if this proves untrue."

"We don't have any sympathy here," Beau answered for me.

"It's true," I said softly.

Octavious walked slowly to the witness stand, his head down. When he was sworn in, he repeated the oath very slowly. I saw that the words were heavy on his tongue and on his heart. He sat quickly, falling into his seat like a man who might otherwise crumple to the floor. Monsieur Polk hesitated and then shrugged to himself and stepped forward on our behalf.

"Monsieur Tate, after your son had first proposed marriage to Ruby Dumas, did you visit Ruby Dumas and ask her to refuse?"

Octavious looked toward Gladys and then he looked down.

"Sir?" Monsieur Polk said.

"Yes, I did."

"Why?"

"I didn't think Paul was ready to marry," he replied. "He was just starting his oil business and he had just built this home."

"That seems like a good time to think of marriage," Monsieur Polk said. "Wasn't there another reason for your asking Ruby Dumas to refuse your son's proposal?"

Octavious looked at Gladys again. "I knew my wife was unhappy about it," he said.

"But your wife has just testified that she was happy Paul was doing the right thing and she testified that she fully accepted Ruby Dumas into her family. Was that not the case, monsieur?"

"She accepted, yes."

"But not willingly?" Before Octavious could respond, Monsieur Polk followed quickly. "Did you believe the baby was your son's baby?"

"I . . . thought it was possible, yes."

"Yet you went to Ruby Dumas to ask her not to marry your son?"

Octavious didn't reply.

"Did your son tell you Pearl was his child?"

"He . . . said he wanted to provide for Ruby and Pearl."

"But he never said Pearl was his child? Sir?"

"No, not to me."

"But to your wife, who then told you? Is that the way it was?"

"Yes. Yes."

"Then why didn't you think he was doing the right thing?"

"I didn't say he wasn't."

"Yet you admit you didn't want to see the marriage happen. Really, monsieur, this is very confusing. Wasn't there another reason, a more serious reason?"

Octavious turned his head slowly toward me and our eyes met. I pleaded for the truth with mine, even though I knew how devastating that truth was.

"I don't know what you mean," he said.

"Please," I cried. "Please do the right thing."

The judge slammed his gavel down.

"For Paul's sake," I added. Octavious winced and his lips trembled.

"That's quite enough, madame. I warned you and—"

"Yes," Octavious admitted softly. "There was another reason."

"Octavious!" Gladys Tate screamed. The judge sat back, shocked at the outbursts, one from each side.

"Don't you think it's time to tell that reason, Monsieur Tate?" our attorney said with a senatorial voice.

Octavious nodded. He looked at Gladys again. "I'm sorry," he said. "I can't go on with this. I owe you so much, but what you're doing is not right, my dearest wife. I'm tired of hiding behind a lie and I can't take a mother from a child."

Gladys wailed. Necks strained to see her daughters comforting her.

"Will you please tell the court what that additional reason was," Monsieur Polk demanded.

"A long time ago, I succumbed to temptation and committed an adulterous act."

The audience took a collective deep breath.

"And?"

"As a result, my son was born." Octavious raised his head and gazed at me. "My son and Ruby Dumas . . ."

"Monsieur?"

"They were half brother and half sister," he confessed.

Bedlam broke out. The judge's gavel was barely heard above the din. Gladys Tate fainted and Octavious buried his face in his hands.

"Your Honor," Monsieur Polk said, stepping forward. "I think it would be in the best interest of the court and all concerned if we could adjoin to your quarters to complete this hearing."

The judge considered and then nodded. "I will see opposing counsels in my chambers," he declared, and rose from his seat. Octavious had not moved from the witness chair. I got up quickly and crossed to him. When he raised his head, his cheeks were wet with tears.

"Thank you," I said.

"I'm sorry for all that I have done," he said.

"I know. I think now you will find peace inside yourself."

Beau came up and embraced me. Then he led me away, people stepping aside to create a path for us. I bit off all my fingernails while Beau and I waited outside Judge Barrow's chambers. My heart was pounding and my stomach felt like it was churning butter. The Tates' attorneys emerged first, their faces so stone-cold, they revealed nothing. They didn't even look our way. Finally Monsieur Polk came to us and told us the judge wanted to meet with us alone.

"What has he decided?" I asked frantically.

"I'm to ask you to go in only, madame. Please."

I clutched Beau's arm, my legs threatening to give out at any moment. If we were to leave without my daughter . . .

In his office without his judicial robes, Judge Barrow looked more like a nice old grandpere. He gestured for us to sit across from him on the settee and then he took off his reading glasses and leaned forward.

"This was, needless to say, the most unusual custody hearing in my experience. I think we have sorted out the truth now. I'm not here to assign blame at this time. Some of this was caused by events beyond your control, but there are all sorts of fraud, ethical and moral fraud, too, and you know how much of that is your doing."

"Yes," I said, my voice filled with remorse.

Judge Barrow stared a moment and nodded. "My instincts tell me your motives for your actions were good ones, motives of love, and the fact that you were willing to risk your reputations and your fortunes by telling the truth in court bodes well in your favor.

"But the state is asking me to judge whether or not you should have custody of this child and be in charge of her welfare and her moral education or whether or not it is better for her to be assigned to a state agency until a proper foster home is found."

"Your Honor," I began, ready to list a dozen promises. He put up his hand.

"I have made my decision, and nothing you say will change that," he said firmly. And then he smiled and added, "I will expect an invitation to a wedding."

I gasped with joy, but Judge Barrow became serious again.

"You may and must become yourself again, madame."

Tears of happiness flooded my face. Beau and I embraced.

"I have given orders for your child to be returned to you. She will be brought here momentarily. The legal ramifications resulting from your previous marriage, straightening out the identities . . . I leave all that to your high-priced attorneys."

"Thank you, Your Honor," I said through my tears. Beau shook his hand and we left the office.

Monsieur Polk was waiting for us in the corridor. "I must confess," he said, "I had my doubts as to the veracity of your story. I am happy for you. Good luck."

We stepped outside to wait for the car that would bring Pearl back to us. There were still people who had been in the courtroom lingering about, discussing the shocking events. I spotted Mrs. Thibodeau, one of Grandmere Catherine's old friends. She had trouble walking now, but she hobbled her way toward us and took my hand.

"I knew it was you," she said. "I told myself Catherine Landry's granddaughter might have been a twin, but she had lived most of her life with Catherine and she had her spirit in her. I looked at your face in that courtroom and I saw your grandmere looking back at me and I knew it would turn out right."

"Thank you, Mrs. Thibodeau."

"God bless you, child, and don't forget us."

"I won't. We'll be back," I promised. She hugged me and I watched her walk way, my heart heavy with the memory of my grandmere walking alongside her friends to church.

The peekaboo sun slipped out from under the mushrooming clouds and dropped warm rays around us as the car with Pearl in it was driven up. The nurse in the front seat opened the door and helped her out. The moment Pearl saw me, her eyes brightened.

"Mommy!" she cried.

It was the best word in the world. Nothing filled my heart with more joy. I held out my arms for her to run to me and then I flooded her faces with kisses and pressed her close. Beau put his arm around my shoulders. All around us, people watched with smiles on their faces.

As we started from the courthouse, I saw the Tates' limousine drive away. The windows were dark, but as the sunlight grew stronger, the silhouette of Madame Tate became clearly outlined. She looked as if she had turned to stone.

I felt sorry for her, even though she had done a very mean thing. She had lost everything today, much more than her vengeance. Her illusionary life had been shattered around her like so much thin china. She was going home to a darker, more troubled time. I prayed that somehow she and Octavious could find a renewal and a peace now that the lies were stripped away.

"Let's go home," Beau said.

Never did those words mean as much to me as they did now.

"I want to make one stop first, Beau," I said. He didn't have to ask where.

A little while later, I stood in front of Grandmere Catherine's tombstone.

A true *traiteur* has a very holy spirit, I thought. She lingers longer to look after the loved ones she has left behind. Grandmere Catherine's spirit was still here. I could feel it, feel her hovering nearby. The breeze became her whisper, its caress, her kiss.

I smiled and gazed up at the light blue sky streaked with thin wisps of clouds now. Mrs. Thibodeau was right, I thought. Grandmere had been with me this day. I kissed my fingers and touched her stone and then I returned to the car and to Beau and to my darling Pearl.

As we drove away, I gazed out the window and saw a marsh hawk strutting on a cypress branch. It watched us and then it lifted into the wind and soared beside and around us for a while until it turned and headed deeper into the bayou.

"Good-bye, Paul," I whispered. But I'll be back, I thought.

I'll be back.

Epilogue

My dreams of having a glorious wedding were still not to become a reality. The publicity and all the commotion surrounding the custody hearing continued to hover about us when we returned to New Orleans. Beau thought it was better for us to have a small ceremony away from the din, and since his parents were not taking it all very well anyway, I couldn't disagree.

We debated for days about whether or not we should sell the house in the Garden District and build a new house just outside of New Orleans. Finally we both came to the same conclusion: We were happy with our servants and we wouldn't find a more beautiful setting. Rather than move, I embarked on the task of redecorating, tearing the rooms apart, floor to ceiling, and replacing the drapes, wall hangings, flooring, and even some of the fixtures. It was as though I were caught in a maddening frenzy to purify the house and purge it of any and all traces of my stepmother, Daphne.

Of course, I kept all the things that I knew had been precious to Daddy and I didn't change a thing in the room that had once been Uncle Jean's. It remained a shrine to his memory, something I knew Daddy had wanted. I put all of the things that even smelled of Daphne into the attic, burying away clothing, jewelry, pictures, mementoes, in large trunks. Then I gathered Gisselle's things together and gave much of it away to thrift shops and charities.

With the rooms repainted, new drapes on the windows, the changes in the artwork, the house took on my and Beau's identities. Of course, there were still memories lingering like cobwebs, but I believed, as did Beau, that time was the best vacuum cleaner and these troublesome memories would someday become vague and insignificant.

After I had done what I wanted with the house, I directed my energies back into my artistic work. One of the first pictures I drew and then painted was a picture of a young woman sitting in a gazebo with a newborn baby in her arms. The setting placed her in a home and on grounds like ours in the Garden District. When Beau looked at the picture, he told me he thought I had done a self-portrait, and then, a few weeks later, I woke with the symptoms of pregnancy and realized that the inspiration for the picture had come from a deeper realization inside myself.

Beau swore it meant I had some of Grandmere Catherine's *traiteur* powers.

"Why can't it be so? Your people believe it's inherited power, right?" he said.

"I never felt anything like that, Beau, and I never even dreamt of healing people. I don't have that sort of mystical insight."

He nodded and thought a moment and then said a startling thing. "Sometimes, when I'm with Pearl and she's jabbering away in her baby language, I see her fix intently on something, and suddenly her face seems years older than four. There's an awareness in her eyes. Do you ever feel that when you're with her?"

"Yes," I said, "but I was afraid to even mention anything like it for fear you would laugh at me."

"I'm not laughing. I'm wondering. You know," he said, "she's even beguiling my parents these days. Mother tries not to show it, but she can't help but dote on her, and my father . . . when he's with her, he's like a little boy again."

"She has her way with them."

"With anyone," Beau said. "I think she's charmed. There. I've said it. Just don't tell any of my friends," he added quickly. I laughed. "Next thing you know," he said, "you'll have me believing in some of those voodoo rituals you and Nina Jackson used to practice."

"Don't discount anything," I warned.

He laughed again, but two weeks into my ninth month, he managed to surprise me with a wonderful present. He had located Nina and he brought her to our house to see me.

"I have a surprise visitor for you," Beau said, coming into the sitting room first.

"Who?"

Then he reached around the door and brought Nina forward. She didn't look very much older, although her hair was completely gray.

"Nina!" I struggled to my feet. I was so big, I felt like a hippopotamus rising out of a swamp. We embraced.

"You be big, all right," Nina said. "And close. I can see it in your eyes."

"Oh, Nina, where have you been?"

"Been travelin' a bit up and down the river. Nina be retired now. I live with my sister."

She sat and talked with me for an hour. I showed her Pearl and she ranted and raved about how beautiful she was becoming. She told me she thought she was a special child, too. And then she told me she was going to light a blue candle for my new baby so the baby would have success and protection.

"It don't be long," she predicted. She reached into her

pocket and produced a camphor lump for me to wear around my neck. "It keep germs away from you and your baby," she promised. I told her I would wear it even in the hospital.

"Please, don't be a stranger. Come see us again, Nina."

"Be sure I will," she said.

"Nina," I asked, taking her hand into mine, "do you think the anger I threw into the wind when I went to see Mama Dede with you about Gisselle has blown away?"

"It be blown from your heart, child. That's what matters most."

We hugged and Beau took her home.

"That was a wonderful present, Beau," I told him when he returned. "Thank you."

"I see she left something," he said, eyeing the camphor lump around my neck. "Figured she would. To tell you the truth," he admitted, "I was hoping she would. Can't take any chances."

We laughed about it.

Four days later my labor began. It was intense, even more so than it had been with Pearl. Beau was at my side constantly and was even there with me in the delivery room. He held my hand and encouraged my breathing. I think he felt every stick of pain I felt, for I saw him wince each time. Finally my water broke and the baby started to enter this world.

"It's a boy!" the doctor cried, and then screamed, "Wait!"

Beau's eyes widened.

"It's another boy! Twins!" the doctor added. "I thought it might be. One was hiding the other, covering his heartbeat with his own.

"Congratulations!" he said, and the nurses held two blond, blue-eyed baby boys in their arms.

"We're not giving either of them away," Beau joked. "Don't worry."

Twins, I thought. They're going to love each other from day one, I pledged, day one.

Pearl was overwhelmed with the news that she would have not one baby brother, but two. Our first great task was going to be finding names for them. We had already discussed the possibility of a girl and then a boy, thinking the boy would be called Pierre, after Daddy. I knew what I wanted to do, but I wasn't sure how Beau would feel. He surprised me in the hospital room afterward by suggesting it himself.

"We should call our second son Jean," he said.

"Oh, Beau, I thought so, but . . ."

"But what?" He smiled. "I told you. I'm a believer now. It was meant to be."

Maybe, I thought. Maybe.

Beau had a photographer waiting at the house the day we brought the twins home. We had pictures taken of the five of us. We were quite the little family now. We hired a nurse to help with the twins in the beginning, but Beau thought we might keep her on longer.

"I don't want you neglecting your art," he insisted.

"Nothing's more important than my children, Beau. My art will take a backseat," I told him. I wanted to be close to my boys and make sure they were taught to love and cherish each other. Beau understood.

A week after I had returned from the hospital with our twins, I sat out in the gardens, relaxing and reading. Pearl was upstairs in the new nursery, intrigued and fascinated with her two infant brothers.

"Pardon, madame," Aubrey said, coming out to me, "but this just arrived special delivery for you."

"Thank you, Aubrey." I took the envelope. When I saw it came from Jeanne, I sat back, my fingers trembling as I tore it open. There was a photograph within and a note.

Dear Ruby,

Mother insisted every iota of anything that reminds us of you be thrown out. I couldn't find it in my heart to throw this away. Somehow, I think, Paul would have wanted you to have it.

Jeanne

343

I looked at the picture. I couldn't remember who had taken it, one of Paul's school friends, I thought. It was a picture of the two of us taken at the *fais do do* hall when Paul had taken me to the dance. That had been my first real date, and it was before I had learned the truth about ourselves. Both of us looked so young and innocent and hopeful. We had nothing ahead of us but happiness and love.

I didn't realize I was crying until a tear fell on the photograph.

"Mommy!" I heard Pearl cry from the patio. I turned to see her running toward me, Beau coming along behind her. "They looked at me! Pierre and Jean! They both looked at me and they smiled!"

I quickly wiped any remaining tears from my cheeks and stuffed the picture and the note between the pages of my book.

"They did," Beau vouched. "I saw it myself."

"I'm glad, darling. Your brothers will love you forever and ever."

"Come on, Mommy. Let's go see them. Come on," she urged, pulling on my hand.

"I will, honey. In a moment."

Beau stared at me. "Are you all right?" he asked.

"Yes." I smiled. "I am."

"I'll take her back. Let's go, princess. Give Mommy a little more rest, okay? And then she'll come."

"Will you, Mommy?"

"I will, honey. I promise."

Beau mouthed *I love you* and carried Pearl back to the house.

I sat back. In the distance a cloud shaped like a pirogue drifted across the blue sky and I thought I heard Grandmere Catherine whispering in the breeze again, filling me with hope.

From bestselling author
V.C. Andrews,
comes the second book
in the exciting *Logan* series.

V.C. ANDREWS®

Heart Song

COMING MID-MAY 1997
FROM POCKET STAR BOOKS

POCKET
STAR
BOOKS

1253

The Phenomenal
V.C. ANDREWS®